PRAISE FOR TEA COOPER

"*The Cartographer's Secret* is a galvanizing, immersive adventure following a family's entanglement with a vanished Australian explorer through the lush Hunter Valley at the turn of the twentieth century, forcing the characters to reckon with the choice found at the crux of passion and loyalty, and the power of shared blood that can either destroy or heal."

—Joy Callaway, international bestselling author of *The Fifth Avenue Artists Society* and *The Greenbrier Resort*

"In *The Cartographer's Secret*, Cooper invites readers into another sweeping tale full of her signature mix of mystery, history, romance, and family secrets. Firmly set within one of Australia's great historical puzzles, Letitia Rawlings embarks on a harrowing adventure, discovering answers to the deeper questions of life—loyalty, trust, sacrifice, love, and the true meaning of family—along the way. Readers will love this gripping tale to the very last page, and beyond."

—Katherine Reay, bestselling author of *The London House* and *The Printed Letter Bookshop*

"Deeply researched. Emotional. Atmospheric and alive . . . Tea Cooper transports the reader to a sweeping landscape of turn-of-the-twentieth-century Australia—from the raw realities of the Australian goldfields to the sophisticated institutions of Sydney—and does so with an expert pen. Combining characters that are wonderfully complex with a story spanning decades of their lives, *The Girl in the Painting* is a triumph of family, faith, and long-awaited forgiveness. I was swept away!"

—Kristy Cambron, award-winning author of *The Paris Dressmaker* and the Hidden Masterpiece novels

"A stunning historic̶ roams through quaint Maitland Tow̶ ̶gh to bustling Sydney and even the ̶ ̶ystery and an

air of romance, this new novel from one of Australia's leading historical fiction specialists will leave you amazed."

—*Mrs B's Book Reviews*, Australia

"Cooper has fashioned a richly intriguing tale."

—*Booklist*, for *The Woman in the Green Dress*

"Refreshing and unique, *The Woman in the Green Dress* sweeps you across the wild lands of Australia in a thrilling whirl of mystery, romance, and danger. This magical tale weaves together two storylines with a heart-pounding finish that is drop-dead gorgeous."

—J'nell Ciesielski, author of *The Ice Swan*

"Readers of Kate Morton and Beatriz Williams will be dazzled. *The Woman in the Green Dress* spins readers into an evocative world of mystery and romance in this deeply researched book by Tea Cooper. There is a Dickensian flair to Cooper's carefully constructed world of lost inheritances and found treasures . . . One of the most intelligent, visceral, and vibrant historical reads I have had the privilege of visiting in an age."

—Rachel McMillan, author of *The London Restoration*

"Boast[s] strong female protagonists, an infectious fascination with the past, and the narrative skill to weave multiple timelines into a satisfying whole . . . fast paced and involving storytelling . . . smartly edited, cleanly written . . . easy to devour."

—*Sydney Morning Herald*, for *The Woman in the Green Dress*

"A freshly drawn, bittersweet saga that draws nuggets of 'truth' with timeless magic and might-have-beens."

—*North & South* magazine, New Zealand,
for *The Woman in the Green Dress*

"*The Woman in the Green Dress* is a fine read, sure to be devoured by . . . all fans of quality fiction. An utterly engrossing story."

—Better Reading, Sydney

THE
CARTOGRAPHER'S
SECRET

ALSO BY TEA COOPER

The Girl in the Painting
The Woman in the Green Dress
The Naturalist's Daughter
The Currency Lass
The Cedar Cutter
The Horse Thief

(AVAILABLE IN EBOOK)
Matilda's Freedom
Lily's Leap
Forgotten Fragrance
The House on Boundary Street

THE
CARTOGRAPHER'S
SECRET

TEA COOPER

HARPER **MUSE**

The Cartographer's Secret

Copyright © 2021 Tea Cooper

First Published 2020

First Australian Paperback Edition 2020

ISBN 978-1-4892-9957-4

© 2020 by Tea Cooper

Australian Copyright 2020

New Zealand Copyright 2020

All rights reserved. No portion of this book may be reproduced, stored in a retrieval system, or transmitted in any form or by any means—electronic, mechanical, photocopy, recording, scanning, or other—except for brief quotations in critical reviews or articles, without the prior written permission of the publisher.

Published by Harper Muse, an imprint of HarperCollins Focus LLC.

Map by Wikimedia Commons

This book is a work of fiction. The characters, incidents, and dialogue are drawn from the author's imagination and are not to be construed as real. Any resemblance to actual events or persons, living or dead, is entirely coincidental.

Any internet addresses (websites, blogs, etc.) in this book are offered as a resource. They are not intended in any way to be or imply an endorsement by HarperCollins Focus LLC, nor does HarperCollins Focus LLC vouch for the content of these sites for the life of this book.

Library of Congress Cataloging-in-Publication Data

Names: Cooper, Tea, author.
Title: The cartographer's secret / Tea Cooper.
Description: [Nashville, TN] : Harper Muse, [2021] | Summary: "A gripping historical mystery for fans of Kate Morton and Natasha Lester's The Paris Seamstress, The Cartographer's Secret follows a young woman's quest to heal a family rift as she becomes entangled in one of Australia's greatest historical puzzles"-- Provided by publisher.
Identifiers: LCCN 2021021234 (print) | LCCN 2021021235 (ebook) | ISBN 9780785267317 (paperback) | ISBN 9780785267454 (epub) | ISBN 9780785267591
Subjects: LCSH: Mystery fiction. gsafd | BISAC: FICTION / Romance / Historical / 20th Century | FICTION / Mystery & Detective / Amateur Sleuth
Classification: LCC PR9619.4.C659 C37 2021 (print) | LCC PR9619.4.C659 (ebook) | DDC 823/.92--dc23
LC record available at https://lccn.loc.gov/2021021234
LC ebook record available at https://lccn.loc.gov/2021021235

Printed in the United States of America

21 22 23 24 25 LSC 5 4 3 2 1

To Carl Hoipo,
chief historian, historical guru, and cartophile,
with more thanks than I can ever express

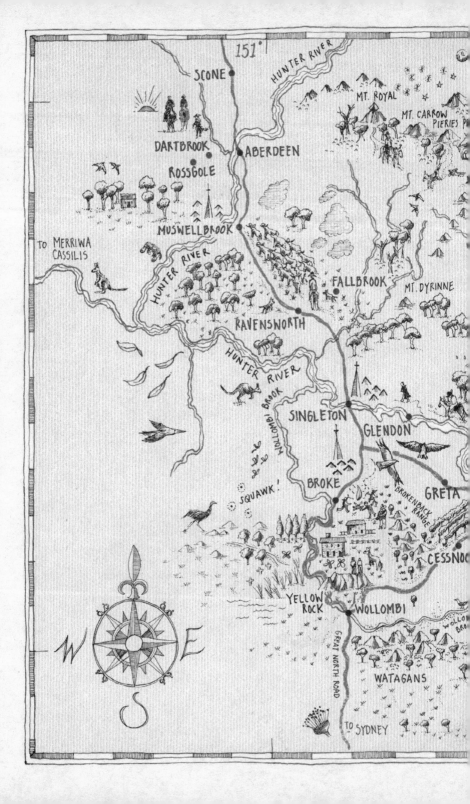

PROLOGUE

SYDNEY, AUSTRALIA, 1911

Ladies, ladies. Your attention, please. It is imperative that we take advantage of this opportunity." An air of despair laced Mrs. Booth's voice. "Miss Fletcher is a very busy woman; her studio portraits are in high demand. We are very lucky to have her here today."

The hands on the wall clock ticked their agonizing way to two. By the time the women were herded into place, it would be well past the hour Letitia Rawlings promised to be standing on the corner of George Street. The boat race started at three, and she had to be aboard before the starter's gun.

Precious minutes lapsed while Miss Fletcher arranged every single member of the Women's Club, seating Mrs. Booth in the center, adjusting drapes, worrying about height, the set of elbows, and the women's ability to remain silent and still. When she'd accomplished those major feats, she spent more valuable moments measuring the intensity of the light while an argument ensued about who should sit next to whom.

Patience worn to a frazzle, Lettie turned to Mrs. Booth and hissed, "I really must leave. I have a prior commitment."

"You cannot." Mrs. Booth clamped her hand firmly on Lettie's arm and held her steady, fixed her eyes on the camera, and nodded. "Continue, Miss Fletcher. We are ready."

A further eternity passed until finally Lettie managed to offer her farewells and escape. She scanned the busy street searching for Thorne's pride and joy—his motor—but the shiny green custom-built Model T Ford with its distinctive khaki roof was nowhere to be seen.

There was no sign of her brother in Pitt Street either, which was hardly unexpected. If he'd waited he'd have missed the pre-start checks. Thorne always won the sprint, and she usually made a fine showing in the ladies' steering race, but she'd promised to attend the luncheon at the Women's Club. There had been several of her cohort from the Ladies Debating Society present, and she hadn't caught up with them since university days. Now she wished she'd refused the invitation.

Clamping her hat over her unruly curls and dodging the crowds, she bolted down the hill toward the Quay. The start line was just beyond Fort Macquarie Tram Depot. It couldn't take more than fifteen minutes. If she hurried she might have time to slip into her well-worn seat at the back of Thorne's boat before the race began.

The first glimmer of the harbor appeared between the buildings surrounding the Quay. Seven minutes until the gun. Even if she wasn't aboard, she'd be there to cheer Thorne to the finish. Tucking her bag under her arm, she lifted her skirts and ran.

The ground shuddered.

A deafening explosion ricocheted from the buildings, thundered through her body, and shook her to her core.

And the sky lit up—an obscene ball of flame and smoke shot into the windless air. Jagged timber shards knifed toward the sky. Flames crackled and her ears rang, filling her chest with a strange, heavy thump.

A limp body arced through the billowing clouds.

All-encompassing silence. No sound, no words, just a horrendous, earth-stopping dread as the dancing blaze and floating debris mesmerized the crowd of onlookers.

And there in the benign waves lapping the small stretch of sand, a straw boater. Not a mark on it, the blue hair ribbon he'd pinched from her dresser that morning still pristine.

The gaping hollow in her stomach sliced its way to her heart, and Lettie knew her beloved brother, Thorne Ludgrove Rawlings, was no more.

1

Lettie lay on her bed, eyes focused on the ceiling rose, waiting for her breathing to settle and the sweat to dry on her skin. She knew, down to the last second, how long it would take to rid herself of the flickering images.

No matter what the papers described, no matter what the eyewitness reports and the scientific evidence suggested, the result was conclusive. A careless cigarette and her brother was no more.

She reached for her sketchbook and flicked through the pages to the last drawing she'd made: Thorne at the stern of the boat, his boater at a rakish angle and his smile blazing in competition with the noonday sun. If only she'd done as she'd promised and hadn't agreed to the ridiculous photograph to commemorate the insignificant achievements of the Women's Club.

Perhaps if she'd made it to the wharf in time, Thorne wouldn't have lit the cigarette. She could imagine his impatience. She'd berated him hundreds of times for smoking in the boat—they both knew the dangers of a naked flame with the engine primed.

They'd dreamed of shared adventures and exploration, made so many plans. The biggest reminder of them sat mocking her in the old stables behind the row of terraces on Macquarie Street. Their future, their way out. And now she couldn't bring herself to lift the dust sheets covering the Model T Ford. She might as well lie buried beneath them; better still, buried with Thorne beneath the open-armed angel in Waverley Cemetery.

"Letitia! I wish to speak to you."

She wiped away her tears and rolled off the bed, squinting into the early morning sun rising over the Botanic Gardens. Donning yesterday's black skirt and blouse, she hurried along the landing in answer to her mother's call.

The creaking door echoed her silent groan as she swung it open, her mouth clamped against the stale air as she waited for her eyes to adjust to the gloom.

Pillows plumped, bed jacket neatly arranged, and breakfast tray balanced across her lap, Mrs. Miriam Rawlings lifted her lorgnette to her eyes and surveyed her daughter from head to toe. "I imagined you'd be up and breakfasted. The time for excuses is over; a routine must be established."

Something Lettie simply hadn't managed to do. Only Thorne made their privileged existence bearable, and since his accident she'd done very little other than mope around the house. Even Pater's cherished grandfather clock no longer ticked away the meaningless hours of her existence, its pendulum tied in place marking the time of her brother's demise.

The half-light softened Miriam's features but failed to mask the perpetual shrewdness in her gaze. "I have made a decision." She patted the side of the bed, inviting her to sit.

Unnerved by the unusual gesture, Lettie parked herself on the corner of the bed, hands in lap, feet tucked to one side, seeking to present the picture expected rather than suffer yet another diatribe about her shortcomings.

"Letitia," Miriam murmured in a soft tone, the one she used when she despaired her standards would ever be met. "You must come to terms with the situation. We can no longer leave matters to chance."

Not this again. Not the endless discussion about Thorne's inheritance. "Have you not written again?"

"I wrote before and after the funeral and, as expected, she hasn't deigned to respond. Why would I write again?"

A very good question, really. To the best of her knowledge, the ridiculous silence between the Ludgroves and the Maynards had been maintained for nigh on thirty years. Lettie examined the cuff of her blouse. "To ensure Great-Aunt Olivia received your letters and knows of Thorne's passing." Great-Aunt Olivia Maynard, the sole orchestrator of the estrangement between the Ludgrove and the Maynard families.

"I've procrastinated for too long." Miriam tapped her lorgnette against her teeth. "There's nothing for it . . . I shall have to make the journey."

Lettie squirmed under her gaze. "Shall I come with you?"

"I'll take Connors, drive down, and spend the night in Wollombi. I believe there is a tolerable hotel there." She picked up her journal and leafed through the pages, letting out a series of sighs and tuts and indulging in a great deal of head shaking. "You have so many engagements."

Lettie's spine gave an involuntary twitch. An ever-increasing pile of invitations lay unanswered, and now, after a six-month reprieve, Miriam had decided the time had come to crank up the

Hunt-for-a-Husband rigmarole and expected her to flutter and fawn and make sheep's eyes at every one of the distinguished gentlemen Miriam paraded in front of her. She had some ridiculous notion that Lettie was the best catch in Sydney, which, with her being twenty-five, was so far from the truth as to be laughable, never mind the fact she wasn't the slightest bit interested in matrimony. She enjoyed male companionship, liked nothing better than to tinker with the engine of the motor car or discuss the benefits of gasoline over electric, but she hated the societal demands Miriam forced upon her, missed her brother like an amputated limb, and was seriously suspicious of the state of matrimony. Most men were looking for a servant and a bedfellow. She craved the type of companionship she and Thorne had shared, but there were few among the upper classes of Sydney who understood the workings of a Model T Ford or the delights of motorboat racing. She refused to marry, to pander to some man's quirks and whims. There had to be more to life.

The string of gentlemen callers, conjured like rabbits from a magician's hat, had reappeared in the last few weeks, and Lettie wanted none of it. She intended to manage her own affairs. She leaped to her feet and pulled back the heavy brocade curtains with more force than intended.

"Lettie, don't, please don't."

The use of her pet name brought her to a standstill. Pater was the only one who called her Lettie. Pater . . . and Thorne.

"We must put this behind us and move on, no matter how painful it might be. Too much time has passed." Moisture leaked from Miriam's eyes, tracking down the fine lines she tried so hard to mask. Lettie had never seen Miriam truly cry. Not when Grandfather died, not when the Depression had stripped the family of many of their assets, not even when Lettie had broken the dreadful news of Thorne's accident. It was something Miriam simply didn't tolerate.

An unexpected rush of compassion took Lettie by surprise. Miriam never offered her any show of warmth or tenderness, never had. Thorne was the sun around which every member of the family revolved; she couldn't remember a time when it had been otherwise.

"You must attend to these invitations." Miriam tightened the matrimonial net.

And in that moment Lettie saw her escape. "Why don't I go and break the news to Great-Aunt Olivia?"

"You?"

"Whyever not? It would save you the trip."

"Alone? You can't go alone." Miriam picked up the hand mirror from her bedside table and peered into it, stretching the skin of her cheeks. "However, I am not at my best. The last months have taken their toll—"

"The very reason I should go," Lettie interrupted. Hopefully alone. "I believe the road once out of Sydney is quite rough. It may aggravate your rheumatic fever . . ."

"And what about these?" Miriam indicated the list of engagements in her journal.

"Surely they can wait, be postponed. A week at most. What difference would it make?"

"You'll have to be careful. Olivia is a difficult character. She's got a tongue like acid and a mind to match. Very fixed ideas. Take Connors."

Lettie had no intention of taking Connors, Mother's lugubrious part-time chauffeur and factotum, but leaving Sydney was an enticing option and one Thorne would thoroughly approve. He'd taught her to drive. *"One day you'll thank me for this,"* he'd said as she'd crunched the gears and stalled for the umpteenth time on the steep hills around Sydney. *"A lady should never rely on a man to see her out of trouble"*—spoken with a wry grin after another of his spectacular failures to arrive at the appointed hour. On that occasion, she'd ended up walking home alone. A journey she'd thoroughly enjoyed, though never admitted. "I'll take Thorne's motor, drive myself. You can't manage without Connors, not while Pater's so busy."

"Oh no. I don't believe—"

"It's the obvious solution, and I have long since attained my majority so there is nothing inappropriate in traveling alone." And very little Miriam could do to prevent her. Her own bank account contained a very tidy sum from her commissions. After Thorne approached the editor of *The Bulletin*, they'd published several of her drawings, albeit under a pseudonym. Fortunately, neither Miriam nor Pater had discovered Raw Edge was, in fact, Miss Letitia Rawlings. "Tell me all I need to know about Great-Aunt Olivia."

"Perhaps it is a solution. Your commitments could be rescheduled." Miriam pulled herself a little higher up the pillows. "There's very little you don't know. Olivia is my mother's sister, your great-aunt on the Maynard side, the last of the line. She's always had an unladylike passion for breeding horses, and she has very fixed ideas." Her lips pursed. "Although I suspect her passion will have waned. She must be close to seventy." An air of evasiveness hung for a moment. "She can be very loose with the truth. Are you sure you're up to it? The meeting will be fraught with difficulties."

Lettie could barely remember the woman. She and Thorne had

visited only once, as children, after Grandfather died. A dark old house, the atmosphere thick with unvoiced grievances, Miriam stony faced, Pater cowed as he hustled them back to the carriage he'd hired, long before the days of motor cars. Thorne had wrangled himself free and clambered into the branches of a majestic angophora . . . She swallowed the lump in her throat.

Maybe a trip would help her wretched lethargy abate, provide material for some new drawings and articles, clear her mind. The editor of *The Bulletin* had sent a card only a few days ago requesting an appointment. She hadn't answered, had nothing to offer.

"Letitia." Miriam patted the counterpane, inviting her to sit again. "I'll be honest with you, there's more to the visit than good manners. Thorne was heir to both properties. You must accept your responsibilities, for the family's sake."

Miriam's words brought Lettie's head up sharply. "With Thorne gone . . ." Miriam raised her hands almost in supplication, and with a crashing realization Lettie understood the plan she'd fallen victim to.

"You want me to ingratiate myself with Great-Aunt Olivia and ensure that Thorne's inheritance . . ." She couldn't finish the sentence. The horror of the prospect sank slowly into her atrophied brain.

"Darling, it's for the best."

Darling! Since when had she ever been anyone's darling? That spot was reserved for Thorne and Thorne alone. No matter what plan Miriam might be hatching, Lettie had no intention of moving into the role Thorne had vacated.

"It is Olivia who, by her callous disregard for your grandfather's wishes, has foiled everyone's intentions. You must go and speak to her. Make her see that now Thorne has gone . . ." Miriam dabbed her dry eyes with the soggy scrap of lace. "Letitia, you must be the one to inherit. Not just for the family but for yourself. You're no longer a young girl. A large endowment will significantly increase your odds on the marriage market."

Good God! Was she nothing but a prize racehorse?

"Thorne planned to drive out and see Aunt Olivia." The words, the secret trip Thorne had promised, tripped off Lettie's tongue.

Miriam's head tilted at an alarming angle and her mouth followed suit while she fished for words. "Why would he have wanted to do that?"

"He thought it would be the right thing. Introduce himself to the woman whose estate he may one day inherit."

"But we don't . . . we haven't . . ."

"Spoken for years. Yes, indeed, and that's why Thorne thought it was the right thing to do. He didn't want to appear grasping or rude." And neither did she.

Miriam lifted her teacup, handkerchief held to the base to catch the drips, and sipped. Over the rim her eyes glittered. Unshed tears from grief? More likely due to the prospect of achieving her aim. A hard, tight smile pulled at the lines around her mouth. "We must never appear rude."

After the claustrophobic months of mourning, the hope of an escape beckoned like a welcoming wave, outweighing the horror of Miriam's contrivance.

Lettie brushed off her skirt. She wouldn't do this for Miriam; she'd do it for Thorne, do as he'd intended, uncover the secrets of the past and bring an end to the ridiculous family feud. "I'll go and get the motor out from the stables and check it over. It'll need an oil change and grease, spare tires, and extra gasoline."

Fired with a long-forgotten enthusiasm, and wanting to get

away before she had to listen to any more of Miriam's blathering, Lettie fled downstairs and into the stables. Ignoring the sudden wrench as she opened the car door and inhaled the familiar scent of Thorne's cologne, she reached beneath the seat and pulled out his matches and packet of cigarettes and lit one.

The exhaled cloud of smoke conjured his grinning face, then faded as the specter of Great-Aunt Olivia rose, tinging the air with the stirrings of the long-forgotten past.

2

The pair of wedge-tailed eagles soared high in the air, circling on the thermal currents rising from the ground below. Evie tilted her face to the sun and threw out her arms to embrace the view that encompassed her world: from the ancient rocks beneath her bare feet to the distant horizon where the pale pink clouds marked the division between reality and mystery.

All she needed and all she had ever wanted. This was her place, where she belonged.

The valley below shimmered like the surface of a vast inland sea edged by blue-gray ridges unfurling into the distance. Over it all lay an intense stillness, broken only by the jeweled flashes of the parrots and the screeches of the cockatoos. A view so indelibly engraved on her mind she could recapture every detail with her eyes closed.

A distant *cooee* rang out, echoed, and bounced back. Snatching up a spray of flowering old man's beard she'd found growing along the track, she slithered down the rock face to the clearing where her horse stood patiently cropping a patch of grass. She threw herself astride Elsey's back and galloped down to the very spot where Aunt Olivia stood waiting.

"If you've been out on your own again you'll be for it." Aunt Olivia dusted her hands and glared.

For as long as Evie could remember Pa had insisted someone should always accompany her, although as she'd gotten older she'd learned to pick her time and sneak away alone.

"I haven't been far. Elsey needed some exercise."

"And that would tell otherwise." Aunt Olivia pointed to the spray in her hand. "Don't give me that rubbish. That grows up the top. You've been up Yellow Rock again."

"I didn't come to any harm." Throughout her childhood she'd suffered from the occasional spell that no one could explain. One moment she would be "there" and the next, someone would be sitting her up and asking if she was all right. She always was, but it was as though she'd lost a fragment of time.

"Your father wanted to know where you were."

"Did you tell him?" She tucked the spray of flowers into the metal tube she used for collecting samples. The last thing she wanted was a lecture from Pa on what Doctor Glennie liked to call *petit mal*. It was in no way evil nor an illness; simply a slipping of time and a residue pain in her head that dispersed after an hour or so. And besides, it hadn't happened for almost two years. "You better get a move on. He wants to talk to you in the study. Now."

Evie's stomach gave a lurch. Pa had never summoned her to his study in such a peremptory fashion before. "Why?"

Aunt Olivia shrugged her shoulders. "I have no idea. I'm going to sit with Alice. She needs some company."

Poor Mama. A pall hung over the house, the air laden with an oppressive ambience. That was why Evie had fled, hadn't even taken her sketchbook or her paints. She'd simply thrown a blanket over Elsey's back and slipped the bridle over her head. Then galloped off, leaving behind the strange, thick silence cloaking the house.

She pushed open the study door and tipped her head around the corner, inhaling the familiar scent of leather, old papers, and ink mixed with Pa's sandalwood soap. And dust—more dust than anywhere else in the house, because he guarded his precious mementos with a single-minded obsession and no feather duster was allowed in his hallowed space.

"Come in, my sweet. Come in." He peered up from the piles of paperwork obliterating the desktop.

She stepped inside, her hand drifting toward the two globes. When Pa was away in Sydney she'd sneak inside and wander among his mysterious collections, her fingers trailing over the fossils and shells, sharpened rocks, and strange artifacts arranged on the mantelpiece. It brought him closer, a way of feeling the essence of him during the long days without him. As she stood and spun the terrestrial and celestial globes, she'd imagine his voice patiently describing the world's wonders that inhabited her daydreams and filled the void of her loneliness.

Pa gestured to the chair across from his desk. Taking care to avoid the sprawled mass of dog on the carpet, she picked her way across the room. Pa's hound, Oxley, the shaggy bundle of bones that possibly loved Pa even more than she did, raised his head and flicked his bedraggled tail in welcome.

It wasn't until she reached the desk that she realized what Pa was studying with such intent. Her palms grew damp and her heart picked up a beat or two. She'd given it to him last evening, asked for his opinion on the task that had consumed her every waking hour for the last year.

Her map.

The map of her life—every place of significance she'd visited, every track she'd traveled, every story Pa had told her of the vast Hunter Valley.

He lifted his leonine head, eyes twinkling. "I had no idea you were so talented."

Heat rose to her cheeks, feet fidgeting, heart thumping as she fought the desire to cover her face. Pa loved her drawings. He'd hung a series in golden frames in the hallway, showed them to anyone and everyone who visited, but she knew why her map had particularly sparked his interest.

He was a surveyor, and if life had treated him more kindly, his name would rank with many of the famous explorers who had charted the wide land the Ludgroves and the Maynards called home: Blaxland, Mitchell, Oxley, Sturt, Hume and Hovell, and of course, Ludwig Leichhardt.

"I see you've marked some of Leichhardt's travels through the Hunter." Pa let out a long sigh and traced the path she'd annotated. "A prince, the veritable Prince of Explorers, the most amiable of men." His eyes took on a distant look as they always did when he spoke of Doctor Leichhardt, staring out to some far horizon visible only in his memory, a memory that still rankled despite the passing years.

"What do you think, Evie? Have you a theory? Leichhardt left us with such a mystery when he and his exploration party disappeared, never to be seen again. Five men, two Aboriginal guides, seven horses, twenty mules, and fifty bullocks cannot vanish without a trace. Can your bright young mind shed some light on this conundrum?"

She tucked a rogue curl behind her ear, then tightened her

fingers around the strap of her collecting box; she wanted to show Pa the spray of lichen she'd found, but she knew better than to disturb his reminiscences.

These were the stories she'd grown up with, her bedtime stories. Fairy tales lulled other children to sleep, fantasies of princesses locked in towers, marauding dragons, and handsome princes. She had her handsome prince, but he was no fantasy. He was a genuine hero.

"I see you have marked the spot where I first met Leichhardt."

Evie didn't respond. She knew the words that would follow as surely as any well-loved fable.

"I came across him horseless and lost on the banks of the Hunter. Here he is. You've drawn him on the map. Are the coordinates correct?" He lifted the monocle he'd taken to wearing on a long black ribbon around his neck and gripped it between his cheek and brow bone. "Why, you've even drawn his hat and long coat. Such an impractical garment. It was the array of pockets he loved. He was on his way to the Scotts' and had missed the path. When I delivered him, safe and sound, they invited our entire family to return for a Christmas feast, and very fine it was too. Tables stretched in the shade of the spreading trees, roast goose and plum pudding, figs, peaches, apricots from their trees." He let out a delighted chuckle and pointed to the little vignette marking what was once the vast property of Glendon. "And here we all are enjoying the Christmas bounty. And here are the drovers at their camp beyond the stables. Your map is remarkably accurate."

For longer than she could remember, the old maps of the Dutch cartographers had held her fascination. She tried to replicate the intricate designs and drawings and at the same time remain true to history and the local landscape. She'd wanted to mark the great ocean beyond Newcastle with the words *Here there be dragons*, but she'd had to make do with *Here there be whales*. Any inaccuracy would have incurred Pa's wrath.

"I've always believed Leichhardt only invited me to accompany him through the Hunter in the hope he wouldn't get lost again." He allowed himself a wry laugh. "You've marked it all. The places we unearthed fossils and the ancient water courses, even our camp on Pieries Peak. A time of my life I will never forget. Armed with little more than knapsacks and notebooks, we roamed wherever we fancied. From Yellow Rock itself to the very summit of Mount Royal, country filled with stands of box, spotted gum, blackbutt and forest gum, ironbark and stringybark." He let out a painful sigh. "We could have achieved so much."

But there was no happy ending to Pa's story, no pot of gold at the end of the rainbow. The evidence sat before her in the shape of poor Pa. Struck down in his prime, to live forever with dreams of what might have been.

"We had such plans of exploration, for the betterment of the country, for you, my sweet, and all who will come after you."

She knew better than to interrupt, but he'd aroused her curiosity. She'd heard so many tales of Leichhardt's expedition, but none that directly affected her. "How?"

"First an overland route to Carpentaria, creating a shorter route to India, an unlimited market for our horses. The settlement at Port Essington would be our *entrepôt* for all traffic in and out of the country. And acres and acres of grazing land, enough for all the generations who would follow." He rolled his eyes and shook his head. "But for the governor. He refused to confirm the vote for supplies. Then, always impatient, Leichhardt took matters into his own hands, volunteered to lead and finance the expedition himself. Many of us in the Hunter bred horses, the finest in the colony, our reputation established. Your grandfather raised a large proportion of the funds to support Leichhardt, and I was to travel with them. Then this . . ." Pa thumped his leg with his cane and heaved upright.

Pa, the man who'd lost most of his leg and all his dreams to an unfortunate accident.

He wasn't alone in his obsession with Leichhardt. The entire country continued to offer theories regarding his disappearance, and had ever since Leichhardt's final, fateful expedition to cross the continent from east to west over thirty years ago. A cornucopia of possibilities continued to absorb the population: Leichhardt and his party were murdered, or mutinied; they drowned in a flash flood or perished for want of water; even that they were eaten by sharks in the Gulf; and more recently that Leichhardt had lived out his days with a tribe deep in the desert—but nothing conclusive, nothing ever proven. "Perhaps he simply got lost."

"They thought him lost somewhere between the Darling Downs and Port Essington on his first expedition, but he wasn't, was he? Bold as brass he sailed into Port Jackson. Three thousand miles in fifteen months. Three thousand miles!" Another whack with Pa's cane on his wooden leg brought her out of her reverie. Pa's life's dream to accompany Leichhardt, shattered by a single misstep.

Her map showed the past, Pa's stories, where he preferred to dwell. Much of the Hunter she and Pa had traveled together—he in the dog cart he favored as he could no longer ride, the faithful Oxley by his side, and she astride a pony that she'd gradually outgrown until she'd received Elsey for her sixteenth birthday. In Pa's eyes the most magnificent Waler ever bred on the property.

Together they'd charted the paths with a compass and sextant, camped, and as the sky darkened Pa would point out the map of the stars, tell her the stories he'd learned from the Wonnarua People, and quote his favorite line from *Hamlet*. "'There are more things in heaven and earth . . . ,'" she murmured.

"'. . . than are dreamt of in your philosophy,'" Pa finished with a wistful smile. "It's time we attended upon your mother, but first perhaps you'd like to show me what you have in your vasculum. Something from Yellow Rock?"

Her cheeks heated; he'd known all along where she'd been. While he rolled her map and secured it with the faded blue ribbon she'd saved from an outgrown dress, she lifted the lid on the cylindrical collecting box and carefully took out the spray of old man's beard.

"Ah! *Usnea*. Unusual to find it flowering."

"It grows on Yellow Rock. I'd like to add a picture of it." She reached for her map.

"I'd like to study it further. I noticed there are sections yet to be completed. We should discuss those."

A flicker of annoyance danced across her shoulders. Her map was something she'd created to amuse herself, to fill the long hours she spent alone. She could hardly refuse, but she had plans for the unfinished sections.

With Oxley panting at their heels, she led the way to the top of the stairs and into Mama's room where, despite the warm day, a fire burned, rendering the bedchamber claustrophobic. It reeked of sickness and the strange air of despair that permeated the house.

The huge mound Mama assured the family was their long-awaited brother simply accentuated her pallor and discomfort. Aunt Olivia sat at the bedside, sweat beading her brow as she attempted to master the latest piece of embroidery foisted on her.

"How are you this evening?" Pa reached for Mama's hand.

She offered a wan smile. "A little cold and a trifle uncomfortable." With both hands, she cupped her stomach. "I haven't seen Miriam today."

Olivia dropped her needlework in a flurry, a look of concern washing across her face. "I'll go and fetch her." She jumped up, her hand on the doorknob before anyone could respond.

"Bailey and the drovers are in. She'll be down at the camp, kicking up her heels."

Pa hovered at the end of Mama's bed, his eyes fixed on the dwindling light beyond the rock, as though his mind still rested on Evie's map, compass points or landforms she might have forgotten to include. Keen to escape the oppressiveness of the overheated room, Evie rose. "I'll go with Olivia and find Miriam."

The plaintive look etching Mama's pale features kept Evie tied to the spot beside the bed.

"Stay with me. I've seen nothing of you today either." She reached for her hand.

"And on your way, Olivia, ask Mrs. Hewitt to serve supper here. I've got work to do," Pa said.

Evie, as well as everyone else, knew this was Pa's way of escaping Mama's confinement. She could hardly blame him. The chances of the baby being born alive diminished with each passing day. The last time Doctor Glennie called he'd taken Pa aside. Evie didn't need him to tell her, nor did Mama. Come what may, she would have to deliver herself of the child, and after the wretched losses of Evie's two older brothers, who hadn't drawn more than a few blue-tinged breaths, Mama's wait was an ongoing agony.

Evie sank down on the edge of the bed and cradled Mama's frail hand.

"I'm sorry. You must be strong."

A shiver traced her spine as she smoothed Mama's dry skin. The endless string of stillbirths, miscarriages, and misery had ravaged her face and stripped her mind and body of her vivacity. "There's nothing to be sorry about."

"I haven't long now."

"Everything will be fine once the baby comes."

A fierce, fevered light shone in Mama's dark eyes as she struggled higher in the bed. "No. You know as well as I. There will be no heir for your father, no brother for you."

How could Mama be certain this baby was a boy? Both Evie and Miriam had thrived. It was only Mama who harbored this mind-consuming belief that she'd failed because she couldn't produce a son and heir for the mighty Maynard-Ludgrove alliance. "Perhaps we will have a sister. I would like that."

"He's a boy. I know."

Only because Mrs. Hewitt had dangled Mama's wedding ring over her stomach, like some ancient water-divining crone. It hung, then slowly spun—a circle for Miriam, the first daughter; from side to side for poor little William and James alone on the hillside; another circle for Evie; and then they'd all held their breath as the ring paused before swinging like an exhausted pendulum.

Mama's face had paled as she accepted her fate. The baby was a boy, and in her mind he would not survive. He would join William and James on the hillside beneath the cedar tree along with Mama's brothers. The Ludgrove and Maynard families were not destined to produce the son and heir the vast properties demanded. "There will be another chance." Evie tried for a reassuring smile and failed miserably.

"There will be no more. God knows I've tried. Tried for you

and for your father. Joshua has already gone." Mama's hands cradled her stomach. "My boys and I will be together soon."

The skin of Evie's arms rose in a horrifying rash of goose bumps. She licked her lips, snatched a moment to force some words of comfort from her addled brain, and failed. She wouldn't have another chance.

3

The sudden backfire sent Lettie rocketing forward. Head down, heart pounding, hands clutched tightly to the steering wheel, furious that even in the country, as far from the sea as she'd ever traveled, Thorne's accident could still haunt her.

She pulled off her gloves, untied her scarf, mopped the layer of perspiration from her face, and exhaled slowly, bringing her thundering heartbeat under control.

No need to check the motor. She'd babied it for the last few miles. It was a gift she'd made it this far. Releasing the hand brake, she coasted down the gentle incline toward a sign announcing she'd reached the town of Wollombi.

Hardly a town, but several yards ahead there was a solid building emblazoned with the words *Family Hotel* and behind it a meandering creek surrounded by neatly fenced, well-tended paddocks and a large market garden. Easing out from behind the wheel she stretched her legs, peeled off her thick dustcoat, and pushed up her sleeves.

A straight, flat stretch of track disappeared into a shimmering

25

heat haze, and to her right a slight incline led to some sort of a general store and a few other surprisingly substantial sandstone buildings. Not her destination, but a necessary stop. Lizzie was going nowhere until she found her a drink. What were the chances of gasoline in a remote place like this?

Pushing her driving goggles up on top of her head, she strode up the hill.

The faded door of the general store, though firmly closed, sported a scrawled sign reading *Open*. She turned the handle and entered the cool, dark interior.

"Stinking out there. Close the door behind you." The words came from the depths of the shop, but the owner of the gravelly tones remained invisible.

She swung the door closed and waited while the shadows took shape and resolved into a long counter covered in an array of wilting vegetables and other knickknacks.

"What can I do for you?" A heavyset man stepped out from behind the counter, his bushy eyebrows quivering as he took in the goggles perched on the top of her head.

"I'm after a can of gasoline."

"That'd account for the extra pair of eyes then." He gave a sigh, which may well have been relief. "Where's the motor?"

"At the bottom of the hill. I thought I'd make it into town, but I had to coast the last little bit."

He peered outside. Must have caught sight of Lizzie because he turned with a smile. "Get a few motors through here nowadays. Not usually driven by a woman, though."

"So you carry gasoline?"

"Nah."

Her stomach sank. She couldn't leave Lizzie skew-whiff on the side of the road in some out-of-the-way town.

"Where are you heading?"

"The Ludgrove-Maynard properties."

"Yellow Rock?" His eyebrows rose. "A good twenty miles. Go see Armstrong, at the forge." He flipped his thumb over his shoulder. "Just across the road. I'll keep an eye on the motor. Not that you'll have a problem. No one in town today. Too bloody humid. Armstrong'll fix you up."

"Thank you, thank you very much."

"How'd you come by the motor?" He scratched his head and studied her from head to toe.

"It belongs to my brother." *Belonged*, she mentally corrected, not wanting to get into the conversation that would ensue.

"Ah! That's more like it. Where's he, then?"

"Sydney." No lie in that. And somehow she felt that if Great-Aunt Olivia hadn't received Miriam's letter, she should be the first one to hear the news of his passing—from her, not from some shopkeeper in the local town.

"You drove yourself?"

"Plenty of practice. I had a good teacher." She slipped through the door before he could ask any more questions.

Across the road a winding flagstone path edged with faded geraniums, and the stench of cats, led to a couple of slab buildings and a sign dangling from a branch announcing *The Forge*. Following the sound of hammering, she wandered down the path and drew to a halt a good few feet from a blazing fire where a sweaty man in a leather apron hunched, belting the daylights out of a blazing horseshoe. He gave a final thump and lifted his head.

"Mr. Armstrong? I'm after some gasoline. The man at the general store said you carried it."

He wiped his forehead on a filthy rag and tossed it aside. "Nat, can you see to that while I re-shoe your horse?"

A lean, muscular man stepped from the shadows, hat pulled low, dark hair curling at the collar of his faded shirt. "Where is it?"

"Out there. Not in here." Armstrong sighed.

The man ambled to the back of the building, ducked his head beneath the lintel, and disappeared.

Lettie scampered after him.

"How much do you want?" he called over his shoulder.

"I've got three two-gallon cans to refill."

Half hidden behind the makeshift bench, Nathaniel poked around and pulled out a few cans, most of them empty. Who the hell was she? There was something about the lilt in her voice, the way she tilted her head when she spoke, something familiar, but he couldn't place her. "Nah! He's only got one. Be another delivery on the Sydney dray tomorrow." He straightened up, snatched another look, didn't want to appear to be staring.

"I'll take that. Thanks." She rammed her hand into her pocket and brought out a wallet, more like a man's than something a girl would carry, though the bug-eyed glasses rammed on the top of her head didn't look much like something a girl would wear either.

"Where are you heading?"

"The Ludgrove-Maynard properties."

"Yellow Rock?"

"Apparently."

"That'll be two shillings and sixpence." Armstrong charged twice the going rate, but she wasn't in a position to argue.

Without a second thought she pulled out a crisp pound note.

He schooled his face. More money than Armstrong had seen in a while. "Got anything smaller?"

She answered with a smile, not much more than a crease at the corner of her mouth, followed by a raised eyebrow above large green-brown eyes smudged with shadows. "Keep the change and I'll come and pick up some more on my way back."

Olivia would be in for a surprise, or maybe she was expecting a visitor, though he couldn't imagine she wouldn't have mentioned it. "You're visiting? For long?"

She shrugged. "I'm not sure. Would the Family Hotel have a room?"

"Maybe. Thought you were going to Yellow Rock. Plenty of room there. The old lady'll love a bit of company."

"You know the Ludgrove family?"

"Everyone knows everyone around here. I do a bit of work there now and again." More than a bit now that Olivia was getting on, but she was determined not to give up the horses. The cattle had all gone, though the drovers still called in on their way north. This woman couldn't know the family well if she was calling Olivia a Ludgrove. She was Maynard through and through, and would take a horse whip to anyone who tried to say otherwise. "Where's the motor? I'll give you a hand."

"Down at the bottom of the hill. I ran out at the top of the crest and coasted into town."

"Right you are." He hefted the can. "We can go out this way."

A whistle slipped out between his lips when he set eyes on the motor, as sleek as the girl standing in front of him. He'd always maintained a horse was all he needed, but he wouldn't mind the opportunity to take a ride. He thumped the can down and stood in front of the car, running his hand over the glossy green paintwork, brushing the road dust away. "I thought motors only came in black."

When he lifted his head, she was watching, lips tilted in another of those half smiles. "Mostly they do. It's my brother's car. It was custom-built in Victoria. He helped, and chose the paint color. It's the only green one in Australia."

And it matched her eyes perfectly.

"I need to fill her up." She held out her hand.

The can would be much too heavy for her. "Let me." The gasoline would have to go in under the front. That's where the engine was kept, wasn't it? He reached across and unclipped the bonnet. A mass of gleaming tubes and cylinders and all manner of bits and pieces greeted him, along with the smell of oil and grease. The tank had to be there somewhere. He lifted the can.

"It's under here." She swung open the driver's door and lifted the seat.

"Ah!" Heat rose to his face. "Right you are." He closed the bonnet. "Pretty engine."

"A front-mounted 177-cubic-inch inline four-cylinder engine, which produces twenty horsepower for a top speed of forty-five miles per hour."

She might as well have been speaking double Dutch, for all he knew.

He fitted the funnel she held out, tipped the spirit in, and replaced the lid. Not too difficult. Maybe he could get the hang of these things. "Will that see you to Yellow Rock?"

"I'll be good for about fifty miles."

"Nowhere near that far. Know the way?"

She pointed down the road to the bridge. "That way."

"You'll cross Cunneens Bridge about two hundred yards down. After that the track gets a bit rougher. Make sure you follow the brook; there are seven crossings. Rain wasn't too bad—you shouldn't have a problem, but don't hang around. There's a storm coming and the water rises fast. Once you ford the last crossing, follow the track and Yellow Rock's on your right. You'll see the drive. Can't miss it."

"Thank you." She pulled the goggles down, covering her eyes, and worked her fingers into her leather gloves.

"My pleasure." He opened the door and glanced down at the three pedals on the floor and some sort of brake. Couldn't be too complicated; he'd seen enough of them getting around on the Sydney roads. "Are you ready to go?"

"It's not quite that simple. There are a couple of things I need to do first." She fiddled with two levers hanging off the side of the steering wheel, then walked around to the front and grabbed hold of a bent piece of pipe poking out from the car. That was it. He'd seen blokes in Sydney winding their motors up. "Let me do that for you, Miss . . ."

She stepped back with a smile. "Rawlings. Letitia Rawlings."

His head came up with a snap. "You related to Olivia?" That would account for the familiarity in her looks and mannerisms. Denman always maintained Olivia had been a looker in her early days; if Miss Rawlings was an example of the family breeding, it would be easy to understand.

"She's my great-aunt."

"And you've come from Sydney."

"Yes."

He gave the pipe a swing. Nothing happened.

"You need to . . ."

He wiped his arm across his forehead, gave another mighty swing. Not much more happened, though he wasn't sure what to expect. Perhaps it wasn't as easy as it looked, and it was bloody hard work. Not something you'd imagine a slip of a woman handling.

"It'll fire in a moment. It's because she ran out of gasoline." She bent down and fiddled with something tucked below the bonnet. "There, that should help prime it. Let me have a go. Stand aside. They have a habit of kicking back." Her shoulder muscles tightened, and she set her feet square before giving the metal bar an almighty swing with her left hand. The engine spluttered and sprang to life. "Thank you for your help." She reached for her dustcoat, slipped it on, wiped her hands, and slid in behind the wheel.

Moments later, with nothing more than a wave, she headed over Cunneens Bridge into the arms of the incoming storm.

4

Evie lurched upright, the distinctive haunting cry of the koel rising in pitch and intensity. It never ceased to shock her. She burrowed under the quilt, knowing the ruckus would continue until the breeding male reclaimed his territory and attracted his mate and she'd laid her eggs in another's nest.

A heavy lethargy suffused her limbs, as though she were floating through the spring mist that rolled across the paddocks, a blissful state between sleeping and waking.

Until reality came crashing back, pulling her into a dawn she didn't want to inhabit. She scrubbed at her face, forced her eyelids open, bringing with the daylight the dismal memory of the past weeks.

She turned to the portrait she'd sketched less than a year ago. Mama tending her beloved roses, her cheeks pink from the warm glow of the sun, her body slim as a girl's. Now she lay beneath the earth, her casket alongside those of her sons, united in death as they'd never been in life.

Pa, a haggard remnant of the man he'd been; Miriam, red-eyed and strangely silent, as though all her brash opinions had flown to the heavens accompanying Mama's and Joshua's souls. Only Aunt Olivia seemed to hold the family together, though perhaps she found solace in the constant orders she issued. Not one funeral but two. Pa would never have the son he yearned for; he'd lost his wife and she her mother. The familiar prick of tears scratched behind her eyes as she struggled out of bed and shrugged into her clothes.

The reek of naphthalene from the taffeta dress she'd worn since Mama's passing hovered in a malodorous cloud above her head as she ran downstairs to find Pa, Miriam, and Olivia deep in discussion over the remnants of breakfast.

The conversation halted when she entered the room. She slipped into her customary seat next to Pa, averting her eyes from Mama's empty chair. Mrs. Hewitt laid a plate in front of her, a pile of scrambled eggs and some slices of ham, and glared at Miriam and Olivia, both of them splotchy faced as they shifted their cutlery around their plates. After a few moments of tortured silence, they left the room, their breakfast abandoned.

Pa cleared his throat, pushed his untouched plate away. "I realize it's unexpected; however, I have no option. Miriam and I will be traveling to Sydney. A suitor has made an offer. I thought to postpone the wedding until after a longer period of mourning, but I find that is not possible."

Evie's fork clattered against the plate and the egg in her mouth turned to paste. "Whyever not?" There'd been talk of suitors before Mama's passing, but none Miriam deemed acceptable. Where had this urgent Sydney suitor come from?

"Matters of the heart move in mysterious ways."

Rubbish! She'd never heard such nonsense pass Pa's lips.

"My mind is made up. Miriam and I will travel to Sydney this week to prepare for the wedding."

Some childish voice in Evie's head wanted to shout, *What about me?* She'd lost Mama, and now Pa and Miriam would leave too.

No need to ask the question. Pa knew her well enough. "You will stay here with Olivia. She will take care of you, as she has always done. Once the dates are finalized and everything organized, I'll let you know the details."

Evie chewed at a forkful of egg, more to give herself time to digest this odd information than to fulfill any desire for sustenance. It was such a contradiction. Pa always said he wanted Miriam to marry into one of the local families. Why suddenly up and rush to Sydney? And if Miriam had gotten her way and that's why they were going to Sydney, why was she sporting such red eyes? She knew her older sister well enough. She had bigger plans than living in the Hunter for the rest of her life. She should be bursting with excitement. She'd spoken of nothing but Sydney since she'd returned from Mrs. M'Ghie's Educational Establishment, a boarding school for young ladies, one Evie had managed to escape due to Pa's cosseting concerns for her health.

She pushed aside the last of the egg, masked a sniff, and plastered a conciliatory smile on her face.

"There's something more we must discuss." Pa unhooked his cane from the tabletop, eased upright. "When you've finished your breakfast, come to my study." And with that he pivoted on his heel and left.

Evie toyed with the remains of her breakfast, risked Mrs. Hewitt's wrath by leaving the mess, and scuttled down the hallway. Some indiscretion, something serious enough to merit a personal lecture. The days of storytelling and gentle reminiscences had disappeared with Mama's passing; she'd hardly spoken to Pa in the past few weeks. Perhaps he wanted to give her back her map. She hadn't dared ask.

As always, Pa's study door was closed. She knocked, then pushed it wide, the smell of the warm, sweet whiskey Pa liked to drink stronger than usual. Twisting her damp hands behind her back, she contemplated a reprimand.

"Close the door and sit down." He gestured to the chair across from him.

She eased around in front of the desk and hovered, her stomach performing a series of neat cartwheels.

"Sit." His voice carried a slight tone of amusement. "It's a bit of a mess, isn't it?"

She perched on the edge of the chair, unsure how to respond, her gaze wandering from the neatly framed collection of maps to the mounds of paperwork and journals littering his desk.

"I have something for you."

She dragged her attention to his face, saw a shadow of the familiar twinkle in his eyes, and exhaled. He knew exactly the effect this room had on her, the treasure house of all the stories he'd told over the years. Stories that had papered her childhood and still held her captive. He lifted a large package from his lap and laid it on the desk.

A wisp of breeze, warm and dry, from the open door behind her grazed her neck and she reached out, then dropped her hand back into her lap.

"Go ahead. Open it."

The wrapping snagged against her paint-stained fingers and a tingle of apprehension lifted the hair on her scalp as she pulled at the knot, working the leather thong until it came free. She slipped it from beneath the package before coiling it to save for another use.

Unwrapping the burlap, she laid bare a leather saddlebag with two buckles at the front and two straps at the back, its rounded edges stamped with a decorative border and brass studs attaching the straps to the bag, as soft to the touch as a pair of kidskin gloves. "For me?"

"Aren't you going to look inside?"

She elbowed aside a stack of papers and undid the buckles. Her breath caught. Inside she found a collection of paintbrushes and wood-encased graphite pencils, each housed tightly in its own small pocket.

"Look further. There's ink and watercolors, a place for your sketchbook, and a matching notebook. I had the pencils sent from England. The best in the world, Cumberland Graphite."

"It's beautiful." The soft calfskin slid smooth against her palms. "Thank you."

"And here"—he leaned forward and turned the saddlebag over—"the Ludgrove-Maynard brand. Should you ever lose it, the brand will be recognized and it will be returned."

"I would never lose it." From her earliest years, Pa had provided her with drawing paper, paints, and inks. And now this. A new set of tools, the most beautiful gift she'd ever received.

"I want you to do something for me while I'm away in Sydney." His words diluted the pleasure his gift had brought—she'd forgotten his announcement in the dining room. He often visited Sydney but rarely stayed for more than a week; arranging Miriam's wedding would surely take much longer.

"How long will you be away?" She couldn't bear the thought. Both Mama and Pa gone.

"A few weeks, maybe a month or two. I need you here to look after Oxley. He'd be lonely if we all left." His concerned gaze brought a rush of heat to her cheeks. Such selfish thoughts. She might not be invited to Sydney, but he cared enough to soften what he knew would be a blow with his thoughtful gift. "I have a plan, and I need your help."

"Of course." She slid forward in the chair, sitting tall, determined not to miss a single word.

"Last time I was in Sydney I met with Mr. Du Faur. We are of the opinion that it is extremely unlikely there will ever be a full and conclusive explanation of Leichhardt's fate."

Her frisson of excitement fizzled and spluttered. Du Faur, fellow of the Royal Geographical Society, was one of the few men, along with Pa, who believed the mystery of Leichhardt's disappearance would one day be solved. "What of the telescope?" Pa had told her all about it. Inscribed *L.L.D.H.D. 1845*, it had been found in the desert.

"Battered and broken, but possibly authentic."

"And the other relics, the missing ones?"

"Lost. Perhaps stolen, as suggested. I'm sure you remember the details."

She nodded. A man had returned from the interior with a satchel he claimed contained a hunting watch, telescope, quadrant, and thermometer, and a canister full of papers belonging to Leichhardt and a member of his party, his brother-in-law, August Classen, but when he opened the satchel in Sydney, nothing was there except for the telescope and some blank sheets of paper, pencils, and ink powder. "What do you think happened to them?"

"Many members of the Geographical Society thought his tale a ruse, but Du Faur and I thought otherwise and chose to fund the expedition. The poor man had been ill aboard ship from Brisbane. Someone could have stolen them while he slept, which was why we supported his further trip into the interior.

"Sadly, he and one of his companions perished in the desert within a matter of weeks. We have been over the story a hundred times. Interviewed the sole remaining survivor, a Mr. Lewis Thompson, and finally the matter has been brought to a close."

Would the mystery of Leichhardt's disappearance never be solved? It had consumed Pa for more than a quarter of a century, and its tendrils threatened to ensnare her as well. Evie lifted her gaze to offer some sympathy and found his lips pursed and his fingers drumming on the desktop.

"What is it?"

He sat back with his arms folded, eyes sparkling, and the first smile she had seen since Mama's passing lighting his face. "I have decided to publish an account of Leichhardt's achievements, lauding him rather than dwelling on his disappearance. The first history of Leichhardt ever written. And I need your help."

"Anything, of course. Anything."

"The time has come to collate my notes and make them available to the world. I intend to start at the beginning, from the moment I first met Leichhardt. I am the only person who has consistent and long-term records of all matters relating to his travels in Australia. Leichhardt's letters to me, my own journals"—he brought his fist down on the table, accentuating each item—"newspapers and articles, Du Faur's notes and reports from the Geographical Society." He rested his large hands over hers on top of the saddlebag. "I want you to produce a series of maps showing the path Leichhardt trod from the moment he arrived in the Hunter until his last communication from Roma, in Queensland. We will divide the book into three volumes—the first will cover the Hunter, the second his trip to Port Essington. I have access to his surviving notes, and members of that party are willing to include their observations. The third volume will cover his plans for his final expedition to cross the country from east to west. Leichhardt's disappearance is one of the country's great mysteries. We owe it to the world to tell the full story and applaud his achievements. It will be the greatest tribute."

The enormity of his idea blossomed, filling every crevice of her mind, and he wanted her help, wanted her to work with him. She could already see the first of the maps in her mind's eye. The view from Yellow Rock, the vast Hunter Valley from the ocean to the plains, Mount Royal in the Barrington Tops and Glendon, Razorback and Ravensworth, Cockfighter's Creek, and the mighty Hunter River. With her new saddlebag, she would have all the tools she needed at her fingertips. "We must start immediately." Her shoulders sank, for they couldn't, could they? Because Pa was due to leave for Sydney with Miriam. "Can you not postpone the trip to Sydney? Or at least cut it short?"

"Unfortunately not, and if we are to make a head start—"

Her heart thrilled at his use of the word *we*.

"—I must have all the facts at my fingertips. While I'm in Sydney I'd like you to go through my field notes, journals, and letters, organize them into groups relevant to each book. Begin with the Hunter. Complete your map—you'll find all the coordinates in my journals. Extend it and mark every piece of information no matter how insignificant. Remember everything I have taught you. Accuracy is paramount." He tapped the saddlebag, making her heart swell at the honor he was bestowing. His private thoughts and words, his journals, his most treasured possessions, meticulous and carefully recorded, his personal letters from Leichhardt . . .

"Anything you think might be relevant. I also have this." He lifted a shabby piece of paper from the desk. "This is a map Leichhardt made, originally of the Glendon property. He expanded it and sent it to me when I was recovering from my accident."

She reached out her hand and took the flimsy piece of paper with reverence. Strange to hold something that belonged to Leichhardt. According to Pa, Leichhardt's extensive notes contained some of the best maps and most detailed information on the wildlife, vegetation, and geology ever gathered.

"Once Miriam is married, we will begin in earnest. Meanwhile, go through all my papers. Perhaps you might find something I have overlooked."

Pa's words sent shivers down her spine, and she resolved to write down everything, and the maps—her maps would be the best, the most accurate and intricate ever produced.

Her skin heated at the prospect, and suddenly her envy of her older sister vanished. Let Miriam enjoy Pa's undivided attention for the time being.

Evie had no interest in Miriam's girlish pursuits, in marriage or Sydney society. She'd rather spend her time at Yellow Rock collating Pa's notes and papers, creating the book that would record the full and true story of Ludwig Leichhardt, the Prince of Explorers.

5

Somehow Lettie felt Thorne's presence closer now than she had since his passing. As though he sat beside her reveling in the speed and the tantalizing scent of adventure. Not another vehicle in sight, the rolling green hills, high sky, and lightly forested slopes creating the kind of landscape he'd promised. Everything they'd imagined, vast rugged tracts of land ripe for exploring.

The humidity brought out the scent of the eucalyptus and a hint of something sweeter along the well-defined track winding its way beside the brook. The first crossing proved nothing more than a watery dip lined with pebbles and shale, the second a little deeper, barely enough to cause a splash. A few houses dotted the clearings adjacent to the brook, small holdings, more than likely, basking under a brilliant blue sky. No sign of the promised storm. The third culvert spanned a much wider section of the creek, and the still, deep water tempted her to pull up and take a break, but the sun was already sinking toward the hills and the shadows were lengthening.

Before long she rounded a sweeping bend and found herself in a thickly wooded section where the overhanging trees created a damp, dappled tunnel. The track became muddy and the wash-away from previous storms had left potholes and a steep drop-off into the next crossing. She edged down the slope and through the water, and by the time she'd reached the other side, ominous clouds hovered above the hills and the light had begun to fade.

She pulled off her goggles and coasted along the track, impatient to reach her destination. To her right the range rose in a massive wall in front of the blue-gray clouds. For a moment she hesitated, debated turning back. She'd covered more than half the distance. A bright flash of lightning slashing down through the clouds made up her mind. She opened the throttle and forged on.

The remainder of the track proved more than acceptable and the final crossing hardly a concern. With a grin of accomplishment, she gazed up at the massive golden landform towering above the valley floor, pitted with channels where the rain had swept down over the centuries, forming sinuous hollows.

If the man's directions were good, she should almost be there. She shifted into top gear, the eddying wind whipping her hair back from her face, and a curl of anticipation, perhaps excitement, twisted her stomach.

Gripping the wheel, she swung into the driveway and slowed to a crawl. Tall, straight trees, their trunks mottled and spotted, arched above her forming a dank tunnel, and Miriam's words rang in her ears: *"Be firm. Don't stand any nonsense."*

Large thunderclouds loomed above a two-story sandstone house surrounded by acres of long grass, swaying and shifting like an inland sea. She drew in a fortifying breath. "Let's go and brave the bunyip in her lair."

The shadows beneath an ancient angophora offered some shelter from the increasing rain, and without further thought she drew to a halt and struck out toward the large house. Built of irregular sandstone in blocks of every imaginable hue, it sat square and squat despite its two stories. A veranda shaded the front of the house and behind it the cliff face towered, throwing long shadows.

From the corner of her eye Lettie sensed movement. She removed her gloves, the palms of her hands sticky with perspiration, and flexed her tensed fingers. A gleam of light shone briefly in one of the upstairs windows and she mounted the veranda, her heart thumping. But for the looming rock she'd have doubted she was in the right place. A deserted, desolate air merged with the cloying humidity.

If only she'd bothered to ask Miriam for more details. The long-standing family feud was a matter of history. As children she and Thorne would threaten each other with excommunication to Great-Aunt Olivia and then run for cover if Miriam heard the name pass their lips. How could anyone avoid speaking to a family member for decades? Thorne's plans to visit had fired Lettie's imagination; it was a rite of passage, he'd said.

Ramming her hands deep into her pockets, she approached the doors. Low clouds barely visible against the darkening sky scudded above the house, almost obliterating the two matching chimneys. The place appeared deserted, no sense of another person, no visible movement inside the house, the original flicker of light extinguished. Perhaps behind one of the shuttered windows Great-Aunt Olivia waited, watching her every move, ready to lure her into her world.

A small bell hung to one side of the doors, a rusty chain dangling. Chiding herself for her foolish fantasies, Lettie rang the bell. The sound, surprisingly loud, echoed and faded and the chain slowly stopped swinging.

At last she heard footsteps approaching. A heavy dragging sound of bolts being pulled sent her leaping off the veranda. Resisting the urge to scramble back to the motor, she held her ground. With a grind of wood against sandstone the doors swung open.

A woman in a faded cotton frock, heavy boots, and well-worn apron stood in the doorway, arms akimbo, silhouetted against the dark interior.

Lettie took a couple of steps closer. "I'm looking for Miss Maynard, Olivia Maynard."

The woman reached to the doorjamb for support, swaying slightly. "And who might you be?" With her head tipped to one side she eyed Lettie for a long moment, leaving her in no doubt that her presence was an imposition.

"My name's Letitia Rawlings."

Something resembling a spasm of despair crossed the woman's face and she dropped her gaze. "Nobody here. What do you want?"

An overwhelming sense of disappointment drowned Lettie's trepidation. "I'd like to speak with Miss Maynard. I've motored up from Sydney." And she had no idea what had possessed her to embark on such a ludicrous adventure. Why hadn't she stopped at the hotel in Wollombi and waited until the morning? Despite the stifling humidity, an icy trickle traced her skin.

"Better come over to the farm—the main house is closed up." The woman's pinched, tense mouth belied her invitation. She slammed and bolted the doors, leaving Lettie scuffing her feet until she reappeared from the back of the house. With a twist of her head she indicated the path, then trudged off toward an area full of fruit trees encompassed by trailing, mildewed grapevines.

Still doubting the wisdom of her actions, Lettie followed her through a small timber gate dangling on rusty hinges, the air redolent with the pungent fragrance of overripe citrus. They skirted a lichen-covered table and single chair beneath a sprawling lemon tree and a series of beehives farther along the path, but it wasn't until they reached the far side of the orchard that Lettie spotted a second house, smaller, single story, a stunted replica of the first.

"Maynard Farm." The woman answered her unasked question and led the way between a series of fenced paddocks. "Where the horses are bred."

Lettie stopped in her tracks. Originally Grandfather's business had revolved around horse shipments. Walers for the Indian army. Then after he died Pater had turned to racehorses. "Have you always lived here?"

"Worked here all my life. For the Ludgroves . . . and the Maynards," she added, almost as an afterthought.

A rumble of thunder shook the ground. "Then you know Olivia Maynard."

"I do." She led the way around the back of the house, stepped up onto the back veranda, and in a well-practiced move, cocked her hip against the door. Unlike the big house, it swung open with barely a complaint. "You better come in."

Before she had time to falter, Lettie stepped into the cool, dark interior and stood hovering.

"Close the door behind you. Keep the humidity at bay."

The kitchen, dominated by a huge scrubbed timber table and blackened range, felt homely. Away from the brooding presence of the main house, Lettie's resolve strengthened.

"Sit yourself down." The woman dumped her basket onto the table. "I expect you could do with something to drink." Disappearing into a small room off to one side, she clattered and banged and then reappeared with two glasses and a bottle. "Lemonade?"

Lettie ran her tongue around the inside of her mouth, dislodging some of the accumulated dirt and dust from the road. "That would be lovely."

The woman pulled up a chair, sat down, and poured two glasses, then pushed one across the table. The deliciously cool lemonade slipped down her throat, and when she put the glass down she'd almost finished it. Not so the woman; she hadn't touched hers. She had her chin rested in her interlocked fingers, studying Lettie intently.

Color blossomed on her cheeks. "I'm sorry. I hadn't realized how thirsty I was."

Without asking the woman topped off her glass. "And who's Miss Maynard to you?"

Lettie resisted the desire to down the second glass. "She's my great-aunt."

The ensuing silence made her feel ridiculously uncomfortable, like a child reprimanded for an unknown offense. "I'm sorry to appear unannounced, but I have a message for her . . . from my mother, Miriam Rawlings," she finished, rather hoping it would add some emphasis to her paltry tale. "She thought it would be better delivered personally."

"And that message is?"

"I really would like to speak to Miss Maynard. It's a personal matter."

The woman's eyes slid to the door, then returned to Lettie's face, resuming her intense observation.

Wriggling under her scrutiny, Lettie scraped back her chair and stood. Perhaps Great-Aunt Olivia had passed and this poor woman, with her stunned, ashen face and faded dress, was mourning her loss. Surely someone would have told Miriam if her aunt had passed.

"She's not available—at present."

It didn't sound as though she was too late, and the man in Wollombi hadn't mentioned anything. "May I wait, or should I come back tomorrow?"

"Sit yourself down. Finish your drink."

That sounded a little friendlier, and when the corners of the woman's mouth hitched in what might have been the beginning of a smile, Lettie noticed for the first time that her dark eyes didn't mirror the dour expression on her face; they held a gentle softness.

Lettie lowered herself back into the chair and picked up the glass, sipping slowly.

"From Sydney, you said?"

"Yes. I left early this morning."

"It used to take a good two or three days to make the trip. Brave girl, though, driving all this way on your own."

"I enjoyed the drive." As she spoke Lettie realized just how true the words were. The fresh air, being alone, nothing to crowd her mind but the twisting, turning road and the passing scenery, something she hadn't experienced for a long time.

"Weren't you worried about breaking down? Those motors can be unreliable. Not like a horse." Again her lips quirked, and Lettie felt as though she was testing her.

"The car belongs to my brother. He taught me to drive, and I'm pretty familiar with the workings." Thanks to *The Woman and the Car: A Chatty Little Handbook for All Women Who Motor or Who Want to Motor*, the neat little book Thorne had presented her with when he'd first given her lessons.

"And you're delivering a message for your mother."

Put like that it didn't make her sound as though she was as independent as she liked to believe. Who was this woman? She looked as though she was some sort of hired hand with her thick gray hair caught in a messy knot at the nape of her neck and her stained calico apron. "I'm sorry, I didn't catch your name."

"Mrs. Brown . . . Margaret," the woman added after a momentary pause.

Lettie lifted the glass and finished the lemonade. "I'll call back tomorrow if I may. Perhaps Miss Maynard will be available then?"

"And where will you be spending the night? We're in for a storm."

"I'll head back to town, to the hotel in Wollombi."

"Got lights on that motor of yours?"

"Yes, I have. I'm quite used to driving in the dark." Had spent more time driving at night than during the day, if the truth were known. Weaving through the streets of Sydney, collecting Thorne and spiriting him home before news of another of his escapades reached Miriam.

"Plenty of room here, and I've got a pie ready for the oven. I can't turn Miss Maynard's niece away."

"Grandniece," she corrected for some unknown reason. Perhaps because Miriam was Olivia's niece and she didn't want to wear the same label. Only Thorne had managed to keep the peace between Lettie and Miriam. And now, well . . . the familiar tightening in her throat caught her unawares. All so foolish, so ridiculously foolish to die in a boating accident on a picture-perfect autumn day.

"Can't choose your family. No matter how much you might wish it."

Lettie lifted her head with a jerk. For the second time, Mrs.

Brown had as good as read her thoughts. "Now, why don't you go out to that motor of yours, collect up your belongings. I imagine you came prepared for a night or two away. While you're doing that, I'll air one of the rooms and we'll eat the pie I've got here and have a bit of a chat."

"Will Miss Maynard be back soon?"

"I'm sure she will. Go out the back here." She gestured to the door. "Walk around the house to the front. Can't get lost, follow the path. And by the time you come back I'll have everything sorted."

It sounded very much the best solution, and she didn't fancy all the bends in the dark or the fords over the creek that twisted and turned along the track. Another rumble of thunder made the decision easy. "Thank you."

Darkness had fallen but hadn't dispersed the heaviness of the air. A sudden squall of wind and a flurry of rain sent her running the last few yards. She pulled her bag from behind the front seat and then, with a nod to Thorne, protected his pride and joy by lifting the roof and latching it against the rain.

The slate roof of the house glinted wetly in the twilight and a bird shrieked somewhere in the distance, then a jagged shaft of lightning illuminated the rock, followed by a heavy rumble of thunder. Drawing in a lungful of the sweet, moisture-laden air, she ran back along the path.

When she pushed open the back door, her stomach rumbled in appreciation, the wholesome smell reminding her she hadn't eaten since breakfast.

Lettie tucked her bag out of harm's way against the wall and moved a colander of green beans from the sink before rinsing her hands under the tap. In her absence, the table had been laid for two, which meant Great-Aunt Olivia couldn't be expected tonight.

She shook the excess water from her hands, then made some effort to tidy her hair by running her fingers through her damp curls and re-pinning them.

"There you are. Everything's ready. I'll show you to your room after we've eaten. No one occupies the main house anymore."

"Have you always lived here?"

"Born and bred."

"Then you must know my family. My grandfather, William Ludgrove, was born here. He married Alice Maynard. My mother, Miriam, is their eldest daughter."

Mrs. Brown gave a cursory sniff and dug the knife into the steaming pie. "Steak and kidney pie was William's favorite, though he liked it cold, took it when he went out roaming."

A sudden sweep of excitement raced through her. Thorne had been right. They did need to discover their roots, learn about their family. "Roaming?"

"Great one for roaming was William in his younger days. Spent time with the Blaxland brothers, learned all he knew from them."

"I'm sorry. No one's ever mentioned anyone called Blaxland."

"Surveyors, explorers. Didn't they teach you anything at that posh school of yours in Sydney?"

How did Mrs. Brown know she'd attended school in Sydney? Lucky guess, more than likely. "I . . . Yes, of course they did." History, she'd loved history. Could recite the dates of the kings and queens of England from memory—though mostly because the learning had been a punishment. "Are the Blaxlands your neighbors?"

"Properties all over the place. Came from England originally, same as all our forebears. Made a name for themselves, though. Taught your grandfather how to draw a map, use a compass."

She had no recollection of Grandfather doing very much other than sitting in his big chair staring out at the trees in the Botanic Gardens. "Grandfather Ludgrove died when I was five. I didn't know him very well."

"Obviously not. Eat up then."

Feeling very much like that five-year-old, Lettie ate quietly and cleared her plate. "Thank you, that was delicious." She smothered a yawn.

"You're tired. Take your bag and go to bed. Down the hallway, second door on the right. You should find everything you need."

"Let me help . . ." She stood to collect the plates. While they'd been talking a heavy blanket of darkness had fallen and all but the area around the table was a blur. "It's much darker here than in the city."

"Just the storm. It'll pass. Leave the plates be." Mrs. Brown held out a lantern. "Good night."

Lettie took the lantern, picked up her bag, and left the kitchen, the sound of the rain deafening on the roof. Her hand slid along the smooth timber dado as she made her way down the hallway, uncannily aware she was following in the footsteps of her long-forgotten family.

6

Evie stayed out of the way working on her map. The house, which for the past weeks had existed under the pall of mourning, became a hive of activity. Every item of clothing Miriam possessed was brought out, tried on, tutted over, cleaned, and in some cases unpicked and restitched. It seemed fashions in Sydney changed faster than the weather, and where once pleats and buttons were the order of the day, now, according to Miriam and her Sydney papers, flounces, frills, and frippery were essential.

After Evie spent a particularly late night checking the coordinates on her map, Olivia burst into her room early in the morning and refused to be ignored. She emptied the contents of her wardrobe onto the bed and shook out several of her dresses. She held them up to the light, turned them this way and that, measured length and width and breadth, then threw her hands up in horror. "There's nothing suitable. They're all too small. Come with me. I need your help."

Pulling a robe over her shift, she followed Olivia down the

hallway. When they came to a halt outside Mama's room, Evie's stomach performed a series of ungainly somersaults. She hadn't entered the room since Mama's passing.

Olivia showed no hesitation. She threw open the door and marched inside.

Evie blinked into the darkness, her throat tightening, half expecting to see Mama's form in the large bed surrounded by the fine net curtains. The room still smelled of her, of lily of the valley, vainly trying to mask an overwhelming odor of something riper, something she couldn't, didn't want to, dwell on.

"Don't be so childish. Life must go on." Olivia pushed back the curtains and let the morning light fill the morbid space. "You have to accept it, and now is as good a time as any."

Evie walked to the mirrored dressing table, the memory of the times she had stood awed by the responsibility of brushing Mama's waist-length hair bittersweet. She picked up one of the silver-backed brushes and pulled several strands of hair from the soft bristles and wound them around her finger.

"Evie!" The bark in Olivia's voice broke into her thoughts, although when she lifted her head she realized it wasn't anger she'd heard in Olivia's voice but grief. She stood, her hand on the cupboard door, gazing at the empty bed, jaw rigid. "You should have those brushes. Let me speak to your pa, but right now we have a job to do." With her lips pursed, Olivia opened the wardrobe, releasing another pungent waft of lily of the valley.

A moment later the first armful of clothes landed unceremoniously on the bed. "Miriam needs several hats and somewhere there's a cloak. More room in that."

Evie and Miriam weren't as close as sisters might have been. Mrs. Hewitt liked to say the perfect example of chalk and cheese, but Miriam was hardly overweight. Well-rounded perhaps and rarely satisfied, always wanting something more, railing against the fate that had seen her closeted at Yellow Rock since she'd finished school. "Will Miriam get married in Sydney or here?"

"That's up to your father to decide. No doubt he'll let us know. Take these hatboxes—we'll see if there's anything that'll suit." Olivia dumped a teetering pile of rounded boxes into Evie's arms. "She's going to need morning dresses, luncheon wear, afternoon tea dresses. For goodness' sake! Why anyone needs four different outfits in one day is beyond my comprehension. I suppose she'll need her riding habit too. That requires attention."

Evie shook out two velvet cloaks, one a rich viridian, the other a dark Prussian blue, the collar edged with rabbit fur. "These are lovely," she sighed, slipping the blue one over her shoulders. "Mama liked the blue one best."

"The green one will make Miriam look sallow. Give her the blue."

Evie stripped off the cloak, wrinkling her nose and stifling a whine. The blue was much prettier, with the soft fur framing the hood. Why would it suit Miriam better? She shrugged. She had no idea. Perhaps she should spend some time with Miriam before she left, find out about this new suitor. She'd imagined, now that she was almost eighteen, they might have more in common, but Miriam still saw her as nothing more than a hindrance, forever under her feet or spying on her, the little sister in need of minding.

"Miriam's not a child anymore. Time to accept her responsibilities, settle down, and get married."

"Who is this man who has offered for her?"

"A friend of your father, a business partner."

"What's his name?"

Olivia frowned. "Rawlings. Edward Rawlings."

Not a name Evie recognized, but why would she? She'd never set foot in Sydney. Pa had deemed it better she should grow up at Yellow Rock, with Mama and Aunt Olivia, though over the years she'd spent more time with Olivia than anyone else. She scooped up the hatboxes and the midnight blue cloak and smoothed the fur wistfully. It would be nice to have something of Mama's to wear. "I'll take them in to Miriam, shall I?"

"You keep the hairbrushes and the green cloak. Miriam can make do with the blue. Make sure you knock first. She might still be abed."

Evie slipped through the door, hatboxes swinging against her legs, clothes piled in her arms up above her chin. She shunted the door with her shoulder and it swung wide. "Miriam! I've got some hats for you and Mama's beautiful blue cloak."

A groan and a clatter greeted her words when she dumped everything on the bottom of the bed.

"Go away." Miriam burrowed down beneath the quilt, but not before Evie noticed her blotched face and swollen eyes.

Evie's heart went out to her. She ran her hand over her sister's hair, remembering the cooling touch of Mama's hand soothing her when she ailed. "Why are you crying? We've found a lovely cloak for you to wear to Sydney and some pretty hats."

Miriam's shoulders heaved and she jerked upright, pushing Evie aside. The movement released a flurry of sour air, making Evie's stomach heave. "Oh! You're truly unwell. Can I get you anything?" The water carafe sat empty on the bedside table. "Some more water? A cup of tea and some dry toast?"

"Go away!" Miriam spat through clenched teeth.

"Let me help, please. There must be something I can do."

"There's nothing *you* can do. I shall be happy to be out of this place and in Sydney where I belong. Pa no longer cares for me."

Evie flopped down on the corner of the bed. "Pa loves you very much. He sent you to the best school, he's taking you to Sydney, wants you to represent him . . ." Her words petered out.

"Just leave me alone." Miriam disappeared beneath the bedclothes.

Evie darted through the door, her mind in a flat spin, straight into a moving mound of clothes reeking of lily of the valley.

"I told you to knock," Olivia hissed.

"The door was open—"

"Go and get dressed."

She didn't need to be told twice. Having both Miriam and Olivia berate her was more than she could tolerate.

The contents of her wardrobe still lay scattered across the bed. A pile of the white pin-tucked muslin dresses she wore throughout the warmer months, a winter dress she hated because it itched, her divided skirt for riding, and the black taffeta dress she'd worn since Mama's passing. For some unknown reason the prospect of another day in starched black seemed senseless. Mama hated black and Olivia had said life must go on. Pa obviously agreed; otherwise, why would he be taking Miriam to Sydney to be married? She rummaged through the pile of clothing until she found a red blouse and pulled it on with her divided skirt. A day out in the fresh air, perhaps a trip up to Yellow Rock with her sketchbook, would clear her head. Miriam's behavior made no sense, no sense at all.

With that thought at the forefront of her mind, she headed downstairs. Pa's study door was ajar. "Morning, Pa." She hovered, her fingers itching to use her new saddlebag, which sat in the corner of the room near the french doors.

Pa lifted his head. "Good morning. I am in no doubt you and Olivia will manage perfectly well until I return."

The outside supervision and the breeding program had always fallen to Olivia and Bailey, and the men Pa employed were more than capable of managing the cattle. When Pa was in Sydney he saw to the shipment of the horses. Nothing would change. "Yes. We will."

"Bailey will deliver the horses and organize the drovers. If there are any problems Rawlings and I will handle the Sydney end."

Her head came up with a snap. She hadn't made the connection before. "Your business manager?"

"The very man. Soon to be your brother-in-law."

Edward Rawlings must have been courting Miriam while she was in Sydney and she'd said nothing of it. "Closemouthed bag of bones," Evie muttered under her breath. "When did Miriam meet Edward Rawlings?"

"She's known him for some time." Pa's face flushed. "The Rawlingses are neighbors in Macquarie Street. He and his mother, Charlotte, also live in Horbury Terrace. They are acquainted with Mrs. Burdekin." He turned and smoothed the cedar box that housed his compass, sextant, and chain.

Now it made a little more sense. Pa had known the Burdekins for many years and was full of admiration for the way Mrs. Burdekin had taken over her husband's business interests when he passed, but more importantly, she shared Pa's passion for the mystery of Leichhardt.

Pa cleared his throat. "I'm leaving my chest here, in your safekeeping. Use it for your map. The coordinates must be accurate. I shan't need it until I return from Sydney."

His surveyor's box, his most treasured possession and a constant reminder of his frailty. He'd spent many hours teaching her the workings of the instruments, always with that distant look of disappointment in his eyes. All the horizons he'd intended to chart, all the miles he'd hoped to travel with Leichhardt. If he was leaving it behind, he couldn't be planning to remain in Sydney for too long.

Evie's chest swelled with pride. "So Edward and Miriam will be married from here?"

"That's what I anticipate. Charlotte has everything in hand. I'll let you and Olivia know as plans progress."

"The church at Broke is so very pretty." Truth be told, she was relieved she wouldn't be expected to go to Sydney. She had no desire to leave Yellow Rock. Her grandparents—on Pa's side, Margaret and John Ludgrove, and Mama and Olivia's parents, Mary and Alexander Maynard—were among the first settlers in the area. They'd traveled from England in search of a new life, made their home here, and once they'd found their slice of heaven embraced it.

The Ludgrove-Maynard properties were everything she'd ever known, everything she wanted or needed. The cry of the koels, the squawk of the black cockatoos as they fought over the nuts high in the casuarina trees, and the ragged peaks of the Broken Back Range held her safe beneath the timeless wonder of Yellow Rock.

Yellow Rock was where she belonged, and she had no intention of leaving.

7

YELLOW ROCK, 1911

Lettie slept fitfully in the simple iron bed while the thunderclouds rolled and the rain beat down on the iron roof. Toward
dawn the rain eased and she slipped into a deeper sleep, only to be
abruptly woken by a strange *wurrow-wurrow, keek-keek* birdcall. She
dozed for a little longer, and it was well past sunrise when she pushed
open the kitchen door and found the room deserted. A boiling kettle
sat on the hob and the teapot stood ready. She poured the water and,
while she waited for the tea to brew, threw open the outside door.

The steep rock face glittered in the morning sunshine. Taking a
few steps away from the house, she shaded her eyes and craned her
neck up to the summit. Stunted trees clung to the rock, while in
other places bare slopes caught the beams of sunlight, turning them
to gold. "Yellow Rock," she murmured. It seemed apt.

A woman appeared from behind one of the outhouses, a shotgun dangling from one hand and a brace of rabbits from the other,
accompanied by a large shaggy-coated hound that loped along

beside her, its nose glued to the rabbits. The dog lifted its head, caught sight of Lettie, and bounded over. Two large paws landed on her shoulders and the smell of warm, wet dog enveloped her.

"Stand down!" the woman brandishing the shotgun shouted. "He won't hurt. Just overfamiliar."

With a mournful look, eyes pleading, the hound dropped his paws and collapsed in front of her like a discarded foot rug.

"Let's start again. Good morning!"

"Good morning!" A thrill of curiosity and pleasure warmed Lettie. Great-Aunt Olivia. She looked nothing like the picture she'd painted in her mind, dressed in rough trousers hitched around her waist with the sort of necktie Thorne preferred and Miriam abhorred, and a ragged homespun jumper with frayed cuffs. "I'm Letitia. Letitia Rawlings."

"Well, well. Fancy that. Let's see if we can find a cup of tea." She marched—there was no other word for her purposeful strides— through the kitchen door, dumped the rabbits in the sink, and wiped her hands on her thighs. "Bloody nuisance these rabbits, but they make an excellent pie. Where's Olly? Does she know we've got a visitor?"

Her words brought Lettie to a standstill.

"Cup of tea?"

Lettie managed to nod her head, her mind racing in circles. "I'm sorry, I didn't catch your name."

"Margaret Brown, call me Peg." She dumped fine bone china cups, without saucers, down on the table and stuck her head around the door. "Olly! We've got a visitor!"

When she received no reply, she turned back to the tea. "Milk? Sugar? She'll be along in a moment. I've just got back from Broke. Spent the night with the grandchildren."

Lettie sank down into the chair and wrapped her fingers around one of the cups, trying to make sense of the woman's words. Perhaps Great-Aunt Olivia was ill, not quite in possession of her wits, and Peg was the one charged with her care. Before she had a chance to think any further, the kitchen door opened and the woman she'd met last night appeared in the doorway.

Gone were the faded cotton frock, heavy apron, and boots; instead, she wore a plain navy skirt and a simple striped poplin blouse, more suited to a meeting at the Women's Club than a farmhouse. She managed a half-hearted smile, but her face blanched. "Ah, Peg, you're back." A look passed between them and she offered a wry smile. "I owe you an apology, Letitia. I intended to—"

Lettie's body tensed and she shot to her feet, the rush of anger catching her by surprise. "Why didn't you say who you were last night?" There could only be one answer. For some reason she didn't want to admit who she was. But why? And more to the point, why ask her to stay the night? Why not simply send her on her way if she didn't want to see her?

A satisfactory hint of color stole across Olivia's cheeks. "It's a long story, which I will certainly recount, but for the time being, suffice to say I presumed you'd be bringing me a message from your mother."

"I am. I told you last evening."

"Life can go awry when we dwell on preconceived ideas and beliefs. I thought it better we got to know each other without the implications of the past."

And what was that supposed to mean? The message she had to deliver was simple, had nothing to do with the past or preconceived ideas, simply facts: Thorne had died and therefore could no longer inherit the Ludgrove-Maynard properties. Lettie opened her mouth to speak, but before she could frame the words, Peg pulled one of the chairs from the table.

"Why don't we all sit down." She glared at Olivia. "Olly?" With a sigh, not far different from that of the huge, shaggy dog, Olivia collapsed onto the chair at the end of the table and poured herself a cup of tea. "Where's the sugar?" she asked, her voice petulant.

"It's coming, it's coming." Peg moved toward the pantry, running a soothing hand over Olivia's shoulder as she passed, as though reassuring her.

The atmosphere prickled and Lettie couldn't see a way out, a way of breaking the news gently. Her eyes flashed to Olivia's hands resting on the table, the tension evident in the clenched fists and tight muscles of her wrists. She wore no rings, no adornment of any sort, unlike Miriam, whose heavily bejeweled fingers threatened to weigh her down.

If Olivia had named Thorne her heir, perhaps she saw him as some sort of surrogate son despite her estrangement from the family and she'd been fearful when Lettie had turned up.

"What is this message Miriam wants delivered? Couldn't she come herself?"

Lettie took a sip of her tea, more to compose herself than anything else. "My mother asked me to come. I'm afraid it's bad news."

The dog rose, stretched, and came to stand beside Olivia. Peg moved closer, too, making Lettie aware of the breadth of her shoulders and her height. "Spit it out, girl. Spit it out."

She sucked in a huge breath. "Thorne died in a boating accident." Tears scratched behind her eyes. She let her lashes fall and exhaled slowly.

A gnarled silence fell. Nothing except the sound of the dog's claws on the stone floor as he moved to rest his head in her lap.

"Your brother?"

Olivia's question brought her up sharp. Surely Olivia knew. She'd introduced herself as Letitia Rawlings. "Thorne's my only brother. We were very close. Did you receive Mother's letters?"

Olivia frowned, threw a look at Peg, who shrugged her shoulders.

Lettie pushed back the chair and stood up. "She wrote immediately after Thorne's accident, and again after the funeral. Six months ago."

"Peg, there's some scones in the oven. I haven't had breakfast, and I suspect Letitia could do with something before she leaves."

Why did the wretched woman avoid answering her questions? Well, she'd delivered the news. Olivia didn't seem upset in any way, nor had any mention been made of Thorne's inheritance, and she could hardly blurt that out. A flush of heat hit her cheeks. Nothing had gone the way she'd imagined when she'd arrived last night. She'd thought perhaps she'd be invited to spend a few days. That the matter of Thorne's inheritance might come up naturally and she'd explain their plans to visit, introduce themselves, and heal the family rift.

And she still wasn't quite sure if Olivia was who she said she was, or if Peg was actually Olivia. Why hadn't Miriam shown her a picture or at least given her a physical description of her great-aunt? The stench of duplicity drifted through the homely kitchen, tainting the smell of baking scones.

She raised her head to find Olivia's dark eyes studying her. "You have the Rawlings coloring. What about your brother?"

Lettie's long legs and whippet-thin body were a stark contrast to Thorne's stockier frame, although they both shared Miriam's dark hair, something they'd laughed about as children. "Everyone says I take after Pater's side of the family. Thorne took after Mother."

She ran her hands through the dog's rough coat and his back rippled. The intricacies of home were not something she felt comfortable discussing, especially given her dubious reception. Dubious? There was nothing dubious about the matter. Why was she making excuses? Olivia had lied, blatantly lied. Pretended to be someone she wasn't. For the first time in living memory, Miriam's character assessment had proved accurate. "I must leave. It's a long drive."

Without waiting for a response, she made her way from the kitchen into the house, intent on collecting her bag from the room where she'd slept last night. The front door stood open and Yellow Rock reared majestically into the bright blue sky. She sat down on the doorstep. A faint breeze blew a wisp of hair across her forehead, bringing with it the scent of eucalyptus and the tantalizing promise of a perfect day. Not a soul in sight, about as far removed from Sydney as she could imagine.

How long she sat there, lost in the calm, she had no idea, but when a cool damp nose buffeted her cheek, she jumped.

The dog wagged his moth-eaten tail and settled down next to her, the perfect companion. "I don't know what to do."

He pressed his wet nose against her cheek.

"I've delivered the message, but I have no idea how to bring up Thorne's inheritance."

Settling onto his haunches, he sighed and rested his heavy head against her shoulder.

"Get out, Oxley." Olivia's gruff tones broke her reverie. "I thought you might like a look at this."

Lettie nudged the dog aside and struggled to her feet.

Olivia offered a sketchpad opened at a picture of a girl sitting in a field of wildflowers, her face turned toward Yellow Rock as the sun breached the highest point. An uncontrolled mane of thick dark hair, a pair of huge liquid eyes framed by thick lashes dominating a heart-shaped face, a hint of innocence belying the full lips, and a faint blush on her delicate cheekbones.

A shiver tiptoed down her spine. "Who is it?"

"Your mother's sister, Evie."

Who'd died in childhood, if her memory served her well. Studying the face of the vivacious girl well on her way to womanhood, she knew with absolute certainty that Miriam's and Olivia's beliefs were at odds. "I thought she died as a child," she murmured.

Olivia cradled the picture against her chest. "Are you in any hurry to get back to Sydney? I'd like you to stay a little longer."

Curiosity, and something more akin to a fleeting touch, traced her skin. Lettie shrugged; not long ago she'd intended to storm out, leave without any further ado, but that was before she'd seen the picture of Evie. A girl who, but for the light in her eyes, reminded her very much of herself.

"Stay a little longer." Olivia reached out and laid her hand on her shoulder, butting Oxley aside. "I expect Miriam has told you about the property. I'm sure you'd like to see it."

"She's told me very little." And certainly, nothing she'd said about Olivia remotely resembled the woman standing before her clutching a picture of someone who could have been Lettie's twin sister.

"I had hoped one day you and your brother would come and visit me. He wrote to me last summer and suggested it."

Thorne had written to her! He hadn't told her. He'd suggested the trip but hadn't mentioned he'd already contacted Great-Aunt Olivia. A surge of bitterness swept over her. Thorne never kept secrets. Was it something Miriam had put him up to, something to secure his inheritance? "He did say we should make the trip, but after his accident . . ." Her voice wavered and Olivia's hand tightened on her shoulder.

"Why don't I bring the scones out here and we can have a chat? It's a lovely spot at this time of the morning." Without waiting for a response, Olivia drifted back inside.

Lettie scuffed her hand across her face and let out a long, slow breath. She had no idea why she felt emotional, had never been one for affection, but Olivia's sympathetic air brought out something in her she didn't fully comprehend.

She cast a look along the veranda and spotted a small garden table and two chairs tucked in the shade at the corner. Once she'd set up the table and chairs in the patch of sunshine she sat down, head tilted back, stunned by a pair of huge wedge-tailed eagles sweeping the cobalt sky.

Nothing broke the soothing silence until Olivia reappeared with a tray. "Peg's strawberry jam took a blue ribbon at the Maitland Show. It's highly sought after." She lathered jam and cream onto a split scone and passed the plate to Lettie. "Tuck in."

They sat in companionable silence and ate their fill and drank their way through two cups of tea each before Olivia dusted off her hands. "Now, which version of your family history has Miriam seen fit to offer? Exactly how much do you know?" she asked, cocking one eyebrow.

The irony in Olivia's voice made Lettie start. "Mother told me everything. All about the Maynards and the Ludgroves. Grandfather Ludgrove died when I was five. He had a wooden leg. Charlotte, Pater's mother, was his second wife, and they married not long after Mother and Pater. Grandfather moved to Sydney to be more involved with the business. Grandma Charlotte died a few years ago. Pater has run the business alone ever since."

Olivia let out some sort of a snort that brought Oxley to his feet.

Lettie jumped to the defensive. "Pater spends a lot of time working."

"At Randwick?"

"Yes. That's right. At the racecourse."

Olivia rocked back in the chair and emitted another derogatory harrumph. "And your mother's sister, your aunt Evie, what do you know of her?"

That was a difficulty because she couldn't for the life of her remember Miriam ever mentioning very much about her sister. "She was sickly and died from a childhood ailment."

"I see." Olivia nodded, her eyes clouded as if her thoughts were far away. "Poor Evie did have a difficult childhood. She was prone to moments of dislocation, the falling sickness they called it. She'd grown out of it by the time Miriam married. What about your grandfather? Did she tell you about his interests in exploration?"

Exploration? "He was a surveyor as a young man but took over the family business when his father died, then moved to Sydney."

"And his accident?"

"I know he'd lost his leg in a riding accident as a young man."

"I think we should take a walk."

Lettie collected the plates and put them on the tray, intending to return to the kitchen, but Olivia stilled her hand. "Leave them there. Peg will sort out the tray. There are two hats just inside the door. Go and fetch them—the sun's hot."

Two cabbage palm hats that had seen better days hung on the hat stand just inside the door. Lettie handed one to Olivia and rammed the other down on her head.

"Fit all right?"

"Just fine." She straightened it, yanked it down a bit farther, not wanting to admit that her thick hair always made it difficult to secure a hat without pins.

"You'll need to unfasten your hair; it'll sit better. Don't want it blowing off."

Miriam would have heart failure! With a grin, Lettie pulled out her hair pins, tucked them into her pocket, and gave her head a shake, enjoying the sense of freedom, then rammed the hat down on her head where it sat nice and snug. "Ready." She turned to Olivia and caught a wistful expression drifting across her weathered face.

8

Before the sun had breached the surrounding hills, Olivia and Evie stood on the doorstep, handkerchiefs waving until the carriage vanished from view and the last dust settled.

"Well." Olivia smacked her hands together as though Pa and Miriam's departure was a job well done. "A cup of tea wouldn't go amiss. What have you got there?"

Evie snapped her sketchbook closed. "Just a drawing." An overwhelming and unnatural desire to hide the sketch swamped her. Something she'd never experienced before. "I thought I'd record Miriam's departure." And the annoying fact that she looked like a Botticelli Madonna in the coveted blue cloak.

Evie trailed after Olivia into the house, through the crushing silence. Only a few weeks ago they'd been a family of five eagerly awaiting Joshua's birth; now only two of them remained to rattle around in the big house beneath the shadow of Yellow Rock. Despite knowing Pa and Miriam would return for the wedding, she felt bereft and a tad envious.

"You can wipe that pouty look off your face. We've got plenty to keep us busy." Olivia pulled the tin from the larder and cut two large slices of fruitcake. "Can't work on an empty stomach. The next lot of drovers will be through soon. We've cattle to go north to the Liverpool Plains, three mares due to foal, never mind the mess in the kitchen garden. The place has gone to wrack and ruin since Alice passed. What are you going to take on?"

After Grandfather and Grandmother Maynard died, Olivia had moved into the main house, fulfilling the role of housekeeper as Mama became more and more frail. Joe, the farm manager, and his wife, Nell, had taken up residence in the farmhouse, but Olivia still insisted on taking responsibility for the mares. Evie knew she'd be called to help and it would mean a night or two in the stables. She didn't mind. Anything she could do to temper the misery of Mama's passing would be a relief, and the sight of the new foals always gladdened her heart. "I'll sort out the kitchen garden. The chook shed needs cleaning too."

"We'll get Joe's boy in for that. He's good on the end of the shovel."

"And Joe will be back from Maitland tomorrow afternoon with the wagon."

"If he doesn't get waylaid by a keg of beer. He's got a list of supplies to pick up."

An hour passed as they planned the chores, and all the while Evie's fingers itched to get into Pa's study. "I've got some work to do for Pa too," she finally admitted.

"Then that's how you'll spend your evenings. And no roaming. We go together or not at all."

Evie swallowed the temptation to whine. How could she complete her map if she couldn't go anywhere alone? The lure of

Pa's study hovered like an intangible treasure, a reprieve after the miserable sequence of events. Mama's confinement, the tenterhooks that had fueled their prayers for poor little Joshua, and their sorrowful passing, then Pa's sudden and totally unexpected decision long before the acceptable mourning period had passed to see Miriam married had left her at sixes and sevens. "Has Miriam known Edward Rawlings long?"

"Never really thought about it. William's mentioned him, of course. I've got some memory of his mother, Charlotte, introducing Miriam around the town, into society, during the school term. Macquarie Street is quite the place to live."

"Mrs. Burdekin lives a few doors down. She shares Pa's passion for Leichhardt. He named a river and a duck after her. Pa was most impressed. She subscribed very heavily to the Ladies' Expedition that went in search of Leichhardt and his party."

Olivia wrinkled her nose. "Throwing good money after bad, if you ask me. Everyone knew Leichhardt and his cronies were taken by the natives. Don't understand why they couldn't accept it."

"No, that might not be true. Pa told me only recently . . ." The look on Olivia's face stopped Evie and she gulped down the rest of her tea. Olivia held Leichhardt solely responsible for Pa's misfortune, and any mention of his name brought forth a torrent of derogatory abuse. Now was not the time to let the age-old recriminations fly. She pocketed another piece of fruitcake. "I'll go see what can be done in the kitchen garden and collect the eggs."

"That's my girl. Mrs. Hewitt will be here soon. Peg started today. Big strong girl like her will sort things out in no time, and she'll need the eggs. She's got baking to do."

72

It was well past eight o'clock before Evie lit the lamp in the study. She easily could have fallen straight into bed, but the opportunity shone like Sirius in a winter sky, alluring and tantalizing. Stifling a yawn she lowered herself into Pa's chair and spread her hands palm down on the worn leather inserts, gazing at the piles of paperwork and journals.

They dated back to 1842 when he'd first met Leichhardt on the banks of the Hunter River. He'd kept a daily journal, field notes he liked to call them, a habit instilled in him by Leichhardt himself; a series of soft, leather-bound notebooks, fingerprints and ink splotches marking their covers, indicators of the happy-go-lucky man he once was.

Her fingers trembled as she picked up the oldest of the journals and turned to the frontispiece.

William Ludgrove—Early Travels with Ludwig Leichhardt, 1842

A rush of guilt heated Evie's skin. Opening Pa's journal felt akin to prying. After a moment or two, his familiar looping handwriting soothed her. He'd asked her to sort out his papers and records, and his journals formed part. He'd given her permission.

Tuesday, 27th December 1842

Yellow Rock: Lat -32.4181 Long 151.3463

She smiled. Ever the surveyor, he'd recorded the coordinates. It would make her job easier. She could cross-reference the locations on her map with his notes.

I cannot believe the great honor Doctor Leichhardt has bestowed upon me. I am to accompany him on his travels through the Hunter. What a fortuitous day it was when I found him wandering on the banks of the Hunter River. I intend to ensure he will never lose his way again.

It was with much excitement that I finally packed my bags. Tonight will see me at Glendon, where I will meet with Doctor Leichhardt, and our journey will begin. The man inspires me with such enthusiasm for the country of my birth and he seems to have a greater understanding than I of its natural resources. I look upon this as a challenge. If I can prove myself, hone the skills I have acquired, then perhaps Doctor Leichhardt will find me worthy of inclusion in his future expeditions.

She paused before turning the page and studied Pa's small penciled drawing beneath the writing—a winding track leading to the Hunter River. A track she and Pa had traveled many times. But this was different—Pa astride his horse, hat tipped at a jaunty angle, and saddlebags bulging—drawn before his accident. Her heart twisted as her finger traced his upright form, a representation of his undamaged self.

Pushing the journal to one side, she opened her saddlebag, chose a fine new brush, and copied his illustration to her map before returning to the journal.

Wednesday, 28th December 1842

Glendon: Lat -32.5923 Long 151.2716

We begin our travels with an exploration of Helenus Scott's

estate. I have my sextant, compass, watch, and chain with me and intend to keep perfect records of precise locations as an example of my abilities.

What then followed was a list of dates and locations, and very little else. She skimmed through the names and coordinates— Mirannie Creek through Wolke Tolke, Mount Tyroman to Bukembelong and Peg Top Hill, all the places Pa had told her of, none she had marked on her map.

The lamp flickered and died. Hours must have passed while she'd sat cross-checking the coordinates and marking the locations, knowing they would have to be rechecked for accuracy—more hers than Pa's; she doubted she'd find any errors in his meticulous calculations. A little light from the crescent moon illuminated the room, so she weighted the stack she had created, picked up the notebook, and trailed up the stairs. She had no need of a candle; every step of the way, every creaking stair riser was as familiar as her own drawings. Once in her room she lit the bedside lamp, removed her boots, and slipped under the quilt, knees pulled up to form support for the notebook.

Wednesday, 11th January 1843

Yellow Rock: Lat -32.4181 Long 151.3463

This morning I had the pleasure of escorting Doctor Leichhardt to the summit of Yellow Rock.

The weather was clear. To the north-northeast Dyrinne appeared in its full glory, such a very considerable mountain mass in darkest blue. All remaining ranges were seen very distinctly. Mr. White's Road Range, Mirannie Range, and Jack Shea. Following the fire and ensuing rain the slopes are covered in kangaroo grass. We caught a kangaroo rat in a tree trunk and later a young kangaroo, which impressed Doctor Leichhardt with its gentleness and tameness.

Pa and Leichhardt, together on Yellow Rock! She could picture the scene so clearly. The kangaroos were still as tame now as they had been then. Perhaps she had Pa to thank. Another picture for her map. Pa would like that. He and Doctor Leichhardt offering handfuls of sweet grass to one of the joeys.

Evie's head gave a lurch as sleep overcame her. She scrubbed at her eyes, bit back another yawn, and slid beneath the covers.

Olivia's rough shake woke her. Light streamed through the open window, scalding her eyes. Her limbs felt as heavy as lead, and the misery of the unwritten ending to Pa's story hovered.

"Look at you! Still in your clothes. What time did you come to bed, may I ask?" Olivia's eyes slid toward the journal on the nightstand.

Evie snatched it away, certain Pa would not appreciate his personal journals being shared. "I was reading and fell asleep."

"There's water in the jug. Wake yourself up and put on something old. We've got work to do, dirty work."

And so the days passed with no news of Pa or Miriam, and gradually the pain of Mama's passing eased as Evie became more and more immersed in Pa's notes. Joe had returned with a mighty headache and a wagon full of the supplies, and before long Yellow Rock once more ran to Olivia's satisfaction. A fact confirmed when she said, "I've given Peg and Mrs. Hewitt the day off. Bring your sketchbook and we'll take a picnic, breathe the air, see what's what. I've a mind to check the boundaries."

Olivia's plan would provide the perfect opportunity to confirm the compass points and the routes Pa and Leichhardt had taken. The chance of escaping on her own was nil. She would make the most of Olivia's suggestion.

By the time she reached the stables, Joe had the horses saddled and their picnic stowed, and Olivia sat fidgeting with the reins, wanting to be gone. "I thought we'd take the track up to the top of the rock."

Exactly what she wanted to do. Her new saddlebag took but a moment to attach, and as she smoothed the soft leather she remembered the excitement in Pa's eyes as he'd confided his plan for their book. She couldn't wait to make a start. Only last night she'd read in Pa's journal of a track through the pass, a shortcut to the Upper Hunter. It came out not far from the route the drovers took north. From the top of Yellow Rock she'd be able to locate that and confirm the path Pa and Leichhardt had taken to Mount Royal.

As they ambled along she brought out her new sketchbook and a pencil. She wanted to notate the track, the larger trees, and any rocks that could be used as landmarks. Foolish perhaps. Why bother when she knew it as well as the lines on the palm of her hand? But this was for Pa's book; others would see it who wouldn't know Yellow Rock as she did.

Olivia picked up the pace, clicking her tongue and urging her horse forward up the steep slope. Before long they would have to leave the horses and climb the last part of the track on foot. Evie took only a moment to sketch a rough indication of the tall outcrop of grass trees, their stems crowned with spear-shaped seed pods glistening in the morning light, then the shallow dip in the rocks, a natural basin where a pair of King-Parrots fought over a pool of water still cool from the fall in temperature overnight.

"Where would you like to stop?" Olivia turned and smiled, the flush on her cheeks an indication of the pleasure she found in being away from the never-ending responsibility of the homestead and the horses.

Evie shaded her eyes and picked out the last sight of the track before it took a sharp right-hand turn to begin the steep ascent. "Just before we reach the crest. I want to see how I've done."

"How you've done?" Olivia cast a look down at the sketchbook.

Evie's hand lifted, the same overpowering need to cover her work she'd experienced when Pa and Miriam left. She'd always shared her drawings with Olivia whenever she'd asked, rather suspected Pa had framed her paintings at Olivia's suggestion. "That doesn't look like one of your usual pictures."

"It's not." Evie dragged in a sigh. What had caused this sudden need for secrecy? Besides, Olivia might well have something to add. She'd known the area when it was nothing more than wide-open spaces. "I'm making a map."

"We don't need a map. I've been bringing you up here since you were knee-high to a wombat."

"It's something Pa's asked me to do."

"He's not going to be coming up here. Hasn't for years. That leg of his wouldn't handle this rugged track, all the bumping and twisting. If his dogcart overturned he'd be stuck like a pig in mud." Something in the tone of her voice made Evie turn. Olivia's smile had vanished and a ferocious frown marred her forehead. "You've been reading William's journals. It's putting ideas into your head."

"He left them for me." She still wasn't certain she hadn't read too much into his words, but his description reminded her of the books Mama liked, novels she'd called them. She'd asked her to read aloud to her as her time with Joshua grew closer and she hadn't the strength to hold the book. "You know I've been going through them. He asked me to."

"No good'll come of it. Obsessed, he is. That man, Leichhardt, brought nothing but despair to this family, ruined everything with his high-flown theories and illusions. Your father would be a darn sight happier now if he hadn't taken off on that fool's errand." She reined in her horse with unusual ferocity and jumped to the ground.

Olivia's fluidity of movement took Evie by surprise. Mama always moved with a languid grace, as though her feet barely touched the floor, and she rarely set foot beyond the garden Pa had built for her around the house. The two sisters were as different as she and Miriam.

"I'll let the horses wander; they won't take off." Olivia removed the saddles and bridles and stashed them beneath a gnarled tree trunk. "Look lively."

Evie slipped her saddlebag over her shoulder, relishing the snug fit and the soft leather. Together she and Olivia slithered and scrambled up the steep track to the summit.

The property spread before them, a fine embroidered quilt, every fence line, every outhouse, the orchards and the paddocks, the homestead and the farmhouse. The mares nothing more than small dots roaming in their neatly fenced enclosures, foals gamboling at their feet. "You came up here to save time. You can see everything. I'd never appreciated the advantage it gave you."

"My secret is out." Olivia raised her finger and pointed. "That's Joe sloping off early to get back to Broke before the store closes." She pointed to a flurry of dust turning onto the Singleton road. "He's run out of ale, I'll bet." The tiny toy-like wagon made a sharp turn and bowled down the track. "And there's Oxley."

"I hadn't noticed he'd left us."

"Took off before we left the horses. He'll be here soon enough for his lunch."

Evie had spent so many hours on the rock, more than Olivia knew, for Evie had paid little heed to Pa's order that she should always be accompanied. She looked down at her crude sketch and extended it, filling in the meandering path of Wollombi Brook, the waterholes, and the track that led from Broke to Wollombi and beyond, and in the foreground she couldn't resist the beginning of a tiny sketch of Oxley's waving tail.

"Here." Olivia offered a large sandwich and an egg for Oxley, who reappeared puffing and panting with something that looked remarkably like rabbit fur caught between his teeth. Then she bent to stoke the fire she'd built within the well-used circle of stones, lifted the lid of the billycan, threw in a handful of tea leaves, and finished by tossing a gum leaf from her pocket into the boiling water.

The warm, tight feeling of a day spent in the sun prickled Evie's skin, something she relished even though it meant she'd receive the rounds of the kitchen from Mrs. Hewitt for tarnishing her poor beleaguered complexion. A rash of freckles would dot her nose and cheeks, thanks to Pa's Scottish ancestry.

Nothing different from past trips, but somehow everything was different. Evie no longer focused on the minute detail of the drawings she usually made but what lay beyond the boundaries of her world and where the tracks might lead.

"Are you all right?" Olivia reached out and touched her arm.

She jumped. "What? Yes, I'm fine."

"You've got that faraway look in your eyes."

Which was Olivia's polite way of asking if she was going to have one of her *episodes*.

9

Lettie tramped after Olivia, marveling at the older woman's stamina and trying hard to mask her snatched breaths.

"It's important to know your roots," Olivia said with a crooked smile as she led the way down a path fragrant with the scent of freshly slashed grass. "Up behind us, that's Yellow Rock, leastways that's what we've always called it." She gave a shrug and spread her arms. "The view from up there gives a good sense of the property. Margaret and John Ludgrove, your great-grandparents, had the first land grant; then my parents, Mary and Alexander Maynard, took the second, side by side. They had plans, big plans for this new country, families joined in marriage, common business interests. My father served in India. It was his idea to breed horses and ship them out to the army. Right from the outset the Hunter Valley was one of the great horse breeding areas of the colony. We imported the best English and Irish thoroughbred bloodlines and bred horses suited to Australia. When the Indian Army began purchasing remounts, we had a head start with my father's contacts. To own and ride a Waler was paramount to . . . What's the best motor car money can buy?"

"A Rolls-Royce Silver Ghost." Or so Thorne had said. "A British car. Six-cylinder, three-speed transmission."

Olivia waved her hand in dismissal. "You understand."

Why had Miriam never told her the stories of her family? More to the point, if marriage and business entwined the Ludgroves and the Maynards, what had caused the long-standing rift between them?

"Come on, we'll go this way and fill in some of the gaps." Olivia swung open a small gate into a clearing enclosed by a low wrought-iron fence. "The family plot." She gestured to an array of headstones in a patch of long grass picked through with waving fronds of wildflowers. "Easier to explain if you've got the names in front of you."

Lettie stood in the center surrounded by the very plain, lichen-covered headstones, her heart beating a ridiculous staccato rhythm.

"This here's my ma and pa, your great-grandparents on the Maynard side, Mary and Alexander, and their sons, Alexander and John." Two tiny headstones bearing nothing but a name and a single date sat between the two larger ones.

"And here's my sister, Alice, your grandmother on the Maynard side." Olivia ran her hand along the top of a stone. "And her sons, William, James, and Joshua." She let out a heartfelt sigh. "As a family we were never good with boys."

Despite the sun Lettie shivered. Standing amid the simple stones made her think of Thorne lying alone beneath the marble angel. Another son taken too early. For some reason she believed he'd be happier here, not buried in the busy, bustling Sydney cemetery.

"Then this here's William, your grandfather, and his parents, Margaret and John Ludgrove."

"Grandfather?" Lettie hadn't thought to wonder if he was buried at Waverley. "He died in Sydney. Mother said he suffered an apoplexy."

"An apoplexy? That's what Miriam might call it. It wasn't. He died of a broken heart. Couldn't live with his guilt. Guilt and grief killed him, plain and simple." Olivia's eyes brimmed, and she snagged her bottom lip between her teeth. "Miriam ought to know that."

A breeze shifted through the trees, making the casuarinas sing. "And Evie? Where's Evie?"

"Well, that's the rub, and that's why I wanted to bring you here. Let you see for yourself that all is not quite as you've been led to believe."

Lettie ran a quick search of the headstones. Surely her mother wouldn't lie to her about her sister's death. "Where's Evie buried?"

"It's a long story, and the heat's building. We'll walk back up to the farm and treat ourselves to some of Peg's lemonade and then I'll take you over to the main house. We keep it closed these days. That's where the answers lie."

And that had to suffice. Olivia closed the rusty iron gate, cast one more look around the small patch, and ushered her along the path.

When Olivia and Lettie broke clear of the treed area, the peacefulness of their walk shattered. An apocalypse of horses and cattle, men and dogs, swirling dust and noise enveloped them. A smile lit Olivia's face. "Ah! They're a day early."

"Who are they? What's going on?" Lettie squinted, protecting her eyes, and covered her ears.

"Drovers are in. Cattle muster, on their way to the Liverpool Plains. They always break for a day or two here. Plenty of water. Good campsite. We're on the stock route, have been since the beginning. Take yourself inside. I've got work to do." Olivia rammed the dilapidated hat farther down onto her head and strode off toward the seething inferno.

Lettie had no intention of taking herself inside. She galloped after Olivia into the large paddock just in time to see her clapping an old man on the back. "What the hell are you doing here? Thought you'd had your last drove."

"Could ask you the same question, you miserable old jenny."

Rather than take offense, Olivia let out a hoot of laughter, then reached for Lettie's hand and dragged her close. "This is my greatniece, Letitia Rawlings. You make sure that bloody team of yours keeps their filthy hands off her."

"Pleased to meet—" Lettie's words were cut short when the old man clasped her in a rough hug, enveloping her in a cloud of sweat, stale tobacco, and something rather unpleasant that she didn't recognize.

"Evie, as I live and breathe."

Lettie wrenched herself out of his embrace and rammed her hat a little lower on her head.

"So, you're Miriam's daughter. Always guessed you'd turn out a stunner. Where's that brother of yours?"

Who was this man?

"Leave her be. Give her time." Olivia gestured to the swirling mass of cattle, saving Lettie from answering the man's question. "Bloody good-looking mob you've got there. How's the route holding up? No problems crossing the Hawkesbury?" Olivia's voice, full of confidence, contained a bubble of laughter. She thumped her hands onto her hips and marched across the paddock, leaving Lettie with one hand on Oxley's collar and her mind whirring. This vibrant woman with the flashing eyes and ribald tongue bore no resemblance to the picture Miriam had painted of an aged, possibly demented aunt.

10

YELLOW ROCK, 1880

The rhythm of the days continued and Evie's map expanded, a sketch here, another there, more coordinates and carefully measured distances.

Mrs. Hewitt's niece, Peg, took over the baking and the garden tasks and their lives returned to the easy pattern of the past. Bailey and the drovers came and went, taking the cattle and their dogs with them, and the foals brought with them a touch of hope as they frolicked in the sunshine. More than anything else, the routines lent a soothing simplicity to life, which Evie relished as she spent more and more time in Pa's study collating his papers and making notes.

And on the seventh day they rested. Olivia and Evie would ride up the winding track to Yellow Rock, make the steep climb, and bask in the warm reflection of the sandstone as they sat surveying the countryside all the way to the coast. Neither of them had time for the God who'd done so little for Alice and her boys, so they stayed away from the small church at Broke, giving instead their reverence to the panorama Mother Nature provided.

Evie's map grew more and more complex. From Yellow Rock the stock routes were clearly visible, and when the sun was high the glint of waterholes, the winding pearls of the brook lined with the bright green of the paddocks set her fingers flying. She took great pleasure in sketching in tiny details to lift the somber outline of the winding road. During the rest of the week, she collated Pa's papers and tried to make sense of the vast amount of information. She made her way through the various unrelated piles and tried to create some order. If Pa had any organizational system, it was lost on her. Invoices, lists of supplies, names of the people in the area who had sponsored Leichhardt, even the Ladies' Expedition and Mrs. Burdekin, her name right at the top alongside the Ludgrove name. The amount of money raised made her scalp itch.

As a form of respite, she'd turn to some of the earlier entries in Pa's journal that she'd skimmed, little anecdotes of his time with Leichhardt that all deserved to be documented.

Monday, 23rd January 1843

Mirannie Creek: Lat -32.4727 Long 151.3772

Went to Mirannie, ten miles from Glendon, to see the caves. We passed some very rough places thickly strewn with sandstone. When we returned to our horses we suddenly came upon a bull. He dropped his head threateningly. I stopped, but Doctor Leichhardt walked toward him fearing nothing, swinging his hammer to chase him away. To my great horror the bull was not scared off but charged. Doctor Leichhardt hid behind a large tree, but the bull followed and repeated his attack three times. On the fourth attempt, he delivered a blow to the animal's head and retreated once more to the trees. The bull stared at us from this distance almost indifferently. Finally, we returned to the stream bed and made a long detour to our horses and back to the road and to Glendon. We had come to no harm and retold the story that evening to much hilarity.

She giggled as she completed the illustration. Doctor Leichhardt hiding behind the tree, the bull pawing the ground, puffs of steam escaping from his nostrils, and Pa fleeing as the bull charged, coat-tails flapping and his hat forsaken in a muddy puddle. Oh, how she missed Pa. Surely sufficient time had passed for the details of Miriam's wedding to be arranged and they would return soon. In the meantime, his journals would have to suffice. She washed her brush and turned to the next entry.

Tuesday, 24th January 1843

Mt. Carrow (Pieries Peak): Lat -32.2110 Long 151.3034
Mt. Royal: Lat -32.1752 Long 151.3252

Today we commenced our journey to Mt. Royal. Doctor Leichhardt has looked longingly from several spots at this magnificent mountain. We tramped up and down hills and passed through forests of spotted gum and ironbark, box and stringy bark until we arrived at Fallbrook. Leichhardt was much impressed by the large numbers of ornithorhyn-chus we spotted on the deep banks of the waterholes. The creatures are the cause of much fascination in Europe apparently.

The anecdote made her smile; as a child she had become totally enamored with the funny little water moles who made their home in the banks of the brook, and she would pester Pa to take her at dusk to watch their antics. Why did she feel Pa's absence so keenly? It wasn't as though he hadn't spent time in Sydney before. With a sigh, she closed the journal and wandered out to the kitchen, a tad forlorn.

The sun was sinking fast by the time Olivia returned from her evening trudge, bedding down the mares for the night and checking on the foals. Evie had set the kitchen table as they always did on a Sunday night and rummaged through the pantry. A side of ham, some cheese, yesterday's bread, and a bowl of last winter's apples still cool from the cellar with a cup of tea and some tomato relish would make a fine supper. She'd just turned the pot when Olivia came in, sleeves rolled to her elbows and her hair windswept from her walk.

Without acknowledging her culinary efforts, Olivia sank down at the table, her face marred by a worried frown, her concentration totally absorbed by the letter in her hands.

"Is that from Pa? When will he be home? It's been ages since we heard from him. I'm looking forward to seeing him. Have they made all the arrangements for Miriam's wedding?" Evie prattled on, and only when she received no reply did she notice Olivia was no longer reading but staring out at the fiery glow as the sun sent its last burnished rays across the rock.

Something wasn't right.

Evie poured the tea and set a cup down in front of Olivia. Still she didn't turn from the window. "Olivia?" She sank onto her knees and clasped Olivia's cold hand. "What is it? What does Pa say?"

After a moment Olivia gave a shrug and offered a wan smile.

She brushed at her cheeks and cleared her throat. "It's not from William. It's from Miriam."

Evie's stomach sank and she clenched Olivia's hand. "Is every-thing . . ." The words caught in her throat.

"Your father is well. Plans are proceeding apace."

"When are they coming home?" she asked again. How very, very exciting. Pa would love the additions to her map, and as much as Miriam annoyed her, she'd missed her sister, couldn't wait to see her and more especially meet her soon-to-be brother-in-law. "She must have liked her beau."

"Beggars can't . . ." The muttered remains of Olivia's words slipped into the teacup as she gave a series of thoughtful sips. "The wedding's gone ahead."

The news sent Evie rocking back on her heels, her outstretched hand saving her at the last moment from an unceremonious collapse onto the flagged floor. "Why didn't he tell us? I thought they'd be coming home for the wedding."

Olivia tapped her fingernail on the tabletop, an irritating sound that set Evie's teeth on edge. "Let me read the letter." Evie reached out to take the single sheet of paper grasped loosely in Olivia's hand, but before she had a chance Olivia whisked it away and stuffed it into the pocket of her apron. "Why can't I read it?"

"We'll eat first. These things are better tackled on a full stom-ach. Come and sit down." Olivia reached across and cut herself a thick slab of ham and dolloped some relish on the side of her plate and sliced a tomato. "Come along. You've been out in the fresh air all day. You can read it when I've finished with it."

"Letters don't usually come on Sunday." Evie picked at a slice of bread, unable to bring it to her lips. Something was wrong, some-thing she couldn't fathom, something Olivia wouldn't share.

"Joe brought it in on his way back from church."

Then why hadn't Olivia told her about it earlier? And why the missing invitation? She'd wanted to see Miriam married, imagined the little church in Broke decked out with wildflowers, Pa escorting Miriam down the narrow aisle, smiling faces mingling with the dusty smell of beeswax and cedar.

Olivia thumped her plate away and stood up. "Let's give ourselves a break from the chores tomorrow. What do you think? You can spend all day in William's study on your map. I've got a mind to sort out the tack."

There was nothing she'd rather do except read Miriam's letter.

"Take yourself off to bed. I'll clear up here. You can read it tomorrow when I've finished with it." The plates landed with a crash in the sink. "Bedtime! Go!" The sight of Olivia's crumpled red face, narrowed eyes, and tight lips sent Evie scuttling from the room.

Clutching Pa's journal to her breast, she settled on her bed and tried to push all thoughts of the letter and Olivia's unusual reaction from her mind. Her breathing settled as she became absorbed in Pa's account of the trip to Mount Royal.

Thursday, 26th January 1843

Mt. Carrow/Pivi (Pievies Peak): Lat -32.2110 Long 151.3034

Our path led us uphill. We gained one terrace after the other, always sandstone covered by forest. Pivi, an elongated mountain ridge, stretches from south to north and is joined with Mt. Royal by a significantly higher embankment. Both mountains are a spur of the Liverpool Ranges, which run from southwest to northeast. We stopped at the foot of

Piri and made our camp in a hollow burned-out tree trunk. The end of a fallen tree fed our fire and the southeast wind blew the smoke over us, protecting us from mosquitoes. The night was cool, the sky magnificently starry.

With an aching heart Evie turned the pages, knowing there would be no further entries written in this carefree manner, for it was on that return trip, in a blinding thunderstorm, when Pa had fallen from his horse.

Friday, 27th January 1843

When we arose this morning, there was a fresh wind and Doctor Leichhardt proclaimed himself to be happy, rich, and satisfied enjoying the magnificent view, a sea of hills and ridges, which vanish in the blue of the horizon. He said he wished to remain for some days.

Unbeknownst to me, Doctor Leichhardt had tied his horse with the bridle and overnight it broke its restraint and vanished. I have volunteered to go in search. I left him happily encamped in the burned-out blackbutt with a supply of tea, bacon, and damper. If I fail to locate his horse, I will return to Captain Maynard's for another mount and further supplies.

She smoothed the faded leather of the journal, the picture of Pa on horseback riding down the mountain trail flickering against her eyelids.

Evie woke with a start the next morning, the memory of the un-read letter crowding her mind. Why hadn't Pa written? Olivia must have been keeping something from her. Surely she would have told her if he'd sickened. Dear God—worse—died. She threw on her clothes and raced to the kitchen. No sign of Olivia and no sign of the letter on the table nor in the big drawer that housed all manner of bits and pieces, the place where such things usually landed.

A half-finished cup of tea sat on the table, which meant Olivia would already be outside moving the horses into their day paddock. With a quick glance out of the window, she confirmed her suspicion and then slipped up the stairs and opened Olivia's bedroom door, her heart thundering at her audacity. Olivia guarded her room, her only privacy, like a treasure chest. She found the letter almost immediately, poking out of the book on the bedside table, *The Vase*, by the poet Eliza Dunlop, not something she would have imagined Olivia reading.

She slipped the letter into her sleeve and closed the door, guilt chasing her down the stairs.

The single sheet of paper crackled as she unfolded it. Miriam's familiar scrawl lurched across the page. *Dearest Aunt Olivia . . .* Why wasn't it addressed to her as well?

You will be pleased to know my wedding went off without a hitch. Pa arranged to have the banns read and everything is as it should be. Edward's widowed mother, Charlotte, has been most kind, and I was married from her house where we will live. It is a delightful terrace, next to Pa's, and will suit Edward and me well.

We haven't seen hide nor hair of Pa for several days. He

has been closeted with a Mr. Du Faur, something to do with a man named Skuthorpe who claims to know the whereabouts of some missing Leichhardt relics, though why Pa would be interested in an old watch and other rusty instruments is beyond my understanding.

Her breath whistled out between her lips in relief. Nothing the matter with Pa. Her gaze darted back to the page.

I am to tell you that Pa will be forced to remain in Sydney for several months. For this I am thankful because I need his support at this difficult time.

The corner of the paper crumpled as she tightened her fist, a livid pain in her chest and a burning sensation twisting her stomach. Why wouldn't Pa write himself and tell her this news?

Resisting the temptation to tear the letter into a thousand pieces, she placed it on the bed, a swirling cloud of anger boiling and bubbling in her chest. She slammed her fist into her mouth, trapping the emptiness inside. How she wished she could go and lay her head in Mama's lap and seek her sympathy.

Always Miriam. Miriam wanted to stay in Sydney. A house was provided. Miriam needed Pa's support. He remained in Sydney.

What about Pa's promise to her, their book on Leichhardt, her map? Was it some foolish sop to keep her occupied? And what was this new information about the Leichhardt relics? Were they the ones stolen from the man's satchel? What of the notes written by Leichhardt and his brother-in-law? Surely Pa would have written and told her of something so significant. Had he any intention of returning home and writing their book?

She slammed down the stairs and burst through the front door, wiping away the foul taste of bile with the back of her hand, and began to sob.

What she truly wanted was for life to return to normal. For life to be the way it had been before Mama's passing.

She skirted the stables and took the track leading up to Yellow Rock. Her thoughts coiled and swirled the faster she ran until she hadn't a breath left. Dragging in a great gulp of air, she slumped down under an old ironbark tree, its trunk rough against her heaving back. Her eyes stung, perspiration covered her face, and her parched throat hardly allowed her to swallow.

She shielded her eyes against the glare of the rising sun. The property lay like a drawing below. The two solid dwellings, the farmhouse hardly more than a child's plaything. The spacious flower gardens surrounded by ornamental trees and shrubs. Ma's rose garden, the western slope and driveway edged with large shady trees. Neat fences running in straight rows, the raceway to the stables, the mares' paddock, all wide enough to allow for Pa's dog-cart and for Olivia to manage the mares, move them from paddock to paddock on her own.

On her own.

The words hovered for a moment and a rush of heat suffused her face, her body responding before her mind. She wasn't the only one affected by the news. Not only had Olivia lost her sister, but Pa had deserted her too. Taking for granted that she could manage the farm, the two properties, the horses, and the cattle. Evie wasn't the only one who suffered by Pa's absence.

Her breathing settled, but not the rasping in her throat. She struggled to her feet and out from under the shade of the tree in search of water.

She'd once stumbled across Bailey and Olivia at the old cave under the overhang of the rock, where the walls were covered in ancient handprints; there was always water in the carved basin there, much like the one where the King-Parrots liked to drink.

She trailed back down the slope about a hundred yards, and there just off the track, running around the swell of the hill, nestled in the shade of an overhanging rock, was an indentation in the sandstone where water gathered.

Rock ferns grew marking the spot, and she squatted down and pushed them aside. Cupping her hands, she drank her fill, then splashed her face and dangled her wrists until her blood, and temper, cooled.

If Pa was going to be in Sydney longer than either he or she had anticipated, then she should make use of the time. Olivia managed on her own, and she would too. She would find out as much as she could from Pa's notes of the story behind these Leichhardt relics. And then when Pa told her about the Skuthorpe man, she'd have all the information at her fingertips.

Miriam had said nothing of the canister containing Leichhardt's and Classen's papers; she'd only mentioned a watch and other instruments. Surely the papers were more important, most important because they could well explain the fate of Leichhardt's expedition.

Regretting her foolish flight, she dried her hands on her skirt and headed down the track to the house.

By the time Evie returned, Olivia was back in the kitchen, a fresh pot of tea in front of her and a pile of papers covering the kitchen table.

"I owe you an apology."

Rubbing at her nose where a piece of burned skin had lifted, Olivia raised her head. "I doubt it."

"Oh, but I do." Evie drew in a deep breath. "I went upstairs, into your bedroom while you were out with the horses, and read Miriam's letter."

Olivia's palms flattened on the tabletop and she stared into her face for long seconds. There was nothing in her eyes to indicate anger. But then, she'd never seen Olivia angry. Upset when Mama passed away, concerned for her if one of her attacks threatened, annoyed when Miriam trailed around after the young drovers, but never truly angry, not the way she had looked last night.

"I should have told you straightaway." Olivia reached for the teapot. "I wanted to save you pain. I know how much William means to you, how much you mean to William. This time . . ." Her eyes skittered aside. "Everything will be for the best, and besides, I should be lonely without you."

"I think Pa knew he would be in Sydney longer than he said." The words sprang from her lips before she had time to process the thought; however, she had no doubt she was correct. "Otherwise he wouldn't have given me the saddlebag or asked me to work on my maps for the book. I couldn't have completed everything in a couple of weeks."

"A book you say." Olivia raised her eyebrows in question.

By way of apology Evie told Olivia what Pa had said. He hadn't told her not to talk about it. It was more her own self-importance that had prevented her from telling Olivia. "He's planning to write a book about Leichhardt—three volumes, in fact. He's asked me to collate his papers and draw the maps."

Olivia's lips twitched and she gave a sniff. "That's a big job. You might be right. Take your cup of tea into the study and spend some time there. I'll call you when food's ready."

Evie turned to leave and remembered the part of Miriam's letter she'd forgotten in her selfish tirade. "Do you know anything more about this Skuthorpe man Miriam mentioned?"

"Not a clue. I thought after all this time they'd give up. What's special about a few relics belonging to some failed explorer? Nothing for you to worry about, my sweet girl."

"I'm not a child, you know." Even though she'd behaved like a spoilt infant—it wouldn't happen again.

Olivia pulled back the chair, reached for Evie's hand, and patted it.

She wouldn't be fobbed off with any more platitudes. "Tell me. I have a right to know if it affects me."

"Yes. You do," Olivia admitted with a sigh. "Our breeding business is not, hasn't been for some time, as successful as it was in the past. Money's tight. Many more people have good stock now, and although ours is the best, sometimes money wins out. William is looking to expand into other areas. He dedicated so much of the family money to this ridiculous obsession he has with Leichhardt, amends must be made. Edward Rawlings has contacts in the racing world, a different type of business. William needs to be in Sydney."

Olivia's shuttered face signaled the end of the conversation. Evie took it as her dismissal, swallowing the urge to challenge her unusual remarks.

"Before you go . . . This came from Sydney. The Bushman's Bible. Put it with the others in the study."

11

YELLOW ROCK, 1911

More cattle and stockmen with their horses and dogs arrived as the day wore on, the campfire grew bigger, and someone opened a keg of rum, at least that was what Peg reported when she sent Lettie down to the camp to join in the fun.

Oxley stuck firmly by her side as she wandered across the paddock surrounded by squealing children and a deal of backslapping as old friends caught up with each other. As the sun sank someone lit a small fire out of fresh gum leaves and grass. Everyone gathered around in a circle, and one of the drovers played a series of haunting notes on a hollow branch while white smoke billowed through the twilight.

With the moon riding high above Yellow Rock and the smell of roasting meat and rum mingling with the scent of the gum trees, the smaller fire was abandoned in favor of the bonfire, and someone stuck a well-loved fiddle under his chin and the dancing began.

Olivia hiked up her skirt, flashed a comely pair of ankles, and dragged Lettie into the fray, teaching her jigs and reels making her lungs heave and her face burn. A far cry from the sedate waltzes and the starched shirts she'd encountered in Sydney.

It wasn't until the musicians took a rest that Olivia's dusty skirt stopped flaring and she accepted a tin mug and thrust another into Lettie's hand.

The fumes burned Lettie's nostrils and she handed it back, her gorge rising. "I couldn't. I'll track down a glass of Peg's lemonade when I've got my breath back." Moving from the roaring fire, she found a convenient spot away from the dancing and settled down. A cool breath of air touched her cheek, and the plaintive strains of the fiddle melded with the murmur of voices.

Oxley let out a bark of relief and rushed to her side and flopped down. She ran her fingers through his rough wiry coat, pleased for his company as everyone stood around catching their breath, chatting and sharing a drink. A star-studded sky far brighter than she'd ever seen in Sydney lit the camp, the Milky Way an untidy splattering of paint sweeping the indigo darkness.

A loud laugh broke her contemplation, and she spotted Olivia talking to a tall, rangy fellow brushing his hair back from his face before replacing his battered hat. The flash of his dark eyes, the red shirt, and his wide smile stirred her memory—the man from the blacksmith's in Wollombi.

The moment she stepped into the light of the fire Nathaniel spotted her, remembered her face, recognized her. It would be difficult not to; she'd stayed in his mind from their first meeting. Dark hair, unusual with her green-gold eyes, a mixture of feisty confidence tinged with that lost-little-girl look. A total contrast, and one he couldn't fathom. So she'd made it as far as Yellow Rock, and in the flickering light he couldn't tell if she'd settled. Family, she'd said, and sure enough Olivia had her in the fray, but then there'd be nothing that would keep Olivia away from a shindig.

Even at her age Olivia still turned a pretty ankle and loved nothing more than a dance. According to Denman, she'd been a lively lass in her younger years, though she'd never married. There'd been talk at one stage of a disappointment, a lost love, but Nathaniel had never seen or heard evidence of such.

His gaze roamed the circle around the fire searching for Letitia again. All the Broke girls were there in force, chasing the drovers; there'd be some shenanigans tonight unless he was mistaken. News traveled fast. He hadn't known the drovers would be in, hadn't intended to camp the night in the paddock under Yellow Rock, but he'd seen the herd run through Wollombi, felt the need for company. Pretty much as the locals had done.

It was good to see the place lit up, and truth be told, her name had sparked his interest when she'd turned up in Wollombi. Rawlings. She had to be related. Edward Rawlings was well known around Randwick; he'd come across him more than once delivering horses.

The plaintive notes of the fiddle slowed the dancing and he found her, back resting against one of the wagons and her arms folded protectively across her body as though frightened to let go. He pulled off his hat and stepped in front of her. "Everyone's talking about Olivia's long-lost niece."

"Yes." A frown flitted across her forehead, then the corner of her mouth lifted. "I remember. You helped with the gasoline in Wollombi."

"Nathaniel Poole." Feeling like a gangling boy, he fiddled with the brim of his hat. "That's a great vehicle you've got."

She tilted her chin. "A Model T Ford—the best motor in Australia."

"Don't see many around these parts."

"It's the way of the future. There are over four thousand cars in Sydney now, never mind almost as many motorcycles."

"Sydney's not my cup of tea. Like it better out in the open country where you can breathe." The only thing he owned was the air that he breathed. This girl, woman, in fact—he ran an appreciative gaze from the top of her wavy hair to the tip of her expensive boots—was so far out of his league as to make it ridiculous.

"Have you never visited Sydney?" The frown drifted back, her head tipped to one side, a curtain of hair falling across the side of her face.

His fingers itched to brush the curls aside. "Now and again, running horses down to Sydney." Sometimes taking the back roads, other times sticking to the stock route, giving him a chance to learn the country and a sense of freedom. Just the way he liked it. No ties, back and forth between Scone, Windsor, and Randwick, sometimes farther afield, putting his head down in a different place most nights. "Cattle are slow. I prefer shifting horses." And a fair enough way to earn a quid, and allow him to choose how he spent it. He'd settle soon, had picked out the spot he fancied, one he and Denman could call their own, up Dartbrook way where the grazing was good. "You got here without any problems?"

She turned to him, the light of the fire illuminating her delicate cheekbones. "Yes. Thank you."

"No trouble with the creeks?"

"No, none at all. Your directions were perfect."

"And that motor of yours ran all right? Had enough gasoline?"

"Lizzie's fine."

"Lizzie?"

"Tin Lizzie. My brother's name for the motor. His car, in fact. She does a good fifty miles to the gallon."

He ran his hand through Oxley's fur, shifting from one foot to the other. Never short of a word, he suddenly found himself tongue-tied. Then the music fired up and saved him. "Would you like to dance, Letitia?"

Her arms rose defensively across her body again. "No, thank you. I don't."

"Everyone dances." He offered his hand, sensing the tension deep inside her, wanting to see her smile again. "Besides, I saw you with Olivia. Bet she taught you a trick or two. This one's nice and slow, a waltz." Wasn't that what they did in society? He had some picture in his head of swirling skirts and cavernous ballrooms. No idea where it came from. Only dances he knew happened around a campfire or if it was real smart in the woolshed on one of the bigger properties. She was ballroom material, without a doubt, with her fine wrists, long, thin fingers, and skin as delicate as one of Olivia's china teacups.

"Lettie, come along. Don't be shy," Olivia called as she swirled past, her girlish laugh belying every one of her seventy years. More of a polka than a waltz, but then, that was Olivia, always at a gallop for as long as he could remember.

Letitia took a couple of tentative steps, and in a fit of outright wishful thinking, he took her hand. When her fingers tightened around his, he led her from the security of the wagon into the midst of the dancers, and before she could change her mind, he slipped his hand to her waist. Light as a spring breeze she came into his arms.

He started to move, more shuffled his feet in the dirt—the

connection between his brain and his body well and truly severed by her closeness—took a step back, then forward. Wasn't that the way?

Her body shook, and he stopped short, lurched back. "Did I tread on your foot?"

"No, no." She jiggled from one side to another. "I'm fine." Her mouth quivered and then she laughed.

Whatever had possessed him? He couldn't dance, not slow like this, not with a lady in his arms. The music picked up. Saved by a fiddle. Who'd have thought?

Taking a leaf out of Olivia's book, he spun Letitia once, then galloped her off through the throng, faster and faster. Her shrieks of laughter filled his ears, ringing in the smoky air. Round and around until the bodies blurred and his head went dizzy.

"Stop! Stop!"

He ground to a halt. What now? She slumped against him, then pulled away, bent double, a mixture of snatched breaths and explosive giggles. "Come and sit down."

"I'm so out of breath. I need a drink." She put her hands on her knees and leaned over, sucking in great gasps of air.

A drink? There was rum—the sweet, oaky flavor permeated the air. Surely she wouldn't want rotgut. "Rum?"

She straightened up, her smile wider than the Hunter, then pulled her hair back from her face and twisted it in some kind of knot, leaving tendrils framing her face. "I'd like water, not rum."

"That I can do." He led her away from the fire to a quiet spot below the rock and settled her down on the grass. "Sit here. I'll be back in a moment. Oxley'll keep you company." Happy the dog would take care of her, he raced off.

When he returned he found her perched on a fallen log, one

arm slung around Oxley's shoulders and her eyes fixed on the rock.

"Thank you." She took the water bag and upended it, dribbles of water trickling from the corner of her mouth, then sighed and wiped them away with the back of her hand. "It's so quiet here after the noise around the fire. It's as though the rock swallows all sound."

"Heard the story of Lizard Rock?"

"Olivia calls it Yellow Rock, so did the man in the general store, not Lizard Rock."

"Different people, different names. You can see his shape better in the moonlight. The old fellas, the Wonnarua People, say that's the head of the lizard. And his body runs along the ridgeline, and that arch up there, that's his eye. See his two front legs stretched out, with the tail making up the ridges running in the direction of Wollombi? Sometimes he gets restless and kicks down a flurry of stones, a bit of a landslide. Some say he created all the valleys and the mountains between the ocean and here."

She gave a little shiver.

"Cold?"

"No. You're right, he is watching."

"Just another of the old stories. Country's full of them."

"Tell me." She wrapped her hands around her knees and fixed her gaze on him.

"The old fellas say Lizard made his way across the land from the coast eating everything in his path, all the animals. He kept on eating and eating and growing bigger and bigger until one day he ate Kangaroo."

"I've never eaten a kangaroo."

"It's good tucker. Saved a lot of the early settlers from starvation."

She tilted her head, the moonlight bathing her in a pale halo. "And what happened to the lizard when he ate the kangaroo? Are you going to tell me something I'd rather not know?"

Not if he could help it. He'd be happy if she stayed right where she was studying him with those unfathomable eyes. He drew in a steadying breath. "Understandably Kangaroo wasn't very happy about being eaten. He started to jump up and down inside Lizard's stomach, making him feel real sick."

Letitia gave her stomach a rub and looked around at all the others tucking into their food. "What's for supper?"

"Kangaroo. Do you want the rest of the story?"

She placed her finger against her lips, eyes sparkling. Long fingers, the nails blunt and practical, a smudge of ink against the quick. Boots that would cost twelve months' wages, yet her fingers stained. Such a set of contradictions. "Kangaroo kept on jumping and jumping, until he jumped right out."

"And then what happened to the lizard?" She sat like a child, as though captivated by his words.

"Ah, well, that's the rub. He was turned into stone. And there he is." He pointed to the rock face silhouetted against the night sky.

Her face paled.

"Nothing for you to be worrying about. Lizard's up there reminding us all not to be greedy. Ask Olivia to take you up there. You can see forever."

"How far is forever?"

"All the valleys and the mountains, all the way to the coast. Pretty much . . ." The rest of his words disappeared in the discordant screech of the fiddle as the player searched for the right note. He held out his hand and pulled her to her feet. They danced again, the singing and swearing and hilarity growing louder as the night wore on. Then they sat again shoulder to shoulder while the moonlight chased the falling stars across the sky until finally she excused herself, declined his invitation to walk her back to the farmhouse, and called Oxley.

"Good night, Miss Rawlings."

Somewhere above the rock a night bird called.

She wrapped her arms around her waist. "Lettie, call me Lettie," she said as she drifted off into the night, her face still turned toward the rock and the dog by her side, where he'd like to be.

12

YELLOW ROCK, 1881

The late afternoon sun lit the study and dust motes danced in the beam slanting across the polished timber floorboards. Evie settled at the desk, spread the magazine on top of the piles of paper, and found a small space to rest her elbows.

Pa was very taken with his Bushman's Bible, the new weekly magazine called *The Bulletin* that he'd arranged to have sent from Sydney. She'd read the odd article or two he'd recommended and recognized the names of many of the contributors. The story of Captain Moonlite and the scurrilous Wantabadgery bushrangers had held her captive, and she and Pa had laughed over the political sketches, albeit after he'd explained their significance. Although their stance that Australia should be for the white man alone was something she found hard to agree with. What of the original inhabitants? Why couldn't they all live side by side? Over the years they'd employed many Wonnarua People; they were among some of the best stockmen and drovers in the country, and harvest time would be nigh impossible without their contribution. Yellow Rock wouldn't have thrived without their labor.

She stared at the date of the magazine: *Saturday, 25th December 1880.* Christmas had passed, and she and Olivia hadn't marked it. No picnic on the grass under the spreading angophora, no games, no croquet, no presents exchanged with neighbors. Just a day like any other. She leafed through the magazine from back to front as she always did, and midway through a headline caught her attention.

THE FATE OF LEICHHARDT ONE THOUSAND POUND REWARD

The proprietors of *The Bulletin* have much pleasure in announcing that they are prepared to pay the sum of ONE THOUSAND POUNDS for the first conclusive and substantial proof of the place where Ludwig Leichhardt, the great Australian explorer, met his death . . .

A reward of one thousand pounds! Her mind spiraled. The government had rewarded Leichhardt with a thousand pounds after his Essington expedition. It was a vast amount of money! Did Pa know about this? Did it have something to do with his meeting with Du Faur? Surely if he had Leichhardt's and Classen's rumored writings they would contain *conclusive and substantial proof.* Her gaze raced across the page:

Subject to the following conditions: The information to be clear and unchallengeable. The same to be kept absolutely secret until communicated to and published by the

110

SYDNEY BULLETIN.

All relics and objects recovered and produced in support of the evidence offered to be handed over to the proprietors of The Bulletin, who will undertake to present them to the Australian Museum. The sum of ONE THOUSAND POUNDS has been deposited in the Australian Joint Stock Bank Sydney to pay the reward above offered.

Further particulars in the leading article.

Leading article? What leading article? How had she missed it? She flicked to the front page, her hands damp and shaking.

It told her little she didn't know. Pa might have written it himself, but for the last sentences.

Thirty-two years ago Ludwig Leichhardt left on this ill-starred journey . . . The mystery remains unsolved . . . We have not given up the hope that the survivors or survivor of the party left some message for their fellow men . . .

She read the words again, her mind returning to Miriam's letter. Pa, like the writer of the article, had concluded there was no hope of Leichhardt being found alive. He'd told her that before he left. *We have not given up the hope that the survivors or survivor of the party left some message for their fellow men.* Could the canister contain some message from Leichhardt and Classen? She pushed out of the chair, intent on asking Olivia her opinion, then stopped short, her gaze returning to the initial advertisement:

... to be kept absolutely secret until communicated to and published by the

SYDNEY BULLETIN ...

She'd never kept anything from Olivia. She slumped down and gazed out into the encroaching darkness, thinking of Miriam's letter. *Pa has been closeted with a Mr. Du Faur, something to do with a man named Skuthorpe who claims to know the whereabouts of some missing Leichhardt relics . . . an old watch and other rusty instruments . . .*

She rummaged through the piles of paper on the desk, searching for the notes from the Geographical Society about the relics. Pa had mentioned a telescope, and a man who'd claimed he had discovered other relics and writings, only to have them stolen from his bag while he slept. Surely if they had been stolen for financial gain they would have surfaced before now. If she could find some reference to the whereabouts of the papers, perhaps it would lead to the conclusive evidence *The Bulletin* was looking for, and who was in a better place to do that? She had every scrap of information, every carefully collected fact on the desk in front of her in Pa's notes, journals, and reports. The lure of the reward dangled like a glittering jewel.

It was the perfect solution. First and foremost, the thousand-pound reward would help Pa. And second, and more important, he could come home and they could work on their book and include the new evidence.

A bubble of elation rose in her breast. The success, the accolades! With the support of *The Bulletin*, Pa's name would go down in history as the man who solved the mystery of Leichhardt's disappearance. Everything Pa yearned for, everything he deserved, achieved in one single swoop. Somewhere on his desk among the notes, letters, journals, and newspaper articles the answer must lie. She could feel it beneath her fingertips eluding her, playing the kind of hide-and-go-seek game she'd loved as a child.

In a flurry of agitation, she leafed through Pa's handwritten notes, putting to one side anything that mentioned the Leichhardt relics. With the help of articles from the *Illustrated Sydney News*, *The Queenslander*, the *Morning Bulletin*, and other newspaper clippings, she created a pile of papers that clarified the story of the man Pa had told her about before he left for Sydney. A man called Andrew Hume.

She wrote his name in large letters, then picked up a cutting from the *Maitland Mercury*. It told of his early life. How he'd come to Australia as a child with his mother and father. His father was a stockman in the Hunter River District, and he'd grown up on a property belonging to the Halls near Dartbrook. Then when the family moved to Maitland and bought a shop, Andrew left to travel to the interior, where he claimed to have met a white-haired old man living with the natives who was the sole survivor of an attack on Leichhardt's party. The old man had shown Andrew a canister containing letters and a roll of papers, a watch, quadrant, thermometer, and telescope. The old man insisted he was unable to make the journey to Sydney, and on his instructions Hume buried everything under a marked bloodwood tree to keep the items safe and then set off for Sydney to inform the government. Who was this old man? Had he really been a member of Leichhardt's party? Were the rumors about them being taken captive by the natives true?

She shuffled through the articles until she found a report saying Hume had been arrested on his way back to Sydney as a bushranger and sent to gaol before he had told anyone of the white-haired old man. With a groan, she let her head fall to the table. Why hadn't she listened more carefully to Pa's stories?

Oxley's plaintive whine brought her to her senses and she threw open the door to find Olivia balancing a plate of sandwiches and a glass of lemonade on a tray somewhat like a peace offering.

Whisking around, Evie covered the papers on the desk with a sheet of cartridge paper, the words *absolutely secret* resounding like the koel's cry over and over in her mind. Olivia mustn't see them. None of them. Especially not the notes she'd made on Andrew Hume.

"I called you but you can't have heard me. Perhaps you were dozing." Olivia handed Evie the tray and settled in the chair opposite.

"Daydreaming." Evie fumbled for more words, came up short, and took a bite of the sandwich instead. Oxley sidled closer, quivering in anticipation, and pressed against her leg.

"You've got quite a job on your hands. Can I help clean up this mess?" Olivia asked.

It was the last thing Evie wanted. She picked up a graphite pencil, examined its well-used tip, and started doodling.

"Do you want me to help?"

"Thank you, Aunt Olivia, but no. Pa entrusted me with his papers, and I feel I would be breaking his faith . . ."

"Piffle and nonsense. What's he got here that I don't know about? William forgets I remember the very moment his infatuation with the man began. Remember delivering Leichhardt's wretched letters, reading them when William could barely lift his head from the pillow." Olivia rested her hands on Evie's shoulders and gazed down at the desk. "What's that you're drawing?"

Without thinking she'd sketched the artifacts Andrew Hume claimed he had buried—a hunting watch, quadrant, thermometer, and telescope lying in the desert, alongside the skull of a long-dead bullock. Thank heavens she'd stopped before she'd drawn the canister with the papers; she'd never have explained that away. "It's just a picture."

"Strange things to be drawing."

"Not strange. Something that will need to go on my map."

"More Leichhardt rubbish, unless I'm very much mistaken."

Olivia stuck her nose in the air and marched out of the room, slamming the door behind her.

With a sigh Evie pushed aside her half-eaten lunch. "Go on, Oxley, you can have it." The sandwich vanished in a single gulp. "Greedy boy. The lemonade's mine." Sipping the drink, she surveyed the mess on the desk. Did Hume get out of gaol? It was worse than reading one of the serials in *The Bulletin*, waiting for the next installment.

More rummaging uncovered a series of pages of Pa's looping scrawl. Notes from a meeting with Du Faur. Hume had talked his way out of gaol by telling the authorities about the old man, and then he was given a revolver, ammunition, and twelve pounds for the journey from Newcastle to the Roper River, where he received a horse, saddle, and rations to enable him to go and collect the papers and relics he claimed to have buried.

Upon arriving back in Sydney, all he had was the telescope, some ink powder, and blank paper, and no one believed his story.

And there it was, written in Pa's rambling scrawl:

On opening the satchel we discovered a large slash had
been made, most probably by a sharp blade, scoring the

underside. The only contents being a telescope, which appears to be genuine, and some blank sheets of paper and ink. Hume said the old man who gave him the artifacts was August Classen. Nothing remained in Hume's saddle-bag of the seventy-five pages of Leichhardt's writings or the statement Hume claims Classen wrote during the month he was with him.

Whatever had made Pa and Du Faur believe his tale?

Her eyes flew across the pages. The government had refused to fund a further expedition. She could understand that, but there had been one, she knew, because Hume had perished in the desert on his final expedition to rescue Classen and bring him back to civilization. Pa and Du Faur had financed it and interviewed the only surviving member of the three-man party. She squinted out the french doors trying to recall his name—it escaped her.

No wonder Pa was so interested in the Skuthorpe man, and short of money. All for nothing, because Hume had died in the desert without meeting Classen again.

Six years ago! The wind whistled out between her teeth. She was chasing shadows, or had she missed something?

After a sleepless night peppered with images of barren tracts of red soil and bleached skeletons, Evie rose before daybreak, completed her chores in record time, and set off for the study. Overnight Pa's obsession had become her own. She could think of nothing else.

Oxley foiled her plans, letting out a sharp bark of glee the moment she entered the kitchen.

"Stop right where you are!" Olivia appeared from the depths of the pantry, her arms full of bottles and jars. "The pair of you."

Evie slid to a standstill, her cheeks rivaling stewed rhubarb.

Oxley's tail curled tightly between his back legs.

"I need you to take something to Bailey." Olivia dumped the bottles onto the table, rummaged around in her apron pocket, and handed her a piece of paper and a small drawstring bag. "Tell him it's the best I can do; there's an IOU for the remainder. I'll have it when they come through next time."

Evie hefted the bag. Why it couldn't wait until the afternoon she didn't understand. "I'll do it later."

"Now. He's leaving this morning."

The drovers only turned up the day before, and they always rested before heading up to the Liverpool Plains. "They've just arrived. I need to . . . What is it?"

"Wages."

"Why don't you give it to him this afternoon?"

"Just do as you're bid and stop asking questions. I told you he's leaving now. And don't forget to give him the IOU and tell him I'll get the rest to him as soon as I can."

"But Pa always gives them the full amount . . ." Oh! Then money must be tight, as Olivia had said.

"William's got other things on his mind, you know that, and contrary to common opinion I'm not the Bank of New South Wales—otherwise I wouldn't have had to let Mrs. Hewitt go." Olivia gave one of her irritated huffs and started shunting the bottles back and forth. "And don't forget your hat. Your brains will cook in this heat."

Evie loosened the pins in her hair and rammed her hat down hard, making sure it wouldn't blow off, then left, Oxley dogging her footsteps.

If Bailey was about to leave, there was only one way to catch him: cut behind the stables and meet him at the main gates; that way she wouldn't be caught up in the swirling furor of irritated cattle and yapping dogs. Fine on horseback, but not on foot.

She spotted him at the top of the driveway sitting astride his big black stallion, Raven, under the shade of the trees. "*Cooee. Bailey!*"

Oxley made a fine imitation of her call and Bailey turned and lifted his hat in acknowledgment, wheeling Raven around to meet her.

She held the bag out, her breath coming in ragged gasps. "Aunt Olivia says it's the best she can do. There's an IOU for the rest because she's not the Bank of New South Wales. Why are you leaving early? What about the dance tonight? Aunt Olivia will miss you."

Evie wouldn't be there—she'd be buried in Pa's study—but she knew Olivia and the drovers loved their night on the common at Yellow Rock. They'd light a big fire and bring out their fiddles and the girls from Broke would come and flutter their eyelashes and dance until their feet dropped off.

"They'll be here for a few more days; there'll still be a knees-up every night. I'm picking up some horses in Maitland to take up to Scone, then I'll meet them at Murrurundi."

On the stock route; she'd marked it on her map. The drovers always went that way to the Liverpool Plains and on to Queensland. He tilted his hat and scrubbed his hand over his face, then gazed up at the house, a pained expression etching his usually sunny face. "Tell Olivia I'll be back through in a month or so. That should give her time to chase up young Mr. Ludgrove for the rest of the money."

It seemed strange that Olivia hadn't spoken to Bailey herself. And why would anyone call Pa young? But Bailey had been with them since he could sit astride a horse and his father before him, boss drovers the pair of them. "What's the rush?"

"Going to catch up with one of my father's old mates. They worked together at Hall's place at Dartbrook." He wheeled his horse around. "Take care of yourself, and Olivia. No wandering off." He threw her a half-hearted smile and popped his horse into a lively canter.

"Have a good trip. See you when you get back," she called after him.

With the warm sunshine on her back she meandered through the long grass, full of a flush of wildflowers, while Oxley pranced around chasing butterflies. Since Pa had been in Sydney no one had time to scythe the grass, and she preferred the picture it presented. Untamed and more natural. A few days ago in a moment of conceitedness, she'd sketched a picture of herself sitting among the wildflowers. "What do you think, Oxley?" She ruffled the fur on the top of his head and he turned his liquid eyes up to her face. "Shall we send it to Pa?"

Oxley lifted his nose to the breeze.

"Vanity, I know." She stooped to pick a bunch of flowers, fastened them with a piece of grass, and made her way up the hill to visit Mama, John, James, and Joshua. Bailey's talk of catching up with old mates had made her realize how neglectful she'd become as the weeks had passed.

She laid the wildflowers at the foot of Mama's headstone, wishing she'd taken the time to care for the white roses Mama particularly liked. "I'll spend some time tending your garden soon, I promise." Skirting the path, she and Oxley sneaked around the back to the house hoping to avoid Olivia. They failed. She stood in the hallway, arms folded and a questioning look on her face. "Out!"

She glared at Oxley and pointed to the doorstep. "Did you catch Bailey?"

"Yes, he said he'd be back in a month and it should give you time to chase up *young* Mr. Ludgrove about the rest of the wages. Bailey's nowhere near Pa's age, and I find it difficult to imagine Pa ever being young."

"He cut a fine figure in his youth. Everyone thought your mama had made the best catch. Mind you, she didn't have to do much. It was never going to be otherwise. He'd only had eyes for her from the time she was still in pigtails. The Scotts' girl, the red-head, hadn't got a hope."

Pa's journals told a different story, but then, who was she to judge?

"If he hadn't got such a bee in his bonnet, things might have been very different."

Evie knew what would come next: another tirade about Leichhardt and the way he'd ruined Pa's life. She, too, was en-trapped, like a lizard in amber, able to think of little else. How could five men, two guides, twenty mules, fifty bullocks, seven horses, and masses of gear disappear without trace?

But it wouldn't be without trace if someone found Leichhardt's and Classen's accounts. How she'd love the opportunity to talk to Andrew Hume. What a pity he'd died.

And then everything went still and quiet but for the sound of Bailey's voice as he'd said, *"Going to catch up with one of my father's old mates. They worked together at Hall's place at Dartbrook . . ."*

Dartbrook! Wasn't that where Andrew Hume had lived as a child before his parents moved to Maitland and he went off wan-dering? Wasn't his father a stockman at the Dartbrook property?

"Evie!" Olivia's fingers snapped in front of her face and her hands came down on her shoulders, guiding her into a chair. "It's all right. Sit quietly. It will pass. I've got you."

Cradled against Olivia's breast as though still a child, Evie struggled for breath.

"I knew this would happen. You've been behaving strangely ever since William left."

Evie wrenched away. "I'm not having a turn. I'm perfectly fine. I need to go and talk to Bailey." She shot to her feet and pushed past Olivia, caught her ankle in her haste, and groaned aloud.

Olivia steadied her, a look of concern on her face. "Go upstairs and lie down."

"I don't need to lie down. I need to talk to Bailey."

"Bailey's left. A good hour ago. Are you slipping?"

Slipping? "No, no, I'm perfectly fine. I have to find some paperwork." She limped to the study and tried to close the door behind her, but Oliva shadowed her footsteps.

She pulled her drawing over the top of her notes, then piled some papers on top. Was it too much of a coincidence? "Do you know anyone called Hume?"

Olivia frowned. "You need to rest."

"I don't need to rest. Do you know anyone named Hume? Bailey said he was catching up with an old mate and I wondered if his name was Hume."

There must have been something in the tone of her voice, because Olivia sat down in the chair and scratched her head. "Can't say that I do. Why?"

"Maitland way. Bailey said he was visiting a friend of his father who lived there. He was a drover, a stockman at the Halls' place at Dartbrook."

"Well, Bailey'd know. Ask him."

But Bailey wasn't here and wouldn't be back for a month, at least. And Andrew Hume had traveled from Sydney north on his final expedition, and she'd found a report saying he'd given a talk in Maitland at the School of Arts on the second of July, just before he left. Surely he would have visited his parents, said goodbye. In the same situation she couldn't imagine behaving any other way.

Her gaze dived back to the papers in front of her, then returned to Olivia. She had to speak to Bailey.

"You're still pale. I'll go and make a cup of tea."

Evie didn't want a cup of tea. She wanted some peace and quiet to get her jumbled thoughts in order. "I'll be there in a moment." That moment turned into an hour and more as she worked her way through the pile of papers again and found something she'd missed yesterday. A letter and a photograph of four men. She flipped it over and read the words on the back: *Andrew Hume (far right) about to leave Sydney with members of his second expedition in search of Classen, 1874.* The face of the man, his long beard and bowler hat, told her nothing, nor did the man next to him in a military-styled jacket, or the other two, sporting knee-high boots and waistcoats, and the six horses with their packs bulging.

Unable to resist, she pulled out her map and sketched them just outside Maitland and wrote the word *Hume* and turned to the letter. It was from Du Faur telling of his trip to meet Hume because the men he'd left Sydney with had become disillusioned when he'd disappeared for a couple of days. They'd withdrawn from the expedition and Du Faur had recruited another man named O'Hea and the expedition went ahead. Where did Hume go in those two days?

And that made up her mind. She didn't have a month to wait until Bailey returned because she needed to talk to Andrew Hume's father and ask what happened when his son visited Maitland and if he knew why he had disappeared for two days.

Supposing, just supposing the canister with Leichhardt's and Classen's writings hadn't been stolen along with the other relics, and Andrew Hume had kept them as some form of insurance. Wouldn't he have left them with someone he trusted while he went off into the desert? Who better than his parents?

13

Lettie jerked upright and blinked the room into focus. She'd lain for hours listening to the muted sounds of the drovers' party, reliving the firm touch of Nathaniel's warm hands and the comforting sound of his voice as he'd told her the story of Lizard Rock, until eventually sleep got the better of her. Now the sky had lightened and the same strange birdcall echoed in the silence of the fragile dawn.

A tray bearing a small pot of tea stood on the bedside table. She swung out of bed and poured a cup, sipping slowly as she studied the empty paddock through the glass. Already the promise of another hot, humid day loomed. No sign of the drovers and their cattle, only the looming shadow of Yellow Rock.

A surge of energy raced through her and she pulled her nightgown over her head and reached for her blouse; instead, she found a soft white dress lying across the back of the chair. She shook it out and held it up to the light. Cool and fine, the muslin billowed in the breeze from the window. Lifting it to her shoulders, she held it against her body—a perfect fit and much cooler than her skirt and blouse, which had vanished. Peg must have brought her tea and taken away her clothes that reeked of smoke and sweat after the fire and dancing last night.

She slipped the dress over her head and pulled on the pair of black stockings and buttoned her boots. Her reflection in the glass startled her, breaking her dream of last night.

A dream so vivid, she couldn't believe she'd woken; a yearning so intense that when she touched her chest she expected to find her heart bruised. Someone was calling her name; she couldn't see her face, but the voice was as familiar as her own.

The hot sun beat down and Oxley panted, the wind blowing his ears back like pennants in the breeze. She stood at the top of the rock, a panoramic view laid out before her right to the sparkling sea. The river's serpentine laziness cut its way through verdant green pastures. Unimportant and insignificant, she stood gazing across the golden gorges and hazy violet hillsides leading to the distant horizon. As she balanced on the lip of the precipice, the air flooded over her and stopped her breath. She took a step back, her spine prickling. Her reflection shimmered and faded.

Her heart beat fast against her ribcage and the hairs quivered on her skin. Ridiculous! She hadn't been up there. Nothing but her imagination working overtime after Nathaniel's story and Olivia's strangely evasive responses to her questions. The unfulfilled promise of yesterday, interrupted by the arrival of the stockmen.

Tomorrow Olivia had said, and tomorrow had arrived.

Lettie found Peg in the kitchen stirring a huge pot over the stove. "Ah, you're awake. Did you sleep well?"

"Eventually. There's a bird that calls before it's even light. It's a strange repetitive sound, a sort of *wurro-wurro* sound and then another bird answers, *keek-keek*. It woke me." Peg would think she was some strange city dweller who'd never heard a birdcall.

Peg let out something resembling a laugh. "You've got it down pat. The *wurro-wurro* is the male koel marking his territory. The *keek-keek* is the female accepting his invitation. They make a filthy noise at the beginning of the season. Perhaps you can tell 'em to bugger off. I hate the things. The fig trees attract them. Nasty piece of work the female is too. She lays her egg in someone else's nest, leaves it, and moves on. The chicks hatch and kick all the other birds out of the nest."

"A koel? I've never heard one before."

"Australia's answer to the cuckoo."

"I didn't hear the drovers leave."

"Up and away at first light, same as always. Olivia said she'll meet you over at the main house when you're ready. She's out with Nathaniel sorting the shipment of horses to Sydney. Like some breakfast?"

Lettie's heart gave an unexpected thud. For some reason she had imagined Nathaniel would have left at first light with the drovers. "No, I'm not hungry. I'll go straight over."

"She'll be at the house before long. Oxley'll keep you company. He's taken a shine to you. Don't forget your hat—it's in the hall. It's going to be hot today."

Without replying Lettie grabbed the old cabbage palm hat from the stand, shook her hair loose, and rammed it onto her head, then bolted, her booted feet thudding on the path and Oxley skittering in excitement at the promise of a walk.

She skidded to a halt, breath hitching, a stitch in her side. No sound of voices, nothing other than her ragged breath, the doors firmly closed and the yards empty. "Aunt Olivia?" Her call bounced back at her, echoing against the walls. "Aunt Olivia?" She rounded the corner of the building. "Nathaniel!"

What did sorting a shipment of horses entail? She imagined paperwork, the sort Pater littered across his desktop. Perhaps not. Maybe preparing horses to travel to Sydney, saddles and bridles and other paraphernalia. Lifting her skirt she raced around the back of the stables to the empty paddocks.

Nothing.

Two heartbeats later she stood staring down the drive at Nathaniel's retreating back, her vision blurred by the cloud of dust whipped up by the horses' hooves. "*Cooee*, Nathaniel!" Her cry echoed, but Nathaniel gave no indication that he'd heard.

When he reached the road he turned and lifted his hat in salute. And despite the distance their eyes met and a lopsided grin flickered across his face, making her heart skip a beat before he disappeared in a cloud of dust.

Dragging in great gulps of air, Lettie slumped against the fence, a confusion of emotions swirling in her stomach. In the smoky air last night she'd imagined the first tangible wisps of friendship warming her skin, yet he hadn't even taken the time to bid her farewell.

A waft of breeze snagged the loose tendrils of her hair and above her Yellow Rock loomed, the light and shadows dancing across its knowing eye, and overhead the wedge-tailed eagles kept watch.

Fragments of her dream slipped before her eyes, the wind whipping her skirt, blowing her hair, and then Nathaniel's face in the light of the fire as he'd swirled her around and around to the frantic music of the fiddle. He'd been the last person she'd expected to see with the drovers, but his company, his stories, and his quiet good humor had made her realize how isolated she'd become since Thorne died.

Unlike the first time she arrived at the main house, now the big double doors stood open and a shaft of sunlight welcomed her. Oxley flopped down across the doorway with a vexed sigh, following some unwritten rule, and she stepped over him to the wide cedar staircase curving upward.

The scent of beeswax and lavender filled the air. The house might be unlived in, but it was lovingly tended. She trailed her fingers across the timber-paneled walls, her gaze drawn to a set of exquisitely painted birds framed in matching gold leaf, worthy of a place in any Sydney gallery. She lifted her hand to the glass, almost expecting to feel the smooth green feathers of the King-Parrot, then turned to the next, the palest gray and pink. *Major Mitchell*, the title informed her. "Magnificent." Far better than any of her efforts.

A door upstairs banged. "Aunt Olivia?" she called as she took the stairs. Beneath her palm the banister slid, smooth as silk, worn by generations. Wavering patterns danced against the pale green walls. "Aunt Olivia?"

The staircase creaked and she spun around. "Hello?" Her voice quavered, overwrought and embarrassed by the possibility of being caught uninvited. She peered over the banister. The silence returned and, unable to resist, she moved on.

The first door stood ajar and she peeped inside. Two matching windows overlooking the garden. Two silver-backed brushes side by side on a small dressing table beneath an oval mirror, a pair of black satin ribbons coiled and ready for use. Not a crease marred the neatly folded quilt or the white lace pillowcases. A bunch of wildflowers much like those that grew in front of the house sat on the bedside table in a glass vase. A pair of buttoned boots were tucked under a small chair where a white cotton dress, identical to the one she wore, lay draped as though waiting for the owner to slip it over her head.

Lettie tiptoed across the room, convinced she'd stepped back into the past. There was no doubt in her mind this was Evie's room. A battered rag doll sat propped on the shelf, a lamp with a fluted glass shade, a leather-bound journal on the bedside table. She reached for it, the cover soft and worn beneath her fingertips. *William Ludgrove—Early Travels with Ludwig Leichhardt 1842.*

A rush of guilt heated her skin. Grandfather's journal. Ludwig Leichhardt? The name plucked some distant memory, of schoolrooms and dusty textbooks . . . What had Olivia said? She'd asked if Miriam had told her of William's interest in exploration. Closing the book, she placed it carefully back on the bedside table. There was so much she didn't know, so much she didn't understand.

The faintest scent, peppery like boronia flowers overlaid with a hint of citrus, wafted in the air, and she knew she wasn't alone. At any moment Evie would step through the door, fresh from the bathroom, slip the dress over her head, button her boots, and head downstairs, which was where Lettie ought to have stayed until Olivia had come for her but for her insatiable curiosity.

A dainty desk stood beneath one of the windows. Lettie perched on the edge of the matching chair, her hands framing the sketch Olivia had shown her yesterday, the picture of Evie sitting in a field of wildflowers, her heart-shaped face turned to the rock.

A step behind her made her leap to her feet, and the chair toppled as she turned. Olivia stood there, framed in the doorway.

The woman of yesterday, down at the drovers' camp, with her

pink cheeks, hitched skirt, and rollicking humor, had vanished. Today Olivia would have put Miriam to shame. Her somewhat dated pale lilac dress, almost severe save for a single strand of pearls, accentuated her austere presence. The expression on her face, a mixture of pleasure and something close to agony, made Lettie's cheeks flush.

She tried to speak but her voice lay lost in the past. She recognized the look in Olivia's eyes, the torment. Grief. More than loneliness; a deep, abiding hollow that could never be filled. Lettie saw it every time she looked in the mirror. Ever since Thorne had gone.

Olivia righted the chair, then lifted the dress and draped it reverently on the end of the bed.

Lettie dropped her head. "I'm sorry." She swallowed, her voice high-pitched and unnatural. "You made me jump. I"—she cleared her throat—"came upstairs looking for you. Peg said—"

"I would meet you here." Olivia came and stood beside her. "Don't be embarrassed. A normal curiosity. I had planned to explain things differently. I didn't want you jumping to conclusions." She took her arm and led her to the bed, sat down, then patted the spot beside her. "It's a lovely room, isn't it? One of the nicest in the house. Shall I show you the others?"

Tell me about Evie! The words screamed inside Lettie's head. Every tantalizing morsel Olivia dropped had her craving more.

"Seeing you here, dressed like that . . ."

Lettie looked down at the white dress she'd found beside her bed. "I thought I'd be cooler. It was on the chair in my room when I awoke."

"It fits perfectly. Evie was a little younger than you. How old are you, my dear?"

Lettie licked her lips, her throat dry. Yesterday Olivia had seemed rational and sensible, and Miriam's version of the truth appeared so illogical; now she wasn't sure. "Much older, I suspect. I'm twenty-five."

"And your brother?"

"He was twenty-nine when he died. Six months ago." Lettie dropped to her knees, took Olivia's gnarled, work-worn hand in hers. "What happened to Evie?"

Olivia lifted her shoulders, then exhaled. "I don't know. I just don't know." Her soft, weary voice wavered. "If you'd like to come into Evie's bedroom again, you don't have to ask. I sometimes sit in here. I find it peaceful. Closer to Evie, as if she's still with me, just outside somewhere with her sketchbook and will be back for afternoon tea in the orchard. That was another one of her favorite places, her outdoor dining room she called it, beneath the citrus trees. The perfume of their blossoms reminds me of her; she's with me still. She knows you're here." Olivia walked to the doorway and waited, hand on the doorknob.

Goose bumps stippled Lettie's skin and she stumbled from the room without a backward glance.

Olivia closed the door gently behind her and led the way down the hallway, opening door after door, just long enough for Lettie to glimpse the neatly made beds and drawn curtains in a series of bedrooms. "I moved out of the main house after Evie left. Peg sees to it now. Keeps the rooms clean." She threw open the final door, releasing a waft of lily of the valley and revealing a large four-poster bed framed by gauzy white curtains. "Alice's room." She snapped the door shut. "We'll go downstairs now."

Despite her bravado, Olivia paused for a moment before grasping the banister, taking each step one at a time. The front door still stood open, Oxley providing a shaggy doormat, and as they descended into the pool of morning sunshine, Lettie's sense of trespass lifted.

"Are these Evie's paintings?" She gestured to the gold-framed pictures of the birds.

Olivia nodded. "She loved her paints and pencils."

"They're exquisite."

"William pandered to her. She never went without."

Nothing made sense. These weren't a child's paintings; they were perfectly executed, better than anything she could manage, better than the sketches for which *The Bulletin* handsomely paid Raw Edge. Not the drawings of someone who'd died in childhood. "Are you going to tell me more?"

"I am. I wanted to do it here, where she belonged, where she was happiest. The story begins here." She swung open the door to her left and a cloud of stagnant air wafted out.

14

YELLOW ROCK, 1881

Evie threw herself into the task of planning her trip. The more she thought about it, the more convinced she became Andrew Hume had spent those two missing days with his parents and had left the canister of papers in their safekeeping.

She had to speak with Andrew's father, and she had little time to waste if she was going to catch up with Bailey in Maitland. She could hardly approach Mr. Hume unintroduced and ask for information about his dead son.

Bailey had said he'd be there for a couple of days. She would have to leave first thing in the morning, no later or she'd miss him. She'd tell Olivia she was going out for a day's sketching and would call in to Glendon and spend a night, maybe two there. She knew the track to Maitland well, had visited several of the people who lived along the way with Pa. A good ride, but nothing she and Elsey couldn't manage. Although she knew she'd be welcome at any of the properties, she didn't dare ask for hospitality.

She neatly tore the reward notice from *The Bulletin* and inserted it into her notebook. If her theory proved correct and Hume had left the papers with his parents, she would telegraph *The Bulletin* and claim the reward from Maitland.

She pulled down Pa's surveyor's box. She couldn't take it with her even though he'd left it in her care—she'd need a packhorse like the one Andrew Hume had in the photograph. While she could manage perfectly well without the chain and the sextant, it seemed sensible to take the compass. She lifted it from the box and wrapped it in her painting cloth and tucked it into her saddlebag, then replaced the box on the bookshelves.

Among the leaves of Pa's first journal she'd found a list Leichhardt had sent him detailing the equipment to take on their travels. She ran her finger down the words: *a woolen blanket*—an excellent idea, as she'd be away overnight—but *four shirts, four pairs of socks, and a hunting coat* were totally unnecessary. *A pair of strong boots* she had, but *trousers* she didn't.

She stopped and stared at the shadows playing on Yellow Rock. Wearing trousers, a thick shirt, and her hat pulled low, there would be little chance of anyone thinking her other than a boy out delivering a message. She cast a quick look over the rest of the list: *a tin pot to make tea in, and a smaller one to drink from, some tea and sugar.* Not necessary. She wasn't going into the wilderness. There were inns along the way. *A rope to tether my horse*: most definitely. She'd get one from the stables; she didn't want Elsey wandering off during the night. *A botanizing tin*: she picked up the green vasculum Pa had given her for her sixteenth birthday and hung it on her shoulder. Would it be useful? Probably not. She dropped it onto the desk and returned to Leichhardt's list. *Some paper or a journal*: thanks to Pa she had that in her saddlebag. She must record everything just as Pa and Leichhardt had done.

Shuffling the papers on the desk, she collected every article she'd read about Hume, except for the report from the Geographical Society of Hume's demise. Surely Mr. Hume would appreciate knowing as much as possible about his son's final days. She slipped it into her bag. What to do with the others? If she left them lying on the desk, there was a chance Olivia might come across them and her secret would be out, and that would place the reward in jeopardy.

Rolling the papers into a tight cylindrical shape, she fastened them with the piece of leather Pa had used to wrap her saddlebag. As much as she hated the thought of lying to Olivia, she couldn't divulge her plans. Apart from the fact Olivia would insist on accompanying her—or worse still, refuse to let her go—the canister of papers had to be kept secret until she telegraphed *The Bulletin*.

Almost as an afterthought she slipped the articles about Hume into her vasculum and jammed it onto the bookshelf between two piles of books, then she locked the glass door.

And her map, what should she do with her map? She couldn't take it with her and risk it getting damaged. Dropping onto her hands and knees, she crawled under the desk.

As a child she'd often sat with Oxley while Pa told her stories, and she'd discovered a central cavity, a hidden drawer, with no handle or lock, which released if hit with a quick, sharp push. She placed her map inside and inserted an old paintbrush into the runner, effectively jamming it shut, safe from prying eyes.

With one last glance around the room she threw her saddlebag over her shoulder. She simply hadn't time to waste. She had to be ready to leave at dawn. Only a pair of trousers had to be found. Pa's would surely drown her and she didn't own any.

Evie eventually remedied the situation by taking a walk down to the farmhouse. She had to wait until Joe left for his daily trip to Broke before she could approach his wife.

"Nell?"

Joe's wife lifted her head from the pile of mending on her lap. "What can I do for you, lovey?"

Evie batted down the flush creeping up her neck. Lying never came easy. Miriam said it was because she had no sensibilities for others' feelings and sometimes an untruth was kinder. She disagreed. She'd rather know the truth from the outset. "I've been helping Olivia out in the paddocks and these dresses"—she held out the skirt of her white muslin dress—"get spoilt traipsing around. Pa's given me a mapping task and I'm going to be out riding. I wondered if you had an old pair of Dicken's trousers I could have."

"I'm not sure you'd want to be seen in any of Dicken's cast-offs." Nell dangled a perfect pair of neatly patched moleskins in front of her. "He's grown out of these. I was going to give them to my sister-in-law for her boys. Seven kids is more than anyone could feed, never mind clothe."

She couldn't take the clothes from the children's backs. She had a cupboard full of dresses she'd outgrown; perhaps she could arrange a barter. "There are two girls, aren't there?"

"Yes, that's right. But it's easier to patch a dress or cut one to size."

"I've got a pile of these white muslin dresses in my cupboard that are too small for me. Do you think we could do a swap?"

"I don't think your pa would be happy with that, those scruffy urchins getting around in your fine dresses."

Well, Pa wasn't there to know, was he? And it didn't look as though he'd be back for quite a while. "No one needs to know where they came from, and I'm responsible for my own clothes now."

Nell shot her a sideways glance. "Not up to anything I don't want to know about, are you?"

Evie swallowed and forced a laugh. "No, nothing but mapping."

"The twins' birthdays are coming up and they'd love a pretty dress. Tell you what. You go and fetch me a couple of your old dresses, and I'll see what I can sort out for you."

Before Nell had time to change her mind, Evie fled. Olivia was busy in the paddocks, and from the smell wafting out of the kitchen, Peg was making the most of the huge crop of plums the orchard had provided. She slipped in through the front door, raced upstairs, and was back at the farmhouse with a delighted Oxley bounding alongside in a matter of minutes, two white muslin dresses wrapped in a pillowslip.

Nell was nowhere to be seen. Evie dumped the dresses on the table and waited, watching Olivia putting one of the mares earmarked for sale through her paces. Unless she could claim this reward, there'd soon be no horses left. The colt skittered behind the mare, all legs and big eyes. He'd be weaned before long and sold too.

A wave of guilt washed over her and she sank down in the chair. Once again Mama had fled from her thoughts. When she returned from Maitland she'd make amends, restore Mama's garden, and tend the roses.

"You didn't take long." Nell interrupted her musings, dumping two pairs of trousers and two faded blue shirts down on the table, then shaking them out. "Reckon these'll fit right; you're just a slip of a girl. And there's a belt and a pair of socks. You won't be wanting to wear those black stockings under the trousers, mark my words. Got good strong boots, have you?"

"Yes, I have, thank you." She unwrapped the pillowslip and held up the dresses. "Do you think these will suit?"

Nell ran her hand over the soft material and let out a sigh. "They'll do a treat. I've got some ribbons for their hair. They'll be the bonniest girls in Broke."

"Thank you, Nell. I really appreciate this." She hugged the clothing to her chest, itching to get back to the house.

"Off you go, then. And if I were you I'd wear the trousers under a skirt, then you won't cause too much of a fuss if you're seen out and about. Mind you, you're the only person I know who goes up that big rock." She gave a shudder. "Doesn't it give you the collywobbles, knowing all those stories?"

"Just stories, Nell. Just stories. I'd never come to any harm up there, and the view is worth the climb. It's not only mapping; I'm going to paint Pa a picture of the eagles. There's a pair. I think their aerie is up there." She would one day, she would. She had to make recompense; she'd told enough lies to last a lifetime.

"You be careful, mind. And I'll make sure the twins say thank you."

"Oh, Nell, I'd rather you didn't tell them where the dresses came from. Make them a present from you." The last thing she wanted was Olivia to know that she'd planned all of this in advance. "That way I won't need to admit to wearing trousers—under my skirt," she added, fingers crossed behind her back.

By the time Olivia came in from the paddocks, Evie had stashed her packed saddlebag in the stable. Unfortunately, Oxley insisted on standing guard as though his life depended on it.

If she left at first light, took a break by the river to allow Elsey a rest and a drink, she would be in Maitland before dusk. Bailey wouldn't be too difficult to find; everyone in the district knew him, and if Mr. Hume owned a shop, then he'd be well known. She only needed a moment of Bailey's time and an introduction to

Mr. Hume. Surely he'd remember when his son last visited and if he'd left anything in his safekeeping. She'd be home the following afternoon.

The only problem was Olivia and her insistence that she should always be accompanied. Taking a fortifying breath, she headed for the training paddock. "Can you manage without me for a day or so?"

Olivia's head came up with a snap, her eyebrows forming a deep vee.

"Pa asked me if I could complete Leichhardt's map of Glendon. I thought I'd go up to Yellow Rock to get a bird's-eye view and then make my way to Glendon and spend a day or two there. The new owners offered their hospitality, and I also want to ask if the Scotts left any papers about Leichhardt. They've always said we are welcome, but we've never visited. We shouldn't neglect our neighbors, and they were very kind after Mama and Joshua . . ." Her voice petered out. She was such an awful liar. She hated it, and even with the fingers on both hands crossed behind her back, the sheen of disgrace dampened her palms.

"Give it a few days and I'll come with you. I can't go with Joe and Bailey away."

"I need to go tomorrow. There's absolutely nothing more I can do for Pa until I sort this out. I promised . . ." That childish whine slipped back into her voice. "Please . . . I know the road like the back of my hand. I'll take Oxley. He won't let anything happen to me."

"We'll see. Let me sleep on it. I'm going to take a bath, get an early night. I've been out in the sun all day."

Evie tossed and turned all night, and when the first streaks of light broke the darkness, she shot out of bed and slipped on her usual dress. If she went partway up Yellow Rock, changed her clothes at the cave, and tucked her dress behind the rock ferns, on her return she'd swap back into her dress and no one would be any the wiser. She couldn't wait for Olivia to give her approval. She had to leave, otherwise she might miss Bailey, and without him she'd have no way of getting an introduction to Mr. Hume.

She slipped through the rising mist to the stables, Oxley at her heels, and saddled Elsey, secured her saddlebag, and with barely a backward glance took the path to Yellow Rock.

15

The moment Olivia swung open the study door, Oxley shot to his feet. "You wait in the hall, you mutt. You know very well you're not allowed inside."

A pang of sympathy streaked through Lettie as the dog hung his head and sloped back to the spot by the front door. "It's such a shame . . ."

"He knows his place, same as all his forefathers. William's father brought the first here. Kept him company while he healed."

She had no memory of William having a dog. Surely she would remember. "Grandfather?"

"This is William's study." The silk of Olivia's sleeve rustled as she extended her arm, inviting her into the darkened room.

Lettie first sensed an overwhelming dusty smell, then the rich scent of leather and a base note of sandalwood and ink. Unlike the rest of the house, a thick layer of the past blanketed the entire room, not just the grime but the very atmosphere, and both seemed to take their toll on Olivia. She sank into a chair, frail and broken as a bird, a lace handkerchief held to her nose as she smothered a sneeze. Decades must have passed since the room had been disturbed.

Heavy floor-length curtains cast a sepia tinge, making everything appear faded and indistinct. A man's study, not a place a young woman would spend her time. How could Evie's story lie here?

Lettie drew back one of the heavy curtains. Motes danced in the air, drifting lazily in the broad strips of dazzling sunlight she'd invited into the room.

Framed pictures crammed the walls, grimy and indistinct under their thick layer of dust. Antiquarian maps dating back centuries, fanciful beasts and monsters, dragons lurking in the unknown waters below the equator, minute illustrations peppering the borders.

The Eastern Portion of Australia, dated 1844, divided into numbered counties all outlined in color, the border illustrated with emus, kangaroos, and men with canoes and spears. Another showed the head and shoulders of a bearded man, the title: *An Overland Expedition to Port Essington*.

"Did these all belong to Grandfather?"

"It was his passion, and his father's. John Ludgrove fancied himself a collector of maps, spent a fortune tracking down anything to do with the early days, and William was set to follow in his footsteps until he became obsessed with Leichhardt. I want you to have a better understanding of Evie, and this is the place to start. William taught Evie all he knew about maps."

A strange occupation for a young girl, even one as talented as Evie. "How old was she when she died?"

"I don't know."

Lettie's knees folded and she dropped down beside Olivia. She racked her brain trying to remember something, anything Miriam might have said. Nothing. Nothing but Miriam's stock phrase: *"She died of a childhood ailment." Childhood* implied a very young girl, but this room, the sketchbook, the paintings in the hallway belied Miriam's terse description of her sister's passing.

"She loved to draw and paint." The wistful tone in Olivia's voice hovered in the scented air and her face paled to a chalky white. "She left early one day, said she was going to Yellow Rock to paint, then on to Glendon. She never returned."

Lettie's skin tightened as she remembered Nathaniel's story. She shook the sensation away. "She had an accident?"

"We found her frock stuffed behind a rock. Up there." Olivia gestured to the rock. "She vanished, taken by the rock."

Ridiculous hocus-pocus. People didn't just vanish. "Mother said—"

"Miriam says a lot of things." Olivia tucked her handkerchief into her sleeve and sat up a little straighter. "Few of them bear much resemblance to the truth. She has her own way of viewing the world, her own perceptions."

The asperity of Olivia's remark struck a chord . . . Miriam's version of the truth was always slanted to put herself in the best light, either the victim or the victor, never taking responsibility for any misadventure. Lettie shook her head. She had no idea whose version to believe.

"I blame myself. If I hadn't waited those three days, if she hadn't gone alone . . ."

"How old was Evie when she left?" Lettie rephrased her question, searching for clarity.

"Just shy of her eighteenth birthday. She'd said she'd wait to celebrate until William came home. By the time he did, she'd been gone for two weeks." Olivia fumbled for her handkerchief, her eyes full of tears.

Decades must have passed since then; surely someone had found out what happened to her. She reached for Olivia's hand, had her own brushed away.

While Lettie waited for Olivia to regain her composure, her eyes roamed over the rest of the room. Tall glass-fronted bookcases, their rich cedar, unlike the rest of the house, dulled beneath the grime, lined the walls. Two globes hung crooked on tarnished bronze axes behind the door. In front of one set of french doors sat a massive cedar desk, spanning at least six feet, piled high with yellowing papers, old newsprint, pamphlets, and smaller leather-bound notebooks. A treasure trove of someone's passion. Grandfather's, and from what Olivia implied, Evie's too.

Lettie moved to pull the curtains farther back, then thought better of it. The light might lift the atmosphere of dereliction and desertion, but it would release another cloud of dust, which would do Olivia no good. "How are you feeling?" Lettie asked. "If this is too much we can talk elsewhere."

Olivia let out a series of explosive sneezes in quick succession. "I haven't been in here for a long time and it has brought back a rush of memories I thought I'd buried, demons I'd kept incarcerated."

"Shall we go back to the farmhouse?" She chafed Olivia's cold hand.

"No, I'd like to stay here. I never thought to come into this room again. Draw back the curtains. Let the light in. It'll chase away my demons."

Lettie hooked back the heavy drapes, slid the bolts on the glass-paneled doors, and flung them open, letting the warm air billow through the room, and then sat in the desk chair.

"When you first arrived, I thought for a fleeting moment Evie had come back to me." Olivia's voice wavered, then steadied. "You look very like her, but then you drew near and spoke and I realized my mistake. Your eyes—Evie's were dark, yours are such a soft golden-green. I shouldn't have pretended to be Peg. I simply couldn't face the questions you might have for me."

It was almost as though Olivia carried some burden of guilt. Had she said or done something that had sent Evie away? Was that what Miriam had referred to? Was that why she had eschewed all communication? What did it matter who she'd pretended to be? She was Great-Aunt Olivia now. "We've moved past that, haven't we?" Lettie offered a gentle smile. "Would it be prying if I asked why you and Miriam don't speak?"

"I've given it a lot of thought over the years." Olivia was silent for a moment. "Mostly a long-forgotten rivalry. It's sad, very sad. But too late to do anything about it now. I prefer to keep my distance. I'm too old to cope with more rejection."

Embarrassed by the sudden insight into this very private woman, Lettie sought to change the subject. "But it was a happy household?"

"In many ways William lived only for the time he would be at Yellow Rock, with Evie. She was much the same. She worshipped him." Olivia seemed smaller today, much older, folded into the vast armchair.

"You said Evie left for a day's painting . . ."

"Not painting. She wanted to complete a map, for William. He'd left to take Miriam to Sydney; she was to be married. Evie was out of sorts. She'd been told to stay here with me. William worried about her. She'd had such a difficult childhood, lost moments, but they'd passed as she'd grown older."

"Lost moments? What do you mean?"

145

"Some called it the sleeping sickness, but it wasn't that. She never had a fit, lost control. One moment she'd be in the present and then her eyes would glaze over and she'd be somewhere else. She'd lose a minute or two and come back to us as though no time had passed. Doctor Glennie said he thought it would fade as she grew, and it did."

Something in Olivia's description triggered a memory for Lettie. A girl at school, lying on the floor. She'd thought her dead, but by the time the doctor arrived she was awake, groggy but awake. The doctor had diagnosed epilepsy. Yes, that was it. "Evie suffered from epilepsy?"

"That's not a word I know. The episodes were very brief: she'd suddenly stop what she was doing and stare blankly, as though she were daydreaming. Just as suddenly she would continue with whatever she'd been doing. When she was very young it happened numerous times a day. Miriam always maintained it was a means to curry attention. She had little time for her younger sister, saw her as a hindrance, whereas for me she was the child I would never bear.

"The episodes stopped as Evie grew; when Miriam went to Sydney to marry, she hadn't suffered for several years, although in the last few days before Evie left I wondered . . . consumed as she was by William's plans. She adored her father. He saw to her education, encouraged her with her painting, taught her about mapping and surveying, astronomy and literature. Her mother, Alice, was constantly unwell, her never-ending quest to provide William with the heir he so desired. She had little time to spare for Evie.

"When William left he asked Evie to collate his notes and journals and draw the maps." She waved her hand at the staggering piles of paperwork on the desk. "Told her he'd be back and together they'd produce Leichhardt's story. Three volumes. The final tribute to his vanquished hero."

"Leichhardt." One of the maps on the wall. The expedition to Port Essington. She crossed to the wall, a memory of the classroom surfacing. "Ludwig Leichhardt, the German explorer? The one who vanished in the interior?"

"Wretched man. But for William's obsession none of this would have happened. He lost more than his leg to the man; he lost his daughter as well."

Lettie bit her lip, trying to control her impatience. If only Olivia would start at the beginning, not throw in these random tidbits of information. They cluttered her mind and she couldn't think straight. "Evie left for a day's painting, mapmaking . . . ," she prompted.

"Same as she'd done before. I was busy with the horses. Money was tight. I'd had to let Mrs. Hewitt, the housekeeper, go. We were selling some mares and I had no one except Joe to help with the horses and Peg in the kitchen. The boys were off on the stock route. Evie said she'd go up to Yellow Rock, then on to Glendon and spend a day or two there. She wanted to ask the new owners if the Scotts had left any papers about Leichhardt. She'd taken Oxley. I didn't start to worry until the third day."

Lettie threw a glance over her shoulder. Oxley had sneaked into the room and now lay underneath the desk. "When was this?"

"January 1881."

"The year Thorne was born." Did that have anything to do with Thorne's determination to come to Yellow Rock?

Olivia lifted her head and brushed away a tear trickling down her weathered cheek. "The days merged into a horrible blur. We combed Yellow Rock, called in the Wollombi constabulary. They searched the house, the grounds, even in here. When the drovers returned they covered every inch of the property and all the tracks to Glendon. All they found was her dress tucked up on the rock in one of the caves. Then Nell admitted to giving Evie a pair of Dicken's moleskins."

"Nothing else?"

"No other sign. And no sign of Oxley. That's when I feared the worst."

Hearing his name, Oxley unraveled himself and came to rest his head on Olivia's lap. She ran her fingers through his moth-eaten ears. "He wouldn't have left her, would he, boy? Peg brought Oxley's brother up here to keep me company. And since then we've always had an Oxley."

"Was there nothing else? What about her horse? Did she have an accident?"

"We never found her horse." Olivia dropped her head into her hands, muffling her voice. "William came back, and as the weeks turned to months, his dismay turned him into a bitter and twisted caricature of the man we all loved. Not only had he lost his mentor and hero, but his favorite daughter had been taken too. He was heartbroken. Ran himself ragged searching. They found nothing."

Lettie flopped down on the floor next to Oxley. "Mother never told me. Why?"

"To be honest, I don't think she cared. She and Evie weren't close, too many years and dead brothers between them. She had what she wanted. Her home in Sydney, marriage. She'd produced the son and heir, done what no one else had managed to do since William's birth."

Thorne, the son and heir. The very first part of Olivia's strange tale rang true. She couldn't imagine Miriam at Yellow Rock. She thrived on the hustle and bustle of Sydney, her friends and luncheon parties, her place in society, as she continually reminded anyone who'd listen.

"That's when your grandmother Charlotte stepped in, insisted William return to Sydney. Six months later they were married. The next time I saw him he was in his coffin. We had a hell of a time getting Charlotte and Miriam to release his body, but he'd had it there in black and white in his will. He wanted to be buried with Alice and their boys."

"Evie couldn't have just vanished. Did she have friends, did she visit someone, what were her plans . . ." Lettie's voice trailed off as Olivia's head moved slowly from side to side.

"I never gave up hope, expected one day to find her standing in front of me. After Evie left I moved into the farmhouse. I couldn't bear to live here alone. My parents, William, his parents, my sister, Alice, and then Evie . . . everyone gone. I couldn't manage on my own. At first I tried to carry on, and then as it became more difficult I sold the cattle and all but the best breeding stock. I'd lost heart, as much as William had, but someone had to be here when Evie came home. When I saw you standing on the doorstep, I thought . . ."

Lettie's heart stuttered and she reached for Olivia's hand and squeezed it. "I'm so sorry, so very, very sorry. I should have told you I was coming."

"You had no idea. And besides, it's simply an old woman's fantasy. Time doesn't stand still, no matter how much we might wish it. Evie would be a grown woman now, not a girl like you."

Lettie suddenly felt every one of her twenty-five years, thoroughly ashamed that she'd put this lovely old woman through hell. "Is there anything I can do?"

Olivia's bone-white face ravaged by her tale stared down at her. "Perhaps there's something someone missed. I always thought one day I'd come in here and find a piece of paper or a letter explaining why Evie left . . ." Olivia gestured to the toppling piles on the desk. "I've never been able to face it. I haven't been in here since the day she vanished. Peg said she'd look but it didn't seem right, seemed like prying. It's a family mystery, not one that should involve others."

"I'm family."

"Yes, you are, my dear, and I bless the day Miriam sent you."

It was on the tip of Lettie's tongue to correct Olivia and tell her that Miriam had threatened to come herself and it was only her own belligerence that had brought her to Yellow Rock.

"When I received Thorne's letter I thought perhaps he was the man for the job." Sorrow dropped Olivia's voice to a whisper.

Had he known about Evie? She couldn't believe that, couldn't believe he wouldn't have told her, but he hadn't said he'd written Olivia. What else had he kept to himself?

"When you go home I want you to ask Miriam, talk to her, see if there's anything she knows that she hasn't mentioned. I can't do it. We haven't spoken since the day she left to be married."

Nothing made any sense. "Why? I don't understand."

Olivia let out a heartfelt sigh. "We were never close. Miriam's made the best of her life, done what she set out to do." Two bright spots of color stained Olivia's cheeks, and her eyes drifted to the door, as though she wanted to say more. After a moment, she returned her gaze to Lettie's face and lifted her shoulders. "Who am I to rake up the past? Perhaps she holds herself responsible."

Highly unlikely Miriam would accept responsibility for anything unless it reflected well on her. "What would you have asked

Thorne to do when he arrived?" Lettie didn't add that she'd more than likely have accompanied him.

"I was going to ask him to go through William's papers. Through the study." She screwed up her face and gestured around the room. "It's a man's room. Maybe there's something a woman might miss."

"Oh, tosh and nonsense."

"There may be something. Something that sent Evie away."

Lettie leaped to her feet. "I suspect a woman might do a more thorough job. I'll do it." The words poured out. "Let me go through all of this. Let me see what I can find. Let me help."

And for the first time since Thorne's body had flown through the billowing clouds, Lettie's blood surged and her sense of purpose returned.

16

Faced with the enormity of her task, Lettie hovered in the study doorway. How she wished Evie were here. She could picture every detail of the drawing Olivia had shown her: every freckle, every corkscrew spring of curly hair, the amused quirk of her mouth. If only she could talk to her. Was there something in William's study that had made Evie leave her home and everyone she loved? There had to be an answer.

The cedar desk dominated the large formal room, and six glass-paneled doors with bookcases between lined the external walls. The framed maps covered every other inch of wall space. Towering piles of paper and notebooks obscured the surface of the desk, some neatly bound by lengths of twine, others haphazardly stacked as though someone had rifled through them. And covering it all a thick pillow of undisturbed dust. Even with the curtains drawn and the doors open to the outside, an air of mystery hung, daring her to disturb the past.

Oxley displayed no hesitation; he sidled past her and settled under the desk, his huge head resting on his paws, staring out through the doors to Yellow Rock.

"Is that where your forefathers sat, Oxley? You better not let Olivia catch you."

He lifted his head, offered a baleful stare, and then settled down again as though she had nothing new to contribute.

"I'm going to get to the bottom of this, no matter what you might think. But first I need to write to Miriam and let her know I'm staying." The last thing she wanted was for Miriam to send out a search party, or worse still, arrive herself and rake up long-held grievances.

A quick look at the desk didn't provide any writing implements, and neither did the drawers that flanked either side, but through the dusty glass of the bookcase doors she spotted a pile of cartridge paper balanced on a polished wooden box with brass corners. A portable writing box perhaps, rather like the one Miriam used when she spent a day in bed attending to her correspondence.

The unexpected weight of the box took her by surprise, and she settled it with care on the desk, then ran her fingers over the brass plaque, inscribed *William John Ludgrove 1840*.

The box contained three compartments lined with faded green velvet. One housed a series of linked chains that clanked and rattled as she lifted them, the other an instrument resembling a microscope with two mirrors and a movable arm not quite a semicircle, and numbers, degrees, engraved like a rule. She angled it toward Yellow Rock and the beam of light reflected through the mirror. The shadow fell against the ruled engravings.

Of course!

Some sort of equipment used for surveying, which meant that the linked chain probably was also a measuring device. She carefully laid the two back in the box and smoothed the empty compartment. A faint circular indentation registered beneath her fingertips.

But no pen or ink.

She had to let Miriam know what she planned before she became too absorbed. She turned back to the shelves. Rows and rows of haphazardly stacked leather-bound books filled the shelves along with corked glass vials full of seed specimens and metal boxes and canisters.

No writing paper, but the sheets of thick cartridge paper would be more than adequate for a note to Miriam. She pulled a sheet from the pile and resumed her search for a pen, a pencil even.

An assortment of rocks and specimens littered the mantelpiece; something that resembled a lump of coal, rocks of varying shapes, sizes, and colors, a series of fossils sitting in a pile of powdery dust, every one of them begging inspection, and finally behind them all she found a bottle of ink and a nib pen. Careful not to disturb the display, she carried the writing tools to the desk, pushed aside a pile of papers, and scrawled a note to Miriam, folded the heavy paper, and tucked it into her waistband.

A slow circuit of the room confirmed her observation from yesterday: maps, maps, and more maps. A double hemispherical map of the world showing Captain Cook's discoveries and ships' tracks during the voyage of the *Endeavour* and the *Resolution*. A chart bearing Flinders's name, another of his two circumnavigation voyages. New Holland, Terra Australis, and then Australia. Printed in London, Paris, Amsterdam. She could spend a lifetime studying them alone.

Resisting the temptation to investigate further, she sat down at the desk and pulled a pile of newspaper clippings, maps, pamphlets, and letters toward her. Before long she'd become immersed in the story of Leichhardt's Essington expedition.

Sometime later a knock on the door brought Oxley to his feet with a soft rumble. Lettie pushed back the chair and massaged her neck. "Come in."

Peg appeared, tray in hand. "It's a bit late but I thought you might like a spot of lunch. You've been here for hours."

A bottle of lemonade sat on the tray, beads of moisture peppering the outside. Lettie licked her parched lips. "That would be lovely." She lifted William's box from the desk and placed it carefully on the floor, making room for the tray, and only then noticed the long shadows cast across the garden. "What time is it?"

"Bit past three. It's more afternoon tea than lunch. There's sandwiches, egg and lettuce, and some fruitcake. I'll leave you to it. Olly says supper is at six thirty and not to be late. I'm on my way home to see the grandchildren."

"Thank you." She searched for a handkerchief to wipe her dusty hands, felt the paper tucked into her waistband crackle. "Peg, could you do me a favor?" She brought out the folded piece of paper. "Could you post this for me in Broke?" Unable to resist a smile at the thought of Miriam's reaction, she scrawled the address on the folded paper.

"You'll be staying then?" Peg asked.

"It's just telling Mother I'll be here a few more days."

Peg looked over her shoulder as though someone might be listening, then stepped closer. "Listen, Lettie. You mustn't get too caught up in Olly's grief. She's prone to periods of melancholia. It'll do her no good to bring it all back."

"I'd like to help, and I like being here." The truth of her words made her start. Evie's story had drawn her in, and Olivia had asked for her help.

"It'll be more than a few days, I'd guess." Peg gestured to the piles of newspapers on the floor and the teetering column of journals and other paraphernalia, then held out her hand. "I can post the letter for you, and tomorrow I'll lend you my feather duster. You can't work in this mess." She pocketed the note, ruffled Oxley's ears. "Watch out for the sandwiches—egg's his favorite. See you tomorrow."

The door closed quietly behind her and Lettie sank down into the chair, Oxley's plaintive eyes following her every move as she downed two glasses of lemonade and lifted the napkin covering a pile of sandwiches, crusts removed.

"Just one, and don't tell anyone."

Oxley took the sandwich from her fingers with a sigh of pleasure, swallowed it in one gulp, licked his slobbery lips, and sat fixated while she demolished the remainder.

By the time the shadow of Yellow Rock had lengthened, she'd created some sort of order and cleared enough space to work at the desk. Calling Oxley, she took the tray, shut the doors, and made her way through the orchard, reveling in the cool fresh air blowing the dust from her hair and the grit from her eyes.

Olivia sat waiting in the kitchen, the table laid. "I don't want to know anything. Not yet."

"I've nothing to tell you. I cleared the desk, made space to sort things out, read a little about Leichhardt's Essington expedition. May I ask a couple of questions?"

Folding her arms tight across her waist, Olivia lifted her head. "Depends."

156

"I'd like to know more about Grandfather. I found a box. Instruments of some sort."

With a nod Olivia sat down. "A cedar box with brass corners?"

Lettie nodded.

"His surveying equipment. Blaxland brothers gave it to him. He had no need of it in Sydney."

"Why did he become a surveyor?"

"Wash your hands and I'll dish up. Peg said you'd let your mother know you were staying."

A flush of heat stole across Lettie's cheeks as she concentrated on rinsing her hands. "I hope that's all right. I wrote to let Mother know. I didn't want her to worry, and asked Peg to post it."

"Quite right. We mustn't worry Miriam. She might think I've done away with you."

"I beg your pardon?"

"Take no notice. Old wounds."

"Why would Miriam—"

"Your grandfather grew up here. It was early days. He was the first child born, the hope for the future. The Ludgroves and the Maynards had a common dream when they secured the two adjacent land grants: to breed the finest horseflesh this country had ever seen." Olivia dolloped a large spoonful of rabbit stew onto her plate. "Until Herr Leichhardt himself arrived and William was smitten."

"Leichhardt was here?"

"Right here. Climbed that very rock." Olivia flicked her fork in the direction of Yellow Rock and a comfortable silence descended while they tucked in.

The rabbit stew was quite the most delicious Lettie had ever tasted. Following Olivia's lead, she wiped the crust of her bread around the plate. "Tell me more about William and Leichhardt. How did they meet?"

"It was coming up Christmas. William went to visit the neighbors, wish them the best of the season, deliver some gifts. He stumbled across this chap, up to his knees in the river. Thought he was in trouble. And William, being William, jumped in to help. Turned out Herr Leichhardt was on his way to Glendon."

"Glendon? Where Evie was going?"

"The very place. Other side of the river. The biggest property in the area in those days, belonged to the Scotts. They'd invited Leichhardt to stay, but somewhere along the line he got sidetracked and lost. William sorted him out, delivered him to Glendon. In a matter of hours Leichhardt weaved his magic and William's heart wasn't in horses anymore. He'd got bigger dreams. From that moment there was nothing for William but exploration. More rabbit?"

"No, thank you. It was delicious."

"All that summer he trailed around after Leichhardt, carrying his bags, helping him collect his samples and specimens, canisters, and collecting tins full of old rocks, lumps of clay, dried plants, and those imprint things."

The display on the mantelpiece, the fossils and samples. "And did Leichhardt find what he was looking for?"

"Not sure he knew what he was looking for. It all started with William's father. He put money into Leichhardt's first expedition along with other Hunter families keen to open up grazing lands and a route to the north. All would have been fine if it hadn't been for William's stubbornness. Seventeen he was, just seventeen, thought he was a man. Had some dream about taking off into the wilds with Leichhardt, and when he was invited along he couldn't leave fast enough. The Hunter was more rugged in those days. The grants took up all the good land along the river, but up in the hills it was still a wilderness. They trekked around for a few weeks, reached the top of Mount Royal, then Leichhardt's horse bolted. William settled Leichhardt in the shelter of an old tree and set off in search. That's when he had his accident."

"When he lost his leg?"

"One of those bloody awful summer storms. By the time he was found it was too late. Been lying in the dirt for days. I remember the night they brought him in. Face like a ghost, stinking to high heaven of blood and gore, and that was that."

"Leichhardt saved him?"

"No. He was tucked up in his camp up on the mountain, knew nothing of it. One of the timber cutters found William. His horse had stumbled in a hole, throwing him to the ground before rolling over him and pinning him down. He had to be ferried back on a flat wagon with no springs to cushion him. His leg seemed to be healing at first, but complications set in. Doctor Glennie had to take it or it would've taken him. He didn't only lose his leg; he lost his dreams. He wanted to go with Leichhardt, but a one-legged boy with a dream wasn't about to be invited on any overland expeditions. Young boy named John Murphy took his place. Poor William. It broke his heart. He never rode again, never mind exploring the interior. He did the best he could, helped raise money for Leichhardt's expeditions, hung on his every word when he finally made it back from Port Essington . . . Prince of Explorers . . ." Olivia let out a dismissive snort and cleared the plates.

"Was the Essington expedition the one Grandfather missed out on?"

"Yes. And just as well he did, more so the next expedition, because Leichhardt never came back. William reckoned if he'd been with them they wouldn't have lost their way. He was convinced he'd have saved the day. He spent all his time trawling through every piece of evidence he could find, every reported sighting, every blazed tree, every piece of gossip, but you'd know all that if you've been through the desk."

"I've really only sorted it into piles. I haven't read very much." She'd been too concerned with Leichhardt's story, not William's. "What does all this have to do with Evie?"

"And that's the rub, isn't it? William's obsession was like a family disease; he passed it on to Evie. From the moment she was old enough she'd sit at his feet and listen to his stories. Like tales of the heroes of old."

"Do you think she went looking for Leichhardt?"

"He was long gone, even William admitted that. Besides, she would have told me. Like I said before, she went to take some map Leichhardt had drawn to Glendon, just a few miles away, and do some mapping of her own. I gave her more freedom than she'd had before. She liked to go up to Yellow Rock, said she liked the view, thought she could see to the edge of the world—said it encompassed her world. She wouldn't have gone farther afield without telling me. We were close. I was like a mother to her."

And that was hardly any recommendation in Lettie's eyes. She couldn't imagine telling Miriam all her plans. Thorne certainly hadn't. "I'd like to go up to Yellow Rock."

"Not a good idea."

"Whyever not? Will you come with me?"

Olivia's face blanched. "No. Not up there. Not unless you can convince me it'll help find Evie."

In that case she'd have to find something to convince Olivia, or work her own way up there.

The days slipped by while Lettie wasn't looking and an easy pattern developed. Most mornings dawned with a rumpled eiderdown of mist wallowing in the valley until the weather warmed up and the afternoons held the heat. She'd breakfast with Peg and Olivia, then make her way to the main house, unlock the study, open the french doors to the veranda, and slip back into the past with no one but Oxley for company.

First she worked her way through the piles on the desk. Much to her surprise there was some sort of order, and many of the seemingly random pieces of paper referred to notes in William's journal. Notes written in block print, not the neat cursive she would have expected a girl to use. The looping handwriting, faded in places, and, most annoyingly, frequently written in pencil, belonged to William.

Olivia never set foot in the study but she would answer Lettie's questions over supper, and gradually a picture of Evie's life formed. It was Peg who'd slip in every lunchtime with a chunky sandwich, a piece of cake, and a bottle of lemonade, place them on the side table, and disappear before Lettie had time to acknowledge her presence.

Rumbling thunder and a heavy humidity forced Lettie from her bedroom early. The cloying heat made her skin damp and her head ache with a heavy lethargy. Peg had beaten her to the study. She'd left the french doors open to catch the slightest hint of a breeze and a bottle of lemonade in a bucket of water next to the desk. After pouring a glass, Lettie stood for a moment, taking in the room as a whole. She'd focused her attention on the desk, which was now in some sort of order, but had barely given the maps and the stacked bookshelves a second glance since that first day.

She made her way around the room studying the framed collection of maps hanging on the wall. Most of them bore the printer's name; none appeared to be by William's hand despite Olivia's assurances he was an excellent surveyor.

The pair of globes shone in a shaft of sunlight, and she shook out her handkerchief and polished the brass casing before spinning them slowly. Every available space between the bookshelves and on either side of the fireplace was stacked with boxes and tin canisters holding fossil samples and even occasionally the remains of some dried plant, but nothing that gave her one iota of information about Evie.

Above the golden rocky escarpment of Yellow Rock the perpetual pair of eagles soared. She eased past the desk, mesmerized by the dominating cliff face. Which path had Evie taken, and how far had she gone before she disappeared? Stepping back, resting on the front of the desk, legs stretched out, she tried to picture the young girl in the sketch taking a path to the top. Would she have ridden partway, walked, run even? "It's hopeless, just hopeless!"

Oxley's ears pricked and he opened one eye, but he'd become used to her incessant chatter. She'd learned a lot about Leichhardt and William's obsession with the man, a case of hero worship, but nothing, not one single thing, spoke of his daughter and her part in his passion.

Swallowing a muffled expletive, Lettie spun around and faced the room, her fingers gripping the underside of the desktop.

A soft and very mechanical *click* broke the silence.

Squatting down, she ran her hands along the underside of the desk. She'd spent hours sitting there but never once had she examined the front. She tugged at the base of the timber apron. It refused to budge.

No sign of a keyhole or a handle of any sort. Head down, on her hands and knees she crawled underneath. A drawer ran the width of the center of the desk, the runners melding into the legs, and there she found the culprit—a paintbrush!

With a grunt of satisfaction, she dislodged it from the runners, squirmed out from under the desk, and eased the apron open. The scent of must and ink rose, bringing with it a faint but tantalizing perfume of boronia and citrus.

A long, narrow piece of paper covered with minute illustrations filled the cavity. After removing the last remaining piles of papers from the desk, she eased it from the drawer, her breathing fast and her vision blurring.

A map. It had to be Evie's. She rubbed her hand across her eyes. There was no doubting the fine illustrations dotting the routes and rivers, nor the simple signature, *Evie Ludgrove*, in the bottom right-hand corner. She leaned forward and sniffed to confirm the distinctive scent impregnating the paper.

Was this what she'd unknowingly been searching for? Could it in some way explain Evie's disappearance? She spread the map out and anchored the corners. A decorative scrolled border marked with the longitude and latitude coordinates formed a frame, and in the bottom left-hand corner an intricate compass rose indicated the cardinal directions.

Roads wove from the coast inland; near the center of the map sat Yellow Rock and the house nestled among the plains sweeping down from the escarpment. To the south a range of mountains neatly labeled in Evie's distinctive block letters—the Watagans; to the northwest a town, roofs visible and a church spire—a town called

Singleton; to the north, another range of hills—the Barrington Tops; and nestled among them Mount Royal.

Tiny illustrations decorated the map: olive-green bush; ragged scribbly gums; small flowers; brown creeks and rough bush tracks; a profusion of birdlife, insects, and animals; tiny figures going about their daily lives; and vignettes of the anecdotes she'd read in William's journal. Leichhardt's escapade with the bull; two men, Leichhardt and William, no doubt, offering grass to a joey on the lower slopes of Yellow Rock; and tiny duckbills feeding on the banks of the creek.

Every image carried Evie's distinct style. Lettie could imagine the smile on Evie's face and hear the murmur of her voice as she admired the delicate drawings interspersed with the winding tracks and the sparkling Hunter River. She wanted nothing more than to immerse herself in the panorama before her. To the east the brilliant blue of the ocean sparkled, tiny ships under full sail and the warning *Here there be whales*.

Curbing a smile, Lettie returned to the image of the homestead, the stables and the farmhouse, the paddocks and the horses. And beyond the stables a scene she recognized—the drovers' camp, the fire clearly visible, people dancing, cattle, and horses and dogs.

From the property, a fine line ran to the north through Broke to Mount Royal, another track to Maitland, and the names of properties or the people who owned them. At the center of the map where the Hunter River wound its meandering course, in a horseshoe bend, she found two men on horseback, one wearing a long dusty coat, the other upright, hat at a jaunty angle, pointing to a property marked *Glendon*.

Seeing the map, running her fingers over the delicate images, sent a ripple of anticipation down her spine. An invisible thread connecting her to Evie. More than any inheritance, more than ties of blood. It had sat for decades waiting to be discovered.

The hairs on her arms prickled. She could hear the music of Evie's whispering voice, her words as clear as if she were standing beside her, and the dream she'd had melded into reality, the night she'd woken to find the white dress draped across the chair—Evie's dress.

Did Olivia know the map existed? The jammed drawer indicated it was something private, something Evie didn't want to share, or maybe something Olivia had locked away?

Lettie returned to the drawer, ran her fingers over the base, and sandwiched at the back was a coiled blue ribbon. She unraveled it and smoothed her fingers over the worn satin ribbon. Why had the map been locked away? Did it hold a secret Olivia or Evie didn't want to share? A surge of panic rose in her throat . . . What if Evie had died out there somewhere, wandering alone, lost in the vast country just as Leichhardt had been? Carefully rolling the map, she secured it with the ribbon and rushed off to find Olivia.

"Have you seen this before?" Lettie unrolled Evie's map and spread it out on the kitchen table.

Olivia smoothed the ribbon between her fingers. "This is Evie's. Her hair ribbon. I've never seen the map before, but I recognize the drawings." Tears glistened in her eyes. "Come with me."

She led Lettie past the room where she slept to the very end of the corridor and threw open the door to a small bedroom. Nothing like the room she'd imagine Olivia would inhabit. Spartan. An iron bedstead and a small bedside table. No wardrobe, no dressing table, just a bowl and pitcher and a row of pegs along the wall where an assortment of work clothes hung. No sign of the lilac satin dress she'd worn on the day she'd shown Lettie the study, and nothing that spoke of the modern woman in the navy skirt and pinstriped blouse.

Reaching into the drawer of the bedside table, Olivia brought out a series of drawings, miniatures. An exquisite watercolor of a grass tree, a tiny pool among the rocks where two red and green birds sat drinking . . . the same meticulous style as the illustrations on the map.

"King-Parrots. On the way up Yellow Rock." Olivia sniffed and handed her the next drawing.

Expecting more flora and fauna, Lettie started. The picture was carefully drawn, almost scientific in its accuracy: a telescope, a hunting watch, a quadrant, similar to the one in William's box, and a thermometer, all arranged as some sort of still life in the middle of a barren landscape, complete with an animal skull. "Are these Evie's drawings?"

"They're Evie's, all right. I sat with her while she drew them."

"Have you shown them to anyone? The sergeant, perhaps, when he searched the study? William?" Surely someone would have known what they meant.

Olivia hung her head, then shook it slowly. "No, I didn't."

"Whyever not?"

"Evie could be quite secretive about her drawings. I found these in her bedside drawer. I wasn't sure . . . I had nothing left of her. I thought the sergeant might take away my pictures." She gestured to the miniatures scattered across the quilt. "These weren't going to help find Evie."

But the map in the desk drawer might have. Surely William would know about a secret drawer in his own desk. "What about William? Did he show the sergeant Evie's map?"

Olivia's head came up with a snap. "Where did you find it?" The accusatory tone in Olivia's voice made Lettie's stomach churn. Had she come too close to the truth, found something Olivia hadn't expected her to?

"There's a hidden drawer in the center of the desk. I stumbled upon it by accident. It was jammed shut with an old paintbrush."

Olivia's brow wrinkled. "William couldn't find her map. Asked me time and time again if I'd seen it. He decided she'd taken it with her. We never spoke of it again. Gave up in the end. Same as he did with life. I think he blamed himself. Saw it as some sort of divine justice for leaving Evie here and going to Sydney. I told you. He died of a broken heart. His hero taken and his daughter."

"Poppycock!" Lettie clamped her hand over her mouth, horrified at her insensitivity. Poor Olivia's face was a mask of distress. "I'd like to go up to Yellow Rock. Will you come with me?"

Olivia's face paled, making Lettie regret her impatience. "I haven't been up there since the search parties."

"I'm sorry, I shouldn't have asked you again. I can go alone. I have a map." She threw a wry grin and immediately hated herself for it.

"And how do you intend to get there?"

"I'll walk," Lettie answered, silently questioning her sudden attack of bravado. Under the cloudy sky, the rock threw jagged shadows across the paddocks.

"Have you any idea how difficult the land is?"

"But there's a track, marked on Evie's map." She had to go up there. It was the starting point. The place where Evie's journey began.

"Yes, there was a track, but no one's used it for years. Then there's a climb. A difficult climb."

For goodness' sake, what had possessed her? In her enthusiasm she'd forgotten she was talking to a seventy-year-old woman. "I'm sorry. It hadn't occurred to me—"

She didn't have the opportunity to finish her sentence. Olivia's finger came up in front of her face. "It's not me I'm worried about. Nothing wrong with my stamina. It's you. Can you ride a horse, or is that something else, along with your manners, your mother forgot to teach you?"

A flush rose to Lettie's face. "I beg your pardon, Aunt Olivia. Yes, I can ride."

"And I don't mean around Centennial Park. I mean ride. Astride, not sidesaddle. This'll be no picnic."

"I believe I can manage."

"We'll see. We'll leave at six tomorrow morning." She cast a disparaging glance at Lettie's neat skirt and pin-tucked blouse. "I'll find you something suitable to wear. Go and get a decent night's sleep. You'll need it."

Olivia's sudden about-face and her determined tone made the hairs on Lettie's neck rise. Evie's story had lured her in. It held an inexplicable fascination crammed with frustrating discrepancies that even decades after her disappearance made the air hum.

17

The morning dawned clear and bright despite the storm overnight, and Lettie woke before the koels. She found Olivia in the
stables dressed very much as the drovers: a pair of moleskins held
up by worn leather braces over a pale pink shirt that might once
have been red and highly polished knee-length riding boots. Olivia
handed her a pair of patched moleskins and a shirt. "Put those on,
the horses are saddled," she barked.

The trousers fit perfectly. Lettie removed her skirt, tightened
the belt, and pulled the shirt over her head, ditching her blouse.

With a grunt of approval Olivia led the way outside and stood
with a bemused expression on her face until Lettie had managed to
hoist herself up onto the broad back of an old bay mare.

Thankfully the horses maintained a sedate walk, no doubt in
deference to her lack of ability. She had no intention of letting
Olivia know that she had described her riding ability with uncanny
accuracy—a gentle trot around Centennial Park, nothing more and
nothing she very much enjoyed. Once Thorne had returned from

Victoria with Lizzie, she'd eschewed the mandatory riding lessons and replaced them with driving lessons.

The path wound ever upward, the vertical face of the rock looming large and far more intimidating now she was closer. The play of the golden light and the inky shadows revealed slabs like giant tombstones, others grooved and fluted by thousands of years of fire, wind, and water.

Just as Lettie was getting used to the rolling gait of the old mare, Olivia dismounted. "We'll leave the horses here and go the rest of the way on foot."

Lettie slid down, rubbing her backside, while Olivia hobbled the horses and left them to graze in the shade of a pair of stunted trees.

They followed no track on this part of the rock, and if there'd ever been one it had long since vanished. Lettie's feet, however, chose a way of their own, weaving through the boulders as if she'd walked the path before.

Olivia reached the summit long before she did and stood shoulders square against the buffeting breeze, her stance belying her age. Lettie moved to her side in silence. The wind dropped and a cloud scudded across the sun. Suddenly it grew cold. Below them a deep vertical drop stretched into an exquisite patchwork tapestry.

As if magnified by a powerful telescope, the vast scene stood out with blinding clarity. The paddocks with the mares gently grazing, a gamboling foal, smoke idly curling up into the sky from the chimney of the farmhouse where Peg would no doubt be stirring her jam. Sam, the young stable boy, forking the hay, tiny figures coming and going along the tracks to Wollombi and Broke, and the wind moving the long grass like waves upon water.

Every detail clearly defined and separate. A vast panorama from the ocean to the farthest reaches beyond the Hunter River. A steep escarpment with a narrow rocky end scrambled down the overhang at the end of the spur.

"Even the lowest and most accessible levels of the rock are treacherous, especially for city girls." Olivia's voice quavered as though she'd woken from a dream, a sleepwalker finding herself in an unexpected place.

The ridge sliced its way across the landscape. Tall trees, deep valleys, rocky outcrops radiating across a wide plateau dissected by deep, steep-sided valleys. The thought that perhaps Olivia suffered from trances as Evie had drifted through Lettie's mind and she rested her hand on Olivia's arm and guided her away. "You're making me feel quite giddy, standing close to the edge."

"Close your eyes and listen . . . you'll hear her."

Lettie's heart beat fast against her ribcage, the hairs on her skin beginning to quiver. The realization spread icy and instant across her flesh. It was the same mood she'd felt floating in the dull hallways of the big house the first time she'd ventured up the stairs to Evie's bedroom.

With her head down and her hands rammed deep into her pockets, Olivia cleared her throat. Lettie craned close to catch her words . . . "They told me the whole affair would be cleared up within hours, that I had no idea how many people got lost if they stray a few yards off the beaten track. I knew well enough. Hadn't we all lived with William and his stories of Leichhardt?

"They brought in a tracker. What could he do that the drovers and their dogs hadn't already done? They knew the area as well as anyone, as well as I did. Then they brought in a bloodhound. He spent more time sniffing Oxley's tracks than looking for Evie. The locals all came and combed the surrounding scrub. News traveled faster than a wildfire, and by Sunday evening William had arrived, though what he thought he could do that I hadn't done was beyond anyone's comprehension. Finally the sergeant closed his notebook. The interviews were written out in full and shown to us later for approval."

"Do you still have those?" Lettie asked.

"They'll be in William's study somewhere."

Along with everything else. Nothing that offered any obvious explanation for Evie's disappearance.

"We'll sit down here for a while. Take in the view."

Lettie's knees buckled as Olivia lowered herself to the ground and sat, legs dangling into the abyss.

"Come and sit next to me. This is where Evie liked to sit and draw. Have you got her map?"

Lettie pulled out the map and unrolled it, trying to get her bearings. "Wollombi is that way, and Broke over there. The coast-line leads up to Newcastle and here is the Hunter River." She traced her finger north, over the herd of cattle moving north. "Where does this road go?"

She waited for Olivia's answer, but none was forthcoming. The ribbon of road, probably not much more than a track, wound its way north into the distance. "Olivia?"

"That's the stock route you can see. It goes through Singleton, Scone, and Murrurundi all the way north to the Liverpool Plains. And over to the west that's Cassilis and Merriwa."

"Here's Maitland." Lettie stabbed her finger at the word nest-ling in the bend of the river. "It's marked here on the map next to Hume and Largs."

"Largs is a small village on the outskirts of Maitland. No place called Hume."

"Perhaps it says Home?"

"Yellow Rock's home. Always has been. Always will be."

"But Evie's got the place marked. It seems quite large, look." Lettie squinted at the map; there was no doubt. "Perhaps it's a property."

Receiving no reply, Lettie rolled up the map and clamped it tight in both hands. With the wind gusting she could imagine it being snatched away. The last thing she wanted to happen.

"Here comes Oxley." Olivia pointed her finger down to the base of the rock.

"I hadn't realized he'd left us."

"Picked up the scent of a rabbit. He'll be up here soon." As Olivia spoke Oxley's bark carried on the wind and the flag of his tail became visible between the scrubby trees eking out an existence on the rocky slope.

"I'd love to have a look at some of these places."

"You're looking at a good day's ride to Maitland, and that's if you're flogging it. I doubt you'd be walking at the end."

As unwilling as she was to admit it, her backside felt as though it had been well and truly tanned and her thigh muscles burned like the blazes. "How many miles is it? I did Sydney to Yellow Rock in a day in the motor." For heaven's sake, now she sounded like one of the locals. This place had seeped into her blood with barely a whisper. She could hear Evie egging her on, as though she'd reached down across the decades and stood beckoning her. "Come with me."

"Me?"

"Yes, Aunt Olivia, you. How long has it been since you went on a trip somewhere, took a holiday?"

"I'm not leaving. I can't. I haven't and I won't." A flush blossomed on Olivia's cheeks.

Lettie's stomach did some strange circus backflip. "What do you mean you haven't?"

"I'm not leaving and that's that." Olivia pressed a palm against her heart. "I'd never forgive myself if she came home and I wasn't here." She bounced to her feet and peered over the edge, making Lettie's stomach do another flip. "Time we were going. It'll take you awhile to hobble down the track."

Lettie struggled to her feet, Evie's map rolled tight, hugged to her chest. Three decades and Olivia had never left the property. She couldn't believe it. What kept her here? Guilt or love?

"I did receive Miriam's letter."

Lettie stopped in her tracks. "Why didn't you say?"

"There didn't seem to be much point in replying." She pulled out a sheet of thick writing paper and held it out, all the while continuing to stride down the steep track.

There was no doubt that the letter was from Miriam. The expensive embossed paper, the scent of her cloying perfume, and the sharp pointed handwriting in purple ink. The words blurred. "Just a minute. Wait. Let me read it."

Both the Ludgrove and Maynard properties will now pass to my daughter, Letitia Miriam Rawlings, the family's sole heir.

The cold, stilted words said nothing of her regret at the loss of her only son, nothing of the quirky, wonderful man he was, his razor-sharp wit or his loving heart or his dreams and aspirations. Nothing of Evie. Nothing of the loss of her sister, who was the rightful heir to Ludgrove. It might have been a demand for payment.

Heat, anger, boiled in her blood. If she'd received such a stark missive she would have thrown it in the fire. "She had no right. I had no knowledge. I'm not expecting . . ."

Down the twisted track they went, without speaking, a great ridge of cloud stretched across the setting sun. It wasn't until they reached the horses that Olivia spoke again. "And I don't think you should be traipsing off on your own. I couldn't stand to lose two of you. Miriam would have my hide."

"Two of us? Thorne's passing was not your fault. A dreadful accident. No one's fault."

"Not Thorne. Evie. Punishment for my sins."

Lettie reached out and placed her hand on Olivia's arm. The intricate web of duty and resentment tying the two women held a morbid fascination. "You didn't lose Evie. It wasn't your fault."

The poor woman held herself entirely responsible for Evie's disappearance.

The following day Lettie hobbled along the path to the main house, every muscle in her body screeching. She'd tried not to wince as she'd sat at the table with Olivia and Peg for breakfast, but their knowing eyes had glittered with amusement. Peg had even gone as far as to offer horse liniment, which she declined.

Oxley eyed her with disdain as she shuffled into the study, then settled in his customary position underneath the desk. As always Lettie threw open the french doors, inhaling the warm eucalyptus-scented air blowing down from the rock before unrolling Evie's map and spreading it out.

Gradually the contrasting shapes melded into a reality that only yesterday she'd witnessed from the top of Yellow Rock, and that brought her back to Maitland and the word *Hume*. All the other properties marked showed a cluster of buildings, fence lines; Glendon, in the horseshoe bend of the river, even had tiny figures sitting around a long table under the trees, the tableau implying some sort of festive occasion. She bent her head, narrowed her eyes, trying to bring the tiny pictures into focus . . . A magnifying glass—that was what she needed. Grandfather had worn a monocle. Perhaps he'd had one.

She pulled open the desk drawers, pushed aside a pile of bills and receipts, a set of keys, found a series of nibs, the stubs of several broken pencils, which she'd somehow missed when she'd been looking for something to write her letter to Miriam.

The left-hand side of the desk proved equally disappointing until she reached the third drawer. Underneath several pamphlets, she discovered a square leather box. She opened the lid and found exactly what she was looking for. A small, folding silver magnifying glass.

Returning to the map she peered at the word *Maitland*, the intricate church steeples drawn with such fine detail as to be invisible to the naked eye, and a mere half inch away the word *Hume*. No sign of a house, fences, or anything to indicate a property.

She pushed to her feet, ignoring the screaming in her muscles, and paced the floor, coming to a halt in front of the bookcase. Olivia had insisted there was no place called Hume. Perhaps it was a German word, a word Leichhardt used, people he knew . . . She ran her finger along the spines of the books—no dictionaries in German, or any other language—then turned to William's journals and leafed through some of the pages. It would take her an age to decipher his looping scrawl.

With a frustrated mutter, she picked up the magnifying glass again and studied the writing; though perfectly formed, it was written in pencil, the paper rough as though it had been erased and then replaced or it had been written in haste. Blinking, she brought the magnifying glass closer, and her gaze came to rest on the tiny unpainted illustrations she'd missed—four men and their horses.

What did the picture mean? That the men lived there, owned a property? That one of them was called Hume?

No! She was chasing shadows, and the shadows outside were lengthening too. Before long Peg would be calling her over to the farmhouse. She slipped the map back into the drawer and sat with her chin resting in her hands. So much for making sense of the contents of the study for Olivia; she'd done nothing more than create an even greater mess.

She scooped up the keys and nibs and slid them back where they belonged, then replaced the magnifying glass in the box and put it into the third drawer. Such a lot to sort out.

Papers still covered the desktop. She reached out to one of the teetering piles. She'd take one each day and go through them systematically. She slid one pile toward her, and to her horror it collapsed, scattering the papers to the ground. Grumbling, she bent to retrieve them.

It wasn't until she'd almost completed her task that she noticed two sheets had drifted to the other side of the desk.

Evie's neat block writing, larger than usual, covered the entire sheet. A long list with the name Andrew Hume blazed across the top.

Andrew Hume
Bushranger—Arrested—Parramatta Gaol
Released to Roper River

Returned Sydney—Relics Missing
Left for Second Expedition—Sydney 1874 Maitland
December 1874 Died in Desert

Lettie sank back into the chair and massaged her temples, forcing away the impending headache.

Hume was a person, not a place. What did he have to do with Maitland, and why was he important enough for Evie to make this strange list? What relics were missing? And Roper River. Wherever was that?

She danced to her feet and paced near the walls looking for the map she'd seen. It was colored, she remembered that, pale pastel colors. She came to a halt in front of *The Eastern Portion of Australia* and there was the Hunter, Newcastle, and Maitland. No mention of the Roper River. Why wasn't her geography better?

The image of Leichhardt superimposed over a map of the Northern Territory and Queensland gazed down at her. She stepped closer and there it was—the Roper River, right up in the Gulf of Carpentaria. Why would a bushranger gaoled in Parramatta be *released* to northern Australia? And more to the point, why would he turn up in Sydney, then Maitland, before dying only months later in the interior?

Scooping up the piece of paper she galloped back to the farmhouse, Oxley skittering at her heels.

With the paper in the center of the table, Lettie fired questions at Olivia and Peg.

"Are you certain you don't remember Evie speaking about this

Andrew Hume? It looks as though she spent some time collecting information about him. Did he have something to do with Leichhardt? The Roper River is in the same area as Essington. Was Hume a member of Leichhardt's party? Did Grandfather know Andrew Hume? Please try and think. It might be important."

Olivia shook her head and let out an irritated huff. "The only Hume I remember is Hamilton Hume. He and another bloke, Hovell, I think it was, found the overland route from Sydney to Port Phillip, Melbourne. That was years ago, before *I* was born, never mind Evie. He'd be long gone."

Peg lifted her hand and rested it on Olivia's shoulder. "Might be time for another cup of tea."

"I don't want tea." Olivia sounded like a petulant child. "I want to go to bed. Always comes back to some explorer. Leichhardt's the worst. Every misfortune this family suffers always comes back to him. You'll be telling me next you think Evie went off in search of him."

"No, I don't think Evie went off in search of Leichhardt. From what I've read he'd been missing for over thirty years. I think she went off in search of Hume."

"Well, that's a load of rubbish because he was dead, too, by the time Evie left. Says that right here." Peg stabbed at Evie's list. "December 1874, died in desert." She stood next to Olivia, arms folded across her chest like some ancient guardian.

"I'm going to go to Maitland and Largs." The words popped out of Lettie's mouth. "I can do it in a day, there and back, and see if I can find out anything about this Andrew Hume. Evie wouldn't have written his name on her map if he wasn't important."

Olivia's face paled. "No. You can't do that. What happens if you get lost?"

"I won't get lost. I'll take Evie's map."

"Better take a compass." Peg nodded her head sagely. "Can you use one of those things?"

"Yes, I can, as a matter of fact. Thorne taught me. But I don't have one."

Olivia lifted her head from her hands. "Take William's. It's in the study, with his surveying tools. In the brass-cornered box."

Lettie frowned. She knew exactly which box Olivia was talking about, the one she'd mistaken for a writing box the very first day she'd spent in the study, when she was looking for paper and a pen to write to Miriam. "There isn't a compass in William's box."

"Don't be ridiculous, of course there is. It's been there for longer than I can remember." Olivia pushed herself to her feet. "I'll go and fetch it."

"I'll come with you." Lettie followed Olivia along the path to the main house. "I'm certain it's not there."

"It'll be there." Olivia pushed open the front door and then hesitated for a moment on the step. "There's a lamp on the hall table and matches. See if you can find them."

While Lettie fumbled around in the semidarkness, Olivia strode into the study.

Lettie found the lamp, lit it, and the shadows retreated. Olivia stood near the desk, shoulders slumped, the brass-cornered box open in front of her. "It's not here."

Swallowing her useless reply, Lettie peered over her shoulder. The empty compartment stared up at her as it had done the first time she opened the box.

"I don't understand. Where's it gone? William wouldn't have taken it to Sydney. He always left it at Yellow Rock."

Lettie eased Olivia down into the chair and gazed into her eyes. "Do you think perhaps Evie took it?"

"Why would she?"

Because she meant to go farther afield than Yellow Rock and Glendon. The possibility that she could be right shot through Lettie's blood like a Chinese firecracker, but how to say it to Olivia without breaking her heart?

There was no need. A mournful groan slipped between Olivia's lips and she dropped her head into her hands. "She thought she might get lost. She wasn't going up Yellow Rock, or to Glendon."

18

Olivia appeared in the morning, eyes shadowed but a look of determination on her face. "I have decided you are right. Evie must have had a plan, something she wasn't prepared to share with me. She wouldn't have needed a compass to go up Yellow Rock, nor to Glendon. Could have done the trips with her eyes shut and both hands tied behind her back. It's got to have something to do with all those papers in William's office. Leichhardt, the Prince of Explorers. Not for this family—more like the Angel of Doom."

"Are you sure you don't want to come with me?"

Olivia shook her head. "I must stay here. Don't forget to get some of that gasoline in Wollombi. You don't know where you'll get more."

"I won't. How large a town is Maitland?"

"Big. Used to be the second largest in New South Wales. Cobb and Co ran through there, and the steamers. Newcastle's bigger nowadays, but the drays still stop there even though they've got the railway. Have done for as long as I can remember. Not, mind you, that bullocks need any of this spirit. I like my bullocks unspirited."

A picture popped into Lettie's head and she felt in her pocket for her pencil and notepad—the image of a train of bullocks being force-fed gasoline or perhaps a motor up to its bonnet in a mound of hay. The inspiration of Evie's tiny drawings had reawakened her own creativity. By the time she got back to Sydney, she'd have a wealth of ideas for *The Bulletin.*

Olivia gave a wry smile. "Thank you, Lettie. Without you I never would have entertained the possibility Evie didn't do as I thought. I must stay here, but I shall be thinking about you every moment."

"I'm planning to return tonight, but if I don't you mustn't be concerned. It may take longer than we expect to find out about Andrew Hume."

"Once you reach Maitland, cross the bridge and follow your nose. About five miles give or take to Largs. Follow the river through the town. There'll be people who remember if there's anyone called Hume in the area."

And that was what Lettie was banking on.

Within an hour, Lettie was ready, Evie's map rolled, wrapped in a piece of oilskin, and placed next to her on the front seat. Dressed in the moleskins, riding boots, and shirt Olivia had given her, and with her gloves and goggles firmly in place, she felt quite the adventuress. She gave the crank a swing. The motor sparked to life, as did Oxley.

Before she'd even opened the door, he'd settled himself on the front seat. "Out you get! You can't come with me."

He gave her a malevolent glare and curled up on the seat.

Olivia ruffled his ragged ears. "Take him. It'll make me happier to know you've got some company, and he'll look after the motor if you have to leave it."

With a grin Lettie slipped into gear, opened the throttle, and cruised down the driveway.

Lettie arrived far sooner than she'd anticipated despite a stop at the forge for gasoline and the twinge of disappointment when there was no sign of Nathaniel. He'd crept into her thoughts more often than she was prepared to admit. Perhaps when she returned to Yellow Rock she'd ask Olivia when she next expected him to call in.

The road from Wollombi to Maitland was wide and clear, and she'd had it to herself for most of the way. No bullock drays, no cattle or flocks of sheep.

When she entered the village of Largs it appeared all but deserted, and it wasn't until she turned into a side street that the reason became obvious. A crowd of people dressed in their Sunday best poured from an impressive sandstone church. Children skittered around, releasing their fidgets with a game of hide-and-go-seek between the neat gravestones behind the church, the shouts of their irate mothers who feared they'd ruin their one good set of clothes dispersing any religious fervor.

Once she'd removed her goggles she realized the game had come to a halt and she was now the focus of every pair of eyes. Young boys bouncing up and down clambering onto the fence for a better look; little girls in pretty frocks, their hair ribbons dangling and their eyes wide.

Biting back a smile she waved and walked up the path. "Good morning." She repeated the greeting several times before anyone acknowledged her. "I wonder if you could help me. I'm looking for the Hume family. I think they live locally."

"Hume?"

"Nah! No one around here called Hume."

"Oh, but I have a map with their name marked." She turned back to the car to retrieve Evie's map.

"Don't need no map. I'm telling you there's no one hereabouts by the name of Hume."

A lad of about ten or eleven, his cloth cap screwed up in his hands, looked her up and down. "Did you drive that?"

For goodness' sake. "No, it flew . . ." She bit back her words. "I'm sorry. That was unkind. Would you like to come and have a look?"

He took off down the path without answering, and by the time she'd reached the gate he'd got himself behind the wheel and sat bouncing up and down like an Indian rubber ball.

"Be careful."

"Can we go for a ride?"

"Please, please." The train of children behind her edged closer. "I really haven't got time."

"I know where the Humes are." The lad behind the wheel plastered a smug smile on his face. A few more years and he'd go far in business.

Her heart gave a little jump. She had nothing to lose; besides, she admired his attitude.

The crowd of children swarmed closer. "Far from here?" she asked.

The lad jumped out of the car and held out his hand to a towheaded little girl with grass-stained knees. "Just me and me sister."

"If your parents say it's all right and you can introduce me to the Humes, I'll take you for a ride."

"Promise?"

Lettie nodded. "See what your parents say."

Much to her surprise he took off down the path around the back of the church, his sister galloping in his wake.

Lettie finally caught up with the two children beside a simple headstone, the little girl stuffing a wilting bunch of dandelions into a jar.

The lad's mouth crooked in a smile. "Here's Mum." He patted the top of the headstone. "She said it's fine if we go for a ride. And here's the Humes. Told you."

He stood with his arms folded and a smug expression on his face.

The gravestone read *David Hume 1809–1893* and next to it *Hannah Hume 1815–1893*. Nothing more. Disappointment shot through her. It seemed strange. Surely Evie would have drawn the gravestones, not four men on horseback. She squinted closer at the engraving: *1893*. Both David and Hannah had died in 1893.

And then she understood. If Evie had come here in search of the Humes in 1881, as she suspected, the Humes would still have been alive. A tug on her jacket disturbed her contemplation.

"Can we have that ride now?"

She didn't want to take the time, but the boy had helped, and maybe there was someone else who could tell her more about the Humes. "We still have to ask someone. Who brought you to church?"

"Aunt Bertha. She won't mind. She's coming now."

A small, rather drab woman, hair neatly parted and pulled back from her face, rushed across toward them. "Come here, Lucy. And you, Davey." She grabbed the children's hands. "I'm sorry. Davey can be a real nuisance. Too smart for his own good."

"That's all right. He deserves his ride."

"If you're sure you have the time."

"Time for a quick ride. I was wondering if I could ask you a question." Lettie gestured to the two gravestones. "Did you know the Humes?"

Bertha nodded. "They were good folks. He started out as a hawker, then they kept a shop in Maitland, did quite well for themselves, and they moved out this way when it all became too much."

"Do they have any family here or in Maitland? I wanted to talk to them about their son, Andrew."

"Andrew? Don't know nothing much about Andrew." She fidgeted with her hair, eyes darting from side to side. "I'm not one to gossip." Her voice lowered. "They didn't like to talk about him. Got himself into trouble."

"Can we please go for a ride?" Davey grabbed at her hand. "Please."

"Davey! Mind your manners."

"It's all right. I promised. Do you know anything else about the Humes?"

"David Hume was an overseer out at Dartbrook in the 1840s for the Halls before they moved to Maitland and opened the shop. Andrew was gone by then."

"Gone?"

"He grew up at Dartbrook, then took off into the interior when the rest of the family came to Maitland."

"Can you tell me where Dartbrook is?"

"About seventy miles north of here. Up past Muswellbrook. Far as I can remember the other children, Andrew's brothers and sisters, were all born in Maitland. My mother was the local midwife in those days, delivered pretty much everyone's children."

"Do any of their children still live around here?"

The woman shook her head. "They've all moved on." She turned to go, grabbed at the children's hands. "That Andrew, he was a difficult one. Never did settle down, near broke his mother's heart. Went off with the natives. She always blamed herself, said she'd left him as a child with one of the servant girls and it had turned him. Then he ran riot, arrested as a bushranger, couldn't leave the liquor alone. They as good as washed their hands of him."

Lettie's mouth dried. Why would Evie want to come here? "You don't remember anyone by the name of Evie, Evie Ludgrove, do you?"

The woman raised her shoulders and shook her head.

"Just one more thing. Could you come back to the car and point out the direction to Dartbrook? I'm not very familiar with the area."

"And Aunt Bertha can come for a ride too?" Davey ducked, narrowly avoiding a clip around his ears.

"You hush your mouth. You've done enough damage for one day."

"Really, it's perfectly all right." She threw Davey a wink. "He's been a great help."

By the time she and Bertha had walked back down the road to the motor, Davey was next to it, a proprietorial hand on Oxley's collar, keeping the crowd of children at bay.

Lettie lifted Evie's map from the front seat of the car, unrolled it, and beckoned Bertha. "That's Maitland, clear as day. See?" Lettie hovered her finger over the word.

"If you say so. I'm not too good with letters, and that writing sure is fancy."

A sinking feeling hit Lettie's stomach. If the woman couldn't read, how could she understand a map? She moved her finger along the road she'd driven. "This is the road back to Wollombi, and then if you go that way you're on the way to Sydney. See, look, there's the stock route going north."

"I see it now. Just follow your nose up the stock route. Dartbrook's west of Aberdeen. It's a good two days' ride, more in a dray." Her face flushed. "Silly me. I forgot the motor. Does it go faster than a horse?"

"Quite a lot faster." Lettie let out a sigh. "Is there no other way? No other tracks?" The route Bertha had pointed out ran straight up the stock route to Muswellbrook and then via Aberdeen to the spot she'd indicated as Dartbrook. It formed two sides of a triangle. Surely if she could cut across country . . . "Is there a shorter way, a track across here perhaps?"

"There's the old trail. You turn off at Muscle Creek, onto the Old Scone Road outside Muswellbrook. Nice country up there. Me dad, God rest his soul, used to use the track. Shearer he was. It's an easy run. Leastways that's what he used to tell us. I ain't ever been that way."

Lettie hadn't much to lose. She could come back on the stock route, a simple drive to Yellow Rock if the road was well used and the scale of the map was correct, and she had no reason to doubt that.

"Aunt Bertha, Aunt Bertha. Pleeeeease can we go for our ride?"

Lettie lifted her head, the two children completely forgotten while she'd studied the map. She raised her eyebrows to Bertha, seeking her approval, and received a nod in reply.

"Hop in. You'll have to sit close together. Thank you for your help, Bertha. We'll be back in about five minutes." She couldn't wait to get going. The sun was still high, and it looked no more than seventy miles on the map. She fitted the crank. "Are you ready?"

With little Lucy perched next to him and Oxley jammed in the middle of the bench seat, Davey wasn't looking quite so sure of himself. Lettie smiled at Bertha and turned the engine over, climbed in, and took off at a very sedate pace to roars of approval and much handclapping.

It took rather longer than she expected to make the careful tour of the main street, past the general store and the pub, all closed because it was Sunday.

By the time they returned to the church, Lucy and Davey were waving like royalty to anyone who'd care to look, their faces flushed and their eyes watering. When she drew up they scrambled out and were immediately surrounded by the group of envious children. Keen to get on her way, Lettie waved to Bertha, shouted her thanks, then headed out of town.

"Today's the day." The old man straightened up. "Nothing wrong with Rogue. You shouldn't have a problem." He ran his hand down the horse's shiny black fetlock. "Saddle him up and be on your way. You've got a fair few miles to cover."

Nathaniel's stomach churned. He'd waited for this forever. Stashed away every penny, done every job he could pick up since they'd discovered Rossgole had finally come up for sale, the property he'd had his eyes on since before he could remember. "Everything will be fine." He tried for a reassuring smile, but nerves still twisted his gut.

"Cup of tea before you go?"

"I want to get on the road. I'm going to call in and have one more look at the place. Make sure Parker has come good and cleared out. And if he hasn't it's only fair to warn him that the place will be ours by the end of the week."

"He'll have gone. Nothing he can do about it unless he's robbed a bank. Got those drafts somewhere safe?"

Nathaniel patted the money belt he'd strapped beneath his shirt. "I'll stop in Muswellbrook for the night. See how I go."

"Be a darn sight quicker to go down the stock route."

"Nah." He was determined to check the place one more time, and he'd spotted a shifty look in Parker's eyes last time they'd spoken. "I've got the rest of the afternoon." He swung up onto Rogue's back, held him tight while he pranced and carried on as he always did. "Take care of yourself, old man. I'll see you in a week with the deed in my hands."

Clicking his tongue, Nathaniel kicked Rogue into a gallop, his heartbeat picking up, making his blood race. An hour, maybe a bit more, and he'd be at Rossgole, plenty of time before the sun fell behind the mountain and the shadows lengthened. The track wound its way along the creek bed, the recent rain having turned the grass to a verdant green, good feed, just the way it was at Rossgole. The vision of neatly fenced paddocks and a string of breeding mares made his heart sing. He had plans, big plans. Ever since he'd listened to the blokes down at Randwick talking about the newly formed Light Horse Regiment, he'd known what he wanted to do. Much the same as the Maynards and Ludgroves had done in the early days, but his horses wouldn't be going to India. Not a chance. He'd breed the finest Walers and they'd carry Australians, and if ever there was another war they'd have the horses and the men. The Boer War had taught everyone a lesson; it was one he was going to act upon.

When he reached the Dartbrook track he slowed, cast a look

up to the old house on the hill. Back in the day Hall had owned all the land, built a fine stone house, and bred the best dogs. Hall's Heelers, they called them, border collies crossed with dingoes, but the place had gone to wrack and ruin when Hall had died and the property had been split up.

About a mile farther on he turned off the main track and crossed the creek down onto the flats. The long grass covering the tumble-down fence line swayed in the breeze. That'd be the first job, get the fencing sorted, then he'd talk to Olivia. He wanted to buy his first stock from her, a couple of mares, and while he waited for them to foal he'd make a start on the stables. The house would have to wait. Couldn't leave it too long though. Denman was getting on. Couldn't expect him to sleep rough much as he'd say otherwise. It was time the old man got a rest. Time to pay Denman back for all he'd done.

The gate lolled from its hinges. He dismounted and heaved it back against the fence line, then walked Rogue down the over-grown path to the old shack Parker used, his ears straining for any sound. The trigger-happy old fool had to be handled with kid gloves, and he didn't want to get into a brawl.

He stuck his hand into the trough outside the shack, took off his hat, and filled it, giving it a good sniff before offering it to Rogue. The horse nudged him aside and stuck his head in.

Rapping his knuckles against the splintered lintel, he peered around the door. A camp bed, one corner collapsed and covered with a filthy blanket, ran along one wall, and on the other side a stone chimney and the remains of a rat-infested cupboard. All suffocating under the pile of rusting iron and rotting shingles that had once been the corner of the roof. No sign of Parker. No sign that he'd been there any time recently. Perhaps at last he'd taken him at his word and cleared out.

With a spring in his step he led Rogue under the tree and let him crop the grass in the makeshift paddock. The home paddock, that's what it would be, and up on the rise beyond the dead gum he'd build a house, use the rocks littering the lower slopes for a good solid chimney. The wide stretches of free-draining soil rising to uplands would develop strong bones and muscles in the foals he'd breed, then he'd stand some stallions, have visiting mares, reap the rewards of agistment, and set himself up with quality bloodlines.

Leaving Rogue happily grazing he strode off up the hill in search of a site for the homestead. Somewhere elevated where he and Denman could sit on the veranda of an evening and keep an eye on the paddocks.

He came to a halt and turned. The perfect spot. The sun close to slipping behind the hills, a rosy twilight falling but he could still see Rogue working his way through the lush grass. Just perfect.

He bent down and scooped up a handful of dark soil, brought it to his nose, inhaled the sweet smell of possession, then stuck it in his pocket. The next time he came this way the place would be his.

Time to go. He'd spent longer than he'd intended. He flew down the hillside in leaps and bounds, the swell of happiness almost crushing his chest. He let out a yell. Saw Rogue lift his head.

In moments they were back on the road, the miles ticking away. Next stop Muswellbrook for the night, back on the road bright and early, and Sydney in a couple of days, in time for the auction.

19

Lettie bowled past the neatly tended workers' cottages of Branxton and Greta, then clambered the steep hill out of Singleton, marveling at the view of the plains below.

She'd covered a good fifty miles before she reached Muswellbrook and turned at the spot Bertha had pointed out on the map, crossing a solidly constructed timber bridge where the wide, well-used track snaked its way between dark-soiled paddocks encompassed by thinly treed hills. Finding a farm gate she pulled off the road. "Time for some food, Oxley."

They made short work of the packet of sandwiches Olivia had supplied and finished the flask of water, still cool secured in its neatly wrapped tea towel. "That's your lot, Oxley. We've got a way to go yet, back in the car. We're saving the rest for later."

With a sigh, he settled himself on the passenger seat and they set off once more. Ahead of her the ribbon of road wound into the distance and with a whoop of excitement she opened the throttle. Oxley pricked up his ears and sat tall, searching for any sign of movement among the encroaching trees.

The speed carried her up an unexpected incline with barely a pause, and as she crested the hill shafts of light from the sinking sun glittered, sending rainbow prisms dancing in front of her eyes. Grasping the wheel tightly she held Lizzie steady and raced toward a dip in the road.

The sound of running water broke through the call of the bell-birds and she swung her head left, where a small but gloriously pretty waterfall splashed over mossy boulders before disappearing beneath a timber culvert.

A wave of water hit the windscreen.

She slammed her feet onto the brake and reverse pedals. Oxley let out a strangled bark and vaulted out of the car.

She turned her head. "Oxley!" The back of the car skewed.

With a screech the wheels locked and skidded.

As if in a dream Lettie sat rigid, anticipating the crunch, her hands gripping the useless steering wheel.

With a screech and a shudder Lizzie ground to a halt, groaned, and settled.

Not a sound broke the stillness. Heart thundering ten to the dozen, Lettie cut the engine. "Imbecile! Stupid, stupid imbecile!" Front wheels firmly hooked between two boulders, water seeping onto the front floor.

Easing from behind the wheel she clambered onto the seat. The car wavered, then settled again. In a single bound she sprang out and landed beyond the boulders, knee-deep in the cold water, shivering in the shade thrown by a stand of ancient casuarinas.

Oxley paddled out toward her. "Out!" She pointed beyond the tree line. The impossible dog took no notice and waded toward her. His tail held high above the water, a wavering distress flag. "Go back, Oxley!"

Inch by inch he edged closer until his wet nose buffeted the palm of her hand. "The map! I've forgotten Evie's map." She scrambled back onto the running board, reached into the car, and pulled the cylindrical package from the seat, then dragged herself upright.

Lizzie lurched again and settled deeper into the spilling water. Holding Evie's map high above her head, Lettie jumped off the running board.

Oxley nudged against her and she slipped her fingers beneath the tattered leather of his collar, and together they edged their way to the bank. With another shuddering groan and a grind of metal, Lizzie sank into the deepest pool of water.

Breath heaving, Lettie collapsed, her clothes sodden and her mind in turmoil. "I made a mess of that, didn't I?"

Oxley gave a huge shake, spraying water in a wide arc, then slumped down next to her. A flick of his tongue against her cheek provided his agreement. She ran her fingers through his damp fur while he sat, body pressed against her, shivering in the fading light.

Poor Lizzie. Back end tipped at an alarming angle against a mossy rock, water lapping over the driver's door. One of the lights dangling, the other gone.

"Stupid, stupid, stupid. What the bloody hell am I going to do?" She stood up and eased her shoulders, tested her arms, and balanced on her tiptoes. No injuries, and Oxley seemed none the worse for his heroic rescue either.

One back wheel propped on a rock, the other bent and twisted well below the water level. The front wheels buried in the soft sand edging the creek. The cascading water provided a picturesque but totally devastating backdrop.

Marooned! Not a desert island in sight, but marooned nonetheless.

Goose bumps covered her skin; the air carried a hint of winter chill, and the wind sang in the overhanging trees, intensifying her sense of abandonment.

Where was Thorne when she needed him? This would be an adventure. Alone, she felt like crying. Shaking away her misery she waded back out to the car and reached into the cold water to retrieve the remains of the second lamp and tossed it onto the back seat. Struts from the roof dangled and the back door swung on its hinges. She bent down, swishing her hands through the shallows, searching. If she ever managed to get the car out, she'd need to get the lamps soldered. Her hands bumped against the sandy bottom of the creek, and she pulled out a random collection of bits and pieces and tossed them onto the back seat, found another piece of metal snagged on the root of an old tree above the water level. No point in wondering where they belonged or how imperative they were, because unless she could get some help to tow the car out, they'd be unnecessary.

Oxley's blanket still sat, remarkably dry and neatly folded on the front seat; she pulled it out and wrapped it around her neck and rummaged for her jacket and knapsack before she picked her way back to the edge of the creek and the smell of wet dog and mossy undergrowth.

Twilight had taken a firm hold, and Lettie's stomach gave a loud gurgle, reminding her how long ago they'd stopped to eat. She rummaged in her knapsack for the remains of their lunch, found two hard-boiled eggs, obviously intended for Oxley instead of the sandwiches she'd shared with him, a slab of fruitcake, and three apples. Never in her life had she appreciated anything as much.

Dividing the spoils into two neat piles, one for now and one, God forbid, for the morning, she munched her way through, saving the second egg for Oxley's breakfast.

If only she'd waited until morning before she'd set out, spent the night at a cozy little inn in Muswellbrook. She could be sitting in front of a fire enjoying a hearty supper before a good night's sleep. Impatience. That was her problem. Too impatient.

Jumping to conclusions, racing off with barely a thought of the consequences. With a sympathetic snuffle Oxley tucked himself at her feet.

Wrapping the blanket around her shoulders, she tugged him close, propped her back against a leaning tree, and pulled her knees up to her chin, prepared for a long, cold night. Better than rain. Dear God, if it rained they might be swept away.

She glanced up at the scudding clouds; if anything, the water had risen and flowed more strongly. What would Thorne do?

He'd light a fire. Boil some water. He'd have brought tea, a billy, a saucepan, even some sausages. And she'd taken off without a second thought, like the ill-equipped city dweller she was. She hadn't even any matches, and the sun was disappearing.

Hunkering down, she made a nest at the base of the large hollowed-out tree, its core burned away in some long-forgotten bushfire.

Nathaniel slowed Rogue, avoided a crumbling pothole, and cursed. He'd spent too long at Rossgole. The twilight had turned to a dusty gray, and although the moon was rising he couldn't risk Rogue stumbling. Another couple of hours at least before he made

Muswellbrook. Maybe he'd pull up somewhere along the creek, throw his swag under a tree, and call it quits.

The track crested a small rise, then dipped where an outcrop of casuarinas lined the bank. It was as good a place as any to camp for the night, and he had plenty of water for him and his horse. He dismounted and made his way to the bank and came to a shuddering halt.

Teetering precariously on the tumble of boulders was a motor. Not any motor; in the first light of the rising moon, the green paint-work glinted. His muscles tensed. There couldn't be another green Model T; she'd said it was the only one in the country. Rogue's bridle slipped from his fingers as he skidded down the embankment, over the slippery rocks to the tipped wreckage.

A growl, followed by a welcoming yap, and Oxley launched himself across the water, then a blanket-encased wraith appeared beneath the trees.

A rush of air and a mouthful of curses billowed. "What in God's name are you doing here?" His words sounded harsher than he intended, relief mostly. He'd imagined her slumped and bleeding, maybe dead in that bloody rattletrap.

"Nathaniel!" Her voice wobbled. "The sun was in my eyes and I ran off the culvert. If you could give me a hand, I'm sure we could push Lizzie out." She disentangled herself from the blanket and stepped into the creek.

"Stay where you are. Don't move."

She took no notice. Picked her way across the boulders.

"What are you doing here?"

"I'm on my way to Dartbrook."

"And why didn't you use the stock route, up through Aberdeen? It's metaled, designed for motors and drays. Any sensible person . . ."

That brought her to a halt and her hands flew to her hips, eyes blazing in the moonlight. "Are you going to stand there with that patronizing look on your face or are you going to help?"

He ambled closer. Felt a smile tug at the corner of his lips.

Nothing but her pride damaged by the look of her.

Arms folded, he waded through the water to the motor. Gave a shove. Stuck solid, no chance. "Going to have to pull it out."

"Correct." She glared at him as though the whole mess were his fault.

"Two of us won't budge it."

"What about your horse?"

"Need some decent ropes, probably a harness. We're going to have to get help." He couldn't leave her here. If he took her to Muswellbrook, no one would do anything at this time of night; they'd have to come back in the morning. The possibility of making Sydney in time for the auction shriveled to a far-fetched dream. Only one thing for it.

The truth of Nathaniel's words sank slowly into Lettie's churning thoughts. He made her angry, or the situation made her angry, and worse, he appeared to be enjoying himself. This wasn't the meeting she'd anticipated.

"Better get a move on if we're going to get home before midnight."

"Home? It's too far to walk." She slammed her hand over her mouth. He'd think her completely insane.

"Quite right. We'll ride back. Be in Aberdeen in time for a late supper."

She didn't want to go to Aberdeen. She wanted to go to Dartbrook.

"Come on, let's make a move."

"I can't leave the car here overnight. Someone might steal it."

"Highly unlikely. Think about it. Night. Dark. Back road. It's not going anywhere." He turned and stalked away, back to his horse. Surely he wouldn't leave.

"Nathaniel?" The plaintive wobble in her voice made her cringe.

He lifted some flap on the side of the saddle and undid a wide belt, then slipped it off and balanced it across his arms. "Even if someone comes across the motor, the chances of them getting it out are even less than ours." He waded into the creek again, his heavy boots splashing through the shallows, and tossed the saddle onto the back seat of the car, then meandered back to his horse. "Chances of them knowing how to handle a motor even smaller." He took hold of the reins.

The huge beast pranced around kicking up its heels, as impatient as its master.

Her stomach turned over and a cold sweat broke out on her forehead. "We can't both ride. I'll walk." But before she did that, she had to get Evie's map. Nathaniel was right about Lizzie, but she couldn't leave Evie's map. She padded back to the bank, reached into her knapsack, and tucked Evie's map inside her jacket.

"Come on. Hurry up!" Nathaniel's deep voice rumbled through the darkness, bringing with it a sense of security and relief at his presence. "Up you get."

For goodness' sake, was he going to ignore every word she spoke? "I'll walk." She buttoned her jacket, trying to ignore the massive creature towering over her and the sinking sensation roiling in the pit of her stomach. The gentle animal Olivia had given her to ride up Yellow Rock was nothing like this cavorting monster. "Or else I'll stay here. If you could send someone to help in the morning, I'd very much appreciate it."

"Not a chance." He gestured to the horse. Its sheer size sent a spasm of terror rippling through her. "I'll give you a hand. Good job you're suitably dressed because it'll be astride with two of us."

"Two of us," she echoed with an embarrassingly high-pitched squeak, her gaze riveted on the tufts of hair poking through the open neck of his red shirt.

Before she had time to gather her thoughts, warm hands clasped her firmly around her waist, her feet left the ground, and Nathaniel hoisted her astride the terrifying animal.

In one swift movement he swung up behind her, reached forward, caught the reins, clicked his tongue, and they were off, Oxley lolloping beside them as though he made a habit of racing through the night next to a massive, snorting beast.

Just as she began to calm, they crested the hill and the track fell away, sheering downhill at an alarming angle, forcing her toward the animal's pricked ears. She slammed her eyes shut, every muscle in her body cramped tense.

"Relax. You won't fall. I've got you."

Which was exactly what was causing her concern. His strong arms cradled her, making her breath come in horrible sharp sniffs. And she was hot, very hot. Perspiration soaked the back of her shirt where it rode up and down against the wall of his chest. "I want to get down."

"No chance."

No chance of so many things. Why had she embarked on this madcap scheme? What made her think she could find out what had happened to Evie when numerous search parties had failed? And now this. He'd just picked her up and tossed her like a bag of flour on the foaming creature and galloped down the side of a vertical cliff face in the darkness . . .

"We'll be off the mountain before long. Far better than sitting by the creek freezing to death."

Freezing. She'd love to be freezing. Perhaps this was what Hades felt like.

She peeled her eyes open. The track had leveled again, cleared to a wide-open plain. A large red moon crowned the mountain backdrop. Her breath came in short sharp bursts, every muscle in her body trembled, and black spots danced before her eyes, illuminated by the obscene red glow. The thundering of the hooves on the track filled her ears, drumming out all other sound.

And then she heard Thorne's laugh. He was up there somewhere enjoying every moment of her agony. "What's that noise?"

"Kookaburras. They always go off at this time." His warm breath fanned the tender skin at the back of her neck. "Almost there."

After an eternity he pulled up outside a small slab cottage. "Frog Hollow. Denman's place. We'll bed down for the night and in the morning take a couple of his horses and pull that machine of yours out."

Hauling herself upright she rubbed her hands over her face, blinked her eyes into focus. Lamplight illuminated a huge barn with great double doors, the word *Smithy* branded into the lintel.

Nathaniel swung down, leaving her perched on top of the great steed, then held out his arms, his fingers splayed. She gulped. There had to be another option. How could she throw herself into his arms?

"The alternative's yours." He whistled to Oxley and turned on his heel.

She gazed down at the ground, fought a wave of vertigo. What else could she do? "I'd like your help."

He steadied her with hands around her waist, she slipped into his arms, and for a split second she relaxed limp and boneless against him as he held her safe, until he placed her gently as a precious keepsake on the gloriously stable ground.

With a heartfelt sigh she stepped from his arms and brought her hands up to her flaming face, thankful for the shadowy moonlight. A man with a heavily lined face and wiry hair dusted with silver stepped down off the crooked veranda. "What're you doin' back here?"

Nathaniel gave a laugh, perhaps a groan. "Brought you a couple of visitors. They need a bed, and we could all do with a bit of tucker."

The man's dark eyes sparkled, then he bent down and ran his hands over Oxley's ears. "In exchange for the story about where you found them?"

"What do you say, Lettie?"

She had nothing to say, couldn't form a single word. Her legs trembled and she could barely hold herself upright.

"Lettie, eh?"

"Letitia Rawlings."

"Are you indeed?" The old man's fingers rasped across his chin. "Yeah. Now you mention it, I can see the family resemblance."

The resemblance? Lettie doubted the situation could become any more surreal.

Lettie's eyelids drooped. The flickering firelight and a full stomach thanks to a remarkably good stew had worked their magic. After a decent night's sleep, even outside under the stars, she'd be ready to return and sort out whatever problems Lizzie might have after a night in the creek. With Thorne's tools and the box of spare parts tucked under the back seat, she'd have Lizzie back on the road in no time.

"You'll have to get her and the dog back first thing. Poor old Olivia will be beside herself. Think history's repeating." The old man's sotto voce pierced her sleepy, befuddled brain. "And what's more, you should be well on the way to Sydney by now. They won't delay the auction. Think she can manage a horse on her own?"

"If her performance on the way here was anything to go by, I don't like the chances."

Lettie shot vertical, brushing aside the memory of his muscular arms cradling her. "I'm perfectly capable of riding a horse on my own."

"Thought you'd dropped off."

"I'm wide awake. And if you'd the first inkling of good manners you wouldn't discuss someone in their presence." Especially not someone whose body refused to cooperate. Pain shot through her thigh muscles as she lumbered around the fire. "I told Aunt Olivia I might be gone overnight. She won't be worried."

Denman gave some sort of snort, though how he would know, or care, what Olivia thought, she had no idea.

Unwilling to ask for any more help, she tossed her choices in her mind. Returning to Yellow Rock without Lizzie wasn't an option. If she set out early, maybe cadged a lift to Aberdeen or Muswellbrook, she could hire a wagon, some horses, some help to pull Lizzie out. The repairs she could manage herself. "I don't need you to come with me. I'm quite capable of going alone."

"You will not go alone." Nathaniel's voice brooked no argument and his words quashed her bravado.

"I can manage the repairs. I just need some help towing the car out."

"I'll take you back to Yellow Rock tomorrow morning and worry about the car later."

"I'm not leaving Lizzie." She couldn't. It would be like leaving Thorne in the middle of nowhere. Deserting him. "Can't you drag the car out on your way to Sydney tomorrow and I'll continue on from there?"

He raked his fingers through his thick hair and sighed.

Denman's mouth curved in a smile. "I'll go with the girl, take the wagon. She can give me a ride in that contraption of hers. Always fancied myself at the wheel of a motor."

Lettie exhaled, unclenched her fingers. "All I need is some assistance righting the motor and dragging it from the creek. The rest I can manage." She hoped, swallowing the bitter aftertaste of her shattered pride.

Nathaniel rocked back on his heels, arms folded and a tilt tipping the corner of his mouth.

"Sit down, Nathaniel. You're giving me a crick in me neck."

Nathaniel dropped down onto the makeshift seat and she followed suit across the fire, contemplating her failed plan in the ashes. The smoke swirled and shifted, blowing directly into her eyes.

"Good cleansing stuff, smoke," Denman said with a grin. "Always finds the person who needs it. Now listen here. Nathaniel, you need to be in Sydney. Letitia must sort out this motor of hers, and Olivia needs to know Letitia's come to no harm. Agreed?"

The voice of reason. She grunted her approval.

"This is what we'll do. Get a decent night's sleep. Nathaniel, you sort out Olivia on your way down to Sydney in the morning. I'll take Letitia back, then we'll get the motor out and bring it here."

"If she can get the contraption going."

"As much as it may come as a surprise to you, I have an excellent understanding of the workings of the engine. My brother—"

"Thorne, that would be."

Her head came up with a snap, a flurry of smoke stinging her eyes. How did the old man—

Before she could ask, Denman turned to Nathaniel. "You'll do as bid, boy. I'll take the wagon and if necessary we'll hitch the car up and tow it back here. Can't be that difficult."

"There won't be any necessity to tow it back. I told you—"

"You get the thing going, then you're on your way back to Yellow Rock and Olivia won't have to worry herself to a frazzle."

No, that wouldn't work. She had to get to Dartbrook. What was the matter with her? She'd almost forgotten the reason for her trip. "How far is Dartbrook?"

"A few miles up the track."

Nathaniel let out a mighty sigh and rubbed his hands over his face as though she'd told him she wanted to go to the moon.

"I am looking for the Halls' place."

Denman pinned her with a solid stare. "Why?"

She opened her mouth to answer and then changed her mind. Something about the old man's knowledge of the family, of her, of Thorne. "How do you know I had a brother called Thorne?"

"Known the Ludgroves and the Maynards a long time." He fixed his gaze on the smoldering fire. And there was more to that story than anyone was offering. She'd rather ask Denman after Nathaniel left.

"I think your plan is the best." She offered what she hoped was a winning smile. "I'd very much like your help, thank you."

At that moment the smoke swirled and sent a cloud in Nathaniel's direction. He wiped his eyes and stood. "Enough of your reminiscing, Denman. Lettie needs her beauty sleep and she's nursing a sore bum."

The old man gave a bark of laughter. "Right then, that's agreed. Nathaniel, you can bunk down with me and we'll let Letitia and Oxley have the barn. Go and get her a couple of blankets. She'll be comfortable enough up in the hayloft. The rest can wait until morning."

20

By the time Lettie woke the following morning, the sun was high and every muscle in her body screamed. Not only that, but Oxley had vanished. He'd spent the night curled against her back, providing a welcome security. She eased her way down the ladder from the hayloft and stumbled outside hoping against hope Nathaniel wouldn't notice her lopsided gait.

The old man sat, as he had last night, in front of the fire, his gnarled fingers wrapped around a steaming tin mug, Oxley at his feet. "Tea?" Without waiting for an answer, he poured her a cup, ladled in a heap of sugar, and handed it over.

Not game to abuse her muscles any more, she remained standing, sipping the brew. When they'd arrived last night, she'd paid very little attention to the property. Neat as a pin, the slab cottage stood central, the barn where she'd spent the night flanking the right-hand side and a workshop, the doors wide open, on the left. Rows of blackened tools hung from the rafters. All settled and neat as though it had stood forever. "Have you been here long?"

"Twenty and a bit years. Once I gave up droving I moved up here with Nathaniel. Got a good little business going. Aberdeen's on the stock route. Everyone needs a blacksmith at one time or another."

Over twenty years ago . . . Nathaniel could only have been a boy. Almost as long as Evie had been missing. What Lettie wouldn't give to be following in her footsteps a few days after she'd disappeared. It was too long. Evie would no longer be a girl, even though Olivia thought of her as such; she'd be a middle-aged woman, married with children, grandchildren maybe. But if that was the case, why hadn't she gone home or at least let Olivia know where she was? "Where's Nathaniel?"

"Left. Decided to get the milk train to Singleton, pick up a horse there. Planning to get to Sydney in two days. Don't like his chances, but we'll see. Coming to your rescue put him back a bit."

It hadn't crossed her mind to question why Nathaniel had been on the road, or whether he had time to rescue her and bring her back here. "I'm sorry. Why didn't he say something?"

"And do what? Leave you sitting up to your neck in the creek for the night?"

"I wasn't up to my neck . . ." Her words petered out as she caught the look on Denman's face. "I could have walked back to Muswellbrook."

"Bit of a trek."

"I didn't thank Nathaniel." A flush flew to her cheeks. She couldn't rid herself of the suspicion that he had been aware of the way her body had reacted to his closeness.

"He'll get over it. And Olivia will know where you are. He'll call in on his way past. Can't have the old girl worried."

Old girl! Denman looked a darn sight older than Olivia, with his heavily etched face, long ears, and flyaway hair. "You know Aunt Olivia?"

He flicked the remains of his tea beyond the fire. "Well enough. All the drovers do. Been passing through since I was a boy. Sorry business, Evie disappearing." He gave Oxley's ears a rub and leaned back.

Of course. Why hadn't she thought of that? Her mind darted back to the night at Yellow Rock, Olivia's swirling skirts and ribald laughter, her familiarity with the drovers and the sheer pleasure on her face when they arrived. And Nathaniel, the dances they'd shared, and last night. She lifted her hands to her warm cheeks. "And you knew Evie?"

"We all knew Evie. Lovely little thing, always with her paints and pencils." He sighed and shook his head. "Joined in the search, we all did. Never found her."

Well now perhaps, just perhaps she might find some answers . . .

"Reckon it's too late now."

Surely he didn't believe that the rock had taken Evie. If she'd come to grief close to home, someone would have found her remains by now. The hairs on the back of her neck rose to meet the memory of the strange sensation she'd felt when she'd stood on the top of the rock looking out over the vast plains, and the dream, the dream she'd had the night before she'd found Evie's dress on the chair beside her bed.

"Enough of this nonsense." Denman rose as if sensing her retrospection. "I'll hitch up the wagon and we'll see about this motor of yours. I've a mind to bring it back here. Always wanted the chance to have a close look at one of them."

Except that wasn't what she wanted to do. She'd far rather go to Dartbrook. See if she could find out any more about Andrew

Hume and why Evie had been interested in him. Heavens alone knew where the answers lay. Never mind the answers, the questions. She wouldn't need any help fixing the car; she was confident Thorne's lessons would hold her in good stead. She had a tire repair kit and beneath the back seat a jack, pliers, spanners, a hammer, a tire pump, and all manner of other bits and pieces.

"Can we come back via Dartbrook? You said it was down the road a bit."

"You'll get a fly up your arse if you're seen with me."

Which was all very strange. She tipped her head, not sure how to ask the question. She didn't need to.

"Bad blood. We'll get your motor out first, then you can go and have a word."

With a thoughtfully provided saddle blanket beneath her fragile backside and Oxley jammed between her and Denman, Lettie settled back to enjoy the unfolding panorama she'd missed cradled in front of Nathaniel in the dark the previous night.

The journey to the creek where poor Lizzie lay marooned was slow and tedious, but the heavy carthorses didn't miss a beat and Denman made no effort to increase their pace. For the first few miles he sat sucking quietly on his pipe, his eyes following every deviation in the track. It wasn't until they reached a large expanse of unfolding paddocks that he spoke, his voice a low rumble.

"Rossgole. Two hundred acres give or take, every one of them good soil, well grassed. Young Nathaniel's always wanted a part of it. Felt a connection to the place. Could call it his life's dream. Once he gets back from the auction in Sydney with the paperwork all signed and sealed, we'll be making the move. Has a mind to put his name to stud stock, settle down." His hand swept out in a wide arc. "Be in the next few weeks."

So that was why Nathaniel had to be in Sydney. Heat rose to her face. "Why didn't he tell me? Will he get to Sydney in time?"

"He'll give it his best shot."

"I wish I'd known, but I couldn't go back with him. I couldn't leave the motor."

"All turned out for the best. It'll be fine."

"I hope so. What about your blacksmith shop?" She couldn't imagine he'd get much business this far from town.

"Comes a time for a man to slow down. Unless I can get meself one of these motors. Denman, the Traveling Blacksmith. Has a nice ring. Like one of them circuses, now that'd be the go."

She shot a look at him from under her lashes. Sitting this close to him in the bright sunlight, she studied the map of wrinkles on his weathered face that pointed to a hard life. How old was he? She chewed her lips, wondering if she dared ask and thought better of it. What business was it of hers? Only idle curiosity, nothing more.

"I reckon I've done me time. Years in the saddle, droving, then me blacksmith shop. Know just about every stockman and drover who's traveled these parts and most of the bullockies. Everyone calls into the blacksmith shop."

Lettie fidgeted on the seat, taking the weight off her sore muscles. "Did you ever come across Andrew Hume?"

"Hume? Not right sure. Why do you ask?"

"He grew up at Dartbrook. His father was the overseer on Hall's property in the 1840s."

"Let me see. That's going back a bit. Memory's not what it used to be. Me dad was a drover up this way before me time."

There was something about the way he sucked on his pipe and stared into the distance that made Lettie push on. "His mother and father moved to Maitland, but Andrew didn't go with them."

"Oh! I've got it now. Hall's place. Where they bred the blue heelers, cattle dogs. The boy who went bush, then got himself into a heap of trouble. Came up before the court. Stealing a horse, brandishing a gun. Probably threw away the key."

And that proved she was on the right track. There couldn't be two Andrew Humes who'd been arrested for bushranging. "Why don't you want to go to Dartbrook?"

He shrugged. "Like I said, bad blood."

"What do you mean?"

"Nothing you need worry your head about."

Nathaniel cantered through Broke, his mind swirling. Denman's idea about the milk train had been a good one. It had gotten him to Singleton in a fraction of the time it would have taken on horseback, and he'd pulled in a few favors and borrowed a halfway decent horse. Shame he couldn't have taken the train all the way to Sydney, but like Denman said, Olivia couldn't be left wondering. He'd had no time to hang around, just long enough to let Olivia know Lettie hadn't come to harm. Well, not much. More dented pride than anything else, he'd guess. Quite why she wanted to go to Dartbrook he'd no idea. Still, he'd leave that to Denman to sort out when, or if, they got the motor out. He'd been too blindsided by the feel of her in his arms. Dancing was enough; a ride down the mountain in the moonlight would turn any man's senses.

When he pulled into Yellow Rock he found Olivia pacing the driveway like a marauding goose. She flapped her arms at him and he slammed to a halt.

"Thank God you're here. I need help. I've lost Lettie." Her face crumpled, and for an awful moment he thought she was going to burst into tears. He wasn't good with women, never mind a crying woman.

He swung down from his horse. "She's fine. Had a bit of an accident, that's all."

"What kind of an accident? How badly hurt is she? My horse is saddled and I've got supplies packed. What are you waiting for?" She spun on her heel.

"Olivia, wait up."

"If you're going to tell me something I don't want to hear, you can keep it to yourself." She threw the words over her shoulder and bolted to the stables.

Women! What was it about them? No doubting Olivia and Lettie's relationship, because they sure wouldn't take no for an answer. "Olivia!" There must have been something in his tone of voice, because she came to a halt and turned slowly, almost flinching, bracing herself for the worst. He sucked in a fortifying breath. "Lettie is perfectly fine, suffering nothing more than a sore bum last time I saw her."

"You better not have been looking too closely at her bum or you'll have me to answer to."

"Are you going to listen to what I've got to say or shall I leave? I've got to get to Sydney. It's the Rossgole auction tomorrow afternoon, and I've got no intention of missing it. Waited too long. Lettie was driving up to Dartbrook, the Halls' old place . . ."

"What? . . . She was going to Maitland."

"Don't ask me. I don't know. She took the back road from Muswellbrook, setting sun blinded her, one of the culverts was underwater, and she ran off the road. I was on my way down to

Sydney and found her. Took her back to Denman's. He's going to give her a hand to tow the motor out. If she can get it going she'll be back with you tomorrow night earliest." There, he'd managed to get it out.

"Denman'll see her right." The beginning of a smile tilted her lips and then a frown crossed her forehead. "He will, won't he?"

"'Course he will. And I'll be back through at the end of the week. If there's any problems we can sort them out then. I've got to go."

"Stay and have something, a cup of tea?"

"I haven't got time. You're just going to have to trust me on this one."

"You're a good lad, Nathaniel." She reached up and patted his thigh. "Let's get you a change of horse. That one looks as though it's due for the knacker's yard. You can take Raven. He's ready and waiting. I was about to leave when you arrived."

Blimey. He must have done something right. Olivia didn't part with her horse for anyone. "Thanks. That would be great. I got the milk train down from Aberdeen and borrowed this nag from the bloke at the Caledonian."

"I'll get someone to take it back. There's a stallion to pick up at Randwick, and see if you can get a message to Rawlings, let him know Lettie's still here and she's all right. It'll keep Miriam off my back." Her face flushed. "Lettie will be back here by the time you get there, won't she?"

"I'm sure she will." He turned to unsaddle the Singleton horse.

"Leave that for me. I'm not totally useless. Take care, and good luck. You deserve that property. It's got your name written all over it."

He swung back up into the saddle. "I hope so." Lifting his hand in a wave, he thundered down the drive relishing the feel of a decent horse beneath him.

While Denman's horses made good work of the final miles, Lettie scanned the road ahead for any sign of the car. She recognized little of the track from the night before, most likely because she'd had her eyes tightly closed and had spent the time praying she'd live to tell the tale.

Finally they rolled down the hill and there, tucked askew over the edge of the culvert, lay poor Lizzie.

"Did a good job of that, didn't you?"

Denman slowed the wagon and she jumped down before he'd come to a standstill. In the harsh sunlight the mess she'd gotten herself into became obvious. What had she been thinking? The road she'd careered down pitched at an alarming angle, and the water across the culvert almost reached her knees. Oxley studied the car, then looked at her and whined. She picked her way over the boulders. One of the wheels looked horribly bent and the tire on another was mangled. The one remaining lamp drooped at a precarious angle and the other lay forlorn on the back seat. There was a three-cornered tear in the canvas roof and several of the struts dangled, throwing it out of alignment.

She edged closer, eyeing the collection of crumpled metal she'd fished from the creek and thrown into the back. Nathaniel's saddle was squashed behind the front seats, the water lapping the sides. The blanket she'd wrapped herself in hung forlornly on the branch of the tree above the hollow where she'd imagined she'd spend the night. She let out a relieved breath. Thank goodness Nathaniel had stumbled across her. Though he hadn't done much stumbling. She was the guilty one. And she'd hardly thanked him. Instead, she'd bitten his head off and complained vociferously.

Denman stood, head tipped to one side, surveying the disaster. "Shouldn't be too much of a problem getting her out. Don't know about those wheels, though. I'll unhitch the wagon and we'll run the ropes around the back of the motor. I reckon the horses can pull it out in no time."

"I can manage the wheels, as long as the axle isn't broken. If you've got a saw, we can take the broken spindle out. It shouldn't be a problem. I've got a spare, a tire pump, and another inner tube."

"And what would that be?"

"It's the—"

He waved his hands at her. "Explain later. Let's get her back on the track first."

It took an eternity before they recovered Lizzie, somewhat forlorn but on all four wheels. Denman had unhitched the horses from the wagon, anchored and buckled all kinds of leather straps, and as gently as if they were dealing with a wounded animal, the two carthorses eased poor Lizzie from the creek with less bumping and grinding than Lettie had caused when she'd run off the culvert.

Lettie paced around the car checking the damage. The wheels were the only major problem and the possibility gasoline might have leaked, but there was very little smell and the two full cans remained strapped to the back. There'd be the question of the carburetor and the spark plugs, but they were easy enough to dry and clean. Thorne kept a neat little steel brush for that job, one she'd done many times.

Under Denman's watchful eyes she unpacked the tool kit from under the back seat and set everything out in neat lines as Thorne had always insisted.

"Looks like you might have an idea of what you're doing. Good thing someone had faith in you. If not, Nathaniel would have had you tucked up back with Olivia by now and this poor old girl would be rusting away." He lifted Nathaniel's saddle from behind the seats, dusted it down, and placed it in the wagon along with her knapsack, then wandered back and pulled out the lamp from the back seat. "Nothing that can't be fixed. Do this when we get back. Now, what about all these other bits and pieces you found?"

Lettie allowed his voice to wash over her while she jacked up the car and removed the tire. All the while Denman puttered around in the creek swishing his hands in the water. "Looking for gold?" she asked, lifting her head from fitting the new inner tube.

"Nah! Interesting the stuff that washes down when we've had a bit of rain." He pulled out a worn piece of timber, the edges blackened. "Can't remember a bushfire through here. Though that tree up there on the bank looks as though it's been through a fire once upon a time." He smoothed the piece of wood, then lobbed it back up the hill.

It wasn't until she'd refitted the wheels and she stood to brush the dirt from her knees that she noticed how quiet Denman had become. He stood, his thick, scarred fingers compulsively tracing an odd-shaped piece of metal.

Something she'd failed to notice missing from the wheel or under the bonnet perhaps. "What's that?"

He jumped as though she'd startled him and looked up, his eyes rheumy. "Where'd you get this?"

She took two steps forward. "What is it?"

He dangled a strip of hinged metal from his fingers. "A bit."

"A bit of what?"

"A bit. Mouthpiece from a bridle. Goes in the horse's mouth to help you control it."

"I've got no idea." Nathaniel appeared to have complete control over his horse when they came down the mountain. And his saddle was all in one piece on the back of the wagon. "It must be something from the motor. I collected all the pieces that broke off." She held out her hand.

Denman stared down at the piece of metal. "I don't know much about these motors, but I'm pretty sure you use a steering wheel to control them, not a bit."

"Of course you do. Don't be silly."

"I ain't being silly." He slipped it into the pocket of his jacket. "Right, let's get a move on. Show me how we get this thing going. I've got no intention of spending the night here."

It took a good four cranks to get the first spark, and just when she'd as good as given up, Lizzie sprang to life. Lettie slipped behind the wheel, determined to keep the engine running.

"I'll be right behind you. Take it easy. Too far back to Frog Hollow tonight, too late for Dartbrook, too, and me stomach thinks me throat's been cut. We'll pull into Rossgole and camp there. You can call in to Frog Hollow on the way back from Dartbrook. I've got gasoline that'll see you back to Yellow Rock, and the road from there's metaled."

She could see the wisdom in his words and had no intention

of arriving at Dartbrook in the dark. She had no idea who or what she'd find. "Do you need any help with the horses?"

He threw her a look that didn't want translating and shuffled back to the wagon.

Praying the wheel would hold, she eased onto the track and called Oxley. He bounded up beside her and settled on the seat. The steering wasn't the best, and the wobble in the wheel with the missing spindle didn't help.

Once she crested the hill the track widened and she pulled to a halt, dug out her goggles from the back seat, and cleaned them off while she waited for Denman and the wagon to appear before setting off again.

She crawled along not far in front of Denman, the road pitted with potholes and the light fading, and after a few miles he waved at her to slow and pulled alongside. "Through that gate. I've a mind for baked rabbit. How does that sound?"

Oxley's ears pricked in response. Olivia would know by now she'd come to no harm, and once she'd called in to Dartbrook she'd have an easy run back down the stock route if Denman was to be believed. She had no reason to doubt him. After the past couple of days, she couldn't think of anything better than an easy run on a metaled road.

21

When Lettie reached the gate she eased to a halt and allowed Denman and his wagon to trundle past and turn down the track. She followed, driving past a tumbledown shack, nothing more than four walls with a couple of holes to let the light in, a dangling door, and a chimney. They'd be better off under the stars with a good fire burning, which was what Denman had in mind, because by the time she pulled up he'd released the horses and collected an array of leaves and branches and lit them within a well-worn, rock-edged fire pit.

"Who lives in the shack?"

"Old Fred Parker uses it now and again. Squatted for years." Denman tucked his shotgun under one arm and grabbed the billy in the other. "Fill this up down there at the creek and collect some more wood. I'll be back." And with that he disappeared into the dusk, Oxley glued to his heels.

The fire didn't seem big enough to cook a boiled egg, but who was she to argue? She ambled down to the creek and filled the billy, collected a few sticks on the way back, and fed the fire. It flickered and dulled, then flared again as she settled the billy. They'd need a more substantial fire to bake the promised rabbit. Buttoning her dustcoat to keep out the encroaching chill, she ambled across the paddock, wishing Oxley hadn't taken off with Denman. She'd seen the glint in his eye the moment the word *rabbit* was mentioned. The dog had a vocabulary many would envy.

A large dead tree—a widow maker, Thorne would have called it—stood in majestic isolation in the middle of the paddock, the ground beneath littered with broken branches. She collected some smaller ones into a pile and then wandered around in search of something larger.

The last rays of the sun made a splashy display, illuminating a thick branch angled across a pile of oddly shaped boulders. Just the size she wanted. She picked her way up the small rise and tried to tug the branch free. The corner of her dustcoat snagged and she bent down to free it.

Lichen covered the slanting stones, their weathered edges smoothed. She sank to her knees and ran her hand over the gnarled indentations; but for their haphazard placement they could have been a group of ancient gravestones.

Ignoring the tremor tiptoeing across the nape of her neck, she released the branch and tucked the smaller pieces of timber under her arm before following the odor of singed fur back to the fire where Oxley crouched, his bloodstained jaws crunching something she didn't want to think about.

Denman raised his head. "Wondered what happened to you." He raked the ashes over a mound at the base of the fire and grunted as he clambered to his feet. "Rabbits are in the coals."

Oxley lifted his head, licked his lips, and grinned.

"Dog's had a feed and ours is baking." He snapped several lengths from the timber she'd brought and arranged them in the fire. "Billy's boiled. Ready for a cuppa?"

Lettie sank down holding her hands out to the flames. "Thanks." She wrapped her fingers around the tin mug and sipped the welcome brew.

"Got some good wood there. The big job'll keep us warm tonight."

She offered a wry grin. "I found it over there. Against the big old rocks. They look like crumbled gravestones."

"Doubt that. Apart from old Parker I don't think anyone's ever lived here. Your imagination's running away with you." He prodded the fire, stood up, and lifted his hat and scratched. "While the rabbits are baking you can show me these gravestones you think you've found. Where are they?"

A red moon had risen above the hill and an eerie light illuminated the skeletal sentinel.

"Just beyond the tree."

They trudged back up the hill. "There they are."

Denman crouched down and reached into his pocket, then pulled out a box of matches and nursed the wavering flame.

"They're covered in some sort of lichen."

"Old man's beard. Fix up a sore throat quick as a wink." He snapped his fingers under her nose, making her start, then ran his hand over the face of one of the stones. "Nah. They're not gravestones. Paddocks around here are littered with random rocks. Back from the time water covered the entire area. Nathaniel will be pleased. He won't have to buy me a headstone." He gave a throaty chuckle, making the hairs rise on the back of her neck again. "Come on, that rabbit'll be ready."

Lettie licked the last remaining drips of rabbit juice from her fingers and wrapped her arms around her knees. The warmth of the fire and the slug of rum Denman insisted on slipping into the last cup of tea left her oddly relaxed. "What do you know about Evie? What happened to her?" She hadn't intended to say anything. The rum must have loosened her tongue.

He glanced sideways at her, scratched at the stubble on his chin. "Everyone knows about young Evie. The rock took her."

A streak of anger rushed through her. "That's a load of rubbish and you know it. Olivia told me the drovers combed the area for weeks afterward. They had the best trackers and a bloodhound. They found nothing except her dress pushed down behind the rocks at the freshwater pool."

"Told you the rock took her."

"Don't be ridiculous. I'm serious. I intend to find out what happened to her. She'd planned her trip, taken her father's compass, marked the name Hume on the map, near Maitland. A man named Andrew Hume lived at Dartbrook when he was a child. That's why I want to go there. Supposing Evie went farther afield than anyone expected."

"Up here? Nah! In those days the tracks weren't like they are today. Young girl like that on her own. Need a bushman, a bloody good one, to cut across country from Maitland. Someone who knew the area like the back of his hand. Why would she come this way? Get yourself some sleep."

What was the point in arguing? There was nothing more she could do. And in all honesty, the whole idea was preposterously far-fetched. She'd be believing the old stories next. She ought to be back at Yellow Rock right now instead of sitting in a godforsaken paddock in the middle of nowhere. She pulled the blanket around her shoulders and curled up with her face to the fire and Oxley's warm body pressed against her back. Through the flames the silhouette of the old man hunkered opposite wavered and trembled in the glow as he sat rubbing a handful of ashes into his palm as though his life depended on it.

Above him the blood red moon rose higher and her eyes grew heavier.

The light from the fire flickered and the flames grew, the heat fanning her cheeks, breath warm and rasping against her neck as she leaned forward into the horse's mane. Helter-skelter down the hill, tree branches slashing at her face, the obscene glow illuminating the skyline, her heart pounding in time with the hooves. She thundered down the track as though her life depended on it, her fingers clawing tight around the reins.

And then she was flying, flying through the air. Flashes of yellow and crimson arcing across the sky, then a thump as she landed, knocking the breath from her lungs. Above her a streaking star sliced the night sky before oblivion claimed her. *There are more things in heaven and earth . . .*

"Strewth! Wake up!"

Lettie shot up. Sweat pouring down her face, her breath coming in ragged gasps, her whole body shaking.

Smoke and the stench of burning clogged her nostrils. A wet tongue rasped her cheek. Oxley gave a plaintive whine and pressed closer.

"You're dreaming, having a nightmare." Denman's face, creased with concern, swam into focus.

Lettie gulped in a huge breath, let it whistle out between her dry lips, and her shoulders sank.

A dream.

No wonder after the past few days. The shock of crashing Lizzie, the harrowing ride down the mountain with Nathaniel, the surreal evening scratching around in a paddock littered with ancient stones, picking rabbit meat from bones like a wild animal. And now this.

"Be light in an hour or so." Denman eyed her with a frown. "I'll get the billy on, then we'll get you on the road to Dartbrook."

Oxley wagged his tail in approval. And suddenly she had a longing to be back . . . at Yellow Rock. She'd been on the point of saying home, thinking of Yellow Rock as home.

Denman's tea drove away the last whispers of her dream, and with Oxley lolloping along beside her she climbed the small rise, sketchpad in hand, and squatted under the tree. Her pencil moved swiftly across the page capturing the essence of the place, and once satisfied she returned. Denman sat by the fire, the piece of metal he'd picked out from her car polished to a bright sheen.

"It came up well."

"Needed to make sure me eyes weren't deceivin' me. See here?" He held up the two hinged pieces of metal. "That's my mark."

"You made it?"

"That I did. Made a lot in my time, only this one's different. It's a snaffle bit, made of sweet iron, from the tines of an old plow I came across. See these bits here? Copper inlay. And these, that's my trademark."

The rings at either end of the bit twisted like fine filigree. "Do you know who it belongs to?"

"I do."

She waited as he swirled the now gleaming piece between his fingers. "Made it before I opened me smithy. Made it for me brother, Bailey."

"Why would he throw it away?"

"I don't think he did. Know he wouldn't." His stooped shoulders trembled and he bent his head.

Not knowing how to offer comfort, she edged close, studying the piece of metal.

Denman's voice wavered. "Last I knew he was collecting some horses, then heading off to catch up with the mob of cattle the drovers were bringing up the main route. He was meant to drop the horses off outside Scone, then meet up with them in Murrurundi. Olivia'd given him the wages." He heaved to his feet. "Time to get a move on. I might come with you, to Dartbrook. Leave the horses here and take that motor of yours for a spin. Then you can get on your way to Yellow Rock."

"What about the horses?"

"Fencing's not the best, but they'll be happy enough with the pickings in the paddock. We'll be back in a couple of hours." He raked out the coals on the fire and looked up with a frown. "You get the motor moving, and I'll throw these odds and ends into the wagon. Be with you in a moment."

Calling Oxley, Lettie made her way back to the car. In the early morning sunshine the wheel looked a lot better despite the missing spindle, and the tire had held up. She piled the broken struts and bits and pieces into the blanket and bundled them to one side on the back seat. Oxley would have to give up his front row spot for Denman. She whistled again. The wretched dog was nowhere to be seen.

Once she'd emptied the spare can of spirit into the tank, the engine sprang to life with hardly a complaint and ticked over nicely. How she wished Thorne was with her. She could hear his crow of triumph and imagine the look of pleasure in his eyes. She ran her hand over the bonnet, ignoring the scratches and dents the trip into the gulley had caused. Easily enough fixed when she got back to Sydney.

Shading her eyes she called Oxley again. He came bolting across the paddock, covered in dirt and stinking to high heaven, and slithered to a halt in front of her. "Where's Denman?"

Oxley turned his head toward the paddock, and sure enough Denman appeared. He ambled over. "Right then. All ready to go?"

Before Lettie had time to answer, Oxley bounded onto the front seat.

"Oh no you don't. That's for Denman. In the back." She patted the space next to the bundled blanket and yanked on his collar. For a moment or two he resisted, then with a curled lip he shrugged her off and slipped into the back.

It took almost as long for Denman to get settled, and from the look on his face there was a distinct possibility he might be having second thoughts. With his hands clutched tightly in his lap and his shoulders rigid, he sat staring through the windscreen as though his life were in danger.

Lettie eased in behind the wheel and let off the brake, allowing the downhill slope to edge the car forward before she opened the throttle. "Ready?"

Denman let out some sort of a groan and settled deeper in the seat. "Do your best." He fastened a neckerchief over his nose and mouth, ending any opportunity for conversation.

Before they'd reached the gate a crack sounded.

Lettie slammed her foot on the brake, ducked below the windscreen.

A shot whistled above their heads.

Oxley let out a yelp and flew over the side of the car.

Denman suffered no such terrors. He simply sighed, clambered out of the car, ripped off his neckerchief, and bellowed, "Cut it out, you stupid old fool!"

A shuffling figure appeared, shotgun dangling. "Get off my property."

"Ain't your property, Parker. Never has been, never will be. Nathaniel'll see about that."

The man tucked the gun under his arm and took several steps closer. "What's that good-for-nothin' lout got to do with it?" He tipped his hat, revealing a grimy, pockmarked face, sulfur-yellow teeth, and a set of cold eyes.

Denman pinned him with a ferocious stare and stalked toward him, the dust from his boots rising in whirling clouds. Fighting an overwhelming urge to drag him back to the safety of the car, Lettie gritted her teeth and sat tight.

"You've had your warning. Your time's up. Rossgole'll belong to Nathaniel before the day's out. And you'll be lookin' for some-where else to exercise your shotgun. Now, get out of the way."

Much to Lettie's relief the man's shoulders sagged, then he tucked the shotgun under his arm and shuffled back toward the tumbledown shack.

She scanned the tree line for Oxley. No sign. The good-for-nothing hound had become a law unto himself. She whistled low and the man's head came up. His unnerving gaze followed her as she walked around the car until Denman held up his hand, palm out, in a gesture of restraint.

Parker shrugged. "Get out of here. Not your property yet. And if the horses are still here tomorrow they'll be heading for the knacker's yard." His words lingered on the breeze.

"Let's go." Denman heaved himself into the car.

"Oxley's vanished." She whistled again and set off in the direction of the shack.

"Get back in the motor."

"I need to—"

"Get back in the motor." Denman placed his thumb and forefinger in his mouth and emitted a piercing whistle. "Let's go."

"But Oxley's—"

"He'll be here." True to Denman's word Oxley came hurdling back from the direction of the shack and in one bound settled himself in the back of the car.

Lettie reached back to pat him. "Argh! What have you been doing?" She dusted her hands, setting loose a flurry of black dirt. "Digging, by the looks of it. You disgusting dog. And what's this?" She pulled a chewed piece of hide from the corner of his mouth and tossed it on the floor.

"Time to go." With no sign of his previous concern Denman leaned forward, hands pushed deep in his pockets, nose almost pressed to the windscreen. Lettie took off, narrowly avoiding a gaping pothole.

Once they were over the hill, the road leveled out to a well-packed track and she cranked up the speed, happy to leave the oppressive atmosphere and the man with his ready shotgun.

The remainder of the trip to Dartbrook passed in total silence, not that Lettie wanted to risk opening her mouth. The continual whiff of something disgusting from Oxley turned her stomach. Not the ripe smell of rabbit from last night but a pungent, musky odor.

A few miles later Denman flapped his hand, indicating that she should slow down, then pointed to a dusty cart track meandering through the trees. He pulled off his neckerchief. "Down there."

She slowed to a stop outside a once-impressive sandstone house, the windows boarded, the roof sagging.

"There you go. Dartbrook. Not what it used to be."

Lettie climbed out of the motor and stood for a moment surveying the house. Despite its dilapidated state, a curl of smoke from a chimney at the back wound its way up into the clouds.

A smaller outbuilding stood at the end of a well-worn path behind the main house, smoke wafting and seeping out of the door. "Hello!" She knocked, peered inside, and stood waiting for her eyes to adjust to the gloom.

"What do you want?"

Heart thumping, Lettie whipped around to be greeted by a florid-faced woman, arms akimbo, sporting a matching expression. "Oh! You made me jump. I wonder if you could help me. I'm looking for the Hume family or anyone who might remember them. Andrew Hume specifically."

"House has been closed for years. I'm the caretaker. Used to belong to the Halls, but they're long gone. Why would you think the Humes might be here?"

That was a very good question. She'd started out with such high hopes, but now that she'd arrived she had no idea exactly what to say. "I was in Largs . . ."

The woman's mouth turned down at the corners. "Where's that?"

"Just outside Maitland. Someone said Andrew Hume once lived here. I—"

"Long way to come on the off chance. Must have taken you a good couple of days."

"I have a motor. It didn't take very long." Except for a small accident and a bit of a diversion with a man toting a shotgun.

"A motor, you say. Never seen one of those." She peered around the corner of the house and let out a splutter before ducking into the doorway.

"I'd like to show you something. May I come in?"

"Haven't got long." She held the door ajar, and Lettie stepped inside the small room furnished as a kitchen but with a stretcher tucked up against one wall. She carefully unrolled Evie's map and laid it on the table.

"That's real pretty." The woman reached out a grimy hand.

A fierce protective wave surged through Lettie. She didn't want this unknown woman with her dirty hands touching Evie's map. There was something disconcerting about her conniving gaze. Lettie pushed herself between the table and the woman and pointed to the word *Hume* on the map.

"Right. Well, that's easy, isn't it. That's the property the Humes bought in Maitland. Who drew the map?"

She did know the Humes. "My aunt."

"David Hume was the overseer here, donkey's years back." She stabbed her dirty finger on Evie's map. "For the Halls. Before they sold up."

"Have you ever heard of anyone called Evie Ludgrove?"

To give the woman some credit, she did look as though she was thinking about it as she stared through the open door, then finally shook her head. "Nope. Is that the one who drew the map? Did something happen?"

"She disappeared and I'm trying to find her."

"Disappeared, you say? That's no good."

"I wondered if you remembered her, if you'd ever met her."

She wrinkled her nose. "I was born here. Lived here all me life. Place isn't what it used to be."

Lettie's head came up with a snap. "Did you know Andrew Hume?"

"Met him once. Came to see old Ginny. She used to be his nursemaid, looked after him when he was a boy."

And that confirmed what Bertha had told her. "Can you remember when that was?"

"Years back. I was just a child." The woman's gaze shifted and she moved toward the door. "Who's that outside by that motor of yours?"

"Mr. Denman, the blacksmith."

The woman scowled, making Lettie regret her words. "He shouldn't be spreading no rumors. The Humes were good people. Good-for-nothing lazy layabout."

Which was as far from the way Lettie would have described the old man as she could imagine. "Mr. Denman is very kind. I had an accident on my way here. He helped me."

Why was she explaining herself? It had nothing to do with this woman.

"It ain't my business to stick my nose in, but you seem like a nice enough girl . . . You watch it. None of them can be trusted. Scoundrels, the whole lot of 'em. Andrew got a pardon, he did."

A pardon! That was the problem. The bushranger story, without a doubt.

"Denman wants to watch himself. His brother were no better. And bloody Denman"—she gave an irritated snort—"reckons he knows nothing about it. He was in with Bailey right from the start. Bloody thieves, the pair of them. They never should have trusted him."

"I'm sorry. I have no idea what you're talking about."

"Said he'd deliver thoroughbreds to a property outside Scone. But what happened? Did a runner, he did. Not only with the thoroughbreds, but with the drovers' wages too. There's many a family around here who suffered. Everyone knew they were in it together. Bailey and Denman. How else would he have found the money to set up that blacksmith business or make a claim on the Rossgole land?"

Bailey? Hadn't Denman said he'd made the bit for his brother, Bailey? "I'm very sorry for any hardship you and your family may have suffered." Lettie rolled up the map and edged toward the door. If only she hadn't mentioned Denman. It wasn't her argument. She wanted to know about Andrew. "Is there nothing else you can tell me about Andrew Hume? About the last time he was here?"

"I haven't got time to sit around chatting." She tightened her apron, a flash of color high on her cheeks, as though she'd said more than she intended. "Can't have been much more than ten, maybe eleven years old. Told you he turned up, stayed a couple of days, saw old Ginny, and took off. Never saw him again. Nor did poor Ginny. But for me she'd have died alone. Now . . ." She cocked her head, indicating the door.

"Thank you very much for your help."

"Nothing you couldn't have found out for yourself in Maitland."

That was about the strength of it. Except for the fact that Andrew Hume had called in here to see his old nursemaid. And she had a wrecked motor in the bargain and a question for Denman.

The door slammed behind her and she scuttled back down the path, the woman's story rolling around in her head. She was missing something.

22

W hen Lettie got back to the car she found Denman propped
against the bonnet, enjoying his pipe. "Any luck?" He tipped
his hat back and beamed.

"Maybe. I'm not sure. I made the mistake of mentioning your
name . . ."

"And you got a mouthful about me and me brother and the
thundering pair of scoundrels we were." He let out a huge bark of
laughter and slammed his hands against his thighs.

"Yes." Unsure whether to join in, she settled for a smile. Truth
be told, her curiosity was aroused.

"Time we were getting a move on if you want to get back to
Yellow Rock tonight." He straightened up. "You better hear my
side of the story."

"But you don't know what she said."

"Reckon I do. You can fill in the gaps if need be. Come along."

Once they were bowling back down the road, Denman turned
to Lettie. "What did she tell you? Let me guess. Bailey took off

with a pair of prized thoroughbreds and the drovers' wages and I was in it with him—that's why I've got me blacksmith business, and that's how Nathaniel's going to buy Rossgole."

"Pretty much."

"Mind you, if that was the case I can't understand why we waited that long to buy a property."

He had a point. "What happened to Bailey?"

He thumped his fist on his thigh and scowled. "He was no horse thief, and he wouldn't have done a runner with the drovers' wages. Wasn't built like that. More honor in that man than in any of these big-nosed squatters and landowners. Ask Olivia. She never believed he did it. He wouldn't have. Simple."

"What happened to him?"

Denman's face fell and he lifted his shoulders in defeat. "Never delivered the horses, nor the wages. Never saw him again."

For goodness' sake. No wonder the woman at Dartbrook didn't believe him.

Lettie concentrated on the road ahead until they reached Rossgole. The property sat bathed in a pool of sunshine, and there was no sign of the old man with the shotgun. She pulled up under a shady tree. Oxley gave a yelp of delight and disappeared over the edge of the car.

"That's a darn sight quicker than a wagon." Denman walked around the motor, smoothing his hand over the paintwork, wiping away the dust, and tutting at the scrapes and scratches. "Once we get back to Frog Hollow I'll stoke up the fire in me shed and see if I can get some of these bits and pieces welded back on."

"Really, it doesn't matter. How far is it back to Yellow Rock?" Suddenly she couldn't wait to be gone. "Fifty miles?"

"'Bout that." He scratched his chin, hovered for a moment

as though he wanted to say something, then shook his head and ambled off in the direction of the horses.

Lettie stuck two fingers in her mouth and blew, trying to emulate Denman's whistle, but achieved nothing but a pathetic hiss. "Oxley! Where are you?" The dog was becoming a nuisance. Better to let him have a wander because they'd be stuck in the car for hours and she was determined to make Yellow Rock before nightfall.

It seemed churlish to leave, but the sun was high and she wanted to be on the road as soon as possible. Her skin prickled; she could sense Olivia's concern.

She made a quick tour of last night's campsite, searching for Oxley, then joined Denman. "Nathaniel will have told Olivia where I am, won't he?"

"Said he would. No reason to doubt him. Not ever."

"I really think I should go. The motor is running quite well and the wheel will hold. I won't need the lamps as long as I'm back before dark."

"Reckon you're right."

They ambled back to the car. "And it doesn't look as though there's too much damage to the body." He bent down and wrapped his hands around the wheel and gave it a good shake. "That'll hold, no worries. Might be a good idea to call in and see Armstrong at the forge in Wollombi when you get back. Get him to check it over for you, fix the spindle and the lights." He pulled out a piece of twine and fastened it around the dangling lamp. "Just in case you need it."

"Thank you. I'll call in to the forge when I get back. Have you seen Oxley?"

Denman stuck his fingers into his mouth and produced a magnificent whistle that sent a curl of jealousy through her. "Will you teach me to do that?"

"Not now. Takes a bit of practice. Next time."

But would there be a next time? How strange. She'd given hardly a thought to Miriam and Pater since she left Sydney, and she was torn between leaving Denman and worrying about Olivia, and at the same time her thoughts kept drifting to Nathaniel. Oxley's wet nose buffeted her thigh.

"Thank you for your help." She held out her hand, then laughed as she realized he had an arm full of bridles and other harnesses for the wagon; instead, she wrapped her arm around his shoulders. "I hope I see you again soon." As she pulled back, the glitter of what might have been a tear in Denman's eye caught the sunlight.

"Off you go now." He cleared his throat. "Don't want Olivia on my back, telling me I didn't look after her niece."

"Grandniece," Lettie corrected. "She's my great-aunt."

"Right. Give her my regards."

Long ribbons of bullock wagons and jolting horses wove their way down the winding road. Carriers taking wool bales and goods to Sydney, passengers perched atop, every space utilized, and once in a while, when the road widened, Lettie managed to pass, waving hands and shrieks marking her progress. Then she'd crank up the speed on the flat, even surface until she reached another group and slowed again until she could pass. Oxley surveyed the scene with a regal stare, perched happily on the front seat, none of his previous desire to leap out of the car evident. There were hills, but nothing as steep as the climb into Singleton, and Lizzie handled everything with ease.

They made better time than she'd imagined and the sun was

still above the hills as she crossed Monkey Creek. Oxley let out a howl of pleasure and jumped into the back seat and stood with his paws up on her shoulders, ears flying in the breeze and his tongue lolling.

"Almost home." Home? That's what it felt like. And as unsettling as her sense of failure. She was no closer to finding out what had happened to Evie than when she first heard of her disappearance. She wanted the truth. Not Miriam's version, nor Olivia's, nor Denman's. The facts. But a thirty-year divide had created an impenetrable barricade.

She flew through Broke. A crowd of children playing on the common rushed to wave as she sped past. Oxley's excited barks, right in her left ear, almost deafened her.

With a sigh of relief she skidded into the driveway, inhaling the sweet clean air, the now familiar tang of eucalyptus and citrus, bowled down the drive, and drew to a halt beneath the spreading angophora.

Before she'd managed to remove her goggles, Olivia yanked the door open and wrapped her arms around her. "Let me look at you." She held her two inches away from her face and stared hard. "I was worried."

Lettie gave her a big hug and then disentangled herself and pulled off her goggles. "Didn't Nathaniel let you know what happened?"

"Yes, yes. But that's not the same. Down, Oxley, down. You're filthy and you smell of rancid rabbit, rats, and rotting leather. Go! Come along, come along. I want to hear all about it. Everything. You are not to leave a single moment out."

Which was exactly what was worrying Lettie. She had nothing to tell. Without answering she took Evie's map from the front seat and shuffled through the bits and pieces in the back.

"I expect you'd like a bath, and one for Oxley too."

Oxley shot a walleyed look at Olivia and slunk off, tail between his legs. "I'll get Peg to do it. She's tougher than I am." Olivia walked around the car, ran her hands over the scratches and dents in the paintwork, and caught sight of the bundle of broken metal and timber on the back seat. "It looks as though you have rather a lot to tell me. Come along."

Each step Lettie took underscored her exhaustion, her aching muscles, the throbbing in her head, and the strange sense of dislocation. The small stone house surrounded by lavender bushes and waving grass beckoned, more like home than the terrace in Macquarie Street.

"Sit yourself down." Olivia held out the chair and Lettie sank down with a sigh. "Stay right there. A cup of tea, and while you drink it I'll bring the bath in here. It's nice and warm."

She rested her head on her arms, the tension in her shoulders easing, and her eyelids drooped. Olivia banged and clattered around and kept up a constant stream of conversation. Some addressed to her, other sentences snapped at Oxley as he sat close to the range, the warm air intensifying his disgusting stench.

A cup of tea appeared in front of her, a plate of oatmeal biscuits, and by the time she'd drunk the tea Olivia had a hip bath in front of the range as good as hidden from sight by the clouds of lavender-scented steam.

Wrapped in one of Peg's enormous homespun jumpers and wearing another pair of patched moleskins, Lettie sat toasting her feet in front of the stove. The smell of roast chicken wafted around the kitchen and a very damp and somewhat bedraggled Oxley lay at her feet. Olivia fiddled around brushing her hair, patting her now and again on the shoulder, her mouth puckering, then opening, but no words issued forth. Lettie knew she would have to recount the story of the last few days and, worse, tell Olivia that she, like everyone else, had found no trace of Evie. It had been nothing more than a wild, and somewhat dangerous, goose chase.

Finally Olivia plonked down in the chair and drew in a deep breath. "I'm sorry. I can't wait a moment longer. I know you're exhausted, but tell me. What did you discover?"

Where to start? Perhaps this was one of those occasions when the beginning wasn't the correct place. She reached over for Olivia's hand. "I'm sorry. I've very little to tell. In fact, nothing."

"Nothing," growled Peg from the other side of the kitchen. "You were gone for days and you've nothing to show for it. Start at the beginning."

"Gently, Peg. The poor girl is worn out." Olivia squeezed her hand tightly, belying her comment.

She drew in a deep breath. "I drove to Maitland. You were right, there was no property. A family by the name of Hume lived in Largs, years ago. The rest of the family have left the area. I found two gravestones, Hannah and David Hume. They apparently had a store in Maitland for many years and bought a small property in Largs when they sold the business."

"And it was the property Evie had marked on the map."

"Yes. No one remembered Evie, only Mr. and Mrs. Hume. A woman I met mentioned the fact they had a son who had grown up at Dartbrook—Andrew. I thought perhaps he was the same Andrew mentioned in Evie's notes. I decided to go to Dartbrook and see if I could find out anything about him. That's when I ran off the road and damaged the car. Fortunately Nathaniel came to my rescue and took me back to Frog Hollow."

"Denman's place."

"Yes, that's right. Nathaniel had business in Sydney."

"To put his bid down on the property up there he's got his eye on."

Lettie nodded, the warmth of the room and the effort of speaking draining her. She covered her mouth and yawned. "Denman and I pulled the car out, but it took longer than we expected. I didn't leave until this morning."

"And what about these Humes?" Peg thumped some plates down on the table.

"They were very old when they died; he was eighty-four and she was seventy-eight."

"Not that old," Olivia mumbled under her breath.

Peg nodded her agreement. "Threescore years and ten plus a bit. It's a good age."

"Enough of that. What has this Andrew Hume got to do with anything?" Olivia asked.

"Well, nothing very much. All I found out was that he had lived at Dartbrook as a child and he had visited, to see his old nursemaid Ginny, but she'd since died and the Hall family have moved on. Maybe Evie went looking for Ginny. I can't imagine why, though. Andrew never lived in Maitland. He and his parents didn't get on. Ashamed by his arrest. He was a bushranger." Lettie's eyes grew heavier and Olivia's hold on her hand tightened.

"Denman came with me when I went up to Dartbrook. The place was deserted. Just this one woman living there. The main house was boarded up. She seemed to be living in the kitchen out at the back. I made the mistake of saying Denman was with me. He was waiting out at the car. She said some very unpleasant things about him and his brother, Bailey."

Olivia's forehead wrinkled into a frown, then she turned her gaze to the fire, blinking and chewing her lip.

"The woman knew nothing about Evie. No help at all, and I don't think she was hiding anything. The only link to Evie's map was the name Hume written outside Maitland. Hume died in the desert in 1874, which we found in Evie's notes, so she knew that before she left." She let out a sigh, the warmth of the fire and her tiredness making it impossible to concentrate. "And then I came back."

"Well, that's all of a fuss about nothing and now you've got a damaged motor for your trouble."

"Peg!" Olivia glared, patting Lettie's hand in sympathy.

"You know what I think. What everyone thinks. Evie never left the area, never made it to Glendon, never mind Maitland, no matter what she might have drawn on that map of hers. Lettie might as well be chasing elephants. It's time you gave this away, Olly. It's doing you no good, and no one else." She nodded her head in Lettie's direction. "This chicken's ready."

They ate in silence, each woman wrapped in her own thoughts. Lettie's eyelids kept closing and her whole body felt as heavy as her heart. She'd set out full of such hopes and expectations, intent on solving the mystery of Evie's disappearance, not only for Olivia but for herself as well. She'd become ensnared by the story, but despite Denman's insistence, she couldn't believe Evie had been taken by the rock.

Was there any point in continuing? This wasn't the reason she'd come to Yellow Rock. Olivia had lived with Evie's disappearance for thirty years. She'd tried, but there was little more she could do.

244

Perhaps now was the time to leave; she'd done nothing but bring bad news and stir up troublesome memories. Yet she couldn't articulate the words to give up.

She pulled herself to her feet, reluctant to leave the comfort and security of the kitchen. "I'm sorry, so very sorry. I wanted to find her for you, to make everything right."

"You have done more for me than you can imagine," Olivia said. "You've brought Evie back to me. Your every movement reminds me of her, the way you hold your pencil, the way you brush your hair from your face and squint up at the sun. That little frown between your eyebrows when you're concentrating. I want you to stay. Stay here where you belong. Are you happy to be here?"

At this very moment she was, not happy with herself and her failure to find out what happened to Evie, but happy to be back home at Yellow Rock. "I am. More settled than I was in Sydney. I can't be what Miriam wants me to be. I needed saving, from myself and from the dark place I'd inhabited since Thorne's death."

Olivia's hand rested on her shoulder and gave it a squeeze. And in that moment Lettie understood that both she and Olivia carried the same pain. A pain that would never go away, should never go away. Because love and loss hurt. She couldn't give up now; she owed it to Olivia to help her at least find closure.

"I'm not ready to give up. I'm convinced there's something I've missed. I'm going to go back over the map and the notebooks in the study, starting tomorrow." She had to solve the mystery. It was the only way to be free of its stranglehold. Evie would have returned if she could. She loved Yellow Rock and Olivia. The only person she loved more was her father. The clue to Evie's disappearance lay in William's obsession with Leichhardt. "Andrew Hume is the person who connects everything."

23

It was close to midnight when Nathaniel arrived at Yellow Rock. Under the full moon the sight of Lettie's car beneath the angophora took some of the weight off his shoulders. Denman would have towed it out right enough, but he knew nothing about engines. Not that Nathaniel did either. He'd like to hear how they managed; quite a story, no doubt. Quite a girl, too, and obviously knew her motor car. His lips twitched, the memory of their first meeting crystal clear, and his mood lightened. There'd be another property, maybe not the one he'd set his heart on, but it wasn't the end.

He swung the gate wide and led the stallion he'd picked up at Randwick into the mating paddock. He'd be happy enough there until morning, and Olivia always ensured the water troughs were full. No other way she could run the place single-handed unless she had a strict set of rules. Her rules. And there were plenty of those. None he wished to get tied up in tonight. He'd bunk down in the stables with Raven and in the morning stick his head in before he headed back to deliver the bad news to Denman.

He sure didn't want to. There was no way to soften the blow.

Outbid. Simple as that. It hadn't occurred to him, or Denman, for that matter, that anyone else would be interested in the lot they had their eyes on.

Nothing he could do. He'd made it to Sydney with time to spare, thought it was a done deal, just hadn't realized how much the land was worth.

He rolled out his swag and threw it down on a pile of hay, a darn sight more comfortable than the last couple of nights at Randwick with the constant hullabaloo. Nothing at Yellow Rock but velvet sky and pinprick stars and the sweet smell of hay.

No lights on in the farmhouse. Olivia'd be fast asleep and Lettie—better he didn't dwell too much on Lettie. She'd been taking up far too much room in his head. Way out of his league, though he couldn't shake the feel of her body pressed against him and the sweet scent of her hair as they'd come careering down the mountain. Probably not the gentlemanly thing to do. He could have walked, led the horse.

He stretched his arms over his head and stomped outside. One single lamp flickered somewhere in the main house, one of the downstairs rooms. Maybe Olivia hadn't turned in, maybe Lettie . . .

A soft growl turned to a yap of pleasure and Oxley threw himself through the darkness, paws landing on his shoulders good as knocking him for six. "Woohoo! Down boy, down." A great, wet, rubbery tongue lathered his cheek before the quivering bundle subsided at his feet. "What are you doing out here at this time of night? Thought you got the kitchen floor."

"He does. That way I know when there's trespassers." Olivia's swaddled form came into view, shotgun propped under her arm and some sort of blanket thrown across her shoulders covering her nightclothes. "Be manners to let me know you'd arrived."

"Didn't want to wake you."

"Oxley took care of that. Where's the stallion?"

"In the breeding paddock. Safe and sound. Good-looking horse."

"Hope so. I'm planning on filling the paddocks with his progeny next year." She unhooked the lamp from the wall, and the rasp of a Congreve match and the smell of sulfur hit before the wick spluttered to life, bathing her in a pool of yellow light.

He raked his hand through his hair. "Been a long day. Thought I'd bed down here." He gestured to his swag laid out over the straw. "That okay with you?"

"You know it is." She frowned and moved a bit closer. "What's the matter with you? You look as though you've lost a quid and found sixpence."

He spluttered out something that might, if he was lucky, pass for a laugh. It didn't fool Olivia. She brought the lamp closer. "What's the matter? Everything okay? Denman?"

"He's fine, least he was when I left him. Did Lettie get back all right? Saw her car under the angophora."

"She did. I owe you thanks for that. She told me what you did. I suppose I should be addressing you as Nathaniel Poole, Esquire."

He scuffed his boots in the dirt. Why did he feel as though he'd failed, and failed miserably? He'd done the best he could. And it hadn't been good enough. He dreaded breaking the news to Denman. He'd set his heart on living out his life on that block of dirt.

"Nah. Didn't get it. Outbid." There, it was said.

Olivia reached out her hand, squeezed his forearm. "I'm sorry. I know you had your heart set on Rossgole. Denman too."

248

"Nothing to be done." He shrugged her off, turned before she could see how deeply the whole fiasco cut.

"Sure you don't want anything? Cup of tea? Something stronger?"

He shook his head. "A decent night's sleep'll see me right."

"Come up to the farmhouse for breakfast before you go. Lettie'll want to see you. Might do her good, get her out of William's bloody study. She's become as obsessed as he was about this bloody nonsense."

"Leichhardt or Evie?"

She nodded her head, acknowledging the truth. "Evie, more'n like. Failure sits hard on young shoulders." She threw him a knowing look, handed him the lamp, whistled softly through her teeth for Oxley, and disappeared into the darkness, shotgun tucked snugly under her arm.

Oxley woke Nathaniel just as the sun crested the rise, sent no doubt by Olivia to ensure he didn't slip away. He doused his head in the water bucket, wiped away the sleep, then let Raven out into the small yard with some oats for company. A quick cup of tea and he'd be on his way. Frog Hollow by nightfall and get the job done, break the news to Denman.

The smell of bacon lured him to the kitchen; perhaps a little more than a cup of tea wouldn't go amiss.

Shotgun replaced by a frying pan, Olivia stood at the stove with Oxley salivating at her feet, but no sign of Lettie. "Morning." She shoveled a mound of bacon onto a plate, added some bread, and dumped it down on the table. "Get that into you. Might bring some color to your face. You look as though you haven't seen a decent feed for weeks."

Correct as usual, though not weeks. Hadn't paid much attention to anything bar the chase down to Sydney and an equally quick escape. If it hadn't been for the stallion that needed to be dropped off at Yellow Rock and the horse he'd borrowed from Olivia, he'd be a darn sight closer to Frog Hollow. A night's sleep had done little to improve his mood. He wedged the bacon between the two slices of bread and bit down. A mug of tea appeared in front of him and Olivia sat down, chin resting in her cupped hand.

"Lettie still abed?" he asked once he'd swallowed the first mouthful.

"Doubt it. She's slept the last couple of nights in the study. I'll take her something once I've got you sorted."

"What's she up to?"

"Thinks she's missed something. Before she left she showed me a map of Evie's she'd found. Had a place called Hume marked just outside Maitland. Told her there was nowhere with that name, but she thought there was something in it—that's why she took off in the first place. Reckoned it was some message Evie had left and that she hadn't told the truth. Had no intention of painting and then going out to Glendon. Was off in search of some fellow, Andrew Hume, something to do with Leichhardt. I can't believe that Evie didn't tell me the truth. She'd never done that before in her life, not ever."

Then everything became quiet. Nathaniel finished the sandwich, pushed away his plate, and waited for the rest.

"Lettie's disappointed, dispirited. I want her to stop this madness. It's consuming her the same way it consumed Evie."

Now matters became a little clearer. According to Denman,

Olivia had always shouldered the responsibility for Evie's disappearance, but there was more to it. Some argument about the property. Everyone knew the Maynard land was Olivia's, and the Ludgrove land was held in trust for Evie. Olivia had hardly a penny to her name but more land than she knew what to do with. Miriam and Rawlings had ended up with the hard-folding stuff.

"I thought perhaps"—Olivia's words broke into his thoughts and his head came up with a snap—"thought perhaps you could take Lettie over some breakfast." She nodded at the tray laid for one, napkin and all. "Have a chat. Make sure she's all right."

"I need to be on my way." Coward that he was. Needed to tell Denman, wasn't fair that he should be the last to know his promise, their dream, had come to naught.

Olivia narrowed her eyes. "I'm not asking for much. Just half an hour of your time. It's not like she's difficult to get along with."

Couldn't argue about that. He huffed out a sigh. "Give me the tray. I'll take it over there, see if I can find out what she's up to. I'm out of here in under an hour or I'll never make it back before nightfall."

"You will if you take Raven. I sent the nag you borrowed back to Singleton."

"I'm not planning on coming back this way for a while."

"And I'm not planning on going anywhere. Get him back next time you come through."

"Thanks, thanks a lot. I'll take this over to Lettie."

Nathaniel shouldered open the front door, then paused. He didn't want to scare the living daylights out of Lettie and wasn't sure how she'd feel about the way he'd up and left her with Denman. He'd have to explain about the land. How important it was to both of them. It would take a lot longer than half an hour.

"Lettie?"

Oxley appeared in the doorway, emitted a mumbled growl, then inhaled the smell of bacon and wagged his tail.

"Nathaniel! Come in." The greeting sounded as though she was pleased to see him.

He stepped over the threshold and came to a grinding halt. He'd never set foot in the main house. It had been closed up for as long as he could remember.

"Are you coming in?"

He stepped into the study where shafts of sunlight shone through the open doors, throwing an almost ethereal aura around her head.

Papers lay strewn on every available space, old newspapers, pamphlets, open books, and maps, more maps and books than he'd ever seen in his life. "Olivia thought you could do with some breakfast." He offered the tray like some sort of dumbwaiter.

She sprang to her feet, and he had the strangest sensation that she might throw her arms around him; instead, she came around the desk and took the tray from him. "What are you doing here?"

"On my way back from Sydney. Had to drop off a stallion, then I'm heading back to Frog Hollow."

"Did you get to Sydney in time for the auction?" He nodded. "Denman will be thrilled. We camped the night at Rossgole after we got the car out. He told me all about it. How long you'd been waiting. Then we got chased off by some old man with a shotgun who reckoned we were on his property. Denman put him right." She pushed aside some papers from a small table and put the tray down, then took a huge bite of the bacon sandwich.

"That'd be Fred Parker. He's squatted on the land for longer than I can remember." No point in beating around the bush. Had to explain that he'd been outbid. "I was going to tell him he could stay. Doesn't matter much now. I didn't get the land. Price was too high. Parker'll have to deal with the new owners." He tried for a nonchalant shrug and failed. "There'll be another property."

Her lovely hazel-green eyes widened in sympathy. "Oh! I'm sorry. I felt guilty when Denman explained that you'd risked missing the auction when you rescued me. And I hadn't said thank you. Will you forgive me?" She threw him a smile, and he could have forgiven her the world.

"Nothing to be done. Not your fault, but I've got to get going. It's a good ride. You all right?"

"Yes. Busy."

"Olivia said she's worried about you. Working too hard on all this." He gestured to the pile of papers on the desk.

"Oh! I don't want to worry her, but I don't seem to have gotten any further than the day I left. I was certain Evie's map held the answer. This Andrew Hume. I'm sure he has something to do with her disappearance."

"Did you get to Dartbrook?"

She nodded, finished the remains of her mouthful, and slipped the rest of the sandwich to Oxley. "They told me about Bailey, how he'd taken off with the thoroughbreds and the drovers' wages. I can't imagine Denman's brother doing something like that."

"He didn't. He wouldn't."

"Why are you so sure?"

"Same reason as you. That family hasn't got a mean bone in their body. Honest as the day is long. I wouldn't be standing here today if it hadn't been for them."

"What do you mean?"

It wasn't something he ever talked about, not that he'd taken

253

Denman for granted—that's what the land was all about. A thank-you of sorts. His turn to do the looking after. "I was born out on the road, and my mother didn't make it. I was in the saddle before I could walk, and Denman took me in after my father was killed taking a mob across the Hawkesbury River. Denman brought me up. If it hadn't been for him . . ." His throat rasped. "He took me under his wing. Everyone thought Denman was in on it with Bailey. He tried and tried to prove Bailey hadn't done a runner. Gave up in the end, couldn't fight the rest of the drovers, couldn't take the gossip and bad feeling. He gave up droving, then started his own blacksmith's shop. Always said he did it so I'd have a place to call home and could go to school. Either way, it worked out for the best. That's how we came to be at Frog Hollow."

"I'm sorry. I didn't realize."

"Nothing to be sorry about. Best thing that could have happened to me."

"And you never found out what happened to Bailey?"

"Nope."

Yellow Rock glinted in the sunshine and the sound of a motor broke the silence. "Time I was going." As he made his way to the door, a large black car slid to a halt outside the house. "Looks like you've got visitors. I'll go out the back."

24

"Visitors?" Lettie stepped up to the french doors and her heart sank. An apparition swathed in a voluminous dustcoat with a huge hat anchored by a vast expanse of gauzy material sat in the front seat of a large black motor car.

Miriam!

An icy rash slicked her skin. Not now. Not today.

Connors helped Miriam from the car. She unbuttoned the dustcoat to reveal her prized ankle-length mink coat. She meant business. With one hand resting on Connors's arm she swanned up the path to the front door. Oxley lifted his head and eased to his feet, hackles rising.

"I don't want to talk to Mother." Lettie clapped her hand over her mouth, trapping her childish whine. What was the matter with her? She had nothing to hide. She'd written to Miriam and told her she would be staying. Miriam knew nothing of her fruitless jaunt to Dartbrook or the accident.

Like a wraith Peg appeared in the hallway. "Why is she here?" Lettie hissed.

"Very good question, and one I haven't got a decent answer to. She hasn't set foot on the property for nigh on twenty years. Why did she send you here?"

"Ah!" Lettie blushed to the roots of her hair, closed her eyes for a moment. "I was supposed to discuss Thorne's inheritance. Well, I didn't . . . I couldn't . . . not once Olivia had told me about Evie. I wanted to help her find out what happened. That's all." She let her hands fall, kept her eyes downcast. Most of her fingernails were chipped and broken. Miriam would jump on that the moment she saw her. And her clothes. Oh, God! She couldn't face her.

Peg raised her fingers to her lips and gestured to the sitting room. "Olivia's in the stables. I'll go down and tell her Miriam's here. You entertain your mother." She quirked an apologetic grin and vanished.

Drawing in a fortifying breath, Lettie opened the door. "Mother. What a surprise." The familiar waft of lily of the valley prickled her nose.

"That will be all, Connors." Miriam waved her hand vaguely in the direction of the motor and marched through the door.

Lettie closed the study door and ran her hands over her hair. There was little point in worrying about what she looked like; Miriam's face said it all.

With Oxley grumbling at her heels, Lettie made her way into the sitting room where Miriam took a seat, hands in her lap, feet crossed neatly at the ankles. Only the tapping of her index finger against her leather gloves gave any indication of possible discomfort, or was it impatience?

"Mother." Lettie leaned forward, intending to drop a kiss on

Miriam's cheek. Before she had the opportunity, Oxley barged between them, lowered his muzzle until it was whisper-close to Miriam's face, and growled softly, his intent clear.

Miriam reared back. "Call him off."

"Oxley! Down!" Lettie hauled him back by the scruff of his neck.

"Revolting hound. He smells possibly worse than his predecessors and has no sense of place."

Lettie pointed to the corner of the room and Oxley threw himself down, his ears still cocked and the corner of his lip caught on his teeth.

"For goodness' sake, child, I hardly recognize you."

Lettie pulled at the frayed cuffs of the homespun jumper. "We weren't expecting company. I was on my way to help Aunt Olivia in the stables," she lied.

"Family is hardly company. I'd like some refreshment. We broke the journey at Wiseman's Ferry and have been traveling since first light. Something for Connors too. He's out at the motor. I presume you can manage to arrange that."

Acid rose in Lettie's throat. This was all her fault. She should have known she'd left it too long, should have sent Miriam another letter. Miriam's curiosity would have gotten the better of her—that and her impatience to know whether Lettie had convinced Olivia that she should inherit in Thorne's stead. Unless Miriam had simply come to take matters into her own hands.

The thought horrified her. It would mean she would have to leave. She didn't want to go back to Sydney. Had no intention of doing so. The continual round of engagements and fawning suitors held even less appeal now that she'd had a taste of freedom.

And then the slow realization dawned. She didn't have to

return to Sydney. It would be Olivia's decision to ask her to leave. She didn't have to acquiesce to Miriam's demands.

The surge of defiance took her by surprise, and she squarely met Miriam's gaze. "What are you doing here, Mother? The whole idea was that I should come and save you the trip. I wrote to you and told you I would be staying." She'd hardly given Miriam the opportunity to even speak. The past few weeks had made her realize exactly how Miriam dictated her life, choosing her friends, determining her schedule. Not anymore.

Miriam lowered her voice to a conspiratorial whisper. "You don't understand Olivia."

Lettie reared back. "I like her and I trust her."

"Whereas you don't trust your own mother." It wasn't a question. It was a statement of fact. "Do I need to remind you that I have known Olivia all of my life? Can't you see the danger you're in?"

Danger? Lettie gave a feeble laugh. No danger other than that of her own making, a foolhardy accident in the motor. "I'm staying, Mother!" It wasn't until the words left her lips that she realized the truth. Yellow Rock had truly seeped into her blood. Yellow Rock was part of her. She wasn't ready to leave. Not yet.

"As much as Olivia might be family, she is not your friend. Come back to Sydney and we will let the solicitors deal with the legalities. It was a mistake, my mistake, in allowing you to come."

An apology? An admission of failure? The likes of which had never passed Miriam's lips before. Lettie tried to reply but the words wouldn't come; she couldn't form a simple sentence. It was ridiculous. Her heart was pounding nineteen to the dozen and she felt as though she'd committed some outrageous atrocity. She drew in a breath.

"What are you doing here?" she repeated.

"What do you think? You have obviously failed in your task. I'm here to take you home. I can only presume Olivia has spun some yarn and entrapped you."

Lettie took a deep breath and swallowed her desire to ask Miriam why she hadn't told the truth about Evie, why she'd said she'd died in childhood, but what was the point? She'd simply say she didn't want to discuss it, repeat some platitude about opening old wounds . . .

"Why do you think your grandfather made me leave Yellow Rock?"

Lettie's head came up with a snap. "Because you and Pater were to be married."

"Letitia, didn't you listen to a word I said?"

Miriam had told her to be careful, that Olivia couldn't lie straight in bed, was loose with the truth, every other cliché she could summon, but nothing else. Nothing about her sister, Evie, who hadn't died in childhood as she'd always maintained. "What about Evie? You didn't tell me the truth."

"For goodness' sake. What are you talking about?"

How much longer was she going to keep this up? "Evie didn't die when she was a child. She vanished when she was eighteen. No one knows what happened to her. I intend to find the truth."

Miriam let out a dismissive huff. "Another of Olivia's fantasies."

"If she died when she was young, where is she buried? There's no headstone in the family plot."

The moment's silence that followed allowed Lettie to compose herself, not be swayed as she once would have been. "I am an adult. I make my own decisions. Choose my own truths. I'm staying here until I decide otherwise."

In a second Miriam was on her feet, her face close to Lettie's. "You must not be swayed by Olivia's yarns. You will do what I—"

Before Miriam could finish her sentence, Oxley sneaked between them, hackles raised, teeth bared.

"If you can't control that dog, I shall call Connors."

"I've always found Oxley to be an excellent judge of character." Olivia's voice held a tinge of amusement as she clicked her fingers and Oxley subsided to the floor.

"To what do we owe the pleasure, Miriam?"

How had Olivia arrived so quickly? She couldn't have been in the stables, as Peg suggested, because she was dressed in her dark skirt and blouse, looking every inch the lady of the house.

"This is most unexpected." Olivia settled in the chair opposite Miriam, arranging her skirt, her back as straight as a die. "Now which specific *yarn* would you like to discuss?"

Unable to stay still for a moment longer, Lettie made for the door.

Olivia glared at her. "Sit down. I'd like you to hear what your mother has to say."

Lettie sank onto the edge of a chair, her gaze darting between the two women. The beginnings of a dowager's hump showed beneath Miriam's coat, whereas years of outdoor work with the horses had served Olivia well, straighter, taller even when seated, despite the generation that separated them.

Miriam moistened her lips and swallowed. "Thorne was to inherit Ludgrove on his thirtieth birthday."

"A birthday he sadly didn't see." Olivia's tone reminded Lettie of the fact she was Miriam's aunt, the matriarch of the family, no matter what Miriam might like to imagine. "I think you've forgotten the intricacies of William's will. In the event of Thorne's demise before he inherited Ludgrove, I remain trustee of the property."

"Lettie is Thorne's heir and therefore next in line." Miriam drew herself up. "Pa's dying wish was that the properties should remain united. Therefore, Lettie should inherit both the Maynard and Ludgrove properties."

"That is my decision." Not a flicker of emotion showed on Olivia's face.

"Both properties must pass to Letitia, if the future is to be secured. The law has changed. Women can own property in their own right. It will not pass to her husband. Letitia is therefore the rightful owner of both the Ludgrove land, and when you pass—"

"Which won't be any time soon. You can wipe that avaricious look off your face. It may have been William's wish for the properties to be united; however, the decision as to who inherits is mine, and mine alone."

Lettie kept her hands firmly in her lap, fingers interlaced, as the two women tossed the conversation between them. Lettie was certain Thorne had never entertained the thought that she would inherit in his place. He'd always said the motor would be hers if anything happened to him. She doubted he'd ever thought any further than that. He'd lived for the moment and died before he could inherit. Just that one idea to come and visit Olivia and introduce himself, the only pointer to the future, a future he'd never see.

Lettie stood up. There was little reason for her to be in the room. Neither Olivia nor Miriam could settle the debate. It would require legal consultation; in that regard Miriam was correct.

A fine sheen covered Miriam's face and she tugged at the collar of her coat. "I am entitled to benefit from the inheritance." Her voice quavered. "I am the only woman to produce an heir in the last generation. Both properties belong to the Rawlings family."

And with a flash of blinding clarity, Lettie understood. It had nothing to do with her and everything to do with Miriam.

"For goodness' sake." Miriam rolled her eyes to the ceiling.

"Haven't you come to terms with it yet? Evie is dead. Ludgrove belongs to the Rawlings family, as will Maynard once you pass."

"It is my decision. Thorne had no legal claim to Maynard. Why should he?"

"Because he was my son, and because it was Pa's dying wish for the properties to be united."

The silence hung long and low like the thunderclouds above Yellow Rock. Color suffused Miriam's cheeks and her eyes widened. She cleared her throat. "Because he is . . . was . . . This is ridiculous. We are going around and around in circles."

For the first time in longer than she could remember, Lettie agreed with Miriam.

"There is little point in raking up old arguments, arguments that cannot be proven, that only go to your jealousy and petty—"

Before Miriam finished her sentence, Olivia jumped in. "There is nothing petty about the truth, nor about the reason your marriage was indecently hasty."

Miriam's cheeks flushed and her lips pinched. "That is none of your business. None of anyone's business." She smoothed her hands down her skirt. "You're nothing but a jealous old woman."

"I might be old, but there's nothing wrong with my memory."

Miriam struggled to her feet. "Keep your malicious thoughts to yourself. Letitia, go and pack your bag. We're leaving."

Lettie jumped. "Leaving?"

"I came here to settle the matter amicably, but I see that was a foolish mistake. I have taken rooms at the Family Hotel. We will spend the night there and return to Sydney on the morrow and seek legal consultation."

No. That was not what she wanted. "I can't return to Sydney. Thorne's car needs repair."

Miriam narrowed her gaze. "Repair? Why does it need repair?"

Lettie cleared her throat. "I had a slight accident."

"For goodness' sake, girl, is there nothing you can successfully accomplish? Connors can see to the car and we will leave in the morning."

Miriam had an answer for everything. "I have to take it to the blacksmith for repairs before I can make the return journey to Sydney." Lettie lifted her chin.

Olivia stood up, walked to the door, and held it open. "I suggest that you leave, Miriam. Lettie will see you in the morning in Wollombi once she has made her decision." Leaving the door ajar, Olivia swept from the room, only the *tip-tapping* of her heels offering any form of farewell.

Sometime later Lettie heard the motor start and the gravel crunch as Connors and hopefully Miriam left. She raised her head and pulled her feet up beneath her, not knowing what to do next. Should she go and speak to Olivia? She wasn't ready to go back to her old life. She wanted to stay and finish what she'd started. Inheriting Ludgrove was of no consequence; until she knew what had happened to Evie, she couldn't consider the matter.

Lettie scraped back her hair and followed the cloud of dust as Connors took the driveway at a ridiculous speed. Almost as much dust and clouds as Evie had drawn around the trail of cattle making their way up the stock route. Lettie's resolve firmed as she slipped out of the sitting room. She would not be a pawn in the age-old chess game the two women insisted on playing.

Reaching down, she scratched Oxley's head, then made her way outside for a breath of air. Despite the chill in the air, the sky was bright and the sun warm. She'd promised Olivia she would attend to the study, and there might well be something she'd missed in her madcap race to Maitland and Dartbrook. Settling into a chair on the corner of the veranda, she tipped her head and watched the eagles riding the currents far above the tension and familial disunity pervading the property.

Sometime later Oxley lifted his head, sniffed the air, and took off. Peg came into view striding across the paddock between the two houses. Lettie walked down to meet her.

"There seems to be some debate about whether you're leaving with your mother. Are you?"

The thing Lettie liked most about Peg was her blunt approach. No words couched in double meanings. She dealt in facts.

"No." The word was out of Lettie's mouth before she gave it a second thought. "I can't leave the motor. It needs some more work. And there are other things . . . William's papers, for example."

"Good girl." Peg gave her shoulder an absentminded pat, rather as she did Oxley, and turned. "Let her ladyship stew overnight, then I'll send Sam to let her know in the morning."

"Will Olivia mind if I stay?"

Peg raised one heavy eyebrow, pursed her lips, and didn't bother to answer.

Apart from the horrific thought of being trapped in a car with Miriam for the best part of a day, she had no desire to return to Sydney. Not before she had done what she set out to do—make sure she'd missed nothing in the study that explained Evie's fate.

25

A lot more than an hour had passed before Nathaniel got back on the road. Hopefully Olivia and Lettie had sorted out Miriam. If the rumors around Randwick were to be believed, she could be as wild-winged as an unbroken colt if she didn't get her way.

Although busy, the road wasn't jammed the way it used to be. Trains were moving more than people these days: livestock, goods, and a whole lot more. Not that he was overly keen on the huffing, puffing monsters, but they had their uses.

Once again it was dark before he and Raven arrived at Frog Hollow, but a light still burned in the house and the old man sat silhouetted on the veranda.

Nathaniel's *cooee* received no welcoming wave. An icy blast gut-punched him. He shot from the saddle and took the steps three at a time.

Denman's head lifted slowly and a pair of rheumy eyes pinned him.

"You okay?"

"Aye." Denman dropped his head, peered into his lap at a piece of metal he was working compulsively with his fingers.

"I planned on being back here earlier, but I picked up a job—a stallion had to be delivered to Yellow Rock. I stopped for the night, got tied up with Olivia and Lettie. Then Miriam Rawlings turned up and there was some sort of barney." He might have been talking to a rock. Denman didn't flick a gaze in his direction, didn't acknowledge his words. "Lettie got back without any worries. You must have done a good job on that motor of hers. It didn't look too bad to me."

Still no response.

Nathaniel dropped to his haunches, rested his hand on the old man's knee. "Come on, why don't we get you to bed." He inhaled deeply—no smell of rum. Denman rarely touched the stuff, just a dash in his tea now and again—he certainly wasn't drunk. More as though he was in a trance or something. Had he taken a turn? Had the trouble with Lettie been too much for him? "Come on, old fella." He tugged at Denman's hand, but he pulled away, stuffed the lump of metal in his pocket, batted Nathaniel back, and eased to his feet.

"Go and look after Olivia's horse or you'll never hear the end of it. I'm fine. I've got the billy on."

Nathaniel let his breath go. Denman looked steady enough on his feet. "Right you are. Won't be a tick. A quick rubdown and some tucker, then I'll be back."

"There's oats in the stable."

That was more like it. Strange he hadn't asked about the auction. Well and good. Better told over a cup of tea. By the time he returned from the stable, Denman was back on the veranda, two cups of tea sitting on the rail, the steam curling in the night air. Nathaniel plonked down next to the old man, took the cup, inhaled, and sipped the sweet black brew. Perhaps bad news was better kept until morning. He studied Denman's familiar face as he peered out into the darkness, one hand in his pocket, the other clasped around his tin mug.

Finally Denman broke the silence. "Here. Take a look at this." He pulled his hand from his pocket and held out his palm, flat.

A lump of metal, big enough to wrap his hand around. Nathaniel picked it up, hefted it, and turned it over.

"What do you reckon it is?"

"Looks like a bit to me." Nathaniel put down his cup, scooted forward into the light, and turned the metal.

Denman grunted his approval. "Not any bit."

Nathaniel squinted down, turned it this way and that. "Got your mark on it. One of yours. And it's heavier than usual."

"That's because of the copper inlay."

Nathaniel whistled through his teeth. He hadn't known that Denman did such intricate work. Usually solid, cheap, serviceable. "Must be pretty special. Looks old."

"'Tis."

Nathaniel handed the bit back to Denman. He slipped it into his pocket and they sat together looking out toward the hills of Rossgole. A view he'd hoped he'd be able to call their own. "I've got news. It's not the best."

"I made this for Bailey."

Not the right moment. Denman had something on his mind; there'd be no stopping him, and if he was talking about Bailey, then it was important. "And you've kept it for him?" That could be the only answer. Perhaps the mob at Dartbrook had another go at him; he still wore the brunt of the local belief that Bailey'd done a runner, though where the hell he'd gone and how he'd managed it no one could say.

"No. He used it from the moment I gave it to him. Never used another. It's the copper in the brass. It produces a sweet taste, makes the horse salivate, then they accept the bit more readily."

Nathaniel tossed the information around in his head. "Where did you find it?"

"I didn't. Lettie did."

"Lettie." It was getting stranger by the moment. Lettie had said nothing about the bit. Only that the woman at Dartbrook had mentioned Bailey doing a runner with the wages and the thoroughbreds.

"Must have been in the stream where she bogged the car. She'd knocked off a lamp and a few other bits and pieces, scooped them all up, and thrown them in the car before you picked her up."

He thought back to the night; his mind hadn't been on what she'd done, more the way she'd nestled against his chest on the ride down the hill. "How the hell did it get there?"

"A question I keep asking myself. Means Bailey must have been close by, could have washed downstream over time. Must have let his horse free too." Denman turned the bit over and over in his hand, compulsively smoothing the shiny metal.

"You cleaned that up since you found it?"

The old man pinned him with a stare. "Told you Lettie picked it up with all the bits and pieces that had fallen off her motor and some charred bits of timber."

"Charred? Like fire, you mean."

"Yep. Lettie and I came across old Fred Parker. Wanted to ask him a question or two. See if he could remember a bushfire through that way."

"And what did you get for your trouble? A bullet in your pants?"

"Pretty much." Denman raised his shoulders. "Had Lettie with me. Wasn't about to risk it. Still maintains the property is his. Squatters' rights, I'm guessing."

Denman's words sat heavy in the night air, but Nathaniel needed to sort out this business about Bailey before he gave Denman the news. "And you think Bailey was up that way."

"Stands to reason, doesn't it? If his bit was there."

It all made perfect sense, but it didn't bode well for Bailey. Why would Bailey be cutting through there? He'd be better heading up the main stock route. Wouldn't want to do it today, never mind thirty-odd years ago. "I'll go and have a word with Parker in the morning."

Denman grunted his approval. "Now, are you going to tell me what happened at the land sale?"

Nathaniel lifted his hat and raked his fingers through his hair. "We couldn't do it."

"Outbid."

"Yep. I know how much you wanted it. Didn't have enough. Just outbid, plain and simple."

Denman raised his hands. "Can't do much about it. There'll be other blocks."

But Nathaniel wasn't sure he wanted to wait that long. In fact, he didn't know what he wanted. Even Denman's company wasn't enough tonight. He needed a change, something had to change. Only trouble was, he didn't know what.

While the moon rose and set and dawn approached, Nathaniel tossed and turned in the loft; Lettie's scent clung to the hay, filling his mind with far-fetched dreams. When he couldn't stand it any longer, he went in search of tea.

Denman had beaten him to it, had the billy rattling away on the fire. He thrust a mug into his hands. "I've been thinking."

"About Bailey?"

"Yeah. We know he left Yellow Rock, collected the pair of thoroughbreds in Maitland to deliver to Scone, then said he'd catch up with the mob they were bringing up the main route at Murrurundi."

Why was the old man going over this again? "And he never arrived at Scone, never mind Murrurundi. Disappeared with the horses, and the drovers' pay. Nothing new there. It was the talk of the district."

Denman growled long and low. "Not his style. He wouldn't have done that. Wasn't made that way. But no one saw him once he'd picked up the thoroughbreds. Why not? I reckon for some reason he decided to bring them over the top—maybe he was in a hurry, needed to make up time. Everyone knew there was a cross-country track through McCullys Gap; perhaps he came to grief there. Could be anything . . . bushrangers, an accident." He hunched his shoulders. "Wildfire maybe. They come through those hills."

"You're telling me he rode through the Gap while a fire was raging?"

Denman's face scrunched into a frown. "Don't know there was a fire. That's what I wanted to ask Parker, but he was in no mood for chatting, and like I said, Lettie was there. He's been squatting up there for nigh on forty years. Suppose there was a wildfire? Bailey got caught. Let the horses go. Hoped they'd survive."

"He wouldn't leave his own horse, but he might let the

thoroughbreds go, let them find their own way out. He'd have a better chance of outrunning the fire on horseback than on foot."

"Unless he thought to take cover. In a cave? There's sandstone caves dotted all through the area."

Nathaniel tossed back the remainder of his tea. "I'll go and pay Parker a visit right now. Tell him he'll not be kicked off the land by us. Maybe he'll remember a bit more about the summer of '81." Which was more than a long shot unless there was something to trigger his memory.

"You watch that gun of his."

"Maybe at this time of the morning I'll catch him abed."

"Maybe."

Nathaniel dismounted and tied his horse under the shade of a large tree and set off on foot. Not quite sure what a visit could do to add to Denman's theory, he'd rolled along with it. The old man had worried him last night—that vacant look in his eyes—although he'd picked up soon enough. Everyone had demons that needed to be laid to rest, and Bailey was Denman's.

Before he'd gone more than a few paces he knew his chances of catching Parker abed were fanciful. A loud bang and a clatter sounded from the dilapidated shack, and a thin curl of smoke rose from the small fire pit outside.

It sounded very much as though Parker was either repairing or destroying the building. He didn't want to surprise him, but he'd far rather take on a man with a hammer than a shotgun.

He stepped into the dim interior, moved to one side out of the direct beam of light, didn't want to take the trigger-happy fool by surprise. "Mr. Parker. It's Nathaniel Poole. Can I have a word?"

Parker straightened up and lowered a large crowbar and rested it between his boots, his hands still wrapped around the shaft. "What d'you want?"

"Just a chat. I was down in Sydney, hoping to make a bid on the block. I failed. Outbid." No need to go into the whys and wherefores. "You'll have to deal with the new owners. Denman's got a mind to stay in the area, and you've been here longer than anyone else. Thought perhaps you could help me make another selection. Maybe we could come to some sort of arrangement if we find something."

"Nothing coming up as far as I know." Parker propped the crowbar against the chimney breast, picked up a filthy leather bag, slung it over his shoulder, and ambled out to the fire.

So far so good. Perhaps Lettie and Denman had caught Parker on a bad day. "I'm thinking about weather patterns and which side of the stock route might be better. I've a mind to breed some horses."

"When and if something comes up and you're not outbid again," Parker added with a note of satisfaction. He swung the bag off his shoulder and, with a low groan, hunkered down next to the fire pit.

"True enough." Plow on. Stick with it; don't get riled by the old fool. "Wouldn't be much you don't know about the area and the weather. Seven-year cycles, they say. Drought and fire. I'd like your advice." Nathaniel pulled a couple of ten-shilling notes from his inside pocket, stashed for the purpose. Folded them neatly and clasped them in his hand.

Parker didn't miss a trick. His eyebrows rose and his tone changed. "It's the hot northwesterlies you've got to watch, hot as a

Chinaman's arse, blow for days and days. Take the topsoil, dry the bloody skin off your bones. Happens about every seven years, you're right there." He pulled a metal canister from the leather bag, unscrewed the lid and dragged out a roll of loose papers, gave them a quick scrunch, and tossed them into the fire. The papers caught and rose, crackled and curled, licked by the flames. "That's when the wildfires come. You're praying for rain; clouds gather, and all you get is bloody lightning. Hills are tinder dry; one crack and up they go. Then the windstorms come, and the grasses catch, whip around like a doxy's skirt." His hand sketched a wide arc to encompass the tall grass waving in the breeze.

"And you've never had one through here?"

He tapped the side of his nose. "Gotta be smart, know when to graze the paddocks out. I remember one year, about thirty years ago, it got real close, real close . . ."

Parker's voice faded as Nathaniel counted back the years. "Didn't know what I know now. Didn't act in time. Didn't have the track through for a firebreak. Wind changed direction and the whole bloody mountain went up. For weeks and weeks we'd prayed for rain. Been over a hundred degrees in the shade for days on end. Then the lightning came and up she went. I burned back into the hills. Wind was in my favor. It didn't come down the hill, didn't get as far as Aberdeen neither, took the ridge around Owens Gap. Then almost as though the good Lord heard our prayers, we got a dump of rain, more a bloody flood. Stopped it in its tracks, but it was weeks before you could get through. Always thought it odd, fire and flood in the same spot within days." Amazing how a few shillings could loosen an old man's tongue.

"This fire thirty-odd years ago . . . That'd make it around the beginning of the 1880s."

"Me memory's not what it was . . . Let's see." Parker reached into the saddlebag and pulled out some more papers, rough and yellowed. "Was before the wife up and left. Me boy was here too. Remember getting her to roll up the bedding, bung it under the doors, seal all the gaps, stay inside. Come to think of it, it was right after that she and the boy up and left. Went back to her family in Scone, said she couldn't hack it around here. Blamed me for the fire." He threw another handful of papers into the flames.

"What's that you're burning?"

"Found it when I was cleaning up. Can't make head nor tail of the rubbish inside. Not, mind you, that I'm much for reading. Thought the bag might come in handy seeing as how I've got to move on." Parker narrowed his eyes and glared at him from beneath his shaggy brows.

"Thank you, Mr. Parker. You've given me a good idea. I'll make sure any property I'm looking at is well cleared." He held up the two notes and at that moment a gust of wind whipped them from his outstretched hand. He slammed his palm down, just beating Parker, and slapped them flat on the bag.

"Close." The old man slid the notes from under his fingers and balled them tight in his fist.

"Here. Let me give you a hand." Nathaniel hefted the bag and stood. Just about to upend the entire contents into the fire, his hand stilled as his thumb grazed an indentation on the leather.

A familiar indentation.

One he'd known since he was a child.

An intertwined L & M. The Ludgrove-Maynard brand. The brand every one of their animals, horse and cattle alike, had carried since they'd first settled in the Hunter.

He snatched the bag upright. As a few more loose sheets of

paper fluttered toward the fire, he clasped it tight to his chest. "Where'd you get this?"

Parker lifted his rheumy eyes and grimaced. "Told you, found it. I'm cleaning out."

Holy hell. Had Bailey been carrying it with the wages? And what were the papers Parker had burned? Certainly wouldn't be cash; the man was too wily for that. He cast a quick glance at the fire. Nothing but charred remnants fluttered in the ash. "This brand here." He stabbed at the symbol on the soft leather. "That's the Ludgrove-Maynard brand."

Parker lifted his shoulders, then turned over the two notes still clutched in his filthy fingers. "Got any more of these?" He waved them under Nathaniel's nose. "I'll sell it to you if it means that much." Before the old codger changed his mind, Nathaniel slung the bag over his shoulder. It had to be Bailey's. The one he'd used to carry the wages. Stood to reason Olivia would give him something to carry the money. His fingers itched to open it, look inside. "You say you found it. Where?"

"Inside the shack, under the fireplace."

Bull. He'd bet the rest of the money he'd saved for the land that Parker wasn't telling the whole truth. "Where did you find it?" He rammed his hand down in his pocket and pulled out a handful of coins, the ones he'd earned for moving the stallion, and some others left behind from his pathetic attempt to scavenge every penny he could for the land sale. He held out the handful and they were gone in a blink. Less.

"Happy to do business with you, Mr. Poole."

"Where did you get the saddlebag?"

"Bit of a long story. Fancy a cuppa?"

No. That was the last thing he wanted. But clenching his

fist to stop the impatient drumming of his fingers, he nodded in agreement.

Parker wedged the billy into the coals and rocked back on his heels. "That fire I was telling you about. The year me missus took off. Wasn't feeling too good, sorry for meself. All me plans gone. Took to wandering in the hills." He slopped some tea into a tin mug and took a sip. "Help yourself."

Nathaniel gritted his teeth. He'd like to grab the old fool by the shoulders, shake the words out of him. He glanced up, saw the glint in Parker's eye. He knew what he was doing. Stringing him along. "Wandering the hills, you said."

"Not straight after the fire, mind. Too dangerous then. Trees falling, rockslides every way you turned. Then the rain turning it all to a quagmire. Was out looking for a fresh water supply." He gestured up into the hills. "'Bout halfway up that hill. Up behind the spot you'd picked out for your house site . . ."

And how the hell would he know that?

". . . there's a spring. Comes out of the rock face, nice little cave. Like a little slice of heaven it was, after the fires. Still green, rock ferns shading it from the sun. Stopped there for a breather. Sweetest water ever. Found the bag in there."

Nathaniel sprang to his feet. "Show me."

"These bones are getting on. Not sure I'm up for the climb. Take your horse. Ride up over the house site—thought that's why you'd decided to put the house there. Fresh water supply ain't to be sneezed at. Maybe you're not as smart as I thought." He threw Nathaniel a squinty-eyed look. "You'll see the wallaby track through the trees. They know what's good for 'em."

Within minutes Nathaniel sat astride Rogue on the flat nub of the hill looking up at the crest of Rossgole Mountain. The wallaby track disappeared into the tree line as Parker described, too narrow for a horse. He tethered Rogue and set off on foot. The overgrown scrub snatched at his face, tore his hands, and his breath came in ragged gasps as he reached the top of the hill. Below him lay a panorama stretching from Muswellbrook out to the Liverpool Plains and north.

The wallaby track twisted and turned, then ran parallel with the hill and dropped down into Parker's little slice of heaven. He pushed through a group of cycads to the crystal-clear pool surrounded by ferns where a splash of water emerged from the rock face and trickled down. Squatting, he cupped his hands, threw the water across his face, then drank his fill.

The tiny waterfall masked a small cave. Dumping his hat, he stuck his head through the spray of water and waited for the shadows to resolve, then crawled on all fours inside.

With his hands raised above his head he straightened up. Not quite high enough to stand, but with his knees and head bent he could get a sense of the space. Cool and dry. Beneath his feet, a sandy loam.

Rummaging through his pockets, he brought out his matches. The smell of sulfur filled the confined space, then the flame steadied, revealing the small cave. The match flickered and died.

The second flared, illuminating the smooth rock walls and nothing else except the sense that Parker had told the truth. It was the perfect hiding spot. Dry and safe from fire and flood.

He pushed back out into the light and hunkered down, staring at the white ribbon of road cutting through the paddocks below, linked to the spot where he sat by the gully. A gully that wove its way down the hill to the very spot where Lettie had come to grief. It made perfect sense.

Once more he needed to speak to Parker, confirm he'd found the correct spot, because if he had, it linked the saddlebag and the bit. Crashing through the bush he raced back, vaulted astride Rogue, let out a whoop of excitement, and galloped down the hill. He might not have been able to secure the land for Denman, but he had a feeling this could be almost as good.

He hitched Rogue's bridle to the tree next to the water butt and strode over to the leaning slab shack. "Parker! You around?" He made a circuit of the shack, strode over to the water butt, scanned the paddocks. No sign of him.

The door dangled from the leather hinge and he stuck his head inside. The stretcher sat against the wall, blankets gone and the cupboard doors hanging wide. Crouching down, he swept his hand over the shelf, scooped out the shredded remains of a packet of tea and more rat poop and cobwebs than he'd seen in a long time.

Nothing else. What had he hoped to find? He wiped his hands on the back of his pants and rested his shoulder against the chimney breast, his gaze coming to rest on the neatly swept hearth. Neatly swept! Nothing else in the ramshackle building had seen a broom in a long time.

Bending, he stuck his head up inside the chimney. No daylight. Possum more than like had taken up residence because Parker had been using the outside fire pit. But why?

Why had Parker chosen to use the fire pit outside? He ran his hands down the inside of the wall, boulders from the property held in place by a sandy lime mix, just the same as any early building. Whoever had put it together had done a good job. Maybe Parker had built the slab hut around an existing chimney.

As he turned, the toe of his boot caught a loose slab of sandstone to one side of the hearth. He crouched down and ran his fingers around the edge, loosened and lifted it.

A hidey-hole, and not a bad one. Two, maybe three feet deep, and equally wide, running under the adjacent slabs. The earth was cool, not damp, but cool. Nothing inside. What had he expected to find?

A series of gouged lines ran across the top of the slab next to the hole. He ran his finger over them, scored indentations as though some animal had tried to claw its way into the cavity. He rocked back on his heels, his fingers still smoothing the groves.

Was this where Parker had hidden the saddlebag after he retrieved it from the cave?

With one last look around the shack, he stepped outside into the fading light.

Nathaniel was off his horse before it even slowed, saddlebag clutched under his arm, as he sprang up onto the veranda. "Denman! Where are you?" He stuck his head through the door, dark as a bottomless pit after the sunlight. No sign, no sound. "Denman?" He shot off the veranda and loped around the back out to the shed. "Oi! Old fella. Where are you?"

Denman ambled out, a heavy pair of box joint tongs dangling from one hand, sweat dripping from his face. "I was beginning to think you'd got the raw end of Parker's shotgun. Any luck?"

"Take a look at this." He held up the bag, good as stuffed it under Denman's nose.

"Nice bit of leather. Could do with a cleanup. Give me a minute." He wandered back into the shed and reappeared a moment or two later wiping his hands.

Nathaniel's fingers itched to open the bag, but he couldn't, not without Denman, not if it had something to do with Bailey. "Here." He thrust the bag into Denman's hands. "Look at the brand on the outside flap. Recognize it?"

Denman turned the bag over, the flat of his hand on the flap. "'Course I do. Ludgrove-Maynard brand. Know it as well as you do." He undid the remaining strap. "Where did you get it?"

"Parker had it. He was cleaning up before he moved on. Offered him some money. He handed it over. Easy as." Nathaniel's breath rasped in his throat. "Reckon it's Bailey's? Reckon he was carrying it? With the drovers' wages?"

The flap lifted and the bag fell wide.

"Nah." Denman reached in. "Nah. Not Bailey's. And if it had the wages in it they'd be long gone by now. Parker's no fool. And besides, Bailey wasn't one for painting." He held up a thin paintbrush.

"Then why's it got the brand on it? Why would he have it?"

Denman upended the bag and dropped it to the ground.

Nathaniel was on his hands and knees scrabbling in the dirt. "What did you do that for?" One side housed a series of brushes and pencils all held in place by neat leather loops and a leather-bound notebook. The other side held a pile of thick paper anchored by two leather clasps and a set of watercolor paints.

He reached into the bottom of the bag, his fingers settling on something round. He pulled it out and twisted it. The air whooshed out of Nathaniel's lungs and his shoulders dropped. He lifted it to show Denman.

A compass, the brass tarnished, but the needle still swinging.

Denman snorted. "It ain't Bailey's. He didn't need a compass."

He'd been expecting something that proved the accusations

about Bailey were false, certainly not a bunch of pencils, paints, brushes, and a compass. He rocked back on his heels and looked up.

Denman had a smile, perhaps a grimace, certainly a look of satisfaction. "That belonged to young Evie."

"Why would Bailey be carrying it?"

"Maybe he wasn't."

"Who, then? Couldn't be Evie. She wasn't out this way."

"Perhaps she was. Perhaps she was with Bailey."

"If she'd been with Bailey, Olivia would've known. And she wouldn't have kept quiet about it."

"She's the only one who can answer that." Denman bent down and unstrapped the notebook. He fanned the pages.

Tidy script and some drawings covered a good few pages, the rest blank. Nathaniel peered over his shoulder, but before he had a chance to read it, Denman snapped the notebook shut. "Don't reckon this is for us to see. Need to put it all back together and get it to Olivia." He slid the notebook back into place, then smoothed the dusty leather with his gnarled hands in something resembling a caress. "One of the straps is missing. Looks like it's been chewed. Parker didn't say where he got it?"

"First he said he was cleaning out and he'd forgotten about it."

"Seems all us old blokes have fading memories."

"Handful of cash fixed his memory."

"Cash? How much?"

Nathaniel shrugged and patted his pockets. "I've got some of the money for the land sale here. Gave him a couple of ten-shilling notes and some coins. I was certain the saddlebag was Bailey's. Thought you'd want it. Managed to get Parker to tell me where he'd found it. Over the top of Rossgole Mountain, there's a cave up there. Reckon it's the head of the gully, the one that runs down to the road, to the culvert where Lettie ran off the road—where you found Bailey's bit."

"And what would Bailey be doing up Rossgole Mountain? No need to go that way to Scone."

And that was the piece of information he didn't want to share with Denman, because in his mind the answer was clear. "Parker remembers a wildfire through there, early in 1881."

Denman's face paled and he reached for the veranda to steady himself. "What are you going to do with the bag?"

The words brought him up short. He picked up the saddlebag and slung it across his shoulder. "Get it back to Yellow Rock, I suppose. You're right. Olivia's the one who should have it." He let out a sigh. Cast a glance at Rogue and Raven, who had their heads down munching on the sweet grass growing on the edge of the creek. "I'll go back in the morning."

"Good lad. I'll be coming with you."

26

Overnight Lettie somehow managed to put all thoughts of Miriam out of her mind, all thoughts of anything other than Andrew Hume. She stretched, shook the cobwebs away. There was no point in trying to pretend the confrontation with Miriam hadn't happened. And she couldn't let Peg send Sam to Wollombi to do her donkey work. She would have to face Miriam herself, but it was still early—she could spend a couple of hours in the study before driving into Wollombi. Besides, there was something childishly pleasing about keeping Miriam waiting.

Oxley loitered at the bottom of the steps, eyeing her with a look of disapproval.

"I know, Oxley, I know I have to go, but there's something I'm missing. Just a couple of hours. Miriam won't be ready to leave until at least ten o'clock."

Everything in the study was as she'd left it the day before. With a sigh, she took Evie's map from the drawer. Aching, aching for Evie, for Olivia, for all that had gone before. She was no closer to finding Evie than on the day she'd arrived.

She ran her finger along the Maitland road. Evie must have gone that way. Why else would she have written *Hume* on the map? And presuming the dates on the headstones were correct, she might well have found Andrew's parents. The question remained: Where had that led her? Had she gone to Dartbrook? Did she know that Andrew had grown up there? What had happened to prevent her from returning?

Lettie unrolled the map, releasing the faint but distinctive scent of boronia, turpentine, and paint. "I can't leave it be."

Tracing the route she'd traveled with her finger, Lettie followed the road out to Maitland and Largs, marveling at the small illustrations, properties and people going about their business, tiny slices of life, and then finally the hastily scrawled word *Hume*, written in pencil, slightly east of Maitland, and the four men with their horses.

She reefed open the desk drawer. The magnifying glass. Where was it? She'd used it before she'd left for Maitland. The men with the horses—not drovers or stockmen; they had none of Nathaniel's easy grace. Their clothing was different, too, their hats. One wore a bowler hat, for heaven's sake, another a heavy, almost military jacket. Was one of them Andrew Hume?

She traced the track to Singleton, and beyond to Muswellbrook, to the spot where she'd turned off the stock route and crashed the car, then to Rossgole and up to Dartbrook and back down to Yellow Rock. All the miles she'd traveled because the woman in Largs had said the Humes once lived at Dartbrook. A place not marked on Evie's map.

Was it all a fantasy of her own creation? How she wished she could hand a pencil over to Evie and ask her to fill in the map, tell her story. Maybe Denman and Olivia were right and Evie had gone no farther than Yellow Rock. All that detail incorporated into the map but nothing where she needed it, a vast blank canvas beyond the narrow confines of Evie's life.

Her eyes stung with unshed tears as she studied the details Evie had drawn around the house, the white rosebushes, the angophora tree covered in blossom, the two wedge-tailed eagles. The tiny figures of the drovers and the cattle around their huge bonfire, so perfect she could hear the music of the fiddles, smell the roasting meat, feel the warmth of Nathaniel's body as they'd danced under the stars, the drays in a semicircle beyond the fire, the spot where they'd sat and he'd told her the story of Lizard.

A strange sensation prickled beneath her skin. She couldn't shake the thought Evie's bones might lie out there somewhere hidden, unknown and uncared for. Blocking her morbid thoughts, she followed the path from the bonfire to the stables. Two horses standing in the small paddock, their eyes trained on the stable door, waiting no doubt for their nightly feed. And there behind the stables—her breath caught and a flush rose to her cheeks. She angled the magnifying glass—two people locked in an embrace. More than an embrace. She bent her head closer. Angled it to the light. Jumped to her feet. She hadn't concentrated on the details around the house, been too taken in her unshakable belief that the answer lay in Maitland. Her fingers gripped the horn handle of the glass.

There was no mistake: two people, a man and a woman, the girl's hair hanging free to her waist, her head thrown back in a gesture of abandon. The man's shirt, a minute blaze of color, his fingers entwined in her long dark curls. Who were they?

The skin on her neck tingled. Had she discovered Evie's secret? Was it another self-portrait? Evie clasped in the arms of her lover? Had they left together? And who was the man? A drover, judging by his clothes.

She replaced the magnifying glass in the drawer and wandered to the open door, gazed up at Yellow Rock. Did the rock truly hold the secret to Evie's disappearance? Maybe Denman wasn't far off the mark when he'd said Yellow Rock had taken Evie. Maybe she'd met her lover there, changed into the clothes Nell had provided, and ridden off to make a life for herself with the man she loved.

Surely she wouldn't have left without telling Olivia, though, even if that meant risking her possible censure and disapproval. She wouldn't have shunned the family she loved, her work with William. From everything Olivia had told her, she and William had shared a special bond.

She scrambled around the desk, slipped the map back into the drawer, wrote a quick note for Olivia to tell her where she'd gone, and made her way to the door. There were too many questions still to be answered. But first she had to go to Wollombi, brave Miriam, and tell her she would not return to Sydney with her.

Lizzie was in no condition to make the trip back to Sydney, still sitting askew where she'd pulled up when she'd returned to Yellow Rock, under a blanket of fading gum flowers from the ancient angophora. One lamp still hung at a rakish angle, tied with the piece of twine Denman had provided, the other tossed behind the seat, and the roof couldn't be lifted because of the broken struts. She tipped the front seat and rapped her knuckles against the petrol tank, the hollow ring telling her what she already knew: enough spirit to cover the twenty miles to Wollombi if she was lucky, but no farther.

She'd see Miriam and, while she was there, call in to the forge and have Armstrong see to the repairs.

The engine fired at the first turn of the crank and Oxley landed on the front seat a moment later. She slid in after him. "We're not going far, and you'll have to behave yourself. No jumping out and following interesting smells. Do you hear me?"

He turned and lifted the corner of his mouth in what might have been a grin and settled onto the seat.

With the wind fanning her hair and the air full of the intoxicating aroma of slashed hay, she bowled along, slowing only when the road curved and her vision became obstructed. There'd be no repeat of her foolish disaster with the culvert on the Dartbrook road.

As she crossed Williams Bridge she spotted a small figure sitting on a guard rail, hat in hand, waving frantically. She slowed to a halt. "Sam, what are you doing here?"

"Trying to cadge a ride back to Yellow Rock."

"What were you doing in Wollombi?"

"Telling her ladyship you weren't going to Sydney."

So Peg had decided to send Sam to deliver the message. "I could have saved you a trip. I'm on my way to see my mother now."

He hunched his shoulders and the corners of his mouth drooped. "Just as well because she wasn't takin' any notice of what I said, miserable old cow. Set the bulldog bloke on me." He rubbed at his ear. "Tossed me out, he did. Said I didn't know what I was talking about."

Poor Sam. She could well imagine the scene. Miriam would have worked herself into a rage. Being thwarted was not something she handled well. "I also need to talk to the blacksmith and pick up more gasoline. If you're not in a hurry you can come with me. I'll be a couple of hours . . ."

He vaulted onto the seat before she'd finished her sentence. "Thought you'd never ask. Shove over, Oxley." The lad was such a skinny beanpole both he and Oxley fit in the space easily.

"Hold tight!" She opened the throttle and Lizzie responded to Sam's whoops of excitement and took off.

A few minutes later they drew to a halt outside the general store.

Sam bounced out of the car. "I'll go and tell Armstrong you're here," he called over his shoulder, heading into the forge.

Lettie pulled off her goggles and cast a look up and down the street.

Before she'd made it to the door of the forge, a heaving, panting noise made her turn around and she found Connors's lugubrious face, shiny with perspiration, glaring at her. "Miss Rawlings, Miss Rawlings. Wait a moment," he wheezed.

Restraining a groan, Lettie came to a halt, hand on the gate.

"Mrs. Rawlings wants to speak to you now."

Habit made Lettie turn to follow him and then she stopped. "Tell Mother that I will come to the hotel when I have attended to my business." The audacity of her remark made a blush spring to her cheeks, but she held her ground.

Connors's eyes widened and his brows crawled up his domed forehead. "Mrs. Rawlings is waiting." He gestured toward the sleek black motor parked outside the Family Hotel.

"I will be there after I have attended to my business," she repeated and walked into the blacksmith's shop, head held high and her heart beating a liberating rhythm.

Sam sat parked on a stool next to the roaring fire, mesmerized by Armstrong's hammer blows. Her tap on his shoulder almost sent him into the fire.

"Armstrong will be ready to work on your motor in about ten minutes. I told him what needed doing," he said once he'd recovered.

"And how would you know that, Sam?"

"Said you wanted gasoline. He's got some, and I told him there were some bits and pieces that had fallen off your motor when you drove it into the creek that needed fixing."

The story of her misadventure must be all over town, probably halfway to Sydney, Lettie thought—and without a doubt the details would have made it as far as Miriam and the Family Hotel. "In that case I'll leave everything in your capable hands while I go and have a word with my mother."

"Want me to come with you? That big bloke's a bit of a handful." Not as much of a handful as Miriam but twice Sam's size.

"I'll be fine, thank you. I'll only be across the road. I'll see you and Armstrong when you come out. I can call for help if I need to."

"Right you are." He settled back on the stool, and Armstrong threw her a nod before blasting the fire with a huge pair of bellows. With a resigned sigh Lettie left the forge and walked down the road to the spot where the large black Cadillac was parked.

Miriam sat with her chiffon scarf screwed into a tight ball in her fingers and her face a perfect match for the car's paintwork.

"Good morning, Mother. I trust the hotel was to your liking."

Miriam stared moodily through the windscreen.

There was little point in stringing it out. Lettie looked down at her. "As I said yesterday, I won't be coming back to Sydney with you. Olivia has invited me to stay longer." Not strictly the truth, but close enough. "I am halfway through collating Grandfather's notes, and it is a job I intend to finish." Again not entirely truthful, but there was little point in starting the argument about Evie all over again.

"And what of your commitments in Sydney?" Miriam tilted her head up. "You have invitations to answer and engagements."

"None that I organized, Mother. Please convey my apologies. I shall deal with them when I return."

"When will that be?"

"I'll let you know."

Miriam's face turned an interesting shade of plum, and from the corner of her eye Lettie spotted Sam and Armstrong emerging from the forge. "I hope you have a pleasant trip back to Sydney. I'll write and confirm the date of my return. Goodbye, Mother." She turned on her heel and strode across the road, barely able to control her feeling of triumph.

Armstrong straightened up, the broken car lamp from the back seat swinging from his huge hands. "No problems here. I can weld them both back on. You won't be needing that anymore." He flicked his finger at the piece of twine Denman had used to secure the second lamp. "Need to take off the back wheel and repair the spindle, otherwise you're going to get uneven wear. And fix the spare. No problems with the roof. Just sort out the struts and hinges and stitch up that tear. Take me a couple of hours."

She felt like hugging the man, even more when Connors revved the engine of the monstrous black motor and Miriam vanished in a cloud of dust, her chiffon scarf streaming behind her like a distress signal.

"I can't thank you enough. Sam and I will take a bit of a walk and find ourselves a drink, maybe even something to eat. Would you like me to move the motor?"

"Take it around the back. Turn around, first on your left, there's a track between the forge and the shop on the corner. Can't miss it. There's a spot out the back where I can do the work." Armstrong raised his hand and disappeared back inside.

Sam shaded his eyes and squinted down the road. "They've gone, and if we're going to have some tucker, I'll go and get Oxley. He won't want to miss out."

She hadn't given a thought to Oxley. "Where is he?"

"Had to tie him up. He had a bit of a run-in with the big bloke while you were talking to her ladyship. Don't think he likes them much."

The memory of Olivia's comment about Oxley being a good judge of character slipped into her mind and she curbed a smile. "Good work, Sam. Thanks. I'll meet you down at the hotel. I expect they'll have something for us."

He rubbed his stomach. "Meat pie, that's what you want. They'll be just out of the oven."

In no time at all, Lettie and Sam were settled on a bench overlooking the brook, meat pies in hand and Oxley at their feet salivating. Sam wiped a dribble of gravy from his chin with the back of his hand. "Good job you're staying. Miss Maynard could do with some company."

A strange thing for a young boy to say. "She's got Peg, and you and the drovers, when they call in." And Nathaniel.

"But she's up there all on her own a lot of the time. Not like it used to be in the old days."

"And how would you know that?"

"Me grandfather, Joe. He worked up there. Was there when young Evie went missing, helped in the search. Everyone did."

Lettie put the pie down in her lap. "Do you think I could talk to your grandfather?"

"Bit hard. Died a couple of years back." Another door closed. "But I heard all his stories. What do you want to know?"

"Tell me what it was like when everyone was living at Yellow

Rock." She couldn't bring herself to say *before Evie disappeared*. Maybe his stories would answer the question about the two people behind the stables.

Sam threw the crust of his pie in Oxley's direction and he snatched it before it hit the ground. "Thought you'd know that, would have heard it from family. You're related, ain't you?"

"Yes, but no one ever talked about Yellow Rock."

"Why not?"

A good question, and one she wished she'd asked years before. "I grew up in Sydney."

"The first Ludgroves and the Maynards, they'd be your great-grandparents, I'm guessing; they got the land grants. Years back. It's one of the few places that hasn't been broken up and sold off. In those days the properties around here were all enormous. Thousands of acres, some of them. Not anymore. That's what changed every-thing, Gramps said. Lots of folk bred horses. Ludgrove-Maynard had a name for themselves, the best stock. Used to send their horses to India for the army, even some of them maharajas used to buy them. Gramps reckoned they lived in huge palaces, wore jewels as big as pigeons' eggs in their turbans. That's those hats they wear, a long piece of material they wind around and around . . ."

She didn't want a story about India; she wanted to know about Yellow Rock.

". . . some say the first Mrs. Maynard had some of that blood in her. Heard tell she had hair way down her back, long and straight and black as . . ."

Which brought Lettie's mind back to the picture on Evie's map. She'd have to show Olivia and see if she recognized the couple behind the stables.

". . . and that's why the business took off. Mr. Maynard served in the army in India, knew lots of toffs, Gramps said. But it all went to pot when young Mr. Ludgrove got tied up with that explorer bloke . . ."

And it all came back once more to Leichhardt. No wonder Olivia had such a set against the man.

"That's when times got tough, spent all the profits on those expeditions, had nothing put aside to see the place through the Depression. Gramps said you've got to look after what you've got. First all the cattle went, then they sold off a lot of the stallions and mares, and poor old Miss Maynard was left all on her own trying to manage with only half the horses and none of the help."

Meanwhile Lettie and the rest of the family had been living in the lap of luxury, the best schools, Thorne's trip to England, her time at Sydney University, his motor imported from America and built in Victoria, the boat. Why had Olivia been left to struggle on alone? Her blood fired. It was outrageous.

"Mr. Nathaniel's been good like that."

Lettie's head came up. "Nathaniel?"

"He likes the horses. Not the cattle. She ain't got no one else to help out with the horses. Don't know what'll happen, though. Mr. Nathaniel reckons he's going to start his own stud, reckons there's a war coming and the army's going to need horses. Cor, wouldn't that be the go. Off to war with your own horse. Gramps said the Boer War showed them all what we could do. The Light Horse, they call 'em. I'll be doing that soon as they'll take me. Armstrong reckons you'll be staying. Learn all you can from Olivia and take over."

Even the local blacksmith thought she'd be staying. "I'm not much good around horses. I can barely ride, never mind run the place."

"You could get people to help you. Mr. Nathaniel, me even."

"You just told me Nathaniel wanted his own place." And from what Sam had just said, he had much bigger plans than she'd realized. He might have missed out on Rossgole, but there'd be other places. He wasn't the kind of man to let go of a dream.

"There's others. They'll need people that can breed good strong horses. That's what the Hunter's good at."

But not what she was good at. She could make money out of her cartoons, maybe in a pinch write an article or do some drawings, but not run a property like Yellow Rock. Most importantly, she needed to talk to Olivia, find out what she envisaged for the future. Why she'd wanted to talk to Thorne—and maybe find out why Thorne wanted to visit Yellow Rock.

27

If Nathaniel counted the number of times he'd traveled the road in the past weeks, he'd never leave again. But then, it didn't look as though they'd ever call Rossgole home. Maybe in a couple of years something else would come up.

The miles clocked by. He and Denman spent the night at one of the drovers' camps along the road, scabbed a meal, slept under the stars, and climbed back in the saddle before the sun breached the horizon. Nothing new, nothing he hadn't done a hundred times before; if he'd been alone he might have ridden through the night, but there was Denman to consider. The old fella wasn't getting any younger, and the news about Bailey had hit him hard.

"Hope Olivia's got something on the stove, haven't had decent tucker for days." Denman threw him a lopsided grin. "Looking forward to seeing the old girl. It's been a long time."

They turned into the driveway at Yellow Rock as the sun slipped behind the Wollombi ranges. Oxley raced out to meet them, yapping like a mad thing, running around their horses in tight circles, letting the whole world know they'd arrived. Nathaniel took the horses and sent Denman across to the farmhouse. It was as much as the old fella could do to put one foot in front of the other. Denman's riding days were well and truly numbered.

He stood and waited until Denman had made it to the house, then turned to gaze up to Yellow Rock. The sight brought him stock-still. On the top of the rock, arms spread as though at any moment she might step out and join the two circling eagles, stood Lettie, her bright red Crimean shirt pinpointing her for all the world to see.

Before he had a chance to let rip a *cooee*, she spotted him, waved her hands, and he'd swear their eyes locked. He gave the horses a quick rubdown and set them loose in one of the mating paddocks, then took off. By the time he'd reached the path up the cliff face, she was skittering down in leaps and bounds as though she'd been doing it all her life. Next she jumped astride the old mare and galloped down to meet him. Her riding skills had improved.

"Nathaniel!" Lettie skidded to a halt, her flushed cheeks and sparkling eyes the best welcome he'd ever received. "What are you doing here? I wasn't expecting to see you. Does Olivia know?"

"She will before long. I brought Denman." He held out his hands and she slipped down from the horse, none of the reticence he remembered from before. Almost as though she'd shed her city skin and embraced a new life. "You've been practicing your riding."

"I have."

"Let's get this animal in the paddock. Got something to show the two of you."

"Aren't you going to tell me?"

"Nope, not until we get to the house." Now that he was here at Yellow Rock, he wasn't too sure about their plan. He and Denman had discussed it on and off during the ride down, but the old fella's interest seemed to be firmly entrenched in Bailey's bit and the possibility that he'd been caught in the wildfire. Trouble was, the saddlebag might well put Evie in the vicinity too. How would Olivia take that? The search had centered on Yellow Rock, but what if she had been with Bailey? His breath shuddered out on a sigh.

Lettie tilted her head and looked right into his eyes. "Is it something bad?"

Not game to begin, he took her hand and led her along the path to the farmhouse.

Olivia had Denman parked in a chair on the veranda, hands wrapped around a mug masquerading as tea, but the aroma in the air told a different story. She sat opposite him, her brimming eyes riveted on his face, the silence between them palpable. In her hand she cradled Bailey's bit.

Denman had broken the news.

Nathaniel held out a chair for Lettie, then slipped the saddlebag from his shoulder and hung it on the rail. And then what? He had no idea. Had Denman already said something to Olivia about Evie? Should he broach the subject?

Olivia looked up. "Come on, son, spit it out. Denman said I had to wait for you."

He swung around to pick up the bag. "Get your nose out of there, Oxley."

The dog took off like a startled rabbit down the veranda steps.

Nathaniel placed the bag, brand up, on Olivia's lap. Her face paled. Denman reached for her hand, squeezed it, and nodded.

"What is it?" Lettie hissed.

He lifted his finger to his lips as Olivia reached out her shaking hand and smoothed the leather. "Where did you find it?"

"Parker's squat on Rossgole. I think you should open it," Nathaniel said.

The poor woman turned the color of chalk. She took a slug of her tea, caught her breath; least it brought some color back to her cheeks.

"Shall I get you a glass of water?" Lettie rested her hand on Olivia's shoulder.

"You open it, Lettie. I can't."

Lettie's eyes drilled into his and he nodded. A smattering of black dirt scattered as she lifted the flap and exposed the neat rows of paintbrushes. Olivia let out a moan and covered her face with her hands.

Denman moved faster than he'd ever seen before, by Olivia's side in an instant, arm tight around her heaving shoulders. He tipped his head toward the stables.

Nathaniel didn't need to be told twice. He grasped Lettie's hand. She resisted for a moment, then walked alongside, bristling with unasked questions.

"Come and sit down."

"I don't want to sit down. Olivia needs me."

"Nah. She doesn't, not right now. Denman'll see to her. They go back a long way. Got more than Evie in common."

She plopped down on the garden bench, eyes blazing. "It's about time you told me what's going on. This is ridiculous. Do you think that saddlebag belonged to Evie? Where did you find it? How long have you had it and how can you be certain?"

How much of this was his story to tell? "Goes back to the day you crashed the motor."

"I didn't crash it. I ran off the road."

He quirked a grin and raised his palm, hoping it would signal a truce.

"I need to go back. Olivia's—"

"You're not going anywhere. Denman'll know when it's time. Olivia's got some mourning to do."

"Even if the saddlebag is Evie's, it doesn't prove she's dead. She could have lost it, dropped it. Someone could have stolen it. Parker. Did you ask him?"

"It's not only Evie. It's Bailey too."

"Bailey? Denman's brother? I heard about him from the woman at Dartbrook. I know all about Bailey. Denman told me. He said he was innocent."

Lettie grabbed at her head. It felt as though it would explode.

"When you pulled the stuff out of the creek you picked up a piece of metal, a bit."

She knew that. "Denman said he'd made it."

"That's right, made it for his brother. Bailey wouldn't have let his horse go, not unless he had no other option. Parker has a memory of a pretty savage wildfire through there in the 1880s, early 1881, in fact. He remembers because his wife and boy up and left after the fire."

Cold fingers tiptoed up her spine. "Are you saying Evie and Bailey were together?"

"No proof."

"But why has she never asked the question? If they both disappeared at the same time, it would be logical." Her mind swung back to the picture on Evie's map, the girl and the drover behind the stables.

"Because there was no reason to believe Evie was with Bailey. The search concentrated around Yellow Rock and Glendon. Bailey'd gone to Maitland to pick up some thoroughbreds for Scone, then he was meeting the drovers at Murrurundi."

"But Evie had Maitland, Hume, marked on her map, that's why I . . . Oh! And if she'd met up with Bailey, seen the Humes, and then . . . How far is Murrurundi from Dartbrook?"

"About thirty miles, less if you cut across country."

"They must have been together—otherwise why would her saddlebag be found at Parker's place? Are you sure it's Evie's saddlebag? Lots of people could have bags like that, with paintbrushes and drawing materials."

"It carries the Ludgrove-Maynard brand, and there's not just paintbrushes in there. There's a notebook, some papers, and a compass."

"A compass." The words dried on her lips. "William's compass." Sadness wrapped around her like a damp, musty blanket. "I need to go to Olivia."

"Might be time. Here's Denman."

The old man shuffled down the path toward them, his wrinkled face desolate. "Olivia's asking for you."

Nathaniel pushed to his feet.

"Not you, son. You can keep me company. Olivia wants to talk to Letitia."

Lettie plodded back to the house. A slight breeze had picked up, bringing the scent of citrus and boronia.

What had she done? Wouldn't it have been better if she'd left things as they were, hadn't interfered, hadn't pushed and pushed, determined to find the truth? She hadn't spared a thought for Olivia and what the truth might mean, that knowledge could be worse than ignorance.

Olivia sat staring up at Yellow Rock, her face pale, tears evident in her eyes, and spread out on the old table in front of her lay the contents of the saddlebag.

The compass sat to one side, the brass casing dulled to verdigris; a leather pouch; paintbrushes all neatly lined up in size order; blocks of watercolor paints in a timber frame; a notebook, open on the first page, Evie's signature block print clearly visible; two or three sheets of hand-torn yellowed paper, covered in a faded scrawl; and something that looked like a newspaper clipping.

Olivia offered her a wan smile. "Sit down. This is Evie's saddlebag. William gave it to her before he took Miriam to be married. He had it made specially, pockets for all her pencils, brushes, and paints, and a new notebook. She told me she was going to record all her thoughts, everything relevant to the book they would write. I didn't pay much heed. I hoped her passion for Leichhardt would pass. Least said, soonest mended." She shook her head.

Lettie took Olivia's cold hand. "You weren't to know."

"But you did. You understood. There's the compass." She picked it up and turned it over to reveal the initials *WJL*. "I didn't even know she'd taken it. Not until you discovered it missing. I'd locked the study, locked everything away."

"Would it have made any difference?"

"Perhaps. I believed she'd gone to Yellow Rock. I didn't imagine she'd follow Bailey. Perhaps if the search . . ." Olivia huffed out a mournful sigh. "They didn't leave together. Evie gave Bailey the wages before he left; she didn't leave until the next morning. She was gone when I awoke."

"And you didn't raise the alarm for three days."

Olivia nodded. "I had no reason to doubt her. She never lied to me. She said Yellow Rock and then on to Glendon for a night or two."

Lettie pointed to the leather pouch. "What's that?"

"That's the bag I gave Bailey with the wages, and that's the IOU I wrote for the remainder."

"Then they must have been together."

"At some time, yes."

The small faded newspaper clipping caught Lettie's eye. "What's this?"

"This?" Olivia picked it up and grimaced. "I believe this is the reason she left, and why she didn't tell me." She passed the piece of paper over to Lettie.

Many of the words had faded, the print blurred but the intent clear. A thousand-pound reward for proof of where Leichhardt met his death . . . "Leichhardt died in the desert," Lettie said. "He sent his last letter from Roma, on the Darling Downs. Everyone knows that; besides, it's all in William's notes. Evie went to Maitland, not Queensland."

"She must have thought she could find something that provided proof of the place where Leichhardt died. But here, here in the Hunter? I don't understand either." Olivia wiped her hand across her face. "And she didn't tell me because of the wretched advertisement." She stabbed at the fragile piece of paper. "She knew we were short of money. I told her to tell Bailey I'd get the remainder of the drovers' wages to them next time, gave her that IOU. This"—Olivia stabbed at the advertisement again—"says it must be kept *absolutely secret* until it was published by *The Bulletin*. That must have been why she didn't confide in me."

"Would you have let her go?"

Olivia shook her head. "Of course not. A young girl racing around the countryside on her own. She should have known better."

"She wasn't on her own. She and Bailey—"

"Bailey would have brought her home. He wouldn't have gone traipsing off around the countryside with her. He'd have looked after her, brought her back to me. Nothing makes any sense."

But it was beginning to make a little sense, and it all came back to Andrew Hume, the connection between him, Maitland, Dartbrook, Bailey, and Evie. "Why don't you have a look at her notebook—perhaps there's something there."

"Not yet. I can't do it yet." Olivia slipped the reward notice between the pages of the notebook and handed it to Lettie. "You take it. You read it. And take William's compass and put it back in his box." Olivia left, Evie's saddlebag dangling from one hand and the other clutched to her broken heart.

28

Lettie tucked the notebook under her arm and tilted the compass. The needle angled from Yellow Rock toward the Glendon track. Not long ago she'd stood on the top of the rock looking in the very same direction, unaware of what the future held. The view gave her such a sense of Evie, a unity and harmony with her. As though Evie stood beside her guiding her into her world. The same sense she'd had when she first discovered the map. She had to conjure a similar rapport through Evie's notebook and pray it provided some answers. More than anything else she had to understand how Evie thought she could earn the reward.

Oxley sat waiting on the doorstep. The moment she entered the house he shot into the study and flopped down under the desk. Once Lettie settled in the chair she opened the notebook. No scent of boronia wafted from the pages. Something else. Damp earth and woodsmoke. Emotion thickened her throat, and she took a deep breath to still her quivering anticipation.

17th November 1880

Today Pa gave me the most beautiful present.

The single sentence blazed above a detailed drawing of the saddlebag, the brand clearly drawn, one side open showing the row of brushes and pencils and the notebook tucked under a leather strap, dissipating any remnant of doubt that the saddlebag belonged to Evie.

Lettie turned to the next page: *I will record everything I find that will lead to the publication of our book.* And beneath it a sketch of an impressive leather-bound tome. And written across the flyleaf the words *The Prince of Explorers by William Ludgrove and his daughter Evelyn.* A story that was never written.

A tight knot of determination twisted in her abdomen—when she solved this conundrum *she* would write the story, not of the Prince of Explorers, but of her aunt, Evelyn Ludgrove, who set out to solve the mystery of Ludwig Leichhardt and, in so doing, lost herself.

The next entry was dated several days later. Remembering the pile of notebooks crammed with William's looping cursive, Lettie could well imagine that it had taken Evie a long time to read them all. She, too, had read some, but his flowery prose spent more time on describing the attributes of Leichhardt than anything that would help in her search for Evie. She flicked through several more pages until she came to 2nd January 1881. The pressure of Evie's pen was apparent, no drawings, the writing hurried as though she couldn't get the words down fast enough.

Today we received a letter from Miriam. I never imagined she would marry in Sydney, without us. I miss Pa so. There is only one way I can reclaim his affection. I must find some conclusive original evidence that will make our book shine—something so significant it will bring Pa home.

Nothing but the ramblings of a disappointed young girl. And then as she turned the next few pages, Lettie found what she was looking for.

The Bulletin newspaper is offering a reward of one thousand pounds for conclusive evidence as to the place where Doctor Leichhardt met his fate. I think I may have found an answer in the notes, newspaper articles, and reports from the Geographical Society relating to Andrew Hume.

Lettie threw down the notebook and burrowed through the papers on the desk until she found Evie's hastily written points about Hume. Nothing about reports from the Geographical Society or any other newspaper articles.

She paced the room, bending now and again to rummage through the piles of paper she'd already sorted, peered under the desk, came nose to nose with Oxley. A slobbered, soaked piece of something repulsive hung from the corner of his mouth. She grabbed it and tugged. "You disgusting dog." The corner of his lip curled and he emitted a rumbling growl. She snatched back her hand. "Take it outside!" She crawled out from under the desk and held the door wide. "Go on, shoo!"

Ignoring his refusal, she resumed her search. She had no memory of seeing anything other than Evie's note that mentioned Andrew Hume. She would have remembered, and if Evie had taken notes with her, they would be in the saddlebag, unless . . .

With the words of *The Bulletin* advertisement, *absolutely secret*, echoing in her mind, she skirted Oxley's sprawled form, flung open the door, and shot up the stairs. Where else would a girl hide something secret if not in her bedroom?

She dived under the bed and found nothing, not even a speck of dust. Of course there would be nothing. Peg cleaned every week. Somewhere else. No space at the tiny desk, the sketchbook taking pride of place still open at Evie's self-portrait, nor the bedside table where the first of William's journals sat. She flopped down on the bed and stared around the room.

There was only one other place. The cupboard tucked in the corner. She wrenched open the door, releasing a cloud of naphthalene with a tinge of lily of the valley and Evie's trademark scent. Dress after dress of white cotton dangled in graded lengths. A divided skirt, a green velvet cloak, brown riding boots of varying sizes, and black buttoned boots.

Down on her knees she burrowed farther into the cupboard, hands flat against the base. Nothing. Just nothing.

Groaning in frustration she raced back to the study. Evie had hidden her map in the desk drawer. Even William hadn't found it. She reefed open every single one of the drawers, took each one out, ran her hand over the runners, made certain nothing had fallen down the back, then slumped back into the chair and slammed her hands down.

The palm of her hand hit the side of the compass. "Ouch!" She picked it up, turned it over. Evie couldn't have hidden anything in the compass. Pushing back the chair she opened the bookcase and slid out William's box, took out the sextant and chain, felt all around the edge, tried to lift each compartment. Still nothing.

With a grunt that sent Oxley scuttling into the corner, she

settled the compass back in its compartment and slammed the lid. "Oxley, come here. Where would you hide something?"

Leaning against her leg, he offered silent sympathy but no solution.

Grasping William's box in two hands, she eased it into the space between the books. One of the piles teetered, slipped, and slid to the floor, the crash sending Oxley scooting through the door.

"Blast it." She restacked the books and straightened the box and the green tin lying alongside. A sprig of bottlebrush decorated it. Evie's handiwork, without doubt, but what was it doing on the bookshelf? All the other botanizing canisters and flasks lay stacked against the walls on either side of the mantelpiece. Why was this one among William's books and possessions?

Curiosity aroused, she lifted it down, placed it on the desk next to the notebook. A long leather strap was attached to either end of the green cylindrical metal container—a shoulder strap perhaps. Lettie hefted it, tried it on for size. It sat snug and well-balanced over her right shoulder and rested neatly on her hip, although it weighed more than she expected. Settling it on the desk, she rolled it over. A small trapdoor provided an opening.

After some fumbling she managed to slip her fingers inside. A roll of papers, crammed tight, filled the tin. How could she get them out without destroying them? She snapped the trapdoor closed and examined the ends of the cylinder and found a screw top, rather like the jars in Peg's pantry. She twisted it. Nothing happened. Exerting more force, she finally heard a satisfying grate as the dust and grime released and she freed the lid.

With the palm of her hand she hit the other end of the cylinder until the roll of papers slid to the end. By inserting her fingers and tightening the roll she managed to ease the papers from the canister. A strip of leather secured them.

Her palms sticky with anticipation, she unraveled it—a copy of *The Bulletin*. The irony almost made her shout aloud until she saw the lead article—*The Fate of Ludwig Leichhardt*—and the date—*Saturday, 25th December 1880*. Mere days before Evie disappeared. She flicked through the pages and discovered the corner torn from one page. She had no need to check. Without a doubt the reward notice had once filled the space.

Putting *The Bulletin* aside she leafed through the sheets of paper. Newspaper articles from the *Brisbane Courier*, an interview with Andrew Hume. The details of his early life. Travels around the country. No mention of Maitland. His arrest as a bushranger and finally the story of the way in which he secured his release from prison. He told of his meeting with an old crippled man, who claimed to be a member of Leichhardt's party. He'd shown him some papers sealed in a metal canister—a hunting watch, telescope, quadrant, and thermometer—and Hume had buried them in the desert. Lettie jumped to her feet, reminded of the tiny drawings Olivia had in her bedside table. She was on the right track.

She read on. Hume had been released to the Roper River to retrieve the relics. Then a report from the *Sydney Morning Herald* labeling him a scoundrel and a cheat after he claimed the relics had been stolen.

More articles, the print faded and paper yellowed, transcripts and pages of notes written in William's hand. And the one thing they all had in common, she realized as she scanned the pages—every single one talked of Andrew Hume and the Leichhardt relics.

Lettie went back through the pages, tossing them aside in her frustration when she found no reference to Maitland. She flicked through another series of articles. The words *Maitland Mercury* jumped out: *2nd July 1874*. Her eyes skimmed the page:

The Travels of Andrew Hume

On Tuesday evening, about one hundred persons assembled in the hall of the School of Arts to hear Mr. Andrew Hume, the person who went out to the north of Queensland to discover the remains of the explorer Leichhardt . . .

So Andrew Hume had visited Maitland before he left on his final expedition. But why had Evie thought Maitland significant six—no, seven—years after Andrew Hume's death?

And then Lettie remembered Davey, the young boy in Maitland, leading her to the gravestones of David and Hannah Hume . . . Andrew's parents. They had died in 1893, well after Evie vanished.

She pulled Evie's notebook toward her and flipped through the pages she'd already read.

5th January 1881

The old gods are surely watching over me. Bailey is heading for Maitland. To see an old friend, Hume, who once worked at Dartbrook. I am convinced he is Andrew Hume's father. I will follow and beg an introduction and ask if his son left the relics in his safekeeping. I will leave tomorrow at dawn. My only regret is that I cannot tell Olivia.

Below was a quick sketch of a young boy astride a horse, dressed in patched moleskins, a faded shirt, and a cabbage palm hat.

Lettie sat back and reread the entry. What had made Evie think Andrew Hume might have left the relics in Maitland?

Maitland, 7th January 1881

Bailey is furious! However, I met Andrew Hume's parents. They are both quite aged. Mr. Hume holds his son in low regard. Mrs. Hume took me aside and with tears in her eyes told me Andrew cared more for his old friend and nursemaid Ginny, who lived on the Halls' property at Dartbrook where her husband once worked. Bailey is delivering horses to Scone just ten miles north of Dartbrook and has agreed to let me accompany him. He made me promise to send a letter to Olivia. And so I, too, may be labeled as much a scoundrel and a rogue as Andrew Hume because I have not written to Olivia. I must find Ginny; I believe she holds the key. And I must keep this knowledge secret.

Lettie buried her head in her hands. No room for doubt. Evie was with Bailey.

Dartbrook, 10th January 1881

I HAVE THE EVIDENCE! I was right! Andrew Hume did leave the papers with Ginny. She had no knowledge of the watch and other relics. I believe Andrew told a half-truth and that the thermometer, quadrant, and watch were stolen when he was aboard ship, but not the canister containing the papers. He must have kept them, intending to bring Classen back and verify their authenticity. Seventy-five pages written by Leichhardt himself and another sixty by Classen. My German is poor, but I recognize Leichhardt's signature. The others are signed by Classen. I am certain they explain the fate of the expedition.

Ginny is such a dear old woman and she hadn't heard of Andrew's passing. I have told her about the reward from The Bulletin. I will claim it by telegram from Scone and see that she is amply compensated.

I cannot wait to return to Yellow Rock! I can already see the smile on Pa's face and his eyes dancing. Skuthorpe might claim to have the relics, but I believe I have the answer to the fate of Leichhardt's expedition. We have succeeded where everyone else has failed!

A lump caught in Lettie's throat as she surveyed the final journal entry, Evie's excitement palpable on the page. In the margin there was a small drawing—a bottle-shaped canister, the metal dented and scratched, a thick roll of papers peeking out of the top. But there was no canister in Evie's saddlebag, no papers other than her notebook. Lettie fanned the remaining blank pages of the notebook. The reward notice from *The Bulletin* fell out, then another loosened page slipped free. Evie's bold print:

I WISH TO CLAIM THE REWARD OF ONE THOUSAND POUNDS STOP
I HAVE IN MY POSSESSION PAPERS WRITTEN BY LEICHHARDT
AND CLASSEN DETAILING THE FATE OF LEICHHARDT'S FINAL
EXPEDITION STOP
EVELYN LUDGROVE

A telegram that had never been sent because Evie and Bailey never reached Scone.

Clutching the notebook and papers tight to her chest, Lettie ran back to the farmhouse and left them on the table. No sign of Denman or Nathaniel. And Olivia, where was Olivia? More to the point, where was Evie's saddlebag?

Sticking her fingers in her mouth, she tried for one of Denman's whistles, hoping it might bring Oxley, at best Denman. Her first attempt produced nothing but a series of splutters and a soggy hand—her second proved more fruitful and Oxley appeared from behind the stables, Denman not far behind.

She ran down the path and skidded to a halt, pushing Oxley down. "Denman, where's Nathaniel, where's Olivia, where's Evie's saddlebag?"

"Olivia's got it. She took it to her room last night. Leave her to mourn."

"I can't. I simply can't. She gave me Evie's notebook. It explains everything. Evie was with Bailey."

Denman's face creased in a frown. "Nathaniel, boy, where are you?" He reached for the stall wall, swaying slightly.

"I'll go and find him."

"In the paddock with the mares." He gestured over his shoulder and sank down on an upturned bucket.

"Stay right there. Don't move. I'll be right back."

Denman's blank gaze, fixed on some far distant horizon, showed no sign that he'd heard her. Why hadn't she been more thoughtful? She'd forgotten how old he and Olivia were. She should have chosen her words more carefully.

Nathaniel's shirt made him easy to spot standing behind the stables, just like the drover on Evie's map. It all came back to Evie's map. If only she'd understood it better—if only Evie had taken it with her and finished it. No. Then Lettie wouldn't have been able to commence the search at all. The map had led her to Maitland and to the Humes, Bertha, and Dartbrook.

"Nathaniel! Denman needs you. And I do too. I've read Evie's notebook. She was with Bailey."

Nathaniel's face paled. "That's not good."

"Yes, it is. It means we know they were together, reached Dartbrook, found the papers Andrew Hume had left there . . ." Her words tapered off.

"They must have tried to outrun the fire." He aimed a kick at the base of the fence post.

"And failed?" Her voice quavered. "You think she and Bailey perished in the wildfire?" Goose bumps crawled across her skin. Just like Thorne. Taken by fire. She couldn't imagine a worse way to die. A choked sob slipped between her lips.

Nathaniel reached over and pulled her against his chest.

"Oh! What am I going to tell Olivia?" Wasn't it better to leave things as they were, better for Olivia to remember Evie as the young girl setting out for a day's painting? She wouldn't wish the images scorched in her memory on anyone.

"The truth. It'll be what she wants." With one thumb, he traced a gentle caress on her cheek, wiping away the tears she hadn't known she'd cried. "Come on. Where's this notebook—the least we can do is make sure we're right before we tell Olivia."

"On the kitchen table. And Denman. I told Denman. He looked . . . that's why I was calling you . . . he looked unwell."

"He's tough. He's not harboring any illusions about Bailey. Reckons he'd always known something dire happened. Always maintained Bailey wouldn't have shot through. It'll be Evie that's upset him, and what it'll do to Olivia. Come on." He clasped her hand and led her around to the front of the stables where Denman stood, leaning against the fence, pipe jammed in the corner of his mouth.

"Who's going to tell Olivia?" Denman asked.

"No one. Not until we've looked at this notebook. Come along, old fella."

"Nathaniel, did you take anything from the saddlebag?" Lettie asked.

He dropped her hand. Stopped dead in his tracks. "I did not."

"It's just that Evie said she'd picked up some papers from Dartbrook. She drew a picture. They were in an old tin canister, bottle-shaped."

"Nothing like that in there." There was an edge in Denman's voice, as though he was jumping to Nathaniel's defense. "I was there when he opened it, back at Frog Hollow. He's no thief."

"I'm not suggesting you have stolen anything; it just seems strange. Here, I'll show you."

She pushed open the kitchen door and there was Olivia, sitting at the table, her face streaked with tears, Evie's notebook in her hand.

29

Olivia lifted her ravaged face. "You were right, Lettie. Right all along. Evie did go with Bailey."

Lettie reached out and squeezed Olivia's hand. "You weren't to know."

"If I'd listened, looked more carefully, put the puzzle together, we might have found her before it was too late. I knew Bailey was going to Maitland, knew he was delivering horses to Scone, knew he was going on to Murrurundi. If only I had paid more attention to Evie when she talked about William and their wretched books. If I'd understood she'd become infected by his passion . . . I thought if I ignored all the Leichhardt nonsense, Evie would too."

Lettie understood Olivia's self-recrimination, but she couldn't keep blaming herself for Evie's actions, any more than Lettie could blame Thorne's accident on her tardiness. The outcome couldn't be changed no matter how much they might wish.

Denman reached across the table and tilted Olivia's chin, gazed into her eyes. "You're mourning—not only mourning Evie, Bailey too."

Lettie's head came up with a snap. There was something in the way Olivia's face had changed, softened, when she tipped her head back to look at Denman.

"Yes, yes, I am. I thought he'd left me. We argued. That's why I asked Evie to give him the wages. When he didn't come back, I thought it was because I couldn't give him what he wanted. Couldn't let the family down. I loved him, you know."

Denman squeezed Olivia's fingers. "He knew."

"Do you think he did?"

"He did. Understood it couldn't be."

Lettie felt the sting of tears as the dreadful implication of Olivia's words sank into her befuddled conscience. Olivia hadn't only lost Evie; she'd lost the man she loved, Bailey.

Nathaniel stood with his back to the room. The tension in his shoulders was evident even under the thick cotton of his shirt.

"Shall I make a cup of tea?" Lettie asked for want of anything better to say. What could be said? This agony was of her making. If she'd delivered Miriam's message and left Yellow Rock, the past would have remained buried, much like the contents of the study and Evie's saddlebag. Oxley rested his head against her leg, his big brown eyes full of misery.

"I'll make it." Olivia wiped the back of her hand across her eyes. "Be good to have something to do. And while I am you can tell me what sent you racing to the stables in search of Nathaniel."

Why hadn't she stopped and thought before she'd flown down to the stables? She should have thought about the effect the news would have on Olivia. "I'd read Evie's journal. I'm sorry, I should have broken the news more gently."

"I've read—read some of it. But you still haven't told me what it was you were worked up about." Despite Olivia's ashen complexion, her determination to hear the truth was clear.

"Evie was searching for something specific. You were right, she intended to claim the reward from *The Bulletin*. It's all there. These"—Lettie pointed to the pile of articles she'd found—"these explain why Evie left. They were hidden inside this green metal tube . . ." She sketched the shape with her hands.

Olivia sighed. "Evie's vasculum. She painted bottlebrushes on it."

"Yes, that's right. What is it?"

"Botanists use them for collecting plants. Evie liked to keep her samples fresh, then when she returned she could draw all the details. I didn't know it was missing, didn't notice it in the study."

"It was on the same shelf as William's box, between some books. I found it when I put the compass back. And these were inside." She fanned the articles. "I think Evie set off believing Andrew Hume had left the missing Leichhardt papers with his parents in Maitland while he went to the desert to bring Classen back. But she discovered he hadn't. He disappeared for two days. He had gone to visit his old nursemaid at Dartbrook, Ginny, and left the papers with her, as some sort of security, I'm guessing. Evie went with Bailey to Dartbrook to try and find Ginny and the papers. And she did. There's a picture in her journal of the papers." She picked up the notebook from the table and turned to the last page—to the sketch of a canister with the papers peeking out of the top. "These belonged to Leichhardt and Classen and I believe they explain the fate of the expedition."

"And we're right back to wretched Leichhardt again," Olivia spluttered.

"I wanted to check Evie's saddlebag. I didn't remember seeing them." Lettie reached over and opened the flap on the bag, ran her hand around the bottom, brought out a couple of old and faded pieces of paper. Nothing like the large roll Evie had drawn, and no sign of the canister. "It's not here." She smoothed out the two crumpled sheets, the writing faded, almost illegible. "I can't read them."

"Who is this Classen person? I thought Leichhardt was the one everyone was looking for." Olivia knuckled the tears from her eyes. "None of this is answering any questions about Evie."

"Classen's the man Andrew Hume said he'd found in the desert. A member of Leichhardt's party, his brother-in-law, I think." She angled the screwed-up paper to the light. "There's a name. It might say Classen, the double *s* is strange, more like a capital *B*. Evie found his papers, it's in her notebook, but what became of them?" Lettie's gaze roamed Denman's and Olivia's faces and came to rest on Nathaniel.

He cleared his throat, two spots of color high on his cheeks. "I think I can answer that question."

Her breath caught. Had he taken them from the saddlebag? Had he lied to her when she'd asked him before?

"Parker, Fred Parker. When I got to his place he was burning some stuff. He had the saddlebag next to the fire. I didn't see the Ludgrove-Maynard brand, not at first. I was trying to get him to talk. I helped him. Threw some old papers on the fire. He said he couldn't make head nor tail of them. Didn't know where they came from."

"You burned them!" Lettie's shriek echoed in the kitchen, brought Oxley to his feet, the hair on his back standing to attention.

Nathaniel stood, his head bowed.

"How could you burn them?" She clutched the two remaining pieces of paper to her breast. "That's all Pa ever wanted. Proof of what happened to Leichhardt."

Olivia's head came up sharply. "Give them to me!" She snatched them from Lettie's hand, opened the range, and threw them inside.

"No!" A strange roaring filled Lettie's ears and her vision wavered. "It's for Pa's book." She grabbed at the burning papers, stuck her hand inside the firebox. The flames licked her skin as the paper crumbled to ash beneath her fingers.

"What did you say?" Olivia's voice, barely more than a croak, came from a million miles away.

"The papers, they're for Pa. Proof of Leichhardt's fate. We can claim the reward."

"No, Lettie. Not for your pa, for William, your grandfather. Evie's pa. This has to stop, and it will stop now." Olivia prodded the poker down into the fire. "They're gone. And that's the end of it. There will be no more. Leichhardt has caused this family enough heartache."

The torrent of cold water sent a spasm of pain slicing up her arm. Nathaniel held her tight against his chest, forcing her hand under the tap. She slumped against him, the agony cutting through the clouds of confusion.

"How long has this been going on, Lettie? How long?" Olivia's dark gaze drilled her from across the room.

The roaring sound in Lettie's head receded. She swayed and Nathaniel eased her to a chair, wrapped a sopping tea towel around her throbbing hand.

Olivia glared at her.

Lettie shrugged her shoulders. Olivia had thrown the paper

with Classen's name in the fire. The proof! A choked sound found its way out of her mouth.

"You said, 'It's for Pa's book. The papers, they're for Pa. Proof of Leichhardt's fate.'" Olivia's voice broke into her confusion.

Shaking away her cobwebby thoughts, she licked her lips. "No, not Pa. Pater wouldn't want them. For Grandfather, for Evie, for their book."

"Here, drink this." Olivia held a cup to her lips.

The steam drifted to her nostrils and she inhaled, then bent her head to sip. Had she said Pa? Why would she say that? She'd never called Pater Pa. Olivia must have misheard her. Nathaniel's reassuring arms anchored her. "I can take the cup. I'm not an invalid." The tea slopped over the rim as she raised it to her lips.

Beyond the window the sky had turned crimson, the rising moon painting Yellow Rock a palette of crimson, magenta, and scarlet, the warmth of Nathaniel's body against her back and his arms around her holding her firm.

Down the mountain, heat scorching her cheeks, tears streaming from her eyes, breath rasping as she bent low. Headlong down into the valley, an obscene glow illuminating the treetops, heart pounding in time with the thundering hooves. The deepening roar of the fire reverberated, turning her blood to ice, and in a flash of blinding clarity she accepted her fate.

And then she was flying, the breath wrenched from her lungs, and Pa's voice as a rogue star slashed the sky. *There are more things in heaven and earth* . . .

"Lettie!" Nathaniel's strong arms lifted her, pulled her against his chest, held her tight.

He wiped the perspiration from her face, the tea towel rough against her skin, the throbbing in her hand bringing her back. "I must have fallen asleep." Her head ached. All she wanted was to lie down, pull the blankets over her head, and sleep. "I need to go to bed." She disentangled herself from Nathaniel's grasp and made for the door, staggered, her feet refusing to cooperate.

"Come along, my girl." Olivia's arm wrapped around her shoulders and she led her to the tiny bedroom at the front of the house. The cotton of her nightdress cooled her skin and the welcome weight of the eiderdown anchored her.

Olivia's hand soothed her hair back from her face. "Go to sleep. It'll be better in the morning."

"What was that all about?" Nathaniel stretched out his legs in front of the stove. The color had come back to Denman's face, either from the tea or the knowledge that Olivia seemed once more to be in control.

"Not real sure." Denman scratched at his hair. "Those words she said about things in heaven and earth—"

"'Than are dreamt of in your philosophy.' Shakespeare. William Shakespeare. From a play called *Hamlet*."

"Wouldn't know. She's said them before."

"What do you mean?"

"Night we stopped at Rossgole. She was dreaming, nightmare more like. Scared the living bejesus out of me. Had to wake her up. Sitting up she was, looked like she was trying to outride the devil, fingers wrapped tight and the sweat pouring down her face. Then she collapsed and mumbled that heaven and earth business."

"Reckon she's wrung out, poor girl. Been trying to work it all out. I felt guilty as all hell about those papers I watched Parker burn."

"Nah. You weren't to know what they were. I'd say you did the right thing. More luck than judgment. Why else would Olivia chuck the others in the fire?"

Nathaniel didn't have a chance to answer.

Olivia marched in and planted herself front and center, hands on hips. "I threw them in the fire because the time has come to put an end to this nonsense. It goes back more years than I'd care to count. And Leichhardt's to blame. If it wasn't for him, William wouldn't have lost his leg, wouldn't have spent the family fortune financing useless expeditions, wouldn't have drawn Evie into his obsession, and we wouldn't have lost her."

"Or Bailey," added Denman.

Put like that it all made a whole lot of sense, but it didn't explain Lettie's peculiar behavior, and he cared as much about Lettie as he cared for Denman.

"Time you two got yourselves off to the stables. Happy to sleep there?" Olivia's voice still held a quaver as she collected up Evie's notebook, smoothed it, and slipped it into the pocket of her apron.

Nathaniel pushed the saddlebag toward her, then stopped. "Why don't you give me the saddlebag? I'd like to clean it up." It would come up well with a bit of elbow grease, the least he could do.

Her hand hovered for a moment, as though she couldn't let it go, then she gave a curt nod. "Thank you, Nathaniel. I'd like that."

"I'll be saying good night then."

Neither Denman nor Olivia acknowledged him. He slipped out through the door into the dark.

It was too early to sleep, too much going on in his head. The moon had lost its bloody glow and sat full and bright above Yellow Rock. He wandered off down the path, the path Lettie had run down to greet him before all hell broke loose. She'd brought the past thundering back like an out-of-control carthorse, stampeding everything in its path. He hadn't known that Olivia carried a candle for Bailey, though Denman obviously had.

Stood to reason. Bailey would have confided in his brother. Denman always said he and Bailey were close, real close. He would have known it wouldn't, couldn't, come to anything. A drover, even a boss drover, didn't marry a Maynard, no matter how much they might want to, or a Ludgrove, for that matter. Old money, big landowners, one of the first Hunter families.

He reached out his hand to the moon, closed his fingers, then opened his palm. Nothing. It would be as impossible as catching moonbeams. Which was a shame, a real shame, because the memory of Lettie would wax and wane in his thoughts for a long time, maybe forever. And they said history didn't repeat itself.

A great sigh whistled up from somewhere deep inside him. He'd never had a woman in his life, no one he cared for, but Lettie had gotten under his skin, right from that first moment when she'd walked into the forge bug-eyed and beautiful. Been too busy trying to pull the money together for the bid on Rossgole. And that hadn't gone the way he'd planned. Nothing wrong with his lot, though he still hankered after a decent piece of land. Somewhere he could call his own, breed some horseflesh. Let Denman live out his life in peace and quiet. He'd meant Rossgole to provide that. There'd be other places. He had to wait for the right moment.

30

Nathaniel rose before sparrows, unable to stand Denman's snores a moment longer. He hadn't heard him come in, but he'd made his presence known during the night. Grabbing Evie's bag, a chunk of saddle soap, a tin of Dubbin, and some soft cloths from the tack room, he headed outside and found a spot of sun.

Mindful of his blunder with the papers, he pulled each one of the paintbrushes and pencils out of the pockets and laid them out in order, then the paint box and tin of colored pencils, the bottle of ink, and the nib pen. He ran his fingers across the two scooped edges, the embossed border, and the row of brass studs. At least he reckoned they were brass. He spat on his thumb and rubbed at the green patina. A faint glimmer appeared. Brass without a doubt. It would clean up, no worries.

The two buckles came away easily and the one remaining strap, and after giving them a bit of a rub he lined them up alongside the brushes and turned his attention to the leather. The fine layer of blackened dust, almost soot, cleaned up with a damp cloth. After a go with some saddle soap and a dry, he'd be able to see what was what. Shame about the strap that was missing. It looked as though some animal had bitten it off. When it was all done, perhaps he'd be able to make a replacement. He'd like to give the bag back to Olivia looking its best. Something to remember Evie by.

With the sun warm against his back, he sat half asleep, the rhythmic movement of the cloth against the leather a balm after the madness of the last few days.

"What are you doing to Evie's saddlebag?" Lettie dropped down beside him.

He flinched and jumped to the defensive. "Nothing that'll do any harm. Just cleaning it up for Olivia. I offered last night." He put the cloth down and turned, regretting his reaction. "How're you feeling this morning? How's the hand?"

Lettie flexed her fingers, stretching the red skin. "It's not too bad. Your quick thinking saved me from a nasty burn. I can't imagine what possessed me."

"Just at odds because of everything that's happened. It's a shock for all of us."

"Olivia especially."

"Denman'll take care of her. They go back a long way."

"Did you know Olivia and Bailey . . ." Her words petered out and a flush came to her cheeks, highlighting the eucalyptus tint in her eyes.

He had no memory of Bailey, only knew the stories Denman had told, painted the man as some kind of hero. His staunch belief Bailey wouldn't have stolen anything was as much of a legend as some of the old fellas' stories. "Before my time. Guess it explains why Olivia never married."

"It's sad. She's lived alone for too long."

"Not really alone. She's got Peg, the drovers, I come by as often as I can to give her a hand with the horses, and now you're here."

"There's no reason for me to stay any longer."

Her words made him start. Not what he'd envisioned. Seen her here with Olivia for good, the pair of them running the place, and he'd call in now and again, maybe buy some of their stock, swap the odd service when he finally got his stud up and running. "You wouldn't go back to Sydney, would you? Not now."

She turned her gaze to the rock, a frown creasing her forehead. "I don't know what to do. After my brother died I lost all sense of myself. I couldn't do anything. I pushed everything and everyone away. I ran and now . . ."

"You belong here at Yellow Rock."

"I have to go back to Sydney, make something of my life. Pater and Miriam expect me to marry; I have to prove to them that I am capable of living an independent life."

"An independent life? Your mother sees Ludgrove as a bargaining chip. All those gentleman callers she's arranged are well known around Randwick. The first thing they'll do is sell any property you bring to a marriage."

Her face darkened and her eyes blazed. He'd overdone it this time. Well overdone. What was the matter with him? Narked because she'd had a go at him for letting Parker burn the papers from the saddlebag? Or was he jealous because the thought of her with any other man made his blood run cold?

Not surprisingly she leaped to her feet, hands on her hips.

Lettie's throat constricted, making her gasp for breath. Who did he think he was? "You've got no right to say that."

A sudden sense of foreboding swamped her and the words of Miriam's letter to Olivia, the one she'd shown her up on Yellow Rock, loomed in front of her eyes. *Both the Ludgrove and Maynard properties will now pass to my daughter, Letitia Miriam Rawlings, the family's sole heir.*

"I presume you know that Rawlings's Sydney business can't keep pace with your mother's aspirations for you."

"No. That's not true." All Lettie wanted to do was turn tail and run. It was none of Nathaniel's business. Pater wouldn't force her into a marriage; he was the kindest, most considerate man, always looking after the family, wanting the best for them.

Both the Ludgrove and Maynard properties will now pass to my daughter, Letitia Miriam Rawlings, the family's sole heir.

The words rang again like a death knell. She'd pushed aside all thoughts of marriage since she'd arrived. The mystery of Evie's disappearance had filled her every waking moment. Did Pater and Miriam truly intend the Ludgrove property to provide her with a handsome dowry? Would she have to choose between Olivia and Miriam and Pater, between Yellow Rock and Sydney? She couldn't.

"Go away. It's none of your business."

"You're right there. It might be time you and Olivia had a bit of a chat." And with that he stood up, turned on his heel, and disappeared.

She shuffled back against the wall, pulled her knees up to her chest, and wrapped her arms around her legs. Finding out what happened to Evie was meant to make things better, not worse.

Oxley's warm, wet nose pressed against her cheek. "Go away!" She shrugged him off. He took no notice, just sat down close, his long body leaning heavily against her. She draped her arm around his shoulders, soaking up his silent comfort.

Sometime later Oxley turned his head. A piece of something soggy and disgusting hung out of the corner of his mouth, the same repulsive thing he'd been carrying around for days, the thing she'd tried to take from him in the study. "Drop it, Oxley," she growled.

He pinned her with a sideways stare, then after a moment opened his jaws, let it fall into her lap, then gave her a couple of nudges. Holding it between two fingers, she turned it over. A strip of chewed leather with equally spaced holes.

Crawling on her hands and knees, she edged toward the saddle-bag Nathaniel had left drying in the sun and matched Oxley's offering to the other strap. "Where did you get it? Why didn't you give it to me before?"

Oxley gave her a long-suffering look, stood, stretched, and with his tail held high stalked across the path to the farmhouse.

There was no sign of Nathaniel or Denman, so she left Oxley's piece of chewed leather next to the saddlebag, unable to fathom when he could have bitten it off.

Nathaniel's words, as offensive as they were, carried a note of truthfulness. The dilapidated state of the Sydney house, Pater's long absences, Miriam's insistence that she should make a good marriage. She had to come to a decision. It was no longer her own existence that hung in the balance. Her family's welfare was a responsibility she didn't want but would have to shoulder.

Yellow Rock glared down at her, the sun glancing off the crystals embedded in the rock. She needed somewhere to think, somewhere peaceful. Without another thought she wandered down the path, through the wavering grass to the cemetery. The past had brought her to Yellow Rock—perhaps the answer lay there among her family, the family she hadn't given a moment's thought to until she'd climbed into Lizzie and set off in a half-hearted attempt to escape her meaningless existence.

She pushed open the gate and stood looking at the tiny stones marking the resting place of all the boys who'd never grown to know and love Yellow Rock. And Thorne was just one more.

What would he have done? She couldn't see him as a farmer, not even a gentleman farmer, yet he'd obviously had every intention of coming to talk to Great-Aunt Olivia about his inheritance.

And that's what she must do. The responsibility lay well and truly in her lap.

Lettie found Olivia in the study sitting statue still with Oxley slumped at her feet, staring out at the willows congregated on the bank of the brook. She hadn't expected to see her in the room crowded with more memories of Leichhardt than anyone else. "Good morning, Aunt Olivia."

Oxley eyed her with a judgmental stare, then dropped his head and rested it on Olivia's foot. A flicker of understanding shot through her. The dog had an uncanny knack of knowing who deserved his loyalty.

Oliva ignored her and continued to stare outside, her fingers drumming on the arm of the chair.

"Is there something wrong?" Lettie clamped her lips closed. What a ridiculous thing to say. The poor woman must be devastated. Only the day before, Lettie had shattered Olivia's belief that Evie might one day return. On top of that she'd received confirmation that the man she loved had also perished.

330

And Lettie was to blame. "I'm sorry. I never should have come. I should have left on that first morning. Never dug up the past."

"If I'd wanted you to leave I would have told you. You stayed at my invitation, and I bless the day Miriam sent you."

"She didn't really send me. I rather jumped at the opportunity to leave."

"Understandable."

"And perhaps if I had relayed her message, everything would be sorted out by now and I wouldn't have caused you such misery."

Olivia raised her head and her expression softened. "I shall be eternally grateful to you. You have answered so many questions."

But not all. There was still no proof Evie and Bailey had perished in a wildfire, and there probably never would be. Just supposition. No different from Leichhardt—there was a strange irony in that.

Olivia turned a piece of paper lying on her lap. "Where did you find this?"

Lettie took the painting from Olivia's hand. "I haven't seen it before." She tilted it to the light, Evie's talent evident. A woman, a Madonna, long hair cascading over a dark Prussian blue cloak, the collar edged in fur, stood staring up at Yellow Rock, the aura of melancholy and anguish surrounding her almost palpable. Whatever had made Lettie think that she could draw? Her sketches, her cartoons were nothing more than childish scribbles compared to the artistry apparent in this piece alone.

"Do you know who it is?"

"I'm not sure. Is it Evie? It reminds me of some of the pictures on the map I found the other day." She looked again at Evie's map, spread on top of the desk. "Come and see. The whole scene is wonderful. I especially like it because it reminds me of the day the drovers came when I first arrived. The night you taught me to dance, the night Nathaniel told me the story of Yellow Rock." The wistful tone in her voice made her cheeks burn. Would they ever dance in the moonlight to the strains of the fiddle again?

"I didn't know Evie had drawn the drovers on the map." Olivia pushed out of the chair.

Pleased to have broken the tense atmosphere, Lettie smoothed the map and pointed to the bonfire and the circle of drays. A man playing the fiddle and another an accordion, and the flying skirts and bright faces of the dancers. "Look, I think this is you. See the way you're holding your skirt."

Olivia peered over Lettie's shoulder and emitted a short gasp. "That's Bailey. I'm dancing with Bailey."

Oh no! It seemed everything Lettie did or said caused another painful memory to surface. No wonder Olivia had left the study closed for all these years. Once she'd given Olivia a moment or two to compose herself, Lettie said, "Can you recognize anyone else? Is Denman there? Nathaniel?"

"Before Nathaniel was born. Denman might be. He hadn't started his blacksmith business then." She bent her head close to the map and squinted.

"There's a magnifying glass." Lettie handed the glass to Olivia. "I was using it the other day. That's when I found the people behind the stables." She pointed to the couple entwined in a romantic embrace. "He looks like one of the drovers. Perhaps it's just the red shirt and the angle of his hat. And I wondered if the girl was Evie."

The magnifying glass clattered as it hit the desk. Oliva stood up straight, turfed Oxley out of the soft chair, and resumed her seat.

What had she done this time? "Have you had any breakfast?" Anything, just anything to change the subject. Was there nothing she could do or say that didn't stir up a flurry of emotions?

"Peg's bringing cheese scones. She's on her way now." Olivia cocked her head toward the view of Peg striding along the path, tray in hand.

"Lovely. I'll go and open the door." Lettie scuttled from the room, leaving the heavy weight of the past and Olivia's devastated expression. She had no idea how to behave. This was unlike Thorne's passing. That had been a dreadful time, but there had been so much to do in those first days—the inquest, the funeral, the trappings of mourning—that at the time she had detested, but perhaps they had served some purpose. What did Olivia have—nothing but memories and uncertainties.

Peg shouldered open the door before Lettie reached it. "Everything all right?"

"I'm glad you're here." Lettie took the tray. "You do know what happened last night, don't you?" She couldn't bear the thought of having to retell the whole series of events.

"Olly told me this morning. Suspect it's only the bare bones, but I've got the gist of it."

"Here are some refreshments." Lettie placed the tray on the desktop, cringing at the false brightness in her tone.

"In a moment." Olivia waved the portrait of the woman in the blue cloak in Peg's direction. "Who do you reckon this is?"

Peg barely glanced at it. "Miriam." The clipped word held all the assurance in the world.

"I thought it might be Alice; it's her cloak." Olivia frowned.

"No. It's Miriam. You remember. Alice's hair was straight as a die. See the curls." Peg's finger traced the picture. "She's wearing Alice's cloak, though. The one she wore when she left for Sydney, after Alice passed, before she married. I remember that day clear as yesterday. Mrs. Hewitt had asked me to come up, thought you'd

333

need a hand, but you hadn't given the final say-so. I was hanging about, waiting for them to leave. Thirty or more years ago."

Curiosity piqued, Lettie took the picture again. Miriam? Her mother? Surely she should recognize her. "Mother's hair is always smooth, tied up, never hanging down her back like that. And I've never seen her wearing that cloak."

"That was then; you're talking about now. This was before she took on all the airs and graces." Peg gave a disparaging sniff. "Besides, look at the way she's standing. That's proof if ever I saw it."

Lettie squinted at the picture again. "Proof, proof of what?"

"If you can't see it, I certainly can. Haven't had four children and ten grandchildren not to recognize that stance. Dead giveaway, that age-old gesture. Hand on the belly, protecting her unborn child. Probably didn't even know she was doing it."

Peg's words took a while to penetrate the fog in Lettie's brain, and then the truth of her words thundered through her mind like a steam train. "You're saying that's Mother when she was anticipating?" How could that be? Miriam had told her that the only time she'd been to Yellow Rock since her marriage was after Grandfather died. Lettie could remember it well. The dreadful drive, the thunderous silence, and Thorne's scratched knees bleeding into his socks from his fall from the angophora tree.

A look flashed between Olivia and Peg. Lettie jumped in before either of them had a chance to speak. "When do you think this was drawn? Peg, you said you remembered the day as if it was yesterday."

Olivia answered. "Twenty-fourth of November, 1880."

Three weeks before Miriam and Pater married. Their wedding date was indelibly imprinted on Lettie's mind, Miriam always insisting Pater recognize their wedding anniversary by providing her with a piece of jewelry from Messrs. Fairfax & Roberts. She would go and pick something out and pretend, when Pater presented it to her, that he had chosen the perfect piece. "Before Mother and Pater were married?" And then heat rushed to her cheeks as the implication settled. Mother and Pater must have . . . She shook the thought away at the sound of Olivia's voice, broken, disappointed, and frail.

"I am such a foolish old woman, eaten up with jealousy. I wanted Miriam away. I believed she'd stolen the man I loved."

Lettie lifted her head. Was Olivia suggesting that she and Pater . . . No, that couldn't be right. She'd heard Olivia quite clearly say that Bailey was the only man she loved. In that case . . . was Pater not Thorne's father? How could that be? There had never been a time when . . . Her breath came in short gasps and she sank into the chair, too dizzy to stand, trying in some way to still the banging inside her head. The realization spread icily across her skin. It was the obvious conclusion, but that meant . . .

Thorne *was* her brother. She couldn't entertain otherwise. "What are you suggesting?" Lettie snapped. Peg was mistaken. "Where did you find the picture?"

"Under the pile there." Olivia indicated the papers she'd found in Evie's vasculum. Olivia must have brought them into the study this morning from the kitchen. "I'm trying to remember Evie drawing it. Her nose was out of joint because she wanted to keep Alice's blue cloak and I'd told her to give it to Miriam. The green would have made Miriam look sallow. She'd been having a terrible time of it, dreadfully sick."

"You knew Miriam was . . ." She couldn't get the word out and instead sketched some sort of shape in front of her stomach.

"Yes, I knew. William did too. That's why the wedding was such a hurried job."

Whom to believe? Miriam or Olivia? A mother wouldn't lie to

her children? It was the same as it had been when she first arrived. Olivia playing her off against Miriam, caught in some age-old battle between two women. Oh, how she wished Thorne were here. Not to hear these dreadful accusations but to make fun of them. To dissolve the horrible thick atmosphere, the seriousness of the implication.

She wanted to tear the picture into a million pieces, burn the evidence before her. If, as Peg insisted, Miriam was pregnant before she married Pater, then who was Thorne's father? The image of his dark eyes filled her vision. As children they had laughed about it. Two sides of a coin, his dark eyes nothing like her muddy green ones. His skin welcomed even the harshest sun, whereas hers erupted in a rash of freckles at the slightest provocation, a throwback Miriam always attributed to Pater's Scottish ancestry.

Olivia shifted uncomfortably in her seat. "I thought Bailey was responsible. Now I don't know what to believe." She pushed herself to her feet with a groan and returned to the map. "Evie didn't lie. Leastways, not until she got a bee in her bonnet about that Andrew Hume fellow. That's Bailey and me dancing." She stabbed at the tiny pictures. "And that"—the table shuddered with the force of her finger—"that's Miriam."

There was no doubt in Lettie's mind that Olivia was right, the waist-length curly hair identical to the larger portrait of Miriam in the blue cloak. But it wasn't Pater on the map. This man was taller, stronger, and dressed like one of the drovers, with braces over his shirt. She'd never seen Pater without a jacket and cravat, and to the best of her knowledge, Edward Rawlings had visited Yellow Rock only once, and both she and Thorne had accompanied him.

Olivia rolled up the map, secured it with the blue ribbon, and tucked it under her arm. "Bring the magnifying glass. I need a second, maybe a third opinion. Are you coming, Lettie? Peg?"

31

They found Nathaniel and Denman in the stables, buckets in hand.

"I owe you and Nathaniel." Olivia slapped Denman on the shoulder. "You've done a wonderful job. You didn't have to, you know."

Lettie's gaze swept the immaculate stable block, the polished tack hanging in neat rows, the stacked bales of hay, and beyond the stables, the repaired fence lines and sparkling water troughs.

"Thought you had other things on your mind and could do with a hand." Denman tipped his hat back and sank down on a hay bale with a sigh. "Nathaniel's got something for you. Go on, lad, go and get it."

Without a word, or even a glance in Lettie's direction, Nathaniel disappeared into the stables.

"I wanted to show you something. See if you can help me solve a puzzle." Olivia unrolled Evie's map and spread it out. "This is Evie's map. The one I was telling you about."

Denman peered over Olivia's shoulder. "Talented girl, young

Evie. Always had her sketchbook with her, used to do pictures of all the drovers, fast as lightning that pencil of hers would skid across the page. There's many a woman has one of her sketches tacked to her wall."

"There's a picture here of one of the drovers' parties." Olivia indicated the fire and the group dancing. "I'm dancing with Bailey."

Denman put his nose within two inches of the paper. "Nah. Eyes aren't good enough. It's too dark in here. Need to be outside."

A shiver of apprehension tiptoed across Lettie's shoulders. "I've got a magnifying glass." She reached into her pocket.

"Outside I said. Get a move on."

Olivia rolled up the map yet again and they all trooped out into the sunshine.

"Put it down here." Denman smoothed the map, his nose as good as touching the paper.

Lettie handed him the magnifying glass. "It'll be clearer if you use this."

With a grunt Denman brought the glass to his eye, angled his head, and sighed. "Yep. That's Bailey. Not a doubt about that."

"Do you know who this is?" Olivia pointed to the couple behind the stables.

Denman let out a hoot of laughter. "Caught in the act."

The thundering noise in Lettie's ears almost drowned out his words. "Who is it?" she whispered.

"Miriam, who else? No one else had hair like that, always reckoned she needed a good shearing."

"And who is that with her?" Lettie stabbed at the picture of the man, his arms encircling her waist, his drover's shirt a bright blot.

Denman quirked a grin. "Bit hard to tell. Got any ideas, Nathaniel?"

Lettie jumped. She hadn't noticed that Nathaniel had re-appeared. He had Evie's saddlebag hanging over his shoulder. Polished up, looking as good as new.

Nathaniel took the magnifying glass, examined the picture, and shrugged. "A drover? Could be anyone. Can't see his face, hat's pulled too low."

"Can tell a lot about a man by the way he wears his hat," Denman said.

Lettie's skin prickled. "Do you have any idea who it might be?"

"Take a guess, it's a bloke called Chapman. One of the drov-ers. Stuck around for a while, then took off to . . ." Denman scratched at his chin. "Liverpool Plains, maybe farther north." He shrugged.

A shiver ran down Nathaniel's back and his hat itched. He took it off, raked his fingers through his hair. The picture was ridiculously small. The man could be any one of the drovers who rode the stock route today, never mind thirty years ago.

Olivia cleared her throat. "Lettie, I know this will come as a shock, but it's for the best. Get it out in the open once and for all. There've been too many secrets in this house for too long."

Secrets? What kind of secrets? Something Lettie obviously didn't want to hear; her face had paled and every one of her freckles stood out like specks of gold dust across her nose.

The tension in the air crackled. He stepped up behind her, slipped his arm around her shoulder.

"I'd put money on it being Chapman," Denman said.

Lettie swayed, sucked in her breath, wrenched away from him, and started to run, her feet tumbling and tripping through the long grass.

He bolted after her. Caught her around the waist.

"Let go of me." Her eyes blazed, her arms flailing as she tried to push him away.

He reached for her shoulders, felt the tremor run through her body, then the tears began.

"Leave me alone." Her words came in a hiccupping sob. "You don't understand. It's Thorne . . ." She pushed away from him.

Without a second thought he swept her up into his arms, cradled her against his chest.

"Put me down." She gave a feeble kick, then her entire body heaved and the fight went out of her.

What the hell was going on?

"Take her up to the house, Nathaniel," Olivia said.

He covered the distance in no time, Olivia leading the way. She held open the door of a small bedroom at the front of the house and he laid Lettie down on the narrow bed.

"Go on. Off you go. She'll be fine."

He closed the door behind him, wishing he could stay, sit beside her, hold her hand until she was ready to tell him what was happening.

He found Denman slumped at the kitchen table, the saddle-bag in front of him, running his finger over the leather. "Olivia will look after Letitia. She's got a lot to take in."

A picture of her mother as a young girl messing about with one of the drovers. Not the best, but not the kind of news that would make a girl like Lettie swoon. "Am I missing something?"

"Dunno. Are you?" Denman squinted down at the map, which had somehow made it to the kitchen table. "Let's see here. Perhaps you don't know everything. Miriam was more than a handful. Best thing that could have happened, William taking her to Sydney to wed. She had a bit of a thing going for Chapman. A Ludgrove wasn't ever going to marry a drover."

So he was right. The old story about a man not being good enough.

"Used to hang around every time we came in, flutter her eyelashes, dance the night away, then it got a bit more serious. Didn't realize quite how serious, though." Denman cleared his throat, picked at his ragged fingernails. "Young Mr. Ludgrove got wind of it and got busy securing what you might call an arranged marriage."

Was he saying that Miriam got herself in a predicament, had to get married?

"Rawlings was Mr. Ludgrove's manager in Sydney. It didn't take much to talk him into it. A great dowry smoothed the ride and pushed their finances into the red."

"Are you saying what I think you're saying?"

"That Rawlings didn't sire the boy? Reckon I am. Lettie's taken it tough—finding out the brother she idolized wasn't who she thought he was."

"He's still her brother. Same way you've been a father to me. Though I've never really understood why you took me on."

"Not sure I did either. Just didn't seem fair to me that a boy should suffer because fate dealt him a raw hand. First your mother, then your father in that godawful crossing on the Hawkesbury."

Not the time to go over his story—it was Lettie's he wanted to understand. "And that's why this Chapman disappeared from the scene?"

"Suspect he got a handful of cash to take with him. Like I said, a Ludgrove doesn't marry a drover, no matter how much she might want to."

And the sooner he got that fact straight in his head, the better he'd get on. What if the drover was a stockman? Owned himself a decent property, a stud? The dream was still there. But lately there'd been another thought or two slipping into his mind. And that's what had cut him when Lettie had said she'd have to return to Sydney. It was one he was going to have to get out of his mind right now.

"You're quiet. Nothing else to say?"

"No, just thinking about Lettie, about the future."

"Taken a bit of a shine to her, haven't you?"

"Might have. Not much I can do about it. Said she's going back to Sydney. Besides, it'd be like history repeating, wouldn't it?"

Lettie hugged her arms around her body, her teeth chattering, her whole body shaking. Olivia pulled the quilt around her shoulders and smoothed her hair back from her face. "Come on now. It'll all turn out for the best. You'll see."

No. It wouldn't. It couldn't. "It can't be true. Thorne *is* my brother." The mere thought brought a rush of bile to her mouth.

"Yes, he was, and always will be. Your half brother, that's the only difference."

"But he and I . . . we were alike, had so much in common, loved the same things, the motor, the boat, adventure . . ." She interlaced her fingers, clenched them tight until her knuckles cracked, and a low moan issued from her mouth. "How long have you known?"

"Some of it for a long time, other bits not as long."

"What about Pater? Does he know Thorne isn't his son?"

"From the outset. William arranged the marriage the moment Miriam's situation became obvious. It was a difficult time. Alice had died. William was grieving, we all were. He did what he thought was best. Turned out he was right. Miriam and Rawlings have had a good life. He accepted Thorne as his son and then you came along and sealed the bargain."

The bargain. It made it sound as though she were some kind of compensation. "And Pater is my father?"

"Of course he is. You only have to see the two of you together to know."

"You've never seen Pater and me together."

"I have once. You came here when you were very small, do you remember?"

"With Thorne. Yes. We thought the house was haunted. He fell out of the angophora."

"The day Miriam brought me William's will."

"But why . . ." Lettie shot upright. "Why leave Ludgrove to Thorne? Grandfather knew he wasn't Pater's son. You knew."

"William accepted Thorne as his grandson. He settled a handsome dowry on Miriam; she inherited the house in Horbury Terrace. Same as my parents did for my sister, Alice, and me. She took a large cash dowry into her marriage to William, and I inherited the Maynard land.

"He settled the Ludgrove land on Evie. We all expected she'd come home. William wanted the two properties to stay as one, just the way his father and mine intended."

"And what do you think?"

"I want William's wishes upheld. The properties shouldn't be divided. Right from the moment the land was granted, the intention was that they should be joined, through William and Alice's marriage, but there was no son to inherit. William was convinced Evie would return, so he left me as caretaker and then, only days before he died, he changed his will. If Evie didn't come home, Thorne would inherit the Ludgrove portion on his thirtieth birthday. William finally accepted that he wouldn't be seeing Evie in his lifetime."

But Thorne had died before his thirtieth birthday. "Why did Miriam think Thorne would inherit the Maynard land? It's yours."

"I have no heirs. Miriam played on my insecurities."

"What insecurities?"

"My foolish misapprehension and my misery. I believed Bailey had left, disappeared, because he and Miriam . . ." She took a deep breath, pursed her lips, and forced the words out. "I thought Bailey was Thorne's father. That's why Miriam and I haven't spoken for all these years. I told her I never wanted to see her again, that she should never set foot on Yellow Rock. I believed she'd stolen the man I loved and married another.

"I was a fool. I didn't have the courage to follow my heart. I couldn't marry a drover any more than Miriam could." She waved her hands in the air, her face suffused with color. "Then as the years passed I wondered if I hadn't made a mistake. I tried to find Bailey, but all I heard was the same old story about wages and stolen horses. I didn't believe it any more than Denman did. In the end I decided Bailey's son, Thorne, should be the one to inherit Maynard; not only would it make amends, it would keep the two properties as one, just as William wanted."

But Olivia hadn't had any proof that Thorne was Bailey's son. "Why didn't you ask Mother?"

"Because I'm an arrogant old woman bent on vengeance, without a shred of forgiveness in my soul."

Dread coiled in Lettie's stomach. She didn't want to leave Yellow Rock, especially not now. With a hollow heart Lettie reached out and took Olivia's gnarled hand.

"I want you to do something for me," Olivia murmured.

"Anything."

"I'd like you to stay and finish Evie's map, finish her story, and Bailey's. Tell the truth. You're the only person who can."

Olivia's unexpected request and the faith she was placing in her brought tears to Lettie's eyes. "I'm not sure I can." She hadn't the skill. She might be able to sketch the odd cartoon, doodle on the back of a piece of paper, but what Olivia was asking was so much more.

"You can. No one else understands Evie as well as you do." Olivia narrowed her eyes. "I was right on the very first day you arrived when I said it was as though Evie had come back to me."

Such a fey remark from the down-to-earth woman buffeted Lettie's senses. She'd pushed the dreams and strange sense of connection she felt with Evie away since her foolish grab for the paper in the fire. "What if I spoil Evie's map?" Or worse, "What if I get the story wrong?"

"You won't. Evie will guide you."

32

Nathaniel didn't want to leave Yellow Rock, didn't know what he wanted, truth be told. He'd cleaned, polished, and repaired everything he could find in the stables. A strange stillness hung over the homestead, an atmosphere he couldn't quite fathom, and all he'd seen of Lettie was her back, walking down the path to the study.

Denman appeared with the horses saddled. "Come on, mate, time we were out of here."

The old man was right, but somehow it felt as though they had unfinished business. "I'm not sure we should be leaving Lettie and Olivia."

"They'll be fine."

"Olivia will be here all on her own if Lettie goes back to Sydney."

"She's got Peg. She can manage. Same as she's always done. Nothing more we can do."

"Wish I'd stopped Fred Parker from burning those papers."

Denman handed over the reins, clambered up into the saddle, and clamped his hat down hard. "Wishing ain't going to change anything. Pull yourself together, boy."

"Should go and say goodbye."

"Already done that."

Then that was that. He led Rogue out to the driveway, threw one last look at the main house, imagined Lettie sitting there behind the desk. He couldn't leave without apologizing for the way he'd spoken to her. He'd no idea what had possessed him to stick his nose in—his remarks had been plain out of line. None of his business what she, or her family, did. "Give me a moment. I want to say goodbye to Lettie." Without waiting for Denman's reply he threw him the reins and sprinted down the path.

Lettie stood, hands resting on the desk, gazing out at Yellow Rock, then down at Evie's map, then back out of the french doors. He cleared his throat. "I'm here to say goodbye."

She spun around. Dark shadows bruised the skin beneath her eyes. "You made me jump."

He stood wringing his hands like some lovesick toad, his heart thundering faster than the milk train. "When are you leaving?"

"Leaving?"

"Yeah, leaving for Sydney."

"I haven't made up my mind yet." She quirked a half smile. "You were right. Olivia shouldn't be here on her own. Not yet. And she's asked me to finish Evie's map."

His heart rate slowed and he took a step closer. "Good."

"Good?"

"You belong here." Next thing he knew he was close, so close he could smell the scent of paint, turpentine, see the spots of gold glittering in her luminous eyes. He reached out and cupped her cheek, wanting to pull her into his arms. "Stay. Sydney's no place for you. Especially not now."

She tilted her face to his, a barely discernible half smile lingering on her lips. "I'll stay until I have finished Evie's map." She released her breath in a long, trembling sigh and stepped away from him. "Perhaps you'll be back this way before I leave."

He'd make sure he was. And he'd make sure no harm came to her when she did return to Sydney. "I'll do my best."

Lettie rested her palms flat on the surface of the desk, gulping the air wafting in from the garden but failing to calm the thundering in her blood. It hadn't crossed her mind that Nathaniel and Denman would be leaving. She didn't want them to go. And worse, she didn't want to return to Sydney, even though she knew she must.

The moment she'd arrived at Yellow Rock she'd changed. Yellow Rock had given her a sense of belonging she'd never known, not even when Thorne was alive. Yet now she felt incomplete, as incomplete as Evie's map. She traced the fine lines of the roads she and Evie had traveled, into the blank void that marked the division between reality and mystery, picked up a pencil, and pulled a blank sheet of cartridge paper toward her.

Sometime later, she felt rather than heard Oxley slip into his accustomed place beneath the desk, his heavy head resting on her foot, but still she stared out of the window, unable to make a mark on the paper. How could she finish Evie's map? All they knew for certain was that Evie and Bailey had reached Dartbrook. What happened after that was still a mystery, though in her heart of hearts she believed the wildfire had taken them both, but what did Olivia believe?

Snatching up the map, she made her way out onto the veranda searching for the familiar figure of Olivia, but there was no sign.

Oxley finally solved the problem, spotting Peg in the vegetable garden fighting with a trellis.

"Peg, do you know where Olivia is?"

"In her room. Said she had some thinking to do."

"I need to talk to her. She wants me to finish Evie's map, but I don't think I can. Not until I know she understands that Evie isn't coming back."

"It's hard to give away dreams and beliefs you've held on to for a long time. She's had a lot to take in."

So much—not only Evie but Bailey too. "Should I disturb her?" People needed time to grieve. How many weeks had she spent sitting and staring out of her bedroom window trying to turn back time, trying to will Thorne back into her life?

"That's her decision. Go and find out. What's the worst that can happen?"

That there'd be no ending to Evie and Bailey's story. She turned and gazed up at Yellow Rock. How she wished Nathaniel hadn't left. Right from the very beginning she'd held him at arm's length, denying the truth about the way he made her feel.

"Oxley can give me a hand in the garden. I need some holes dug. You go and talk to Olivia. It's time the past was laid to rest."

Pushing her hair back from her face, Lettie drew in a deep breath of the fragrant air, rich with the scent of citrus blossom, and made her way to the farmhouse, past her room to the very end of the hall.

Olivia's private sanctuary. Only once had Olivia invited her inside—the day she'd shown her Evie's drawings. Lettie clenched her knuckles and knocked on the door.

It swung open.

Olivia sat rigidly upright on the edge of her bed staring at the wall, her hands folded in her lap and her feet neatly aligned on the floor.

"I'm sorry. I knocked, but the door . . ." Lettie's words dried up as she studied Olivia's tearstained face. "I'm sorry. I'll wait until you're—"

"Sit down." Olivia patted the quilt beside her, then scrubbed a balled handkerchief across her face.

The bed groaned as Lettie lowered herself next to Olivia, wanting to take her in her arms and comfort her.

Olivia must have sensed her intention because she drew herself up even straighter, accentuating the space between them, and stuffed her handkerchief into her sleeve. "I want to ask you some questions."

Lettie let her eyelids drop for a moment, then nodded. She'd opened a Pandora's box and now she must face the consequences.

"Why did you come to Yellow Rock?"

"Because Miriam sent . . ." No, now was not the time to hide behind Miriam's skirts. She owed Olivia honesty and truth. "Because I was running away, because my life had no meaning after Thorne died."

"And have you found meaning to your life now?"

"I found you, a family I didn't know I had, the past . . ." A past perhaps Olivia wished Lettie hadn't unearthed. "I just wish I could have found the answers."

"Proof, you mean? Proof that Evie and Bailey are gone."

Lettie bowed her head. How much pain she had caused this poor woman. Wouldn't it have been better if she'd left after she had delivered Miriam's message, not stirred up this hornets' nest?

Olivia's cold hand clasped hers. "I asked you to stay. I asked you to help me find Evie and, as I have told you before, I bless the day Miriam sent you." Silence hung and Olivia's grip tightened.

"Because of you, because of everything you have discovered, I can take solace in the knowledge that Evie and Bailey are together. He will take care of her until our spirits meet." A frail smile flickered across Olivia's pale lips.

Olivia let go of Lettie's hand and reached down to the floor. She lifted Evie's saddlebag and placed it gently in Lettie's lap. "Now you can finish Evie's map. Finish Evie and Bailey's story."

The days merged as Lettie worked, directly onto Evie's map, no longer concerned that the task was beyond her. The words in Evie's notebook echoed in her mind as the pictures took shape. She marked Dartbrook and Rossgole and drew Evie and Bailey, their horses turned toward the north, toward Scone. Evie's excitement visible in the set of her shoulders and the tilt of her head. Bailey, his hat pulled low, a pace or two ahead, a guiding presence as he led the way down the hill, and behind them the red ball of the setting sun hovering above the hills.

There was so much they would never truly know. Evie's physical presence had gone, but she was here at Yellow Rock. She vibrated in every glimmer of sunlight, in every line on the map. The map Lettie would complete.

Her first addition proved she had not only the ability but the inextricable bond with Evie that Olivia had predicted. She could see the difference in their drawings, the difference in style, but together they made a harmonious whole that she believed would please Olivia. Not that she'd seen anything of Olivia since they'd spoken. She'd remained in her room.

Every morning Lettie helped herself to breakfast, went into the study, became absorbed in her drawings, forgot about lunch, and in the evening, she found a meal waiting for her in the farmhouse kitchen along with a note from Peg telling her Olivia had taken her meal in her room. As much as she wanted to offer comfort, she understood Olivia's need for solitude. The need to realign her world. She'd felt much the same after Thorne's death, and she could do no more than be there if Olivia needed her.

Lettie sat at the kitchen table picking at a piece of bread and jam, debating the merits of including Fred Parker on the map. When Olivia bounded into the kitchen, dressed in her very proper pin-tucked blouse and black skirt, carrying a smart straw hat, a pair of gloves, and the first smile Lettie had seen in a long time, she simply gaped.

"I've got some business to attend to in Cessnock. I'll take the coach from Wollombi. And I've decided I'm going to open up the main house again. It's been closed for too long. Peg's attending to it right now. You can take Evie's room. I'll move back into my old room, and we'll clear Alice's and William's rooms for guests." Olivia pinned her hat in place. "I've a mind to ask Denman and Nathaniel if they'd like the farmhouse. Denman said he's packing up the smithy. Since they didn't get Rossgole they can base themselves here. And I want you to treat this place as home. After all, the Ludgrove property will be yours one day soon."

Lettie's head came up with a snap. She didn't want that. Visions of the ensuing argument with Miriam were more than she could stand. How could she finish Evie's map and then see Yellow Rock divided? "I wouldn't know what to do with the place."

"You wouldn't have to do anything. Life could go on just the way it is. You can come and go as you please. Nathaniel and Denman and I will run the stud."

"Nathaniel wants to breed Walers for the Light Horse." Lettie clapped her hand over her mouth. Whatever had made her say that?

"Does he indeed? Always knew that boy had his head screwed on."

"He didn't tell me himself. Sam told me. I shouldn't have said anything."

"No harm in knowing these things." Olivia brushed her hands together as though removing the last little crumb of doubt. "I will telegraph Miriam from Wollombi and tell her of your decision to stay. I'm not ready to deal with her just yet."

Whatever did Olivia need to do? "Deal with her?"

"You concentrate on the map and I'll concentrate on my business. Now off you go. Peg will move your belongings into the main house. You've got work to do. I'll be back in time for supper. We'll eat in the dining room tonight." And with that Olivia swept out the door.

Lettie sat for a while at the kitchen table pondering Olivia's change of demeanor, then returned to the study. She, too, had a plan, one she would discuss with Olivia over supper.

33

While Peg gave the massive cedar table a final polish and arranged carafes of water and lemonade and glasses on the sideboard next to plates of sandwiches, Lettie sat chewing the end of her pencil, her fingers itching to help. "Are you sure there's nothing I can do, Peg?" she called from the study.

"Positive. You get on with that story. I thought you had a deadline."

She did. Her alter ego, Raw Edge, did. The response she'd had from *The Bulletin* when she'd pitched her idea for Evie's story was as swift as it was surprising, and now instead of an article, as she had originally suggested, she was putting together the final proposal for a book. Not *The Prince of Explorers* but the story of Evelyn Ludgrove, an adventurous and brave woman who set out to solve the mystery that consumed and baffled the world.

Olivia swooped into the room and dived like a kookaburra after a lizard for the corner of the desk. "I don't want this available until everyone is here." She snatched the foolscap leather wallet and marched across to the dining room.

Neither she nor Peg knew what Olivia had planned, but it had to be important because she'd worked herself into a frenzy ever since her visit to Cessnock four weeks ago. And she'd invited Miriam and Pater to Yellow Rock and—much to Lettie's surprise—they had accepted.

Nathaniel and Denman had arrived a day ago and, as Olivia had suggested, taken up residence in the farmhouse, although Lettie had a sneaking suspicion Nathaniel might still be sleeping in the stables—something about needing to keep an eye on the horses.

The morning wore on and the temperature climbed almost as high as her curiosity. She packed up her notebook and decided to take a walk. First and foremost, she wanted to see Nathaniel. She'd gone looking for him last evening, but Denman had mumbled something about a job he had to do. In the end, she'd given up and gone to bed, only to lie awake listening to the cicadas.

She'd thought long and hard about what he'd said about Miriam's plans for Ludgrove and tried in a million ways to decide what she should do. Olivia's request that she should finish Evie's map and her submission to *The Bulletin* had provided her with yet more excuses to procrastinate making a decision. There was no practical reason for her to stay at Yellow Rock anymore, just the sense of belonging, one she didn't want to slip through her fingers.

She found Nathaniel out in the paddocks, one of the young colts on a long rope bucking and kicking and carrying on a treat. She hung over the fence, admiring his patience and gentle words. The thought he might be avoiding her crossed her mind, and when he took little notice of her arrival, she found a spot in the shade to wait. Pulling out a piece of paper and pencil, she started to sketch Nathaniel with the colt. Although she'd finished Evie's map, there were little vignettes she continued to add, rather as she suspected

Evie had. This would be one of them. Nathaniel deserved a place on the map as much as anyone else. Without him, they never would have found Evie's saddlebag.

Lettie stretched and let out a long sigh when the large black Cadillac swept into the driveway, Pater behind the wheel and Miriam trailing her trademark chiffon scarf. They pulled to a halt outside the main house. Lettie pushed the sketch into her pocket and rose.

The moment she rounded the corner of the farmhouse Pater bounded from the car, arms extended, a huge smile on his face. "Lettie, it is such a delight to see you." He held her away from him. "You look happy, the happiest I've seen you since . . . The country air must agree with you."

Her gaze raked his face, taking in the telltale signs of concern, the deepened lines around his mouth and his florid complexion. "It's lovely to see you, Pater." She disentangled herself from his grasp and turned to Miriam. "Mother."

"Is there someone who can see to our bags? Your father refused to allow Connors to accompany us." She unwrapped her chiffon scarf and peeled off her gloves. "It is appallingly hot. Not a breath of air."

"I'll take your bags. Peg has prepared rooms for you." Lettie bent down to pick up the two leather cases and hatbox.

"I can manage those. You take the hatbox." Pater grasped a bag in each hand, gave a huff. "Lead the way."

Lettie skittered up the path, a rush of apprehension drying her mouth. Whatever had Olivia planned? No matter how many questions she'd asked, how she'd phrased them, Olivia had refused to enter into any discussion, and now that Miriam and Pater had finally arrived she couldn't pretend everything would stay the same.

Once she reached the top of the stairs, she gestured to the bedrooms. "Olivia said you were to take your pick."

Miriam marched across the landing and threw open the door to Alice's bedroom with a proprietorial air, gave a nod of approval.

"Your father will take Pa's old room. I shall be down once I have refreshed myself." The door closed with a bang, reminding Lettie that she had promised Olivia she would change her clothes.

"I won't be a moment, Pater." She gestured to her moleskins. "I need to put on something more appropriate."

"Very good, very good." He tossed his small bag onto the bed in the sparse room adjacent to the main bedroom. "Try not to take too long. I'll wait for you here."

Lettie slipped into Evie's room and opened the cupboard door. Peg had hung up her clothes, but there was nothing that suited her mood; finally she pulled down one of Evie's white muslin dresses and slipped it over her head. If nothing else she would be cool. She pulled a brush through her hair and fastened it with a black ribbon, slipped on a pair of stockings and boots, and within moments joined Pater.

"Now you can tell me everything that has been happening. I've quite missed my favorite girl." He threaded his arm through hers and they made their way back down the stairs to the dining room.

There was no sign of Olivia, but Denman stood deep in conversation with a couple Lettie had never met before.

Peg appeared carrying a plate of fruitcake. "Ah! I see your parents have arrived." She led them across to Denman. "Mr. and Mrs. Lovedale, may I introduce Olivia's great-niece, Letitia Rawlings."

"Delighted to meet you at long last, my dear." Mr. Lovedale's eyes sparkled as he reached out and took her hand in both of his. "I've heard all about you."

Lettie stammered some sort of welcome and extricated her hand. "This is my father, Edward Rawlings."

"Ah, yes. Rawlings. Good day. I hope your wife will be joining us."

"She will." Pater turned to Lettie. "I should go and find your mother. She won't want to miss anything."

More likely she'd wait until everyone was seated before she made some sort of entrance. As if to call her a liar, Miriam appeared. Quick to grasp the opportunity, Pater rushed across the room and settled her in the chair at the top of the table just as Olivia and Nathaniel entered the room.

Olivia moved to the other end of the table, away from Miriam. She gestured to the seat to her right. "Lettie, I'd like you to sit here, Mr. Lovedale next to Lettie, and then Mrs. Lovedale. Peg, perhaps you'd like to sit opposite Mrs. Lovedale. Nathaniel on my left and Denman next to Peg." Then she stood at the head of the table, leaving Miriam and Pater marooned at the end.

Olivia raised the empty glass in front of her and hit it with a knife. The murmur of conversation stilled. "I've asked you all here today because the time has come to settle the future. Our future. The future of Yellow Rock."

"Before we go any further, I would like to introduce Mr. Lovedale and his wife. Mr. Lovedale is my solicitor. I have known them for many years and value their opinion."

Miriam's face flushed an interesting shade of purple. "Edward," she hissed. "Credentials. What are his credentials?"

Before Pater could answer, Mr. Lovedale rose to his feet and took matters into his own hands. "I believe my credentials are more than adequate. I worked in Sydney for many years and more recently confined my practice to the local area. Shall we continue, Olivia?" He gave a tight bow of his head and sat down.

Olivia's lips tilted. "First, I would like to thank you, Miriam, for sending Letitia here to Yellow Rock. She has helped me move forward, and I now find myself able to look to the future." Olivia reached out and grasped Lettie's hand.

A smile danced across Miriam's face and she sat back, hands neatly clasped in front of her. Pater cleared his throat and mopped at his forehead with a large silk handkerchief. Lettie's stomach turned. Had Olivia gone mad? Was she about to fulfill Miriam's appalling demands? The words of the awful note Miriam had sent to Olivia danced in front of her eyes. *Both the Ludgrove and Maynard properties will now pass to my daughter, Letitia Miriam Rawlings, the family's sole heir.*

Was Olivia finally going to acquiesce to Miriam's outrageous claims? Did Olivia not understand what this would mean? Why hadn't she discussed it with her? The fighting and the bickering that would ensue when Miriam demanded that one or, worse, both properties should be sold made her blood run cold. "No!" The word was out of her mouth before she knew it had happened.

"Letitia, calm yourself. Everything is as it should be." Miriam could hardly contain her jubilation. "Let Aunt Olivia finish."

Oh, how she wished Thorne were here. His inheritance, not hers. Nothing she wanted. What would happen to Olivia, to Peg, to Denman and Nathaniel? To Evie's map, her story?

Miriam sat up a little straighter, possibly considered standing, but Pater rested his hand on her arm and mumbled something Lettie didn't catch under his breath.

"I have asked you all here to tell you my plans for the future," Olivia continued.

"Discuss *our* plans for the future." Miriam pushed Pater's hand aside.

"*My* plans for the Maynard property, which, as Mr. Lovedale will attest, are mine and mine alone to make, and as the trustee, the decision is also mine regarding Ludgrove, due to Thorne's unfortunate demise."

The bald statement was too much for Miriam. She flew to her feet, knocking a glass of water across the pristine white tablecloth. "It is only right and fair that Letitia should inherit. She is—"

Olivia didn't give Miriam the opportunity to finish. "Mr. Lovedale, perhaps you'd like to explain." With a slight smile tipping her lips she sat down.

Mr. Lovedale opened the foolscap wallet Lettie had last seen on the desk in the study, rose to his feet, adjusted his waistcoat, and cleared his throat. "First, I would like to address the Ludgrove portion of the two properties. William Ludgrove's will stipulated that the land and the dwellings built on the original grant should remain in trust for his daughter Evie. He settled a significant endowment on his eldest daughter, Miriam, when she married, and on his demise the title to the dwelling in Horbury Terrace passed to her. He saw no reason for further compensation. Olivia's role was to hold the Ludgrove land in trusteeship until Evelyn Ludgrove returned or her demise could be proven. It would then pass to Thorne Rawlings on his thirtieth birthday."

More huffings and puffings echoed from the other end of the table, but no one paid any attention. Lettie lifted her gaze and locked eyes with Nathaniel; he offered a small, somewhat sad smile and looked away. Something was going on, something she didn't understand.

"And Maynard?" Miriam couldn't restrain herself.

"I have decided to sell Maynard," Olivia said.

A strangled gasp slipped between Miriam's lips. "You cannot. That is part of Letitia's inheritance. The Rawlings family is entitled to it. The Maynard and Ludgrove properties were to remain intact and pass to Thorne, the family's only male heir."

Once more, it all came back to Thorne.

"I have taken Mr. Lovedale's advice on the matter. The Maynard property belongs to me. I am within my rights."

Miriam thumped her fist on the table. "What about Father's will? It specifically said that the two properties should not be divided. This is manipulation and fraud. I will not sit here and—"

"Perhaps I should explain." Mr. Lovedale rose again and with a benign smile raised his hand to stifle Miriam's tirade. "I have perused William Ludgrove's will at length. You are quite right, madam, to say that it was his preferred option that the two properties should not be divided. However, he did not own the Maynard property and was not in a position to make any stipulations regarding it."

"But my mother, Alice, was a Maynard. She and Olivia inherited the property when their parents, Mary and Alexander Maynard, died."

"And that, I am afraid, is where you are mistaken. Alice Maynard received a large dowry, which passed to her husband, William, on their marriage. That dowry did not include the title to the land. That title rests solely with Olivia Maynard, as it has done since her parents' passing. In much the same way as you have no claim over the Ludgrove property."

As though awaking from a coma, Pater jumped to his feet. "I wish to purchase the Maynard property."

"Unfortunately that is not possible. An offer has already been accepted." Mr. Lovedale paused, no doubt expecting Miriam to interject, but strangely she remained silent.

Lettie slumped back in the chair. How could this be happening?

How could Olivia be sitting there with such a beatific smile on her face, not the slightest bit concerned about the ruckus her announcement had caused? More to the point, how could she sell the only home she had ever known? Her gaze roamed the table. Mr. Lovedale sat calmly, his chin resting on his interlocked fingers rather as though he knew he held the winning hand. His wife by his side, composed, no frown upon her face. Only Oxley, perched next to Peg, with his lip caught on his tooth, showed the slightest hint of the ghastly tension swirling around the table.

And there in the middle, Denman, his pipe clasped in his hand, waiting to take a surreptitious puff, and Nathaniel refusing, refusing to catch her eye. It seemed that the Rawlings family—she, Miriam, and Pater—were the outsiders and being played by a master puppeteer.

Amid a series of rattling glasses, Miriam struggled to her feet, grasped vainly at the cloth Peg had carefully placed on the table. "Olivia, Edward and I came here in the spirit of reconciliation—at your request, I might add. You have seen fit to make a mockery of our families' heritage. I shall be seeking legal advice in Sydney. I have no intention of letting the matter rest. Letitia, we are leaving. You went to great pains to tell me that you were capable of making your own decisions. Now is the time to decide where your loyalties lie. Edward . . ." Miriam groped for his hand. "I wish to retire."

The silence, heavy, charged, and ominous, settled as Lettie strove to make sense of her jumbled thoughts. Olivia had sold Maynard! Never in her wildest dreams had she imagined it would come to this. The scraping of Olivia's chair against the floorboards brought her from her reverie. "Aunt Olivia—"

"Not now, Lettie. I have matters to discuss with Mr. Lovedale. Peg, would you please serve the tea and sandwiches."

Unable to sit a moment longer, Lettie left the room. She walked directly into the study, leaning her back against the door, hoping for some peace to collect her scattered thoughts. Oxley sloped in and settled under the desk as she sank into the chair and cast her eye over the room she had come to love.

Maynard to be sold! Whatever was Olivia thinking? She'd said she wanted to keep the two properties as one. What would happen to the horses, the farmhouse, her business? She buried her face in her hands, trying to settle her racing heart, trying to understand Olivia's motives.

"Can you spare me a moment?" Nathaniel's grave voice sent a wave of despair through her.

What about Nathaniel and Denman? Hadn't Olivia told them they could live in the farmhouse? Would that still be the case? Where did the Ludgrove property end and the Maynard property begin? The main house was on Ludgrove land, that she knew. What about the farmhouse? "Nathaniel." She lifted her head, pushed back the chair. "I am so sorry, so very, very sorry."

A frown creased his forehead, as though he didn't understand a word she'd said. "I have to speak to you. I hoped to be able to tell you this before Olivia's announcement, but both she and Mr. Lovedale felt it better to keep quiet until after the meeting."

Oh! The poor man, all his dreams shattered about Rossgole and now this. And what of Denman? He'd given up his smithy, left his livelihood. "Keep quiet? How can you keep quiet? What Olivia has done is outrageous. She has disenfranchised both you and Denman." She slammed her hands down on the desk, her building anger a respite from the overwhelming sense of sorrow enveloping her.

"Lettie, listen. Olivia has accepted *my* offer for Maynard."

Every breath sucked out of her lungs. "Your offer?" The words choked in her dry throat.

"Yes. Once the contracts are signed, I will own Maynard."

She shook her head, the last remnants of despair replaced by a swelling fury. How dare he! How dare he manipulate poor Olivia, take advantage of her while she was at her lowest, mourning the loss of Evie and Bailey.

She covered the distance between them, thundered her fists against his chest. "You! You selfish, unthinking"—her voice rose with a quiver of hysteria—"you conniving rat!"

His arms wrapped around her and pulled her close, imprisoning her flaying fists.

"How could you?" No matter how much she struggled, he held her firm.

He made a noise deep in his throat and locked eyes with her. "My hope is that you will stay, stay here with Olivia." Concern, a flicker of anger, and something else she couldn't place crossed his face. "Will you?"

The note in his voice made her blood tingle. She pushed away, her palms flat against his chest, her eyes searching his face. The change was startling; the barriers between them fell. His hand cupped her jaw, sending heat streaking through her. She breathed in his scent, leather and saddle soap, fresh hay and eucalyptus. Her breath shuddered and she stretched up on tiptoes, then paused, barely stopping herself from pressing a kiss to his lips.

With a long-drawn-out sigh he tightened his grasp, drawing her closer. He smoothed her hair from her face. "It's what Olivia wants. She'll have Ludgrove, live out her life here at Yellow Rock surrounded by the people she loves, and the two properties will continue to function as one. You haven't answered my question . . . Will you stay?"

Nathaniel's heart pounded as he tried to steady his breathing. He wanted to say so much more—there were so many hurdles to overcome.

Lettie's lips moved, her breath fanning his face as she framed her answer, then froze.

He whipped around. The door swung back on its hinges to reveal Rawlings.

A wave of guilt rocked him. How would Rawlings feel about his only child, his much-loved daughter, caught in the arms of a drover?

No. No longer a drover. A stockman perhaps, a landowner once the sale was finalized. He straightened his shoulders, looped his arm around Lettie's waist, and pulled her against him, hip to hip. He'd start the way he intended to continue. He would be courting Lettie. No doubt, no second thoughts.

"Congratulations, young man. Olivia has just told me you are the proud owner of the Maynard property." Rawlings beamed at the pair of them. Not what he had expected, not at all.

"Never doubted your ability, and I hear you're set on breeding Walers again, carrying on the family tradition."

And how the hell would he know that? He turned to Lettie, saw her cheeks pink. He hadn't been the only one talking to Olivia. "It's a thought I had. Seems the Light Horse are looking for good animals."

"Indeed, indeed. Oh, I almost forgot. Lettie, your mother is asking for you."

The pretty flush in her cheeks faded instantly, replaced by an ashen pallor.

"You'll find her upstairs, resting. The afternoon's events have exhausted her." Rawlings settled himself in a chair, crossed his legs. "I don't suppose there'd be a drink anywhere? Matters we need to discuss."

Lettie hovered, the look on her face identical to the night she'd stood beside her crumpled car, plucking up the courage to mount Rogue. He couldn't pick her up in his arms and carry her to safety this time, no matter how much he wanted to. "Would you like me to come—"

"No, no thank you. This is something I must do." She rummaged around on the desk, picked up a drawing. "Talk to Pater. There's a bottle of brandy in the cupboard underneath the bookshelves, and some glasses. Celebrate your success." She threw him a wry smile, left him wondering if he'd ever know what she was thinking.

Nathaniel had to pull open a series of doors before he located the brandy and the glasses; meanwhile, Rawlings wandered around, hands behind his back, surveying the maps on the wall. Maps Nathaniel hadn't even had a chance to take in. He could count the number of times he'd been in this room on one hand, never thought he'd be standing here providing Rawlings with a drink. Not that it would ever be his study; the main house sat fair and square on Ludgrove land. He had no doubt that one day it would belong to Lettie. She had her book to write, her drawings, Evie's map, and she and Olivia would live here, if he could convince her to stay. The farmhouse was more than adequate; besides, it would leave him close to the stables, where he wanted to be. Not that there'd be much going on for a year or two. Although Olivia had accepted a ridiculously low price for Maynard, the same he'd expected to pay for Rossgole, it left him with very little to make a start. He'd have to keep working off the property to make ends meet. For the people at Randwick, there were always horses that needed moving. Rawlings even. His head came up with a snap. He poured a generous slug of brandy into a glass and offered it to Rawlings, then a smaller one for himself. He sniffed the contents, wondered if he wouldn't rather it contained the rum Denman favored.

"Right, young man. Now, where were we? You have a mind to breed Walers again. Something I might be able to help with."

Oh no. He wasn't going to be under anyone's thumb. This was something he was going to do for himself, for Denman, for Lettie and Olivia. He raised an eyebrow and took a sip of the brandy, let it slide down his throat.

"I'm sure you're aware of Lord Kitchener's recommendations. Compulsory part-time military training and the establishment of twenty-eight regiments of Light Horse. The Royal Military College opened last year. They'll be needing horses, stronghearted animals bred for speed, strength, and stamina."

Which was exactly what Nathaniel had in mind when he set out to buy Rossgole. No reason his dream couldn't transfer to Yellow Rock. He and Olivia had discussed it at length. But he didn't want to be at anyone's beck and call, least of all Rawlings's.

"It's a project I very much admire. Sadly, though, it's time for me to stand aside. Let you younger men step up. Which brings me to my next point."

"You're going to sell the racehorses?"

"No, that wasn't exactly what I had in mind. I thought we might come to an agreement. I'd like to offer you a partnership. Bring the animals back here. Stand the stallions at stud, sell the offspring. Let's face it, my record on the track isn't the best. And I'm getting on. I've a mind to retire, dedicate a bit more time to Miriam. She's been sadly neglected over the past few years and neither of us are getting any younger." He took a long swallow, licked his lips. "Nothing like a decent brandy," he added almost as an afterthought.

Nathaniel was on the point of refusing.

"Complete control and a 50 percent share in the sale of the offspring and an introduction to the people you need to meet if this idea of yours is to take off."

"Why are you doing this?"

Rawlings pursed his lips. "I've got my daughter to consider."

Nathaniel slugged the remainder of the brandy before he blurted out something he might regret. Now was not the time for pride.

With every step on every stair Lettie's courage drained. By the time she reached the landing her legs could barely carry her. She slipped into her room and sank onto the floor next to the bed. Evie's painting fell from her hands and she bent her forehead to the counterpane, relishing the smooth, cool feel of the satin. It was something she had to do, nothing she wanted to do. Until she spoke with Miriam, asked the question that plagued her, she couldn't move forward.

She pulled the painting toward her, beautiful in its simplicity, a Botticelli Madonna that could have graced the walls of any of the art galleries in Sydney or Melbourne—maybe even Paris or London. But somehow she doubted Miriam would see it that way.

Lettie had to know the identity of Thorne's father, had to hear it from Miriam's lips. There was no doubt in her mind that Olivia was dancing with Bailey, but it didn't prove that Bailey hadn't sired Thorne, or that the drover—Chapman—had. Only one person held that knowledge, and it was a secret Miriam had kept for over thirty years.

She peered at her ashen face in the mirror, ran a brush through her hair and retied it. What did it matter what Miriam thought about the way she looked? Surely she had left that childish nonsense behind. Ignoring her fluttering heartbeat she grasped the picture in her shaking hand and set out across the landing.

Her knock elicited no response. She swung open the door, mouth clamped against the cloying scent of lily of the valley, and waited while her eyes adjusted to the dim surroundings. Nothing she hadn't done before, yet somehow this time it was different.

The fine net curtains around the bed billowed, but Miriam was barely visible. Not sitting, pillow plumped, as Lettie expected, just a mound beneath the lace-edged sheet.

"Letitia." Miriam's muffled murmur pricked her ears and her tearstained face appeared. She held out her gnarled hand, the rings hanging loose on her thin fingers. "This never should have happened. It is all Olivia's fault."

Lettie stood, unable to speak, hand clasped around Miriam's, each bone as frail as a bird's beneath the loose skin.

"You shouldn't have come. Legal counsel should have dealt with it. Olivia is . . . Olivia cannot be trusted. I knew this would happen; I warned you, and now you have nothing. Your rightful inheritance stripped from you by a greedy, unforgiving old woman."

Lettie took two steps back as Miriam spilled the torrent of venom, and her resolve firmed. She bit her lip, trapping her threatening scream. "Mother, we must talk." She held out Evie's picture.

Miriam's eyes closed and she rolled across the bed, her face to the window.

Determined not to be put off, Lettie crossed to the other side, perched, uninvited, and held up the painting again. "Is this a picture of you? I believe Evie drew it the day you left Yellow Rock to marry Pater."

Miriam's eyes remained firmly closed, the lines on her face taut with frustration.

"Mother, open your eyes. Have you seen it before? You're wearing a blue cloak that belonged to Grandmother, your mother, Alice."

After several agonizing moments Miriam raised her head and peered at the picture through narrowed eyes. "It's difficult to see in this light." She flopped back against the pillow.

Infuriated, Lettie leaped to her feet and reefed open the curtains around the bed and then those covering the windows. "Look at it, look at it closely." She returned to the side of the bed, the picture held in two hands, and stuck it under Miriam's nose.

"It's an excellent likeness. Evie was such a clever girl, always with her paints and pencils. Such a shame, such wasted talent, to have died so young."

"Mother!" Lettie's shriek filled the room. "Will you please accept the truth? Evie did not die in childhood. She disappeared. She left here thirty years ago and was never seen again." An overwhelming desire to bang her head against the bedroom wall overcame her. There was no gentle way to get through to Miriam. It was as though she lived in a world of her own making, one that bore no resemblance to reality. "This is a picture of you on the day you left Yellow Rock. Look at it. Were you carrying a child?"

"Impossible." Miriam squinted at the picture. "That was before I married Edward."

"And that, Mother, is my point. Olivia remembers. Grandfather knew. That's why he arranged for you to marry Pater."

Miriam shot upright, her shift slipping from her bony shoulder. "Thorne was Edward's son. William's grandson. Your brother. I will not have you speak ill of him, or me. You will not accuse me of such contrivance. I gave birth to the family's only male heir."

Either the victim or the victor. Never the perpetrator. Now she could understand Olivia's reluctance to ask Miriam for the truth. "Yes, you did. And yes, Thorne was my brother, always will be. However, Pater was not Thorne's father."

"Olivia has poisoned your mind." She rolled beneath the sheet. "Edward!" Her frail cry barely broke the charged silence.

Lettie stared out at the lengthening shadows. Was it her place to force Miriam to acknowledge the truth? What would anyone gain? Her shoulders slumped—suddenly it seemed unimportant. An unpleasant and unnecessary haranguing of a woman who had made her own truths and continued to live by them. Thorne would always be her brother regardless of his parentage. Pater had accepted him, William had, and so, too, had Olivia. She picked up the picture and closed the door behind her.

EPILOGUE

Lettie and Nathaniel stood at the head of the table under the angophora tree, the long white cloth anchored by sprays of flowering boronia and gum leaves.

He reached for her hand, brought it to his lips. "Happy?" he murmured.

"Happier than I ever imagined."

They'd made their wedding vows in the little church in Broke amid a profusion of wildflowers. After much debate she and Miriam had agreed on her wedding dress, a simple soft white muslin dress that Peg's daughter made, and she wore Miriam's Irish lace veil fastened with a coronet of flannel flowers. Pater had escorted her down the narrow aisle, the smiling faces of the congregation mingling with the scent of beeswax and cedar. Then they'd returned to Yellow Rock for the wedding breakfast.

"There's something I'd like to do before we sit down. Do you think we can leave?"

"We can do whatever you wish."

She didn't tell Nathaniel where she wanted to go. He simply took her hand and they followed Oxley through the long grass and wildflowers up the hill to the family plot beneath the spreading trees.

Carefully she untied the ribbon securing her bouquet and laid the flannel flowers on the newly placed stone memorials. "I feel as though Evie, Bailey, and Thorne are with us in spirit, home where they belong."

"I'm not sure they ever left us."

A breeze stirred the leaves of the trees above them and the air flooded over her, stopping her breath, catching her heart. "You're right. And I believe they're happy too." She interlaced her fingers with Nathaniel's. "We should go back."

Every seat around the table was filled. Oxley presided over one end of the table, a silk tie knotted around his neck, flanked by Denman and Peg and her bevy of granddaughters, their coronets of flowers already askew and their dresses showing the marks of their tumbles in the grass. Mr. and Mrs. Lovedale sat on the opposite side with Sam, who was looking quite the young squire. At the top of the table Olivia hovered, jiggling from one foot to the other, one hand resting on Miriam's shoulder, the other on Pater's.

"Olivia's up to something," Lettie whispered as Nathaniel held the chair for her at the center of the table. "You haven't hatched another plan and forgotten to tell me, have you?"

Nathaniel took one of her hands and pressed his lips to her wrist with such warmth and tenderness her knees trembled and her heart pounded.

She rested her cheek against his palm and sank into the chair. "I have no idea what she's up to. And no, no plans beyond tonight," he whispered, his breath fanning the tender skin behind her ear.

Color flooded her face as the implication of his words settled. She'd hardly seen him in the weeks leading up to their wedding. He had been back and forth to Sydney bringing the horses to Yellow Rock while Denman issued instructions to Sam and a troop of young boys from Broke as they prepared paddocks and kept the stables running with almost military precision. Lettie had spent all of her time in the study putting the finishing touches to the first draft of her manuscript.

The sound of metal against glass brought the assembled company to order and the crowd settled into their seats, all eyes fixed on Olivia.

"I've never been a great one for tradition; rather than follow the accepted progression of events, I would like to speak first. I believe as the matriarch of this family I may claim that right." She pinned Miriam with a stare and received a nod of acquiescence and something that might have passed for a smile.

A smattering of applause greeted her words, but Lettie doubted anything would stop Olivia. The determined look in her eye and her general air of excitement had infected everyone around the table.

"We gather here today to celebrate not only the wedding of Lettie and Nathaniel but also the future. The past twelve months have taught me that we must take what we can when it is offered, pay no heed to convention and expectation. We must grab happiness in both hands and embrace it.

"This is the beginning, not only for Lettie and Nathaniel but for all of us, as we celebrate the coming together once more of the Ludgrove and Maynard families." Olivia paused and produced a thick white envelope from her sleeve. "And this, my darling Lettie, I am handing to you for safekeeping.

"I am very much hoping that William's wishes will be honored, but my time for intervention is over. I will leave that to the two of you—in the hope that one day you will fulfill the dreams of your forefathers. And now a toast—to Nathaniel and Letitia, and the future." The words echoed around them and Nathaniel slipped his hand into hers.

Everyone stood, glasses raised, and echoed Olivia's words. Lettie had no need to unfold the paper Olivia handed to her. She knew it contained the deed to Ludgrove. Olivia had managed, in her roundabout way, to ensure that the mighty Ludgrove-Maynard alliance would continue just as William wished.

And as Lettie sat surrounded by everyone she loved, a deep swell of happiness filled her, as though the clouds had parted to reveal the future.

She had truly come home and need never leave again. She and Nathaniel would live in this house, and their children would grow here and prosper, protected by the guardians of the past and the promise of the future—an outcome Thorne would thoroughly applaud.

HISTORICAL NOTE

As with so many of my books, *The Cartographer's Secret* is a mixture of fact and fiction. I've always had a fascination for maps, particularly those of the early Dutch cartographers. When I discovered that most of those early cartographers were women, working in their family business and obliged to sign their maps with their husband's name, I was more than a little outraged!

However, I like to set my stories in Australia, and so the fictional character Evie Ludgrove stepped onto the stage. I then started researching nineteenth-century Australian maps. What a gold mine I found, and most of them are available online. (I recommend a visit to the David Rumsey Map Collection at davidrumsey.com.)

Not so strangely, nineteenth-century maps led me to Ludwig Leichhardt and the many other explorers who disappeared during that time. Imagine my excitement when I discovered that Ludwig Leichhardt had spent time exploring the Hunter before he set out on his ill-fated expedition to cross Australia from east to west.

Local historical sources informed me that many people in the Hunter had sponsored Leichhardt's various expeditions, and not only that—a copy of the map he made of his Essington expedition was in the local museum!

Off I went on my own journey of exploration. I tracked down Leichhardt's diaries (available through the Mitchell Library and on-line via the University of Queensland), and sure enough Leichhardt had visited the Hunter and the Broken Back Ranges, an area I know and love, and more importantly he'd climbed Yellow Rock.

The property, Yellow Rock, does exist, though not in the manner I have portrayed. I was unable to gain access or contact the current owners, and then in that wonderful, serendipitous fashion that seems to haunt my research, I was put in touch with a member of the family who had originally owned the property.

The Ludgrove and Maynard families are figments of my imagination, and I have woven their early story through Leichhardt's travels in the Hunter.

And then there's Andrew Hume and the Leichhardt relics. Andrew Hume is not a fictional character. He arrived in Australia as a child; his father worked as a stockman on the Halls' property at Dartbrook, NSW; and he spent many years exploring the interior. His parents did own a shop in Maitland and then moved to Largs, and they are buried in the area (although for fiction's sake I moved their resting place a few miles down the road). After that things get a little vague and varied. Was Andrew Hume "a rogue and a scoundrel," or was he telling the truth about the Leichhardt relics? We'll never know because he died before he could prove his claims. I stuck to the reported facts until almost the very end, when I took the liberty of offering a totally imaginative ending.

And so to Evie's fictional map—for the sake of continuity between the two timelines I have used the modern spellings; for example, the 1883 map of NSW shows Muswellbrook as "Muscle

Brook." Leichhardt's journals also include many and varied spellings, and I have standardized those as well.

Perhaps most importantly, I learned from researching *The Cartographer's Secret* that fact truly is stranger than fiction!

ACKNOWLEDGMENTS

First, I would like to acknowledge the Wonnarua People as the Traditional Owners of the land on which this story is set and pay my respects to Elders both past, present, and emerging.

As always there are so many people I must thank, not only for their help in turning a very confused first draft into a book, but also for their interest and willingness to share snippets of information that became integral to the plot along the way.

Carl Hoipo, chief historian, for introducing me to the map of Leichhardt's expedition to Port Essington; Denis Brown, chief engineer, for his advice and extensive knowledge of all things mechanical, including the Model T; Lynda Marsh, for tracking down Andrew Hume's parents; Luke Russell, cultural director; Wylaa Buuranliyn, for advising me on the story of Lizard Rock; the Pynes, for their advice and assistance with stock routes and snaffle bits; chief researcher, who is also my hand holder, plot wrangler, and alpha reader; and critique partners Sarah Barrie and Paula Beavan, for their support in more ways than I can count. And Jane, whose lurcher, Mouse, inspired Oxley.

The wonderful Alex Craig, my Australian editor and my savior, who seems to understand my plot better than I do—thank heavens! It is a privilege to work with her, and I live in constant awe of her ability.

Jo Mackay, my publisher, who is always there for me and manages somehow to unscramble whatever seems insurmountable; Annabel Blay, who keeps me on the straight and narrow when the time comes to turn my manuscript into a book; the fabulous sales team, who embrace my stories with such enthusiasm and take them into the world; and, of course, the brilliant Darren Holt and the HarperCollins design team, who continue to produce the best covers an author could wish for. I am truly blessed. And in the US my thanks to Amanda Bostic, Julie Monroe, and every member of the Harper Muse team. It is an ongoing pleasure and privilege to work with you all.

And finally, to my wonderful readers, thank you for all your support, reviews, emails, encouragement, and enthusiasm. Without you my stories would languish in some forgotten drawer, a bit like Evie's map!

DISCUSSION
QUESTIONS

1. Lettie is a privileged and progressive young woman who shared a deep bond with her brother, Thorne, who taught her not only how to drive his Model T but how to maintain and repair it! Thorne's car, "Lizzie," plays an important role in the story, aiding Lettie's quest to unearth clues to her aunt Evie's disappearance. Can you think of some other ways Lizzie was a help to Lettie?

2. After Thorne's death, Lettie feels alone and lost and jumps at the chance to visit Great-Aunt Olivia at Yellow Rock. What are the benefits of taking a break from "life as usual"? What are your favorite ways to give yourself a break from life's demands?

3. Evie was kept in the dark about her sister Miriam's out-of-wedlock pregnancy. Later, Lettie was kept from knowing that Thorne was her half brother, not her full brother. Although Olivia knew about the pregnancy, she incorrectly

assumed the identity of the baby's father. This family secret had far-reaching effects, none of them good. How can humility and honesty lead to forgiveness and freedom from shame?

4. Miriam, Lettie's mother, is described as "a woman who had made her own truths." She has a rigid worldview and a strained, formal relationship with Lettie. In what ways do you think her cold and controlling demeanor could be linked to the indiscretions she committed in her youth?

5. Though they never knew each other, Evie and Lettie shared a special connection. Besides being similar in appearance, they both had an independent streak and loved to express themselves through drawing and painting. How much do you know about your ancestors? Would you like to learn more?

6. Olivia's life was filled with regrets after she lost two people she loved deeply. Instead of dealing with her grief and heartache head-on, she admits she simply "locked everything away." Have you ever adopted this strategy in the aftermath of heartbreak or tragedy? If so, how did it work out for you?

7. Nathaniel experienced the pain of being orphaned as a young boy. His life could have been much different if Denman hadn't stepped into the role of caretaker and guardian. How can you be a guide and role model for the young people in your life?

8. At one point in the story, Lettie feels she has hurt Olivia by uncovering clues to Evie's disappearance. She wonders if she could have spared Olivia pain by letting the past stay buried. She hadn't considered that "knowledge could be

worse than ignorance." Can you think of a time when you wished you would have remained ignorant?

9. Lettie found Evie's map hidden in the desk, and later she unexpectedly discovered the bit belonging to Bailey's horse. Then Nathaniel stumbled upon Evie's saddlebag, which contained her journal. All these seeming coincidences came together to help solve the mystery of both Evie's and Bailey's disappearances. When has a "coincidence" in your life turned out to have greater meaning?

DON'T MISS THIS *USA TODAY* BESTSELLER FROM TEA COOPER!

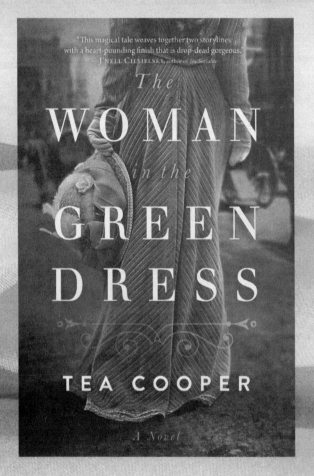

A cursed opal, a gnarled family tree, and a sinister woman in a green dress emerge in the aftermath of World War I.

AVAILABLE IN PRINT, E-BOOK, AND AUDIO!

ALSO AVAILABLE FROM TEA COOPER

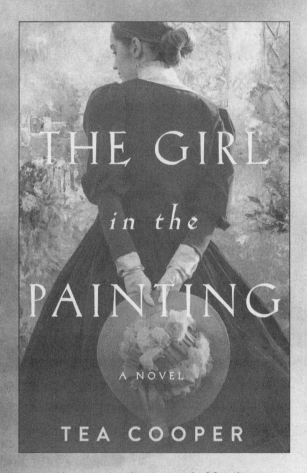

A young prodigy in need of family.
A painting that shatters a woman's peace.
And a decades-old mystery demanding to be solved.

AVAILABLE IN PRINT, E-BOOK, AND AUDIO!

ABOUT THE AUTHOR

Copyright © Katy Clymo

Tea Cooper is an established Australian author of historical fiction. In a past life she was a teacher, a journalist, and a farmer. These days she haunts museums and indulges her passion for storytelling. She is the winner of two Daphne du Maurier Awards and the bestselling author of several novels, including *The Horse Thief, The Cedar Cutter, The Currency Lass,* and *The Naturalist's Daughter.*

teacooperauthor.com
Instagram: @tea_cooper
Twitter: @TeaCooper1
Facebook: @TeaCooper
Pinterest: @teacooperauthor